D0451304

Also by Joan Chase
Published by Ballantine Books:

DURING THE REIGN OF THE QUEEN OF PERSIA

THE
EVENING
WOLVES

Joan Chase

BALLANTINE BOOKS · NEW YORK

Library of Congress Catalog Card Number: 88-7864

ISBN 0-345-36285-3

This edition published by arrangement with Farrar, Straus & Giroux

Manufactured in the United States of America

First Ballantine Books Edition: June 1990

I want to thank the Yaddo Corporation and the Ragdale Foundation for the time they gave me, and the Illinois Council on the Arts and the Whiting Foundation for support. Thanks again to Hayden Carruth and also to Ellen Levine and Jonathan Galassi.

TO ALEC

PART I

In No Man's Land

'' '*Y*OU AIN'T BEEN BLUE. NO, NO, NO. YOU AIN'T been blue, till you've had that mood indigo.' '' Dad's singing steams from the muffler he wears in the frosty night and we hang up the wash by the light of the moon. When the wind sweeps, pitchforks and tuning forks scaling the corner of the house, he's drowned out and lost to me. The muslin sheets steam too, drag with water and freeze stiff as we pull them from the basket into the air, spread and catch them to the line with pins. Then we have to yank the folds speedily as the ice wrinkles pucker and shatter, the weighted cloth snatched by the wind rustling like sails—oh, climb onto the yardarm, we're off to Zanzibar. In places thinned and frayed from wear, I see the moon when I look through.

Ruthann and Tommy peer out the basement window, Tommy on a chair, and sometimes we wave back and forth and holler. It's lively as a puppet show. Dad says the next time out I'll have to wear my mittens, that at this rate we'll take flight, connive with that slattern of a squaw who laments on the face of the moon—see her with her woven blanket jagged around her. Dad never forgets his time in the West when he saw real Indians, most of them sprawled headlong on the sidewalks, punched out and drunk. Insulted to the marrow of their bones. My maiden of the moon, indefatigable, had eyes that from their depths glow with dreams I can't express. Dad says he was once a romantic too.

When the basket is empty we return to the basement

3

to stir another load of clothes through the rinse water and set more rub-dubbing in the washtub. I ease my frozen hands into the warm soap scum, show Dad how red and wrinkled they are, rave how they ache and sting. All this time while Dad listens I am smiling. He looks amused too but distant, his thoughts far away, sloshing to the rhythm of the clothes agitating in the water. I chatter along freely, like singing, my heart on a string, bobbing and cherry red. Dad says I am like a rugged squaw myself, that I will skin many bears, coax smoke from green saplings. He bets I can eat dog when I have to.

Ruthann and Tommy are listening from the basement stairs and Tommy sputters out and squeals, "Eat a dog, eat a dog." Ruthann tickles him and they tussle until Dad cries, "Halt, you ruffians!" sending Ruthann scowling back to her homework, which she holds on her lap, and Tommy fishes again over the side of the stairs, dangling an opened safety pin fastened to a string and stick. I helped him make it and he calls it tackle, describes the sort of fish he catches, their colors and habits, how they lie in wait to trick him. He's a smart little boy. We plan that sometime we'll rent a boat and push off into a misty lake at dawn and Tommy will run the motor. Last summer in Michigan Dad taught me to row a boat and I'd prefer that, but Tommy drones, "Bruhmm, bruhmm," and won't hear of it. Dad says Tommy and I are free to take our chances but he won't be joining us. He never catches a fish no matter how early he gets out.

Tommy's only two and a half and doesn't remember Mother at all. When I tell him little stories, things I go over not to forget, he's at a loss to know what I expect from him, smiles or tears. Mother used to let me take care of him all I wanted and I dragged him everywhere like he was my own pride and joy. But after the accident, Tommy went away to live with Dad's aunt where we hardly knew a thing about him. Until Dad bought our house in Virginia so Tommy could come back and we'd all be together. Dad thought the three of us ought to be able to bury the hatchet and make a home for one small boy, no matter our limitations. "It's no secret your

4

mother and I never got along,'' he reminds me, staring me in the eye while I pray nobody else can hear. It feels like a secret to me. I know I try to make Tommy feel at home, but there's been such a lot of coming and going in our lives, I think Tommy's still mixed up, and part of the time he thinks I'm his mother and other times he thinks he came straight from heaven and has no natural attachments. A frantic look engulfs him right before he throws one of his temper tantrums.

The clothes are rinsed and Dad and I snag them from the hot water with a pole, guiding them into the wringer; they squeeze from the roller plates in long, joined lengths, folding down into the basket set on the floor. Tommy calls it fishing and begs to help, but Dad won't allow it. He might get his fingers caught in the wringer. Dad's heard the saddest tales, arms and legs going in, whole loins flattened to pancakes. Tommy grins because I do, but he's worried and rubs his elbow. Dad ruffles his son's curls. Then it's time to face the perils of the night and the clothesline again, and Dad and I bundle up. He says we should consider mooring a lifeline to the chimney, warns Ruthann and Tommy that this might be the end, the last they'll see of us. He urges them to keep up the mortgage payments. Ruthann snorts, ''Oh, yeah. Maybe I'll lock the door.'' Dad warns her, ''Don't get fresh.'' We all titter when he ties a scarf around his head and skips, tra-la, circling the basement jack.

Our little house lies on a plain in No Man's Land. Dad said it was the best he could afford, our move, like most of his life, arranged at the last minute—a change of job, a new locale, a fresh start. At one time he had sworn off music forever, not the first resolution he's broken, life going on a lot longer than any youngster could imagine— see if I don't find out. Anyway, it won't kill him to associate with the breed and it's probably nothing contagious. He is now registrar at the American Conservatory, teaching Music Theory 101 on the side, but he can take it. Just as long as he never has to go near the concert stage. I was too young to recall his swan song; no need to go into that. But the upshot was that even his mother

5

had to admit he didn't have a performer's temperament. He'd toted his erstwhile master's degree along on a variety of jobs across the land: carpenter, supervisor on the line at Bendix, his bit for Uncle Sam; eventually his nights given over to the study of accounting in a last-ditch stand to earn a decent living. At last an old friend, grand master of the piccolo, had taken pity on him and brought him on board at the conservatory. So what if it wasn't Juilliard. We did have to eat.

Ruthann and I were excited because we'd never lived in a house before, although we get lonely this far from the people we used to know, the places we used to be. Dad says he knows we do. There's no denying we travel under a curse and in this wilderness of the soul we're bound to wander and labor until we are purged, humbled, and terrified. Or just plain dead.

Lots of times I'm bewildered by what Dad has to tell us and he sends me to the dictionary, makes me look words up over and over to figure things out—half the time he doesn't know himself what he means. He says my interest is flattering and touching. The fact I can't spell makes it harder. That's no excuse. Dad says it's only the hard things in life that are worth a damn.

Dad admits he was born to gripe and give everybody a hard time. He hopes we kids will find another way, learn to count our blessings. There are some: our house has a fireplace in the living room; the dining room, where on Sundays we dine like the Cabots, has roses on the wallpaper; the tiny yard is fenced against the barbarians. There are times when Dad says he wishes he'd thrown everything over for a covered wagon instead of a bungalow. We're lucky to have him, the will-o'-the-wisp, the lone plainsman.

I don't feel the cold, my cheeks burning. My coat, losing its buttons, flies away and the knitted scarf unwinds like a bobbin. When the basket is empty Dad says, "Thanks, Margy. You're true blue." I tremble with emotion I try to hide—the slightest praise and I'm on my knees. Off in the dark around us the surrounding brick houses rise like the towers; off goes the mysterious highway. The moonlight's iridescent sheets imprint eternity on the December lawn. Chain-link fences fortify the neighborhood, sparkle with frost, pink an edge on the night. They establish the entrance to the forbidden plain. I imagine the courage it must take to venture out there alone. I'll make it if I have to file through iron bars, plunge into a cauldron. Dad says I tend to be on the hysterical side.

In the kitchen after the wash is hung, I heat milk for hot chocolate while Ruthann does more homework at the table. She could concentrate in a hailstorm, according to Dad. Of course she never thinks to help me, won't lift a finger unless Dad says. Probably she knows I'll go ahead and do everything, and even if we only had plain boiled water to drink, she'd make a joke and wouldn't care, just like she wouldn't care if Dad threw up his hands, said he'd had all he could take, and walked out the door.

"We're going to hell in a hand basket," he says to me, one arm slung over the refrigerator. "And how you'll ever find a husband with those hands the color of poppies, I'd like to know." I smile all the broader. Mother taught me a lot about cooking and I'm over the worst. The first time I made dinner for Dad I had to sit on top of the refrigerator to wait for his report. Somehow it felt as though my whole life had been laid out on a plate.

I keep busy around here. Then I don't despair about husbands, or that I've let my homework go again, that I haven't ironed a thing for school and will have to pay Dad a dime to heat the iron an extra time. I try not to brood about the past because what good would it do. I can make the time with Mother seem like stories that happened to somebody else.

A person as determined to excel, as organized as Ruthann, makes me want to get back, excel at sloth, and fail in the grand manner. I think Dad has similar inclinations; he says he's losing heart, doesn't know what to do with us now that he's got us. He promised himself he'd keep the family together but he fears he's not man enough—"I'd sure hate to see them come and drag you off to the children's home."

That's his way, Dad says—hyperbole and umbrage. We're not to take him seriously. But I know this, he won't hesitate for long. Act now and regret later is his motto. He's the first to admit it. Last year Ruthann and I lived with his mother in Florida. It was decided and we were packed and on the train in two days. Now we're here. Tomorrow it may be "Wagons ho!"

Already, in the seventh grade, I've been to more than ten different schools. When I want to find excuses I count them up. With all the traveling around and adjusting it's a wonder I can read. In some schools they emphasize grammar, in others it's long units on civics or science. I never know what I should be doing. Still, I've had more than my share of experience, and if that's the best teacher, I ought to be about to graduate and get a menial job— the kind I'm destined for in Dad's opinion. He agrees it's not all my fault. Everywhere I'm the new girl in class, the tallest, felled like a tree and propped against the building, waiting out recess and noontime, willing my- self to disappear. The boys point me out and snicker— such a sight with this frizzy hair and already at twelve the figure of a grown woman, suited up in my aunt's old office clothes. Once, the boy they call Slick murmured "Tits" when he passed by. I could have cut off my head. About the time I begin to make new friends, we're off again. Dad's apologized about a million times for his unsteady nature, but I'm in training to be a fatalist, and when all the blood in my body whooshes to my head and I nearly fall on the floor, I wait for the level to lower, focus on the third eye—which Dad says sees where it's all headed.

I'm what Dad calls overstimulated. Winter and sum- mer I bang out of the house without my shoes, dance on the lawn amid fireflies and flurries. I'm a little plump but in my heart I'm graceful as a wind-bell, yearning toward what I can't name. The airy stillness trembles with my life's breath and I fling my arms madly, twirl with such a vengeance I lurch twenty paces before I regain my bal- ance.

* * *

Grandma gave me a book, a keepsake from Florida, *One Hundred and One Famous Poems*, including the Gettysburg Address. It has more than a thousand and one exclamation points and as many capital letters. Stand! Oh Shame! To Be! Time! Roll On! The poets do me a world of good, point to a better way. I open up the book and stick in my finger. A plum: "In a dell of dew." For some reason it carries like a clarion call.

I flourish my cooking spoon in Dad's face. Declare myself a bar wench, a dumb cluck, brag how I hate school and dare him to let me quit tomorrow. Dad counters, "Oh, don't be in such a hurry to start in at the laundry, Blondie. You're headed that way fast enough." He tips an imaginary hat to my failure. He doesn't care what happens to me. I think: Well! If he likes that so much. Well, if that's his opinion of me! I'll just end up and be a flop. See how he likes that!

But I wouldn't like it. In fact, sometimes I dream that I'll make something of myself, whatever that might mean. At school most of the girls say they want to be wives, the others nurses. I announce that I will be an actress. They stare—I certainly don't look like an actress, especially beet-red with my lip stuck out, defiant in the face of their disbelief. And of course Dad would be laughing up his sleeve. He's the one who knows exactly how self-conscious I am, sees in my expressions a scandal of ungovernable feeling. He says he'll be amazed if I master even the simplest skills, typing and shorthand; which makes me remember Mother's slim green notebooks filled with line after line of hieroglyphics, neat as print. He harps on the struggle I will have to keep my weight down.

I don't know whether to laugh or cry. At times I think I'll explode. But being dramatic would serve me well on the stage, I tell myself, so I toss my head in the air and ignore Dad when he taunts me to perform at the drop of a hat. "All right, Miss Bernhardt. Recite 'The Highwayman' if you're bound for the boards."

It runs in the family to be theatrical, among other things. Long ago Dad had his hopes set on vaudeville, then musical comedy, and when he's not disgusted with me we work together to develop any talent I might have. He taught me to sing "Pale Hands," marking time with a ruler, and we've sung through all the parts in *H.M.S. Pinafore*. Once, all in the same day I was Martha Washington in a school play and delivered a dramatic reading from *Huckleberry Finn*, still wearing my powdered wig. Dad does look like an actor or a singer, someone outstanding, his dark red hair gleaming, tall, with a chin of iron. His hard, laughing face changes in an instant too. I never know what will happen. In all seriousness he says I'll probably be a knockout, if ever I master my appetite. Kind of a Gibson Girl. It's in my favor that I'm a natural blonde with a complexion of peaches and cream, discounting a hive or two when I'm upset. It's my turn to be astonished. For his money my future lies in the cultivation of wifely virtues; but all the same, in school I did my careers project on the theater and read a biography of Katharine Cornell for extra credit.

Dad watches me stir up the chocolate sauce for cocoa, working from scratch the way Mother taught me, and he says he's impressed. Maybe I will be all things to all men. But then the reality of our predicament, the fact that another week has gone by and still we don't have a housekeeper, makes him weak in the knees. Tomorrow he'll begin anew, advertise again and see what turns up this time: an escapee from the nuthouse, a prison matron out to pasture. He hates to give up his bedroom, but who else can he ask to sleep in the cellar? When I offer, Ruthann glares up from her arithmetic. "Well, I'm not sleeping with Dad. His room stinks."

"Hold your tongue, lass, or I'll bring out the pilliwinks." Dad has us in stitches and we become giddy, beg to sleep by the furnace, imagine ways it might be fun. Dad says we have enough in common with orphans, no need to huddle in the coal pile. Which reminds him: "What we really need around here is a bride. Maybe I'll come right out and say so in plain English. 'Handsome widower, something of a ladykiller, gainfully employed, with three adorable children, desires female who will cook, clean, and provide child care in return for endless

10

love and devotion.' '' We smirk, suspecting we don't have that much to give.

I've seen different pictures of women in Dad's wallet. With his looks and charm he probably is a ladykiller; like Rhett Butler he doesn't give a damn. He says so anyway. Considering how impulsive he is, anything seems possible and those women should watch themselves unless they want to waltz in here and end up without a prayer— exactly what Dad predicts.

When I'm angry with Dad I think the worst, remember the worst. I know I glower like Genghis Khan and hope the look will last forever. I'd cast out hope to make him suffer. But other times I'm just the opposite and it seems no one in the world understands me so well, feels just the way I do. Like when we carry the tray with hot chocolate and cookies into the living room and lie in the dark to watch the fire. We know we're going to sing and probably be sad too. Something will remind Dad of Mother and he'll speak her name. "Phoebe always wanted a house with a big front veranda." Or, "During the war Phoebe worked for the State Department." I lie very still, holding my breath, heart racing. I want him to say more but I'm afraid, too. Once I overheard him talking to Grandma: "It's a fine thing to never know if you'll get home and find your wife with her head in the oven."

Another part of our ritual is taking turns at the window, invoking the snow, Dad and I taking our chances with natural disaster, in a reckless mood and loving it. Just to be snowbound and no school tomorrow. Dad says he knows what I mean. Even though he will probably have to march off to work, right on schedule, sit remorsefully over an adding machine and carry the grail of the diminished fifth, he'll feel briefly more lighthearted. As though things might have been different. Snow allows for the work of the imagination, lays scaffolding for illusion. Who else talks like that? If Dad gets that close to the women in his wallet it's no wonder they lose their wits and long to be his bride.

It's a good thing I'm getting to know him, for Dad gets on better than he says. In the morning he sings along

11

with the radio while he's shaving and he reads both the morning and the evening papers. We have subscriptions to *Life* and *Time*. Women are always inviting him to dinner, and lots of nights I have to sleep on the couch until he gets home, just like a hired babysitter.

Around our dinner table, Dad quizzes us on foreign affairs, drills us on logical syllogism and the structuring of formal argument, something he learned in college when he was in the debating society. He's full of surprises and of course he's too much for me, hurting my feelings, boxing me into a corner of contradictory assertions. It's all in good fun—he wants to make up—the pros and cons of capital punishment in the soup, likewise the existence of God. The biggest question of all: Is anything worthwhile? Dad hopes I'll forgive any insults in the interest of looking at both sides of an argument. Nothing makes any sense, he reminds me. How to explain Hitler? One of his Peabody friends, of Japanese descent, spent the war behind barbed wire and that was in California. Although it isn't easy to be his daughters, Dad says, the proof is in the pudding and he's proud of us. So far we're meeting the challenge. I don't have to ask why he's nicer to Ruthann. She doesn't like to argue about every little thing.

Dad's hopes are even higher for Tommy, who has come into our lives when Dad is older and he hopes wiser. Certainly not so much of a wiseass. He figures he has at least some idea of what a son might need, although it undermines his courage every day to see a little boy without a mother.

I try to be like a mother to Tommy, although Grandma says it's too much for a young girl and calls every week to see if Dad has found a housekeeper yet. Much as I want to remain the person Mother knew and trusted, Ruthann tells me, "You've changed," arch and superior, watching to see how I'm taking it. Sometimes I think I'm losing my grip.

"I'm the only one who knows what you're really like," Ruthann goes on, black eyes impersonal, as though I'm someone she's reading about. I don't want to prove her right but sometimes I can't help myself. One morning I was late for school, rummaging through my drawers for something to wear. I found a blouse and put it on, standing in front of her, smoothing it down. "Is this too wrinkled to wear?" I pleaded. Ruthann scrutinized me, had me revolve slowly like a model. "Yes, it is," she determined. I drew back my arm and slapped her hard in the face. She turned her back, hunched before me, shoulders shaking in her thin print dress, her head up to my chest.

"I hate myself," I said, the way Mother sometimes did, her head in her hands. "Hit me. Go on." I held out my arm. "I'll give you all my allowance. Don't tell Dad." There would be no explaining.

Most times, though, Ruthann beats me to it, her hand out, demanding the payoff or she'll tell. Just because I hid the pieces of a broken plate or laughed when she said "Shitfire." I pay her; even if she wouldn't ever tell, it's a relief to make some reparation. I entirely lose sight of the fact that Mother kept us both home from the fair after Ruthann dropped the car keys under the porch and lied about it, and that she used to shut me in the closet and hold the door whenever she got the chance. Somehow Ruthann seems like the good one to me. Finding the guilty party doesn't interest Dad. He says he's aware extortion flourishes under his roof but he doesn't want any details. Tranquillity is cheap at any price.

I can't explain what goes on in me. At school when I came back from my mother's funeral the other girls and boys watched me sideways, wide-eyed and silent, waiting for something from me. I outdid myself, friendlier than ever before, laughing at the slightest pretext, volunteering for dodgeball, first on the diamond at noon. Finally my best friend in that town said, "I thought you'd be different. I thought you'd be sad."

I gave her my brightest smile. "Oh no. I know my mother's in heaven, where she's so much happier, looking down on us. She wouldn't want me to be sad." It was clear that girl was no real friend, had known me only a few months, but at least she was satisfied and never brought up the subject again. And then we moved away,

13

and after the first time, when they found out about it and stared, the new kids forgot. I don't talk about it. It's enough to hear Ruthann sometimes at night.

Dad, Tommy, and I fool around in front of the fire, but Ruthann leaves the room, turning on the kitchen light to finish her homework. "That's my girl," Dad whistles in to her, his finger wiping shame at me, the poor example. "With that kind of attention I'll have her eating out of my hand in no time," he whispers. Then he has me get up and shut the swinging door to keep it dark for us poor dreamers; I just laugh, never knowing whose side he's on. "Your sister could actually amount to something," he tells me. "I don't even resent the electric bill for her reading light. It's an investment that might pay off. Maybe she'll take care of me in my dotage—although at this rate I'll have to win her over fast."

By firelight Dad's eyes have the bitter shine of drill bits. I almost get a taste in my mouth. "You there, Blondie," he fires at me. "Title and author!

The venerable woods—rivers that move
In majesty, and the complaining brooks
That make the meadows green; and, poured round all,
Old Ocean's gray and melancholy waste,—"

Instead, I show off and go on with the poem until I'm stuck and Dad helps me, through the whole of "Thanatopsis," resorting to the text off and on to keep us going. After that it's a round with "Snowbound." The fire, Dad's melancholy, Tommy's delight at lying in Dad's elbow, these draw me too close, make my chest heave like old ocean's waste, and I go out to the lighted kitchen for a cold drink of water.

Ruthann, hard at it, frowns into her notebook as though it contains her fate. Her overlong bangs straggle over her face, and peeping through she quips, " 'Abou Ben Adhem,' a-hem," clearing her throat of a bullfrog. She draws the grid for tic-tac-toe and gives me first crack at the center. When I win she sticks out her tongue. Dad says Ruthann was the only baby he ever knew who laughed at a spanking even after she'd been caught. He admires her spirit. I'm the one who makes everything a federal case.

Some things roll off my back. My untouched home-work lies stuck off in a book with curling edges, probably under my bed in a pile of dust. I can't seem to concentrate. And if I do manage to finish it, it will be sloppy and inaccurate. My teacher will shake her head and say I could do better. She knows my father is a teacher.

But what if I couldn't? I get a sinking feeling when I start to think maybe Dad's got me figured and really I am a limited person. Mother had a high opinion of me, and when I got flustered and forgot my times tables or mixed up trying to tie my shoe, she only laughed and said I had to calm down and I'd do fine. Dad doesn't believe in mollycoddling; "You have to face up to things," he says, pacing the room, tattooing his finger-tips together. "Not everyone can go to college. Maybe it's enough to be a blonde." He shrugs.

Last time report cards came out I dreaded going home with mine. I considered forging Dad's signature, but of course Ruthann couldn't wait to raise the flag over her string of A's, so I forked it over. To himself Dad read: "Three B's, three C's." When he handed it back he bit his lip, then smiled and said, "Very good." He didn't hit me or call names and in the first flush of relief I thought I was happy. It was only later, when I told Ruth-ann that her legs were bowed because she hadn't had enough vitamin D, that the full import of being a limited person hit home.

Tommy lands on Dad's foot for a horsy ride, his eyes illuminated upward by the fire as though he's an astral figure floating overhead. "I want to be a fisherman," he squeals on the way up. Dad says once he aimed to be a fisher of men like his dear departed father. That led to three months in a Presbyterian seminary, an ordeal all around that ended when he was caught in the bell tower at midnight working with two other students to disassemble the summons to chapel. Even the resulting cacophony had not deflected justice and he had agreed to leave quietly—one more disappointment to his mother, who still believed you could get blood from a stone.

"You can be anything you want, my boy." Dad swoops Tommy to the floor. Tonight nobody minds that he's the favorite, the family pet. "A boy has to work overtime to be a failure with society on his side. This child isn't even three and already he's got an eye to his future. Take a lesson from him, daughter. Myself, I've sunk this low as a gesture of pure defiance."

"You're not a failure, Dad," I tell him. I can't imagine what he means. "Grandma says you had the highest I.Q. of anybody in Charleston and your teacher at the conservatory said you were a genius." I'm proud of him and hope it won't make him angry to be reminded of the past, of all his hopes and dreams.

"That woman is dreaming still," is all he says. If there's one thing Dad says he can't stand it's an indulgent, good-hearted woman who thinks she knows everything because she's never been out of the house. I'm glad Grandma doesn't hear him now; she looks up to him. But it keeps me on my toes. I might as well be learning what I can from Dad, since, more than most, he tells me what he's thinking. I'm flattered too, although sometimes I'm not certain he knows I pay attention.

"Oh well," Dad says, "when night falls and you're stretched in front of your own hearth, your children close at hand, poetry in your heart, life doesn't seem so bad. Although I sure wish I could mainline get-up-and-go. At this moment every go-getter in that rinky-dink academy is struggling to find the lost chord." Which reminds Dad, and he whistles Ruthann in to join us—he can take only so much of a good example. We all lie on the rug before the dying fire. I've read that in Sweden whole families will bed down together over a warm tile oven. It sounds cozy, but Ruthann keeps resting her leg against mine because she knows I get the heebie-jeebies, and for Dad it's Indian burns, so everything is howling and pestering. Later I will be glad to go off to my cold sheets, warm

16

them myself, and have some peace and quiet. After a fire, the rooms upstairs are hazy with currents of sweet smoke. Dad says it's from burning apple wood.

Grandma doesn't forget us. She writes Ruthann and me frequent long letters to keep our spirits up, her stated mission last year when we lived with her in Florida. As though it might help, she repeats how much Dad loves us, that he is determined to keep us together no matter what. We are not to take his complaints to heart but do our best to make a nice home. What else does Dad have? And if he should want to remarry, we should be the first to rejoice. Because, if ever a man needed a woman! Someday, she says, we'll know what she means.

I know it's lonely for Grandma too, now that Ruthann and I are here and she's all alone in Florida again, years since Aunt Nila died. Not that they were ever much company for each other, Dad says, the little they were willing or required to say to each other passing through him. Until he wised up and pretended to be stone deaf, or made up blatant lies. Dad says he doesn't want to talk about it, caught in the middle between a grieving widow and the miserly spinster who was his dead father's sister. No wonder he took off for the open road.

I like it that Grandma worries about us even though Dad says she can't help herself. Last year she took me to the doctor because I was sighing all day long, couldn't get a deep breath, couldn't yawn. The doctor said I was all right, was probably just adjusting to my mother's death and time would be the cure. Grandma didn't think he was a lot of help; she could have come up with that herself. Home remedies would have to do: piano lessons, tapioca pudding, and jokes. What she called getting a perspective on life. That still comes through the mail. She teases me, writing that she hopes I'm getting plenty of rain and kisses. Last year I complained that the constant sunshine in Florida was boring, and when I ran away from David Mason he chased after me and kissed me on the leg while I was scrambling and twisting. In Grandma's opinion I'm going to have an unusual life,

17

because most young people don't want to wear black and stand out in a downpour. She fears I'm too much like my father. For emphasis Grandma writes big and underlines, uses poetic punctuation. In person she rolls her eyes and drops her false teeth. But when she's serious, she looks us straight in the eye and says Ruthann and I should be allowed to settle in one place and get to know other young people. Florida isn't for young people—they don't need constant sunshine. At the end of her letters, in the biggest blackest print, she directs us to burn them. Immediately! She doesn't want Dad to know she worries. But I can tell that Dad never doubts he's the star of her letters, his poor deluded mother.

Most of the time now Dad does his best, and Ruthann and I have agreed not to tell Grandma when he loses his temper. She can't abide fighting; even Ruthann and I gave her angina with our bickering and she had to rest on the couch; rests that went on so long and were so deep we had to take turns tiptoeing in to be sure she was breathing. Dad is reforming, he's told us. It's only kidding around when he declares that self-control is not natural to him, that he has the killer instinct and is a son of Belial. When he does slap us around, he comes later, humbled, to ask our forgiveness, his eyes shifting, shy and uncomfortable, as though confession is what is unnatural to him. How could we turn our backs? I swallow my tears and right away he's joking again, ordering us to forgive him under penalty of the bleak alternatives. Laughter sputters through my locked jaw, the knot in my chest dissolves. Then I am humbled. I feel certain Dad would dash through fire to save us. He has the flamboyance of a hero.

Across from where we lie in the living room is a small wood, hardly larger than our house and lawn, but it reminds me of what can never be, of wild horses, a labyrinth, and Lapland. I haven't gone to explore—I'm bound to be disappointed, expecting too much and the wrong things. I'd rather keep imagining than know what Dad knows. He suspects poison ivy and a fetid smell. Besides, he says, why get attached to the landmarks of suburbia. Here today, gone tomorrow.

Ruthann would go in with me. Just today she asked if I still want to run away, something we used to plan all the time. We'd do better than Dad did, and never come back. We could use the money from Mother's bankbook, she urges, a secret I told her about and something we keep hidden from everyone, even Grandma. To me it's invaluable, but still I'm in a rage when Ruthann mentions it—as though all we'd have to do is wave a wand and turn it into gold. For all I know, at the bank there's nothing but a pile of dust.

And where would we go? Ruthann's face, dark and square, is oddly womanly on her thin child's body, reminds me of Mother's tense wistfulness. The fragment of metal stuck in her temple since she was a baby glints like a true beauty mark. And her arms, dangling beside her, fidget in the jitters. With her nature, Ruthann would sit down in the road halfway to somewhere and refuse to budge. Leave me standing at the altar. I remember when she locked herself in the Sunday-school room, once when we were little. Finally I got fed up and walked away. Hours later they got to her where she was huddled in a supply closet fast asleep, her head on a Bible. I had told what she did and she got a spanking, but I was supposed to take good care of her and I cried too. That evening I gave her my dessert, which she ate, savoring every bite as though it soothed an actual wound. I wonder if one of these nights I'll have had all I can take, get out of bed, march to the kitchen, and pour Dranō down my throat. It might be done before I could stop myself.

"We're really going to get it, girl," Dad says, hoping and praying. "Just look at that stuff come down." I stand beside him at the window and feel the same thrill. Snow swirls in the halo of the streetlamp and I'm inspired, describing it as a fire or, on the other hand, a ewer foaming with mist, while Dad shakes his head, half smiling and dubious, his hand on my shoulder. "You're too much

19

for me." He says maybe it would calm me down to read some history, bone up on the physical sciences.

From the kitchen Ruthann calls, "How much is a furlong?" Dad salutes her way, calls her diligent and level-headed, just what the doctor ordered, goes in to help. He says it's rare to meet up with a young Einstein, in skirts no less; although he has noticed she seldom cracks a book unless there's an assignment due—Dad's not one to be caught napping.

Of course, he finds fault with my reading, too much and all the wrong things. Even *Jane Eyre* doesn't meet his standards. Anyone can read for fun. I answer back that I've read a biography of Paul Revere and a book on the Lewis and Clark expedition, but he's not impressed. "You can't fool me with the Landmark Series."

Dad surveys our neighborhood as though he's a displaced person, lost and in danger among so many other houses built to the same dismal plan, traffic on the fronting road heavier every day. A small-town boy, he never thought he could exist a stone's throw from the nation's capital, in a place where so many others had chosen to live, cheek to jowl with the organization man. Whatever possessed him to buy on the nether side of the Mason-Dixon Line. How will he ever get his money out, the sidewalk already taken up to widen the road, every spring the watermark in the basement a little higher. The new airport may not leave air space sufficient for breathing. All Dad can say to lift his spirits is: "In this neighborhood I'm Jones." It's true there are really poor people on our street, kids who walk along with us to school, seem to do without lunch or eat some other place. I often see them at the corner grocery buying candy. One girl is in my class and I ask her questions she seems too shy to answer, pulling her hair into strings. She wears a skirt that always has the same big tear, fastened with a safety pin. I imagine taking her home for a needle and thread, then combing out her hair.

The phone rings. "Don't answer it," Dad says. "No one can help me." It may be Grandma calling. She'd detect his mood in a second, but before she could get in gear he'd hand the phone to Ruthann or me. Sermons from *Coronet* and *The Reader's Digest* don't appeal to him. It's no secret what Dad thinks of self-help.

Listening to the long ringing I miss Grandma. I can almost hear her dreamy waterfall prelude to "Beautiful Saviour," the overture pounding to "Onward, Christian Soldiers." Which is only a tease. Grandma is a pacifist, something that is part of her old-time religion, and she won't sing hymns about war. Her music makes me think of Mother, although she never played hymns at all.

Early on Sunday mornings, when we lived with Grandma, we took a bus out into the country, leaving behind the lakes, palm trees, and camellias for sand and open fields, thin stands of pine she called "the barrens." We had to walk a long way down a sandy road, Ruthann and I holding Grandma's arms to steady her where weeds and heavy rains had broken up the level, moving slowly toward Grandma's special church, which shone in the distance like Beulah Land. Inside, the faded whitewashed walls reflected all the pale morning colors like a glass bowl of saltwater taffy and the tinny piano gave the hymns the same frothy, tinsel feel of enamel candies, tasting of salt and molasses.

Clear windows overlooked cotton fields and I stared out during the long sermons, off into the emptiness, pretending that the colored people were proceeding along the rows as they did on weekdays, dragging loaded tow sacks. I would imagine going out to join them so they would know there were white people who cared, who knew they were God's people, as good as anybody. I'd go ahead and invite them in to sing and pray with us, and then I'd have to fight when some of the church members tried to turn them out and called them names. When murderers came riding out of the night with flaming torches, I would have to put my body between the Negro people and danger. If I had to die that was all right, because my grave was never forgotten and people always gathered there to sing and keep me company.

Grandma has strong opinions concerning brotherly love, and every day Ruthann and I found little adventures

21

in Florida to take home to her, going out of our way to use the water fountains for colored only, approaching Negro ladies on the street to politely ask directions. In church we put all our money in the envelopes that went for the African missions. Sharing those moments of solidarity that had become so rare between Ruthann and me; I never knew which might be the last. Our arms stretching out as one to drop a widow's mite into the collection plate.

During the service the ladies fluttered paper palm-leaf fans depicting famous Bible scenes and advertising local funeral parlors. Their summery dresses lifted in the little breeze, wafting talcum; the few men who remained in the congregation of mostly elderly people were sweet with aftershave. I felt transported directly to Galilee. So many tiny images of the Saviour in motion, the visible heat. I could almost see Him walking on the waves.

I feel the lonesomeness of our life in the house in the dark where we lie by the fire in No Man's Land, company for a disappointed man. Sometimes I positively delight in being like Dad, the lone wolf, beyond the reach of telephones, engulfed by morbid tendencies. But they catch up with you, and I think Dad probably misses Mother, although he doesn't say. She used to declare him handsome as the day is long, laughed at his jokes, and encouraged him to believe in himself. Everywhere we went the piano went too, and there was music night and day. Even when Dad was gone, suddenly and without explanation, there wasn't any worry about when he'd be back, returning in some surprising way. I can't remember that I ever asked Mother about him, even after I'd heard them fight and saw she'd been crying. I trusted her to take care of it. I'd like to have a way with Dad myself and make him feel better, but I'm too susceptible. I think sometimes I may actually be a lone wolf too.

Partly; the other part hoping and hoping that Billy Richardson is coming back for me. He said he'd wait, and I look out the window every night before I settle down to sleep, expecting him rain or snow, imagining his kiss on the air. He just might be coming along on his motorcycle, braving the worst conditions to see if I am ready. I can recapture the exact feeling: my arms around his waist, his jacket, leather soft and stirring as skin, crushed against my blouse. It was too exciting not to hold on tight, the wind about to take me away, while he grinned back over his shoulder again and again, the silver of his profile in moonlight, smoky yet distinct. Everything else blurred, trees and houses engulfed in the roar of iron and oil, the scattered sparks, the only clear shape his body in front of the moon.

The ride was swift, dramatic, like his cigarette thrown off in the dark. Too soon we were back home with Dad waiting at the curb, still in his light seersucker suit from work, and I felt shy about saying anything to Billy except thank you, never knowing what might come out of my mouth, whether it would be dumb or something Dad wouldn't like, and in his silence we would all see the sorry sight of me in my tight blue jeans. I went right off to bed with Ruthann when Dad said. From my window I heard them, Billy doing most of the talking, Dad drawing him out, asking questions and murmuring, ''Yes,'' and ''You don't say,'' making another admirer. Regardless of what he might be thinking, if he even listened.

But I don't care what he thinks of Billy. I know what I think. I sneaked into the hall to listen to them talking while they had their beers. Billy said, ''I haven't found the right one yet, I guess. Margy's growing up. Maybe I'll wait for her.'' Alone in the dark hall I began to tremble, hardly able to believe my ears. Until Ruthann came creeping, to pretend we were enemy spies or some such thing, and I went in to bed. She doesn't care a fig for Billy Richardson, wouldn't care if we were caught listening in like little children. She even passed up her turn on the motorcycle and plugged her ears while it idled. He's part of why I can't talk to Ruthann now without it turning into a fight. Not that we'd ever fight over the same man. I can't forget the way I felt when Mike O'Brien walked me home from the swimming pool. He was wheeling his English bike. The wheels hissed and

23

clicked. When he raised his eyes and looked at me under a streetlamp, the moment froze. I was aware of even the veins laced to his heart. Ruthann wouldn't forget he's Catholic, smokes cigarettes, and is scraping the bottom of his class.

That night, after the motorcycle ride, I woke up, remembering abruptly that years before, when we'd lived in Washington with Mother, I'd known Billy Richardson in the old neighborhood. Once he took me down into the basement of his apartment building to show me a rat drowned in a toilet, a vision I couldn't get out of my mind. Closing my eyes after that, I wondered if under cover of darkness all things happened by premonition.

It stops snowing, so emphatically Dad and I take it as a personal insult. Next we're off to Alaska, we agree. He bets igloos neither appreciate nor depreciate. Probably they never heard of eminent domain—the fate of our sidewalks. And maybe in the Yukon I'd make a name for myself. In extremity men are drawn to a woman who's stubborn as a mule. He thinks, whatever my shortcomings, I have the instinct for survival. But I have only one wild thing on my mind. I imagine myself captive in a tepee, embraced by a love-struck savage who wants only me and at the last will even forsake his pagan ways. Later I will think about my homework, I tell myself as I lug sleepy Tommy up to bed, counting the hours that separate me from my doom.

Sundays are the worst for me, living under the gun, and I prepare myself for Monday mornings in various ways. I could set the alarm for six o'clock and do some studying then—a plan I've yet to stick to. Dad says, "You better learn to stick to something, girl. Unless you want to end up like your old man, sick at heart, a menace to animals and small children." I hold Tommy over the toilet, then worm his limp body into pajamas. I imagine myself standing before Billy while he begins to open my blouse.

Grandma used to help me with my homework, to get me started. She played the clown, pencil stuck into her blue hairdo, her forehead furrowed, looking down her bifocals hopelessly into the opened textbook. I had to tell her everything, the simplest facts; it had been centuries since she'd used her head for anything but a hat rack. She crossed her eyes and lolled her tongue. When I got through with that lamebrain, it was a breeze to answer the questions at the end of the chapter.

But when Dad tries to help me, we're wrangling first thing. He jiggles his foot and sighs, clears his throat, drums the pencil. We both despair, and in no time he's out of patience completely, calling me "Dumbo" and "Last-Minute Charlie."

I'm insulted, huffing and puffing. "I don't like school, that's what. I like to be dumb. I don't want any friends." I watch his green eyes thicken like a stormy sea.

"Then what the hell do you want?" When I get on my high horse, making the most of my dissatisfactions, Dad is disgusted. I tell him, "I like to complain, that's what! I like to be disagreeable." I could say more, but I watch his face, see how he's taking it, see what I can get away with, my tone half joking.

If Dad's in the mood he draws me out, just like I'm company, and I find myself singing the blues for real, revealing my hopes and fears. I live to regret it though, for at the very next meal he reminds me that I want to lose weight, or he interrupts my reading: "I thought you were going to try to bring up your grades."

I'm afraid Ruthann gets the brunt from me. I hear her making a dash for the bathroom, to beat me into the tub, first into the water which we have to share to save on the gas bill. I start to race her but she's winning, and because I'm angry that it stopped snowing and she did her homework and I didn't, I let her go ahead and win. I know how to get back.

When she's out of the tub I pass her in the hall without a glance, cold as stone. I don't say good night when I get in bed and right away I turn my back. She could be dead for all I care. She switches off the light and says "Good night" a second time, hoping she can win me over, get me to laugh and talk. I'm on a distant star. The light goes back on and she high-dives on the springs, then tries another tack. "Who'd you rather have for your boyfriend, Marlon Brando or Roy Rogers? Remember Grandma's teeth in the bathroom glass? When the toilet water was purple?" I'm not to be reached, and in the silence she bangs her fists on the headboard.

"Why did the moron drive into the building?" She horse-laughs, bounding on the bed. Dad calls out, "Cut that out," and he means it. In the stillness I reach out and turn off the light.

Just like that, Ruthann is undone. The springs make muffled shifting sounds and in the faint light I see her shaking. The silent treatment seems like cruel and unusual punishment and I hate myself, long to make up and be her best friend. "Good night," I venture, but it's too late. For someone so spunky and organized, Ruthann crushes more quickly than I believe and I think I hardly know her. Right then I'd offer her anything—first into the bathwater the rest of her life. Both she and Dad get to me. Sometimes, in spite of all my enthusiasms, I wonder if I'll ever have a life of my own.

Ruthann cries and I get up to straddle her back, beginning to connect her head bone to her neck bone and so on down her back and legs—"Now hear de word ob de Lord," I sing into her ear, feeling her relax, forgiving me. I go on and make up a song, like when we're riding in the car, making it soft and dreamy, about Dad when he was a boy and ran away to the mountains. The white curtains shining in the moonlight, Mother's dotted Swiss with their illusion-lace border, all stippled at this hour, are misty, drifting like a fog. In the oval mirror at the dressing table, our world seems to be dear and precious, something to hold on to. A train whistle, near and far, tells me this is all we have.

We're asleep a little while and then Dad comes to wake me. He's going out, now that the snow has come to nothing and everything's a dreary same. It seems I am scarcely ever really asleep and I don't remember my dreams. At a summons I could rise up to fix a meal or take the graveyard shift, and I follow Dad to the living room, dragging

26

my blankets to the couch. Ruthann isn't far behind, settling at the other end, our feet and legs entwined.

Dad goes out to walk the highway, along the old route toward Richmond. Although he may end up at a roadhouse, he says he goes to be alone, refusing any rides, walking the blue devils out of his system. One of his friends told me he sees Dad sometimes at night, but Dad won't stop, just waves and keeps going. He's on my mind while I lie, waking and sleeping, keeping an eye on things.

I like it when he's gone and I'm in charge. Ruthann and I get on better, and sometimes I can pretend Mother is upstairs sleeping and I'm taking care of her too. I hate it most when Dad's friends are over, drinking beer and playing poker, sprawled at the dining-room table in suits wrinkled from the day, ties yanked open, lips and eyes moist and loose. If I have to go in there, they make a production of it, stand up, straightening their clothes, and, like Southern gentlemen, bow in mock formality. I must use my manners and say "How do you do?" and shake hands, make polite conversation, unless I want to hear from Dad. The friend who is the dentist won't let go of my hand, insisting I am a beautiful girl while I blush and feel their eyes appraising me. Although Dad calls musicians prima donnas and fuddy-duddies behind their backs, one of the teachers from the conservatory comes occasionally and he's the only one I like. Sometimes he passes on a hand of poker and opens up his violin case and plays for me. Afterward the men clap from the dining room. When I had to interrupt their game, to remind Dad to give me money for my gym suit, he asked, "What have you done for me lately?" The friends laughed as though I were the farmer's daughter.

I hear a strange noise in the house, from the basement it seems, and Ruthann and I prepare to meet the danger. We search high and low, armed with the baseball bat and the broom. I am weak and trembly and when unexpectably a broomstraw tickles my arm, I leap and yip, nearly falling down the stairs. We know how we carry on and laugh at ourselves, though our excursion, lighting the

27

house, makes us feel more at home, and once again we can imagine we'll always be together, wanting nothing more. Even as I'm pretending, I wonder if it will ever happen again. The last time I played dolls passed without recognition. When we tell Dad we get scared alone in the house at night, he accuses us of hysterics and play-acting. It's unlikely anyone would bother us, he says—whatever would they do then?

We settle back on the couch and I begin to worry, counting the hours until school. The school I go to now is called "progressive" and I'm less afraid. So far this year I haven't seen a teacher hit anybody, and if a girl has cramps there's a private place to lie down. When boys come back from the principal's office I can see they haven't been crying. I misspelled twenty words in my careers report and the teacher wrote, "See me after class," and didn't make me a laughingstock.

I miss Mother the most at lunch. I sense that everybody notices my dilapidated sandwich, which I threw together right after breakfast when I wasn't hungry, sees my crumpled lunch bag has lost its starch. Sometimes I pretend I forgot it and leave it in my coat. It's too pathetic. But Carol Rollins didn't help when her mother included an extra sandwich for me, leftovers from the Sunday roast, or perfect layers of pre-sliced cheese, cut on the diagonal. Charity was ashes in my mouth. Dad says he'll brook no complaints concerning his shopping; potted ham and canned corned beef are cheap and edible. If we don't like gelatin we can contact Children's Aid. Usually I resort to peanut butter and jelly. Although I like that best, it's the most woebegone of all, the bleeding jelly staining the white bread gray.

Progressive education is full of itself. Big ideas, Dad says—in his day I would have been black and blue, not getting an afternoon a month off to "instrument the approaching sociability of boys and girls." I dream about these monthly tea dances, but the actual affairs, huddled masses of boys and girls at opposite ends of the gym, the shining floor between like a shallow sea, each crossing made at hazard and in open view, remind me of notes

I've found on my desk. One read, "Roses are red, violets are blue." Inside was a drawing of a naked lady with curly yellow hair. The few couples who can dance in the face of such insinuation put the rest of us to shame.

But now it seems I will be among them. Last Friday Henry Wilson came up to me in the hall and asked me to go with him the next time. I said yes, but now, Ruthann's legs on mine, I feel hobbled. I can't dance, except the fandango, which I do by myself. I have nothing to wear. Girls invited by boys are expected to dress up and wear stockings and heels to school, all day the chosen ones. Dad will shrug and ask if I think he's made of money. He'll tell me to wear my saddle shoes and hold my head high: learn to bear the lesser humiliations gladly.

Maybe Henry won't mind what I wear. He's liked me all year, ever since we had shop together and I flinched every time the saw sliced through a piece of wood. He seems easy to please, calls me "Chiquita Banana," so I will laugh and toss my head. Although if we sit down together at one of the little side tables it seems I'll have to find something to say.

I like to be teased by boys, which is how it started with Mr. McMasters. I don't want to think about him but he's one of my worries and sneaks up on me in the middle of the night. There he is when I close my eyes, the braided gym rope with the whistle looping through the golden hair sprigging the opened V of his shirt. Once I imagined it was a silver cross and he a wandering troubadour, not my everyday shop teacher, coach of the boys' lacrosse team. But when I got down to his office I felt like one of those girls who deserve to be strangled or worse.

For a couple of months we'd sort of been friends. He teased me about my curly hair, naming me Athena. In the hall he always picked me out, calling "Man-o'-War" or "Citation," calling attention to my track record in Florida, where I won the county fifty-yard dash. The boys turned to notice. Mr. McMasters said I looked like Ingrid Bergman. All the attention went to my head and I quite forgot I'm just a silly girl and began to dream Billy Richardson would have to fight to win my favors.

The day it went wrong between us, I met Mr. Mc-Masters on the stairs, all eager, a chicken for the plucking. "I want to see you in my office," he said, his eyes on my shoes. I tried to think: had I been careless when I sanded my pump lamp or somehow neglected to respond when he'd spoken or teased me? Did he like someone else? Was I going to fail? He seemed distracted, moving off, a little hop in his walk. "Something's come up," he said over his shoulder. "Maybe you can help me." I wanted to—a wink, a grin. If Peter Piper picked a peck of pickled peppers. Maybe he was disgusted with me because over the summer I'd gained some weight.

I trudged along to his basement cubicle, past the mimeograph room with its draughts of heady chemicals, through aisles of steel lockers to the ceiling. I didn't see anyone but him, the echo of our footsteps sounding as though we'd entered a cave; far off above us in daylight, classes in session behind closed doors, the order of the days holding us like prisoners.

Mr. McMasters turned into his office, snapping on the light. I'd never been there before, in the windowless room, a dusty circular saw propped in the corner, the air stale as though we were in a closet. When I hesitated by the door he said, "Well, come in," impatient. I stationed myself just inside, my papers rattling against my chest where I clutched my books. The newspaper on the desk was opened to the crossword puzzle. In his triangular face his small dark eyes swarmed like a mass of fruit flies.

I held my breath, waiting, my eyes unfocused and faraway as though the better to hear. He moved his papers, stepping in a careful silent trail he seemed to have followed before. For the first time I realized I was taller than he. Perhaps he'd noticed too, for he spoke then: "You seem more grown up than the other girls." His voice sunk in exhaustion. "I thought maybe you'd been around, the way you look. Maybe I could talk to you." He turned his back to bubble a drink from the bottle of springwater suspended behind him, the tiny pointed paper cup overflowing in his hand, splashing the floor. His brown trousers hung against his canvas shoes, slapping the soles as though he padded in bedroom slippers. I watched myself watching him, not quite ready to give up hope that we would still be friends.

When he came close to me, I backed into the wall. My neck prickled from his breath as though it had come out of him cold. He leaned on the wall, one hand on either side of my face, angling his close to speak. "I thought you would have heard stuff going around. Some tough talk. I mean some of the girls have been saying stuff. I thought you might have heard. You know. Words. Like 'fuck,' 'cunt.' '' Rasping from his throat, his words repeated while I stared into the far bluish water of the cooler, which seemed to be filling the room and drowning us. "You know. I know you know. I've seen you looking at me." From the boys' locker room a basketball whacked the wall, releasing me, and I kicked over the metal wastebasket beside us. Mr. McMasters jumped as I whirled out the door, running through the empty corridor and up the stairs without looking back. The double doors at the front of the school stopped me by the principal's office. I don't know where I thought I was going, into the rain, no umbrella, no one at home. Rain sheeted the glass, swirls of paper and twigs sucked along to the storm drain. It was a good thing no one came around until I got control of myself, because I wouldn't have been able to hide my feelings. Although when your mother's dead everybody thinks they already know your troubles.

When I was a little girl Dad played a game with me until I got big enough and wouldn't do it anymore. He was in the living room in the dark, calling me to come in, snapping and growling. "Come here, little girl." His voice wavering, secretive. "Come here. Step into the den of the wolf of old Siberia." Sly whispers and shrieks of laughter. Mother, half smiling, shook her head at me. "No, you don't. Don't go in there. You end up crying every time." She turned back to the sink.

31

"Don't listen to your mother, little girl," the wolf begged. "Come closer. A fire burns in the heart of the cave. A bed of eiderdown waits. A dreamless sleep. His hot breath will give you the shivers. Don't be afraid, although the wolf is hungry. Don't listen to reason." If only I could sneak in and spy on the wolf. I edged closer.

Then I was caught, pulled in and down, the wolf in his glory. Gleeful and superior, he howled and ground his merciless teeth. I wailed, crushed in his bones. I kicked and twisted. Caught. It wasn't fair.

Mother arrived, hands on hips, the overhead light showing the wolf plain as day. She stood over us. "Honestly. A grown man. I'd think you'd be ashamed."

The wolf sat up, rolling down his sleeves and fastening his cuffs. "She knew what she was getting."

Mother took my hand and pulled me away. Under the lights, beside her, I was brave again and stuck out my shoe, nudging the wolf. "I told you." He grinned up at Mother. "Every little girl wants to play with the wolf, wants to see if she can get the best of him."

"Nonsense," Mother said, and led me away to the kitchen.

Mr. McMasters is the first wolf I've met since. I knew him the instant I approached his den. Now we don't look at each other or talk in the halls. He wonders if I've told. I shouldn't have gone with him, shouldn't have played along. At least I know a wolf when I see one. Mother told Dad he was scaring me. "I didn't make the world," he said.

Ruthann sighs, her head under the covers. I wonder what she thinks as we roam from place to place, our possessions narrowed down to a few clothes, some special keepsakes. Mother's things disappeared before I thought to notice, and now there's only one small snapshot of her left, which I keep in my Bible. Sometimes Ruthann and I can still be the best of friends and we remember we're sisters, lucky to have each other. When Dad's girlfriend was at dinner, bragging on and on about her peppery salad, which we only ate to be polite, she leaned on the table so her bosom shot up over the top of her halter dress in two fat hearts. Ruthann bent to pick up her napkin, muttering, "Hot peppers." Now every time we play jump rope Ruthann yells, "Hot peppers," and we fall on the ground and hoot.

But then without any warning it's suddenly more fun for Ruthann to see me on the spot. "I'm telling," she accuses me, a solemn stranger. "You laughed at Dad's girlfriend."

"You're telling! I'm the one that should tell," I ought to say. Put an end to that and tough it out. But each time I fall to pieces and start to beg and plead with her, showing all my weakness. I can look back and see how tempting it might be, how it would astonish her. Why, she might want to see if it will happen all over again. I am the perfect candidate for blackmail.

The trouble is, I feel bad. I believe there's something to tell. That must be why I came out with it and told Dad about Mr. McMasters. The minute he asked me if I was worried about something, I started to cry and it spilled out, the whole story, except Dad had to say the bad words himself while I nodded my head.

He didn't say anything while I cried. Then he asked, "Do you want me to speak to him? Talk to the people at school?"

"I'd rather die," I swore, although I knew he would despise me for a coward. But I couldn't help it. It felt like it would be the end of me, for people to know.

"Have it your way," Dad said, and left me alone. The subject didn't come up again, but it was something between us, and the next time I needed a box of Kotex in a rush, I gave the money to the lady next door and asked her for the favor. She handed them to Dad when he answered the door and he appeared in my room and threw the bag in my face. "Why in hell didn't you ask me? I'm your father. You better learn to face facts, girl, or the next time you may get more than an earful." That time I thought I would never stop crying, but if I did, I would never cry again.

In spite of all she knows about me, Ruthann takes my

failures as a mortal blow. She's deeply disappointed—at least until she collects. And for the really big things she is beyond even that. There was a game I played with Tommy sometimes when we took our walks. The last time was the day I showed it to Ruthann and I didn't even finish.

When we got to the place where it happened, I sent Ruthann to stand behind a tree to watch. Near to Tommy, but hidden, so he wouldn't know she was there. Then I knelt beside him and began, my back to Ruthann; though I could feel her shock I plunged on, as though under an obligation. "Tommy," I said, "Margy has to leave you now. She hates to go but she has to and you can't come. She won't ever be able to come back to you no matter if you cry and cry, no matter if your heart should break in two. You won't ever see her again." His chin quivered and I kissed him over and over into the cuddly folds, before I stood and turned away, to leave him standing there in his miniature tailored man's hat and coat with the string-fastened mittens dangling at his wrists, his narrow shoulders drooping.

The next part was when I would walk away from him, before he was crying hard, to vanish behind the hedge, then circle back to get close by him to watch him cry. Until I would be crying too. This time, though, Ruthann stepped forward into plain view, a dark unpitying angel sent to judge the quick and the dead, and immediately I abandoned the game, forfeiting the tears and the joyful reunion that came at the end, after Tommy had given up hope and thought I was lost forever. I just turned my back and went on down the street in open daylight, letting them come along, slowing when Ruthann yelled "Wait up," although I could not imagine there was any damnation that would scald like the forgiveness of the innocent.

Lost River

O LD WIDOW SLIPPED OUT IN THE NIGHT. BEFORE SHE was thrown out. Margy was in disgrace and I was humming, "Cat's in the cream jar, what'll I do?" weaving a terrible sight of wilty dandelions through the fence wire, when Dad said, "I can't stand it anymore."

When Dad doesn't know what else to do he gets in the car and drives like hell, to use his expression. He arranged us. I was to sit up beside him so he could keep an eye on me since I'm the troublemaker. I liked that, sitting up with Dad in the sunshine like the wife. I got to hold the map and he showed me the way South. It was a long haul and then some, straight into the land of rattlers and rednecks. Into the heart of Dixie.

"Got that straight, whippersnapper?" Dad's eyes threaded through his face, green like the rivers over the map, narrow and tricky.

"The latitude is thirty-seven degrees north," I informed him, giving the map a thump. Dad scratched his ear and admitted I had my endearing side. He cleared his throat and tuned up: "Carry Me Back to Old Virginny," the down-South place we were going, on our way to visit Dad's old chum from college. And wouldn't he be thrilled to see the four of us coming his way, our chins on the ground. Incidentally, one of Dad's sweetie-pies lives in that same burg and I knew we'd check in on her. Last night when I was in bed I heard him buzzing to her on the phone, spreading the news of his troubles. We went to visit her at her house once and had a boring old tea party. Dad calls her Gloria, but secretly I call her "Glory Bee."

In the morning it was "Pack up, girls, we're hitting the road." We were killing two birds with one stone, because Tommy might end up staying with Dad's old pal where there was another little boy. Dad had Margy get his clothes together, just in case. Tommy was easy to get rid of, Dad said. Folks were standing in line. We girls presented the problem—Saturday's children, we'd have to work for a living. Not me. I'm a student.

I thought Margy would give Tommy a love knot bound with her own yellow hair, or take a lover's leap, but she didn't even shed one tear that I saw. Probably she'd come to agree with Dad that she's not to be trusted, not since Tommy got the burn. It's on his chest, no bigger than a silver dollar, and the doctor said it would take off only a little hair. But given a choice, Dad said, count on Margy to overreact—just because he yelled at her didn't mean he wanted to kill her. But she doesn't know what she might do next, what she'll be to blame for. I'd think she'd welcome the day, some peace and quiet with nobody pestering. I'll have to watch out, though. I don't want her getting away without me.

Dad gave Margy and me a paper bag for our clothes, and then we helped him pack some things from the kitchen to save money on the trip by eating in the car or at a picnic table. For all I knew we'd never be back and I hid a silver candy kiss in the corner of the spice drawer to surprise somebody.

I've lost track of the places I've been, the apartments we've moved into and out of, the people we've known, adventures along the way. Sometimes Mother followed Dad. Then he came along after us. There was no way to figure it. Some places there were rats and Dad had to concoct his special poison of arsenic and ground glass— the certain end of a rat. Other places, all of us had to sleep in one room, which Dad didn't like a bit. Every night I got a spanking, up to all hours. Margy went to five different schools in the first grade, a disadvantage Dad says he tries to keep in mind when report cards come due. I guess I've had only advantages. At school they were amazed and they skipped me ahead from the fifth grade to the sixth.

I had decided to do my part to make this the most enjoyable trip Dad ever had, so I watched him and every time he looked at me I smiled, until he said I was making him self-conscious. Then he held my hand for a while. I wanted to tell him his hand felt like a hair shirt, like in Bible days, just to be interesting. But it was too peaceful. I hardly minded that Margy was stretched out in the back seat, where they had the pillow, taking care of Tommy— which I wouldn't want to do for longer than five minutes anyway, fun as she makes it seem. Margy has a way of making the grass greener on her side. She makes it seem like a holiday when she's scrubbing the floor. She even likes car rides. The longest trip doesn't faze her, not with that imagination, eyes glued to the horizon, scenery inside and out, contented as though she could ride to the ends of the earth and never have to pee. That's another time I get lonely and dream up ways to get her goat.

She started droning out a song to Tommy. Probably a made-up one about the mean boy that ran away who she says was Dad, although I don't like to think so. It would make me too sad. I tried to hear but she kept her voice soft and mystery-mysterious and my neck crinked trying to stretch. When I got on my knees Dad said, ''Sit down before I knock you down,'' which made me testy even though he was smiling. Still, I thought maybe he and I could have a conversation rolling along, so I asked, ''How much money do you make?'' I'm a pistol.

''Not enough,'' he said. ''Why do you ask? Is there something you want?'' His eyes swarmed as though they had a million holes with bees. It's a sore point. Margy and I are not allowed to want anything. It just grinds Dad's nose in his poverty. We're supposed to do without and smile since he can't help it.

I can't help wanting everything in sight and letting him know about it. Margy, of course, tries to be perfect, tries to cooperate. Until, like at Christmas, her shoe had such an awful hole in it, everybody could see it flapping when she was up on the stage with the school chorus, and when Dad got her home he took hold of her neck and held her head against the wall, yelling in her face. She made the whole family look like white trash, parading around like that. When Dad couldn't darn well afford to buy shoes for his children he'd better throw in the towel. Margy cried and cried. That time she got new shoes without asking, shiny new saddle oxfords, size nine and a half. No wonder she tries to stay out of shoe stores.

"The best things in life are free," I told Dad, delivering one of my specials, a long slow curvy wink, something I practiced up in my free time.

Dad said sometimes he had to admit he and I were cut out of the same cloth and that's not a compliment. I take it as one. I was beginning to tell him about my report on South American agriculture, for which he ought to be grateful every time he drinks a cup of coffee, when he interrupted without a never-you-mind, telling Margy to speak up.

Margy didn't want him to hear her made-up story, since he'd accuse her of being soft in the head, so she came up with: " 'Abou Ben Adhem (may his tribe increase!)' " and went on to finish the whole poem.

"What's that I see in yonder fir tree? A dreary old widder, plain as can be," I was muttering to myself.

"What's that?" Dad perked up his ears, but I wasn't telling and gave him another wink. See how he liked being left out. When he noticed I was jabbing a pencil into the upholstery he grabbed it and it sailed out the window. He told me I'd better behave myself if I knew what was good for me; then he went back to Margy-Pargy, telling her about a special place he was going to show us, a lost place where he said he hoped to find the strength to go on. We were even driving out of the way. "I've about reached my limits," he said. That's one of the things Dad and I have in common: we have our limits.

I reached mine with the widow, which was Dad's pet name for Mrs. Winkler, the old woman he hired last fall to be our housekeeper. She was a bad pick, like our house

38

chosen at the last minute, and things went from bad to worse. I know I did. At first we were friends. She stirred up delicious cornbreads for supper, fried corn mush for breakfast, and came up with sausage gravy for noontime. At night she let us watch while she shot her medicine into her big fat leg where it always stayed yellow and blue at the top. Once she let me feel the place where one of her fingers used to be and it was like when my tooth fell out. But in no time it got so she and Margy were whispering grown-up secrets and they didn't listen to me a bit better than Dad did. And she gave Tommy a helium balloon and there was nothing for me. It was a shocking sight when I sat down at the kitchen table in my birthday suit.

"Ruthann!" Mrs. Winkler gasped.

"That's my name. Use it but don't break it." The cold air was already nipping at my heels.

"A great big girl. That ain't no way to behave." Her eyes were fixed out the window like it would be a pain to have to see me, nothing on my chest bigger than a goosebump.

" 'Ain't' is not a word," I informed her. Mother used to say that, although it sounded like one to me. "My blouse is all wrinkly," I pouted. "You better get a move on." By then my teeth were chattering and Margy had to bring me a coat. She was supposed to tell Dad, and Mrs. Winkler said she would too. But everybody forgot after Mrs. Winkler paid me a nickel to act decent and put my clothes on.

While she listened to Dad, Margy's forehead stayed knotted like a rope, like she couldn't get enough. If she paid that kind of attention in school, she wouldn't be the dumb one. She can't let Dad and me alone for a second and I wanted to reach back and plug up her ears. Or ask her her favorite color so she could say "Blue" and I could say "Black." Unless I said blue first. Instead, I sneaked my fingers behind the seat, pinch-pinch on Tommy's leg, my creepy hairy spider crawl. He yowled and his coloring mood flew out the window. He pinched back,

39

jacking around, giggling up a storm, until Dad spoiled that with a quick-stop by the side of the road to ask me if I wanted a spanking. I had a mind to say, "Yes, thank you very much," but his golden eyes gave me a chill like he was an idol brought to light in a cave. "I'm bored," I said, a hasty glance at the sky where an endless blue scared me even worse, and I started winking.

"Enough of that idiot business," Dad said. "Study this a while and learn something useful." He handed me the map book, giving me a tap on the head. "When you know all forty-eight capitals I'll give you kids a quiz. You'll be the winner because Tommy can't read and Margy doesn't have the native industry to master a thankless task." Probably Margy didn't hear that, even though she was right there. She falls off into a daydream like the sleeping sickness.

I got right to work and learned Montgomery and Phoenix while Dad went back to his driving and taking up Margy's time, wilderness mumbo-jumbo. "The Old Chisholm Trail." I wouldn't be surprised if any day he rides off on a horse into the wild blue yonder and that will be the end of that.

We had our sandwiches after a while. "I don't know," Dad said, smelling his before he bit in, eyeing Margy in the mirror. "Warm bologna. Smells a little funny. Risky business in this weather." We were already gulping ours down. It smelled like dog food, so I kept chewing—one thing I tell Margy, "Dog food is perfectly edible."

"Dad," Margy said, "I've almost eaten mine. Am I going to be sick? Oh, I know I will. I'll die." She reached over to take Tommy's away and he yiped. "Dad. He's eating it! He is. Dad." Margy looked like a cherub blowing up a storm. "Tommy, don't. You're going to be sick." I was chewing away but I guess she didn't care what happened to me.

"All right, Margy," Dad said. "Take it easy. I'm just playing the fool. I'm sure it's fine. Go ahead and finish up. As long as I eat mine. We can all go together."

"But I don't want to be sick. Are you sure it's not going to hurt me? Tommy, don't," she yelped, and I was up on my knees to see. He'd tossed his sandwich on the floor and there was gravel and dirt in the mustard. I pointed and laughed.

"I sick," Tommy said, squealing and laughing.

"Boy, if this road wasn't a veritable sidewinder, I'd pull over and give you a slap. One of you girls will have to do it for me. And make it count."

"I will. I will." I was practically falling over the seat into the back while Tommy squiggled down onto the floor to get away. Then there was mustard on his shoe. "Oo-oo oo-oo, step in dog-do."

Tommy did not appreciate that and started to whine and cry, wiping at the stuff, which smeared all around. Margy tried to help him, but I kept laughing and he kicked and flung himself out straight and stiff, screaming blue-bloody murder. I plugged my ears.

The car stopped and I was down on the seat in a flash. I started winking to myself and my shoulder was hunched for when I got hit. But nothing happened. Instead, the door opened and Dad got out of the car, so little by little I let myself come alive and hear and everything was quiet. I got up to see and there Dad was, walking away down the road. "That's the end of him," I shrugged. Tommy pulled up on his knees, not crying, just the jolt of a sob shaking him like the hiccups. Margy wasn't looking Dad's way.

"It's his fault," she said. I thought it was mine, but I'm not one to argue.

Dad stepped off into the woods and we couldn't see him. "Daddy" came Tommy's little sob.

"He's peeing," I said.

He nodded as though that explained everything. That second Dad came back in sight, walking our way, his red hair glowing against the green forest like he was part of a picture on velvet and a deer would be found drinking off in a shady glade.

He got back in the car and started driving without a how-do-you-do. I do fine myself, I was about to say, only he was not in the mood to be friendly. Outside my window a row of hollyhocks marched by and I told Dad what

41

I had learned in school, that they were in a category with loosestrife and pigeonberry and should be shot on sight, but he didn't show any interest so I shut up. Tommy was asleep then and I went back to improving my mind by learning the capitals, keeping an eye on Margy, who was reading. She was droopy-eyed and any second would be nodding off. I'd have to catch her and wake her right up, because I have strict orders not to let her sleep with her mouth hanging open, the whites of her eyes staring like a blindman's—which is how most people get to look the second they can't help themselves. Leave it to Margy to resist fate, as Grandma would say. Sometimes I even do it at home, wake her up. "You were doing it," I say, the truth or not, and she has to be grateful. I really don't care how she looks. I just want her to be awake when I am.

Without Mother or Grandma around I'm more myself every day. Mother had a complete list on the refrigerator, the dos and don'ts of good behavior. Grandma was so impressed she made a copy to have with us in Florida and she followed it to the letter, better than Mother. It gave me something to live up to. There were rules like: Wear your apron at meals, no backtalk, clean your plate, no bad words. Now Dad doesn't have the patience for such matters and Mrs. Winkler never had a chance with me around. I don't know what's happened to the list but I think Margy is still living by it, although she never wears her apron to meals, I have to admit. I especially break the rule that forbids talking with your mouth full.

It was Grandma's opinion that I was a neglected child. Even my mother didn't love me, at least not as much as Margy. In Florida she founded her own mission society, consisting of Margy and her, designed just for me. Grandma gave me everything good, piano lessons, a pencil sharpener, and whatever I did brought on a chorus of praise. If Margy hasn't learned to appreciate me she's convinced she ought to try, and I see her trying to control herself. Which makes me lonely as can be and I interrupt her reading and sleeping and make her fight me.

I depended on Mother too. No matter how she felt

about me. I made her mad, I could see that, but she ended up with hugs and kisses, exclaiming, "Whatever am I going to do with you?" Explaining for the millionth time about manners and cooperative behavior. I was improving right along, but she didn't get to finish me, and sometimes I have to wink seventeen times before I let myself get out of bed.

Margy was the mother's darling. Once she got cut and sat there in the sandbox, bleeding down into the sand. We were playing with tin-can lids and she didn't know she was cut, up in the fat squishy part of her leg, until the blood was spread about her white skin like a broken necklace of beads. Then she wouldn't move, as if the rest of her would spill out, just crying down her cheeks. I went to find Mother, but I forgot and caught some fireflies for a jar. Mother came out to see about us. I forgot to say, swinging upside down on the porch railing, my skirt whirling a turban around my dizzy head. Mother heard Margy and went to see. "You little brat." She glared at me, carrying her past into the house. Margy went off in the car to the doctor and Mother gave me to the neighbor lady. She didn't want to see my face.

After Margy was stitched back up and tucked in bed safe and sound, I was up with Mother. I didn't know she had such a sad face and I turned up her lips with my fingers and made a smile. She gave me a bath, and when I was stepping over the high rim of the tub she scooped me into a bundle inside the towel and hugged me tight, saying I was Mother's little doodlebug. She knew I wasn't really a mean person. I had a very sweet heart. I just wanted me to learn to help other people and not be selfish. She was sorry she'd lost her temper and got so angry. I was only a little girl. In time I would learn, she was sure, and she would help me all she could.

I must have fallen asleep on the way South. There was a wet spot on the seat, so probably my mouth was hanging open a mile, since nobody has orders to disturb me. When I sat up and looked out the window the low-down sun stabbed me in the eye. Dad was blabbing away, telling Margy he hoped she'd be different from the other women he knew. In his opinion most women were downright pitiful, living their lives for some man. I've seen some of them in person and others have their pictures in his wallet. One of them was a bleached blonde and I asked him if she was a hot number.

I guess Dad wouldn't want his Margy to end up like that, lips puckered for a smooch, on her way to a wingding. He wants her in an old wrapper, chopping wood and lugging water from the spring. Always and forever Dad's little fat boy, his nickname for Margy when she was small. The funny part is, Margy could fall for it. It's in her face while she's listening to Dad, as if on the inside she's saying, "Hark!" Her dreams coming at her from somebody gazing in a crystal ball. I'm not sure what Dad expects of me. Probably he'd be content if I'd let everybody alone.

There's another part to Margy, though, the part that wants to be an actress or a singer, anything so she gets all the attention. That's one of our fights. When we go to the movies and it's about one of those sad-sack girls nobody notices or understands, Margy thinks it's her life story. Any day she expects she will rise up in a crowd or appear on the street, singing her heart out, and amazing everybody with the beauty they never saw before. I keep my eyes on Margy instead of the movie, cruising for a bruising. Margy hisses for me to quit staring. "Leave!" Which I would never do, though I can hardly wait to get out of the dark and see something bad, maybe an old drunk peeing in the park or two dogs stuck together.

Margy might as well have been watching a movie, the way she was looking while Dad talked, parading himself over the range on Old Paint, describing a tree that had seen the birth of Christ, as though a tree would care. I asked how we were going to be able to see a river that was lost, but nobody cared what I thought so I began to say, "I'm hungry." By my count I said it every six seconds, until Dad had to look my way. He already knows I don't give up. When he spanks me he asks if I'll ever

44

do it again. "I might," I say. "Doesn't hurt." The spanking goes on and on. He eyed me from the side of his face, a tiny elephant-eye slit in a sea of squints. I squinted him back. "I'm hungry." He reached out and took my hand to hold. "I think I'm in my dotage," I said, and he got a kick out of that.

I want to fight Margy when she hogs all the attention or gives hers away for free. Margy and I don't have the conversations we used to, because I make her mad. She says we don't have much in common and I get her back by dozing off in the middle of one of her important ideas. I got up twice at the movies and filed in front of her during the scene when the gypsy was lying dead on the bed, his hair in a wild tangle, not to mention his golden earring. Listening to Dad she got all uppity and la-di-da, as though she was the only true and wonderful person in the world, staring off without a thought for me.

When Tommy woke up from his nap, Margy was reading to him and Dad and I were left alone. I kicked my feet against the glove compartment until he told me to cut it out. I looked in there to see the gloves, but he didn't think that was funny. As long as we've been together, Dad and I have been strangers. Sometimes when we're alone he picks his nose just like there's nobody there. That puts me in the worst mood. He wouldn't even notice if I picked mine—too much of a "don't" even to make Mother's list.

It doesn't bother Dad that we're strangers. Probably he doesn't realize it, because I've had my reputation since I was a baby crying all the time; then I had to be rushed to the hospital, dying with the croup. I think I've changed, but it's hard to get anybody to notice, not when they've known you since the day you were born.

The best way to get Margy's chicken gizzard is to look her straight in the eye and say, "You've changed." I guess she believes she was born perfect and could only go downhill. Or maybe she thinks Mother would walk right past her in heaven. I don't question her, though. Not since she began on a long explanation when I'd just asked if she believed in God. A simple yes was what I had in mind. I turned around and left her, mid-sentence, my ears stoppered with blood, shaking like a leaf. Margy gets everything complicated. She's sure she's to blame for the trouble we had with Mrs. Winkler, and she socked me in the chest when I merely mentioned the séance. And here I'd thought all along it was my idea.

Mrs. Winkler couldn't do a thing with me. I'm famed for that. When she told me to pick up my room I said, "It's too heavy." When she called me a mess, I said, "Takes one to know one." Then I threw everything I owned under the bed and had to hunt in the dark for something to wear, pulling it out dusty and more ratty-looking with each passing day. I made up songs I hummed to Margy, right under Mrs. Winkler's nose. "Wee Willy Stinkie" and "What's that I see in yonder fir tree? A dreary old widder, plain as can be." "Yonder" was her old-country word, nothing I would ever say. All day long I was jumping from black widow spiders. When she said I was a smart-aleck, turning purple from her blood pressure, I stared her down, the most blankety-blank puss in town. I certainly would rather be dead than say a word like "nigger," while she doesn't know a bit better. Margy still takes the blame, though, probably because she got such a big laugh from the things I did when I was the boss.

Dad didn't know a thing about what was going on until he came home in the night and Tommy had the burn. Most of the time he was out on his dates, and when he was with us he was like the guest, someone we visited politely in the basement, where he'd fixed a place to sleep and hang his clothes. While he washed his face at the washtubs and put on a clean shirt, I showed him my school papers so he could go on being impressed. Tommy had pictures he'd colored in nursery school and we taped them to the wall over Dad's cot. Dad said it was too bad Margy didn't have anything more tangible to exhibit than her smiling face, but he had to admit her good nature was what made our world go round. That made her smile all the bigger. "Is everything under control around here?" he asked, knotting his tie, squaring Margy in the

46

eye through the mirror. She shrugged—he could see for himself.

"You better go easy on the cornbread if you expect to have a romantic life," he told Margy once when he lined us up to say good night, kisses for Tommy and me, a handshake for the grown-up girl. But Margy wasn't having even that. She would eat what she wanted. Deep down Margy had her limits too, and by the last night when we had the séance with Mrs. Winkler, she was in the whiskey too, sneaking in and out of the pantry, where it was stashed behind the flour canister. I'd been trying to tell her that it tasted just like cherries and she found out that it did. When we were gathered around the card table with the candle burning, trying to get the whole thing to rise into the air, we all had lips as red as Tommy's, which are naturally like the red, red rose.

Then, out of the blue, calamity struck. Even before I could figure out for myself if the widow and her spirits were for the birds, Tommy leaned over the candle while our eyes were pinched shut and suddenly we smelled smoke. Margy was the hero, did exactly what they told us in school when the firemen came, pulled him into her own body and smothered the fire. After that we lay around on the couch until Dad came home and called the doctor. We forgot that part. Mrs. Winkler stayed locked in her room and was gone in the morning before we got up. The whiskey was gone too. I checked. That was when Dad said we should all climb overboard before our ship sank for good.

At first he took it out on Margy for not calling the doctor first thing, for not telling him all along how things were. He was disappointed in her. He'd thought he could count on her. Everybody, including Margy, forgets she's a person too. She bawled and bawled. When his voice got so loud it hurt my ears, I went out into the yard. I drew some pictures in the dirt by the garbage cans, and fixed a trap with a nail and a piece of glass, in case a rat came by.

When it got quiet I went in. Dad was to the part about asking Margy to forgive him. After all, it wasn't up to

47

her to make up for everything that had gone wrong with his life. He patted her shoulder and gave her a speech. He knew she did the best she could. As isolated as we were, no wonder she'd forgotten there were hospitals, ambulances, places to turn for help. For a frontierswoman she'd done pretty well. We can't resist Dad when he's sorry. I didn't especially blame him either. I must say I expect the world of Margy too.

Dad must have been feeling pretty good about his life, driving us in his car, on the way to see Gloria, his special girlfriend who sent Margy and me *A Tale of Two Cities* after we didn't go to the cartoon show. Dad was singing, "Polly Wolly Doodle All the Day," and even before we asked, he pulled into a place and went inside to buy us dinner. We had to take potluck—otherwise it was too complicated, and besides, this way Margy couldn't order dessert and he wouldn't have to leave a tip. Maybe we would give him a tip. I dug a penny out of the floormat and presented it when he came out with the tray.

At the motel I was fit to be tied, running on the bed, touching the four walls, leaping for the ceiling light. Paper cups, a fresh one for every sip. I calmed down when Dad let us color before bedtime while he walked circles around the motel and smoked. Then he went to make a phone call and left Margy in charge. We were never enough for Dad. Margy sang a made-up song about the boy who ran away from home and left his mother crying. That was Grandma and it made me feel like crying too. Tommy and I were always begging Margy, but then the story was long and sad, and as soon as it was done I wanted to make everybody suffer.

Dad came back and announced bed. A battle cry. When I was little I caused more trouble, spankings every night, sometimes two or three. Laughing in the window when the neighbors came home at all hours. Mother was beside herself. As a last resort, Dad tied me in bed with some ropes. There, that'll fix you!

I'm better than that now. At the motel I just made a general nuisance of myself, scrambling and racing, everything bright as day with the yellow light blinking out front saying this was a quality motel. I tickled Tommy's leg where it flopped over my face, off the side of the bed he was sleeping in with Dad. Margy got Kleenex in the face, drifting out of nowhere. When Tommy got tired he started in whining until Dad lost patience and whirled out of bed to put a stop to it. My personal sandman. A couple of wallops and I was off to dreamland. "Why in hell can't you settle down and act like a reasonable human being?" he yelled. "I can't say. Doesn't hurt," I murmured into the pillow. One way or another I've managed to get to sleep every night of my life.

I shut my eyes and it was morning. All that fuss for nothing. Margy was up greeting the day, thrilled all over again because she could see mountains on down the road. I kind of liked them myself, but I wasn't going to say so. An excitable person gets on my nerves in the morning when all I want to do is snuggle down.

Then Miss Cheerful was whipping around the room, dressing Tommy, picking up clothes, folding blankets. I slipped into Dad's bed and played dead, even when he came out of the bathroom. "Get up, you lazy good-for-nothing daughter." First I can't settle down, then I can't get started.

Dad got me going. He stood there, hands on hips, mean as a snout-nosed beetle, I was thinking. I squiggled out the other side to get away, but I was up and went ahead and pulled on my clothes from the day before. I liked my clean ones all folded in the paper bag. Margy offered to comb out my hair, but right away she hurt me, yanking away, so I kicked her leg a light one and asked her if she wanted to snatch me bald-headed. I laughed, but old Early-to-bed-early-to-rise wanted to hold a grudge and wouldn't talk, just staring at me while I went ahead and fixed my own braids right on top of the tangles, just the way I go ahead and iron anything I want to, dirt and all. I put in my pink barettes too, slipping them in to hold the tangles. They're my favorite, with tiny flower baskets on top, some Grandma gave me. Tommy tried to get his hands on them right away and his finger got bent in the drawer.

Dad flew out of the bathroom when he heard the shriek, Mr. Burma Shave in a cloud of steam. "Christ, you girls are going to cripple him before you're done." He took Tommy into the bathroom and slammed the door.

My hair, even the way it was, looked better than Margy's. Hers is a briar patch, not pretty, no matter who says so. I myself am sick to death of yellow hair and I've made a vow to cross my eyes every time the subject comes up. Mother used to warn me they might get stuck that way, but now I take my own risks. My hair is straight, quiet hair and my head feels peaceful, at least where it shows. Margy said I had shaving cream on my ear, but what did I care. I might shave the whole thing off. I look after myself. I don't need old bossy-boss. My hair was aching and I stuck out my tongue like a five-year-old.

Dad got dressed and asked what we wanted for breakfast. Without a thought Margy said, "Doughnuts," which got her a look and a half. We're all watching Margy's weight. I wouldn't even look at Dad because he didn't give me a chance to say I was sorry about Tommy's hurt finger. "I guess you'll take what you can get," he warned, and off he drove for the food we were going to eat in the room to save money. When we made up I was going to ask him what he did with the money he saved.

I was never going to speak to Margy again, but she started coloring patterns on the paper shower mat and I wanted to help and she let me. Tommy said my colors were like the mountains we could see and I whispered, so nosy wouldn't hear, that I was sorry about his finger and gave it a butterfly tickle to feel better. He let me fasten one of my barrettes in his hair and I hid it down in his curls. Another Goldilocks.

Mother wouldn't even braid Margy's hair, for fear of spoiling the curl. Like it belonged in a museum. My hair, she said, was straight as a stick. Went with the rest of me, the bag of bones. Grandma said I couldn't help it that I wasn't as pretty as Margy, and besides, I had my gifts. She said I was talented on the piano and begged Dad to let me continue my lessons. "Over my dead body," he said, and raised my allowance by a quarter when I agreed to stop bringing up the subject. But afterward I felt like a heel, serving Mammon instead of God, and told Dad to keep his money—which he was glad to do. Truthfully, I didn't mind that much about the piano. Without Grandma to brag on me, I probably wouldn't have the heart to practice.

Mother was the gifted one, and it was wonderful to hear the "Moonlight" Sonata coming out to me like a lifeline wherever I was playing, even down the street. Margy said that once there was a man sitting beside Mother on the bench and they were singing a song. Before I had to hear about that I plugged my ears and now I never discuss Mother. She's my own private vision, and sometimes at night I think she flies in the window and sits on the end of the bed, singing to me.

Dad came back with cereal, sugar, and canned Pet milk. "I'm not eating," I announced. At home when he pours that in his coffee, Margy and I gag and have to run out on the porch. He pried open the can, prying at me with his eyes. He said I must not be hungry, not if a little thing like that was in the way. I turned my back on him and the spotted cow.

"That's mean, Dad," Margy said. "You know we hate it."

"Are you girls ganging up on me?" Dad was fixing Tommy a cozy place to eat at the dresser. "That's my boy," Dad said when Tommy started right in to eat. I was going to ask Margy to run away and we'd find porridge in the woods, honey in the comb.

"You know, sweetheart," Dad said to Margy, "you're getting old for this sort of thing. The small fry delight in contrariness of all varieties, but frankly I expect more of you."

"I can't stand it," the sweetheart said. "I just can't."

" 'Can't never did anything,' " Dad said, one of Mother's favorite expressions.

Margy's head drooped. "All right," she said. "One taste." So much for running away.

51

"Eat all your vittles for Daddy dear," I told her. We used to laugh till we choked, eating our "vittles."

"Don't even ignore her," Dad said. "She's not dry behind the ears yet." I held my nose to watch. Margy poured a little milk on her cereal, thrilling as though she was about to be poisoned. A deep breath and some was in her mouth. Nothing happened. Then her brown eyes bulged and her cheeks puffed, with a rocking in her throat. I ran with her to the toilet and stood beside her, both of us gagging, spitting, and laughing, me at the very thought.

Dad said he'd never seen such a pair of weak sisters. We sure had a way to go before we made the grade. He couldn't help thinking of the millions all over the world without a bite to eat and here he was, giving us an opportunity to overcome a smidgeon of . . . I stopped listening when Margy started to blubber, "But, Dad, I tried."

Dad ended up shouting, "Goddamn it. Go on and throw it out. Perfectly good food but you're too finicky. Eat it dry. Just eat." He kicked out the door and we jumped. I was glad he didn't kick me. Margy was trying not to cry, and if that meant she was going to shiver and shake, I was going to call her fat and dumb. But then I got to laughing when she spilled the cereal in the toilet and Tommy came to see. He spit some in too and we thought it was great, flushing and spitting, living for the moment. Margy sat on the bed and crunched dry cereal. The sugar sparkled on her lips and I took her a glass of water. "Wasn't it awful?" I could smell Dad's smoke coming in the window.

Margy nodded her head. "This is pretty good," she whispered. "You should eat some." I considered doing it so we could stay friends, but Dad came back in the door.

"I give up," he said after he gave me the count of three to start eating and I didn't move. He told Margy she could eat for me too. "It's a long time to lunch," he reminded me. When I was a baby I made myself quit breathing even, sad and blue lying on the floor.

Margy got to work and cleaned up from breakfast. Dad lay on the bed and smoked, his feet crossed, one arm behind his head, joking that he would forgive us whenever we asked. He sang "You Are My Sunshine" while we tried to keep frowning, except for Tommy, who was spitting cereal in the toilet. I went in and we had a giggling contest.

"That's more like it," Dad said, "though what a pity it is when filth is all that will move a crowd." Then he begged us to forgive him. He couldn't stand to be in bad with the women folk. It reminded him too vividly of his childhood. If I'd rub his feet, he told me, I'd be back in his good graces in no time.

I started right off tickling him, because I was mad, and he rolled around on the bed and moaned as though I was killing him. I chased him, trying to pinch his fat, until he swooped me up in his arms and pinned me flat between his knees.

I'd been there before. Dad and I used to play wolf when Mother was here. Every time I ended up hurt and Mother had to stop us. Dad said it was my own fault, nodding to Mother, who was trying to hold me back, digging her fingers into my shoulders. "She knows what happens." I couldn't help it. I liked the wolf the best of all.

"Who's afraid of the big bad wolf?" I sang on the motel bed. Margy came over. "Dad, don't," she said.

"I'm hungry," I yelled.

"Please, Dad. Let's go." Poor Margy with her load of care. Tommy came too and hung on Dad's waist, his head on the bed. They never left us alone.

Dad uncrossed his legs and sat up, smoothing his clothes. "All right, honey, settle down." He was holding me off while I was fighting him.

"Don't honey me." I wasn't ever going to quit, but I banged myself on his bones and I was killed, falling on the bed to cry while Margy and Dad put stuff in the car.

"I nearly forgot," Dad said. "It's time to write to friends and relatives." I knew mine would be best, since Margy's writing is messy and her spelling so atrocious

53

Dad says she must do it on purpose. I thought I'd write Grandma, but Dad thought we should write Gloria Stevenson, to show we were literate as well as beautiful. Since I knew we'd be seeing her at the end of the trail, it seemed funny to write.

Dad guided Tommy's pencil to write, "We are having a wonderful time with dear Daddy." He happened to spy my barrette in Tommy's hair and it flew out the door. I tried to fight my way past.

"No, you don't. First your letter. You girls don't think I'm going into bondage for the sake of this boy to have him in skirts?" He glared as though I'd figured that out.

"Dear Mrs. Stevenson," I wrote, using a formal construction. "I am hungry. Dad made me eat canned milk but I wouldn't. He socked me and threw away my barrette. I hate Dad." She wouldn't know truth from fiction.

Dad read the letters out loud, except his, which wasn't fair. Of course Margy's ran the word "mountain" into the ground. Dad shook his head, sad to read mine, then folded it in with the others and licked the stamp. "You sure you want to tell everything you know?"

Outside, I got my barrette out of the dirt and polished it off with spit. I showed Dad the flower basket, pinning it in my hair. "These are the best I ever had." Dad said I had him twisted around my little finger and took my hand. "You've got a real sweet smile." We mailed the letter before we rode off. Dad shrugged. "I guess she might as well know what she'd be in for."

We hit the road and drove for hours. Sometimes Dad and Margy sang Western songs. For a break Dad did the donkey part of "The Grand Canyon Suite," and Tommy and I laughed. The way Margy sings, even "Pack Up Your Troubles in Your Old Kit-Bag" sounded like somebody ran away and I was glad when she wound down, although then we had to hear how beautiful everything was, the flowers and birds, the babbling brooks. I couldn't see much, slumping on my spine, the world shooting past like a banner saying life was real and earnest and the grave was not its goal. After a nap Dad said

I could climb out of the quagmire and sit with the white folks—which meant up on my knees. But only if I kept my face to the front and didn't start trouble. I was bored in no time. I told Dad his freckles spilled like brown gravy, glistening in his sweat. Then I said he looked like Howdy Doody. That got Tommy going and we yelled until Dad threatened to stop the car and crack our heads together.

"I'm hungry" was my answer to that. I really was. Dad gave me a finger flick on the cheek and said he'd warned me. We were having a late lunch. I said it again. He flicked me. Then he kind of faded away, dreaming about his girlfriend. I reached over and pinched a tad of Dad's skin in my fingernails so he jumped. "I'm hungry." I eyed him.

There were trees all around. Dad swung off the road into a little grassy place, skidding the car to a stop. "Get out. I'm sick to death of your pestering." I did what he said. I had my rights. I went around to the trunk with my legs going wibble-wobble, not looking at Margy, like I was going to be stepping onto a fast ride at the fair and couldn't stop myself. Snap, Crackle, and Pop were having a party in the sunshine on the trunk lid. My lip was dry and pinned to my teeth where it couldn't shiver.

Margy was out on the grass holding Tommy. Selah. Words like that, from the Bible, kept going through my head. It felt like it was being clanged in the cymbals and my hair was strung up like a lyre. "Therefore will we not fear, though the earth be removed, and though the mountains be carried into the midst of the sea." Selah. Margy was going to cry. Selah. "Make a joyful noise unto the Lord."

Dad stuck a cereal puff on the end of his nose, flicked out his tongue, snapping it into his mouth. His eyes flickered red as jewels. I grinned with my lip stuck up and it hurt. He put a puff on the end of my nose. I couldn't reach it with my tongue and it got loose, spinning away to the ground like a whirligig. I bent down to get it. Dad grabbed my neck in his elbow, yanking me close to his face, tilting the cereal box over my mouth. "Open your stupid mouth if you're so hungry." The cereal flooded down my face, but I didn't open my mouth. It was in my nose. Margy was next to me. "Dad," she said. Her yellow hair flashed by on the wings of the morning. The cereal stopped coming.

"Just what do you think you're going to do about it, Blondie?" Dad let go and I fell on the ground. It was quiet; then the car door opened and the motor was going. "We went through fire and through water." Selah.

I opened my eyes like a new day. Margy was wiping Tommy's nose with her skirt, and I found the cereal box and started stuffing myself as fast as I could. I knew what Dad meant when he said, "You get hungry enough, you'll eat." He found that out when he went door-to-door to beg and all his pride was gone. Bring on the canned milk. Peter Piper picked a peck of pickled peppers. Selah. "If I take the wings of the morning, and dwell in the uttermost parts of the sea." I dug out the dregs of the cereal and the motor stopped. Dad was sitting in the car, resting his head on the steering wheel.

Without looking up he called, "You kids want something to drink?"—the miracle worker in the wilderness. I wasn't talking but Tommy ran to the car and they drove away. Now there was no reason for him ever to come back. Margy would go with me into the forest to find blackberries and live in a hollow tree. I'd keep her in stitches for something to wear.

When Dad came back, Tommy was sitting on his lap, driving the car, drinking a grape soda with a big bag of chips to share. There was a Coke for Margy and lemonade for me. I don't like Coke, so I knew we were smoking a peace pipe, and brushing off my mouth I had a guzzle. Dad said, "Now that we've got that settled, I hope you're happy." He gave me a hug.

"Will you marry me?" I asked, all shuddery.

A kiss dropped from heaven onto my barrette. "You don't carry a grudge, do you, good-looking? That's your sister's department. You kids must realize what I mean when I tell you I'm no good at this mother-father business. In fact, I couldn't do much worse. I hope you'll

56

believe me when I tell you I'm sorry. Now, come along and we'll find some water, wash your faces, see if we can cool off the hothead.'' Dad, Tommy, and I walked away from Margy, letting her lag behind, carrying the grudge. Missing out on the chips.

Dad took me piggybacking. He said I was light as a feather and just as wispy. '' 'We're walking farther into this rotting grave and shall we ne'er get out?' '' Dad was sharing his poetry with me and I dreamed I was Bess the landlord's black-eyed daughter. I yelled back to Margy to stop her lollygagging and get a move on, showing whose side I was on. Bugs were attacking us like birdshot.

A splashing waterfall, white through the green leaves, solved all our troubles. "The Lost River." I was as excited as Margy, wiggling to get down when she went running by. She couldn't stop in time and ran clear into the water with her shoes on. Luckily, Dad didn't see when he came whipping along without his clothes on and ran into the water. Tommy jumped up and down, speechless and pointing. "I see your heinie," I kept yelling, yanking off my own clothes as fast as I could down to my underpants. Margy helped Tommy take off his shoes, then he undressed. She only tucked up her skirt, setting her shoes on a rock to dry.

"Guard that boy with your life," Dad called. "If anything happens to him you may as well jump in too. Your life won't be worth a plugged nickel." He was grinning, waiting for me to dog-paddle through the deep part to get to him. Margy and I couldn't swim a lick. Mother said Dad had scared us too much and she wouldn't let us go out where he was, to fight the monster of the deep. Now I do what I want.

Dad grabbed hold of my arms and we bobbed and floated in silvery bubbles. I took rides on his back far down into the caves and whirlpools, where it was cold as ice. I was having the time of my life and I tried to get Margy to watch, but she was too busy saving Tommy from drowning. I hugged Dad's neck so tight he said I was drowning him. And he needed every hair he had left.

Once I gave him a kiss on his backbone when we went riding down. Maybe he thought it was a sly little-bitty minnow. Selah. I hugged him with all my might.

Then a hand was on my head, holding me down, and I was lost in the water and couldn't see. Up was the same as down and everything was cold and drear. Monsters slithered everywhere and came inside, and I was drowned in the dark, too drowned for Margy ever to find. Heaven shone over me in a field of ice. I thought I heard Margy singing the saddest song.

What a surprise when I was free in the air, coughing my guts out, and the monster was gone. I wanted to cry forever and ever so I would stay warm with the tears raining down. Dad was pushing me away, over where Margy was. He said I deserved it. He'd warned me repeatedly about hanging on his neck and pulling his hair. He didn't need a big baby to take care of that couldn't even take her medicine. I was spattered blue and chicken-skinned, stabbing myself on the rocks, wondering about the medicine I was supposed to get.

We didn't have a towel. Margy bundled up leaves and grass, and she and Tommy gave me a rubdown. There was a big warm rock for me to lie on and we turned me all around for a baking. I was coming to life again and got dressed. I told Margy I'd drowned but she said I didn't. It was Dad holding me down. I told her I was going to make him pay. She said, "Don't cause trouble." Trouble's my middle name.

Then Dad caught us napping again, leaping out of the woods, and we didn't know how he got there. He was Pan, he said, covered with vine and leaves, dancing and blowing over his hands and a blade of grass. "This tune will make you poor girls forget every trouble you ever had." Then he saw me all shivery and gathered me in his arms, wrapping me in his shirt. While he got the rest of his clothes on, he made us do jumping jacks to get the blood moving. I told him it wasn't a joke to drown somebody. He said I'd been a thorn in his side the livelong day.

"You don't give up." Dad ruffled my wet hair, smiling

down. It had more of the feeling like it was curly and I thought I'd keep it that way all the time and be just like Tommy and Margy, giving it little sprinkles all day long.

"Come on, waterbugs. Quick-time to the car. We'll fire up the heater and see about a decent meal. I've exhausted patience with myself today. Shake hands all around and we'll be friends to the end." Dad stuck out his hand. Only Margy wouldn't be friends, keeping her hands behind her back, her eyes straight ahead. Dad shrugged and we got going, leaving Margy to follow the best she could. "Hurry up. Your sister's going to catch her death," Dad called back.

"I'm coming," she said. She was carrying her shoes.

"Put those on and step it up. You want her to get pneumonia?"

Margy came stepping, with her yellow hair. "My feet are tough."

"What the hell's wrong with you? Here, let me see those shoes." Selah. All around was the cold lonesome place Mrs. Winkler used to see when she stared out at the rain last winter. I moved a little away from Dad and Margy.

Margy hid the shoes behind her. "They got wet," she said, her lip stuck out and wobbling. I would have worn my old sopping shoes, size nine and a half. So what if they squished like a swamp and were twice too big forever and I had to wear seven pairs of socks to keep them with me. Selah. Margy was in trouble. Her head was down.

Dad let go of Tommy's hand and grabbed Margy's neck. "I'm sick and tired of you. You big lummox." He pushed her into a tree. Run, Margy, run and run. Get to the river, cross over and go on, run until you're so far away you'll never be found, not even by me.

"They got wet," she said, a broken record, her cheek flattened against the bark.

"You big dummy. They didn't just get wet. Shoes don't throw themselves in the water and ask to be ruined. Some dumb cluck has to put them there." Dad had Margy's head in his hands, smack against the tree. Her shoulders

59

were shaking up and down. The whole tree was shaking like it was about to wake up.

I saw Tommy skipping along the path, going back toward the river, and I went after him. I'd be the hero, the one to save him from drowning. Then everybody would be happy.

"I don't know how I'm supposed to manage everything. I can't make ends meet as it is and there isn't a single solitary soul I can depend on." I heard Dad's high silly voice as I was leaving it behind, taking step after step into the green leaves and the rushing loud sound of the water. Tommy grinned when he saw me following and started running. It was easy to get away from a baby and I passed him by and ran on, to hide and spy and hide again. When he didn't see me peeping out, Tommy soon gave up the ghost and turned around, heading back to where Dad was, rubbing his eyes. I didn't want to be with Dad and Margy when they were mad so I kept on going along, hiding in the trees. They'd have to come for me. If they wanted to. When I ran I tripped on a root and had to stay put until my breath was back inside. I fixed on a big shining rock to be my guiding star.

At the water I thought I'd go in wading, being careful like Mother taught me, doing whatever I wanted. Tommy didn't come again and I was following after a little bird that hopped from tree to tree like it was leading me somewhere, maybe where Mother was. I'd ask her why she wasn't more careful. Some little fishes were swimming in a pale quiet spot and I tried to snag one for a cold meal. Three bitter berries were popped in my mouth before I knew it. Margy better come soon if she knew what was good for her. When she was done with her spanking. Before I was lost and gone. Selah.

Mother spanked me with the hairbrush. I hung down over her knees with my face in her tight stockings, looking into the rims of her black shoes. I was never to ask Mrs. Jackson if she was the bearded lady. That was not funny. Why couldn't I listen? Did I want to hurt other people's feelings? She'd been so embarrassed she wanted to die. The brush banged along on my behind. It had a carved horse and rider on the handle and a wooden curl of a whip. The rider was having a wild ride, galloping over hill and dale. When he broke off he flew across the room and hit the wall. Mother and I gave each other the eye and I didn't know what was going to happen, until she began laughing, threw her hands to her face, and I slid off her lap into a heap on the floor. "You make me feel like a brute," she gasped, crying a little at the same time. Afterward she gathered me up and pulled me into a hug, rocking back and forth. "All skin and bones." She rocked. "My little doodlebug."

Margy didn't come and the sun got lower and lower. How would she find me in the forest when all the animals were loose, out looking for their food? I took a drink out of the violet water, snorting my nose over the surface like a horse. "She better get a move on," I said to a fish swimming by, "or I'll give her something to remember." I didn't know if he heard me, because I couldn't hear myself with the water rushing by. "I'm hungry," I yelled, my voice haunting me like a ghost. Maybe Margy was still getting her spanking and couldn't come. Maybe it would never end. Margy was never lost, because she was always with Margy.

I used to go after her when she went to school. I wanted to be a first-grader too, but it wasn't time, Mother said. I could read already, and I sneaked out and went along behind so she didn't know. I spied and saw her meet the boy Mother made her walk with, to cross the streets. Margy didn't want to because he always held her hand. Everybody was after Margy. Skippety-skippety. Along the busy street the cars honked and made me go faster with my eyes shut so I wouldn't know. Margy was gone but I'd find her. When she saw me having all the fun she'd come out to be with me. My sash came undone and dragged, like a bride coming over the grass. In the big yard there were swings, seesaws, monkey bars, all the grass scratched bare. I was at school. Everything was mine and I ran around using all my stuff as fast as I could. I skinned the cat blind.

Margy was at the window of the school, waving her

61

arms. "Go home, go home." I ran to another swing. She'd be down in a second. Then dark hands caught me, pinching, and a stick smacked my legs and then my hands, when they got in the way. "How dare you sneak off like that. The second my back is turned." I kept myself laughing all the way home, yanking and fighting for the stick.

After that I was mostly at home. Unless I made a getaway. Dad had the rope fixed pretty good, though, and usually it stayed around my middle. Margy came home for lunch and played with me beside the tree. When she had to go back, I trailed to the end of my rope and cried. Sometimes I ate some grass. I spent a lot of my time working to untie myself and they called me "Houdini." Mother said she hated to do it, but I was too little to be out in the neighborhoods alone. Whatever would she do if I got lost? She rocked me. "Oh, it's a crime. Why can't you be good?"

My legs were chattering and I sat down for a rest. A squirrel gave me a scolding from his tree. Well, I would never eat canned milk. I picked a yellow flower to fasten in my buttonhole. Mother said raising me was not a primrose path. When Margy and I ran with the other kids who were running after a car of colored people driving down our street, yelling "Nigger, nigger," Dad was waiting by the front door. "I'll do all I can to save you," he said, "but I don't know. Generally these people come back in the night and cut off the ears of trashy white folk." He shook his head. "Maybe they'll give you a break, considering your age." Margy couldn't get to sleep and she kept breaking into tears. Whenever she got quiet I sneaked up to the window and yelled, "There's one," getting her riled again. That went on until Mother made Dad come into our room and, with the light on, tell Margy he was only kidding. Nobody was going to hurt her.

"I'm so ashamed," Margy cried, and promised she'd never do anything that bad, ever again. I kept saying, "I will," until I got my spanking.

It was getting darker and darker until the last bright

spot of sun was gone, like Dad when he's come to his dotage. My knees were staring up at me like hollow eyes. I started winking to see what would happen. Selah. "They mount up to the heaven, they go down again to the depths." There was a tiny scooped-out place by a log and there I curled up like an animal in its den. When I was asleep it would be the place where I was lost in the water and heaven was brimming through. One potato, two potato. Selah.

Light was shining then and I thought it was Mother saying my name, only there was a man talking and I stayed still. Maybe it was the man who carried the little girl out of her bedroom and down a ladder, wrapped in a blanket. He didn't mean to kill her; it happened in the blanket. Afterward, when he tried to get money, she was already dead. Dad said he'd never pay a dime so we should watch our step.

"Thank God." A different man was talking and there were lights all around and people, like a party. My eyes stayed shut while someone lifted me up in his arms. He loved me, I could tell. He said so, kissing my cheek, he was so happy. By then I knew it was Dad who had come to get me and it was a little like heaven. I stayed very still to make it last forever. He whispered that he'd never been more afraid in his life, that I was his dear little girl and he couldn't bear not to have me. Somehow everything had turned out right again. I listened carefully, in case Dad called me his doodlebug, but then I fell asleep while he carried me out of the forest in his arms.

They told me I was sick as a dog and slept for a year. All I knew was waking up in a strange room where Dad's girlfriend was sitting beside me reading a book. I was trying to remember her name, but then Margy said, "I think she's awake, Gloria," and I had to open up wide to see her. She didn't look mad but happy to see me, and Gloria's red hair made me think of Dad, the two of them like a matched pair drawing a golden chariot. It seemed I'd traveled such a long way to be home again.

Little by little Margy told me the adventure of how I

was lost and then found, a story I didn't mind because of the happy ending. Tommy hadn't been any help finding me, although they'd gone along the path to the river, calling and calling. But Dad was afraid everyone would be lost when it got dark, so they went to the police for help. It had been very scary when they were driving away from the woods, leaving me behind. Tommy and Margy had stayed with a policeman's wife while the men went into the forest. Dad had insisted on going too, even though he'd been warned about snakes and quicksand. "What kind of man do you take me for?" he said. "That's my daughter out there."

After I was found, Dad drove through the night to Gloria's house. Her friend was a doctor and he looked me over for free and left some aspirin. They watched me carefully, to be certain all was well, and, once, I'd opened my peepers and winked, before I went back to sleep. Everybody laughed at that and knew I'd be myself again. Gloria said, "It made us so happy when we knew you were getting better. We just had to celebrate." She looked like the cat that ate the canary.

Everybody seemed happy, including Dad, who was brought in to see me after my face was washed. We put off fixing my hair because of the tangles. In fact, Gloria and I thought we'd have it cut and solve the problem for good. She'd take me to her beauty parlor. Dad stood at the foot of the bed, hand-delivering my barrettes, which he'd found on the ground beside me. I pinned them in for maybe the last time. Margy didn't say one word about her spanking or that I'd run away and left her. She wasn't carrying a grudge anymore. She promised she would color with me or play Old Maid, anything I wanted. I wanted to say I was sorry, but the words wouldn't come. Gloria seemed to be watching everywhere.

Then came the real surprise. A very big one. "It's time for you to know, Ruthann. Yesterday, after we knew for sure you were better, your father and I were married. He popped the question, and I just said yes, and off we went." Gloria was smiling until she broke out sneezing and had to leave for a Kleenex.

64

Dad eyed me as though he'd played a good trick. "Can't keep up with your old man, can you, kid. Turn your back and he's on his honeymoon. That's how I expect you to do it, quick and dirty. You'll get used to it sooner or later. That one has." He nodded at Margy, who was reading. "Why not sooner?" his palms spread like a collection plate. He went out and from the living room the march began on the piano: "Here comes the bride/All fat and wide." I had an urge to march out and drop the lid on Dad's fingers, but I was dizzy when I sat up. When my strength was back they'd hear. I'd practice my scales until they'd think a ghost had come to stay.

Maybe that was what Gloria thought happened to her picture. During the tea party when we first met her, I was checking out her room when somebody was coming. Caught red-handed, I jammed a little picture I'd picked up into my pocket, shrugging when Gloria looked in and saw me. She didn't have the nerve to ask, I was acting so devil-may-care. Then I forgot to put it back.

By the time Gloria came in to see me again, I had everything figured and asked her if she'd mind if I called her Mother. Tears in her eyes broke like glass, and I had to stick my head under the covers and stare at the knobs on my knees. "I want that more than anything, Ruthann," she said, sneezing again. When I came out she gave me my first kiss. She talked about her happiness then, her plans. How exciting it was to have children, now at long last. To be moving into a home of her own, and she would be able to quit her job at Southland Chem. Not that she hadn't liked it and been a great help to her boss, doing much more than typing and shorthand. But this was the life she'd always dreamed of. Even for the little bit of time she'd been married before, she and her husband had been living right there with her parents. Before he went to war. Nodding, smiling when Gloria did, we were getting along fine until it was another sad story coming up and I was going to stop listening. But Gloria looked out the window and was quiet. It was embarrassing that everybody was dead.

Dad called in from the other room. Gloria didn't fool

him. It was really his home and children she wanted, not him. Gloria got up and her tinkling laugh went in where he was. She was probably applying one of her kisses in the silence then. I examined mine in the mirror, where it launched from my cheek in the dip of a tiny bird. I didn't wash the spot but it faded away; although I always knew where it was, like the invisible print of an admission stamp at the fair which a violet light can find.

Margy said she felt we were starting over and she confided in me. She wasn't going to call Gloria Mother, because it didn't feel right. She remembered Mother too well. However, that didn't mean she wouldn't be as nice to Gloria as she could be. She would help her with all the work, and Dad had given her a lecture about Tommy, about how important it was for him to have a mother of his own. How she must not interfere, and she had given her promise. Margy's determination showed as plainly in her face as once before when she'd told me she was going to learn to keep her mouth shut around Dad and not tell her secrets, even if it killed her. Even if they were total strangers. But I knew that if Margy never spoke another word to me in her life, I'd know exactly who she was, her image shining out of her eyes in two clear cameos.

Leave it to Margy to make a federal case. If Tommy could call Gloria Mother, I could too. Mother was gone and had to take the consequences. I was putting her out of my mind.

Then Margy said she wanted to ask my forgiveness. She was ashamed for the times she'd slapped me and yelled at me for nothing, just because she felt ornery. She'd agreed with Dad that I was mean and sneaky when she was the one who was mean. But she was going to change. I could say the last good night for the rest of our lives. She would never hit me again. I pretended to fall asleep while she was apologizing so I didn't have to hear. Things were too mixed up when Margy thought she needed my forgiveness.

Dad was a happy man. He said so over and over, and sometimes he hugged Gloria in plain sight. I thought maybe when he was alone he jumped in the air and clicked his feet to keep the magic coming. Maybe I would get to be as beautiful as Gloria, if I paid attention and did the things she did. Even though I was the bag of bones and didn't have such fancy red hair. Gloria said she couldn't wait to help Margy and me learn how to become young ladies with all the fellows and good times she had when she was a girl. Margy turned up her nose in a polite way, but I was all ears. I'd be wearing a bra when I got to junior high school, ready or not.

It was as though I woke up from being lost and found myself in a new life where everybody loved everybody, even me. The troublemaker was a thing of the past. Now Gloria would ride up in the front of the car with Dad in the sunshine and I would be in back with Margy and Tommy, giving my all for a feast and the new moon. I would do my best with Gloria, study her like a map, learn her ways like the capitals of the states, and grow up to be like somebody Dad would choose to be his wedded wife. There was the little matter of the picture I stole from her room, but it was so small she probably never noticed.

Dad rode from place to place, went all over the world to find his bride. She was going to make him happy and I was going to do my best for Dad. He went searching for me and found me in a hollow stump, picked me off the cold ground. I felt the warm water trickling down my neck a long time before I knew how sad Dad was, how hard he could cry. His chest went rocking up and down underneath me, heaving and thundering like I was being carried along on a strong horse that galloped away the miles over those endless plains he and Margy imagine are just around every corner.

The Blue Ribbon

THOSE GIRLS. THEY MAKE ME WANT TO LAUGH BUT I don't say anything because they'd only resent it. Such romantic notions. Parroting those things they've heard their father say. They come into a little town like Fort Crossing and it's ooh and ahhh. If they had the least idea of what a bunch of nobodies live around here, gossiping and prying. Well, someday.

Although Francis says it's hard to teach them a thing. Mostly they want to argue. Especially Margy, who will declare something like she doesn't ever want to get married or go to college—she will sing and dance. Like her mother, I suppose. But then she doesn't have the nerve to open her mouth in front of the family, let alone on a stage. Francis says she's closed up like a clam this last year or so though she's no less contrary. For a while she insisted on going to church with the Pentecostals, where they roll on the floor and raise Cain. I guess they'd come to the door asking for money and Margy is easily influenced, with a soft heart. Francis says she'll probably become Jewish next—she has such a streak of compassion. Considering what happened to the Jews, anyone feels that. But I'd find it highly unlikely Margy would convert. I knew this woman once who had a fit when someone borrowed her frying pan without asking. Apparently it was a sin to cook meat in it. I can't think anyone would put up with that sort of thing if they didn't have to. Although I listened to the things Francis said, I've known too many young girls to get excited about a few whims. Let the fellows come knocking, they settle right down.

Francis and I had been dating five weekends straight, talking on the phone long distance sometimes twice a day in between, when he suggested it was time I meet the girls. Tommy had been to see me several times by then and no one would have believed how I felt about him the moment I first saw him. It was exactly as I had imagined a mother would feel when they brought in her baby for the first time for her to hold. I thought of Mother too, losing her little baby boy who was my twin, and sad as that was, it was like God making it up to both of us, that darling Tommy coming into our lives. He seemed to feel it too and let me hold him on my lap while he searched in my purse for some candy. Although it was a wonder he didn't slide off, the way my legs trembled beneath me. It would be different with the girls. I knew that. They were older and remembered their mother, though I never doubted they'd be just as sweet and eager, coming in time to accept me and my love.

But meeting them for the first time, I felt some uneasiness. I didn't know just how they would feel about me, their daddy bringing a new woman into the home to replace their mother. I'd heard people talk all my life. One woman I knew had been left to care for her invalid stepmother for close to fifty years, until the old woman died. That was forty-six years after her daddy was gone. The moral of that story: "What is pomp, rule, reign, but earth and dust? And, live how we can, yet die we must."

It was Mother's idea to have a tea party on the veranda for the girls, something to make a good first impression. It seemed like extra work for Mother to haul out all that stuff when we could as easily have drunk lemonade in the dining room where the light would have been more soothing for my eyes. Besides, it seemed like something to impress old women from the church more than young children. But Mother was certain the girls would like it.

She was right, of course. They went on about it until it seemed almost silly, although I knew it was their way

of being polite and friendly, so I kept my smile to myself.
When they were coming down the front walk toward me,
I began to shake all over, a funny way to feel in front of
young girls, considering I'd be doing them the favor if I
decided to come into their home and be their mother and
they should have worried about what I thought of them.
But my mind was a blank and I couldn't think of anything
to say, feeling as though I might actually burst into tears.
I'm certain I was affected by knowing all they'd been
through, losing their mother so young. And in a way,
too, I could nearly feel her presence, as if Phoebe were
coming along, watching over her children to be certain
they would be well taken care of and truly loved. It
flashed through my mind how someday I could be out
walking on High Street, all three of the children with me,
and pass someone like Dolly Potts, with them looking
up to ask me something, showing on their faces that they
depended on me, that I was their mother. My voice would
hardly rise over the lump lodged in my throat when I said
hello, and the smile I was holding burbled and broke
repeatedly on my lips, like a bubble.

A lot of the people from this town couldn't be budged
with the atom bomb. Live and die with the Alleghenies
behind you and, somewhere over yonder, the delta. My
cousin used to declare, like it was gospel, "High Street
is the hub of the universe." No more sense than to repeat
it out loud; she was the same one who threw live frogs
in the woodstove when I was a child. I was awake for a
year with nightmares from that, recovering in time for
her to tell me her version of the facts of life so I could
about give up sleeping altogether.

A mighty stupid way to be, if you ask me, but what
can you do. I mean, they don't want to be any different.
Bite my tongue. All the time I was growing up, all I
thought about was getting away to see the world, getting
away from Dolly Pottses and Lila Simmonses of the fish-
pond. It didn't take being brilliant to know there had to
be more to life than wagging tongues, scandal, and back-
biting.

That attitude never made me popular, certainly not

with the other girls. The day I entered first grade, Dolly was waiting. Jealous, no doubt: I always had nice clothes and came from a respectable home. Although my daddy was mostly a self-made preacher, training at a small Bible college nobody ever heard of, he was no snake handler and some of the nicest people in town went to his church. I'd a lot rather have been a Masters than a Potts. In spite of my hair being a bright red then, Mother told me I had nothing to hide, and she took pride in fixing curls that hung to my waist. While she dipped a comb into a glass of water and swooped the dampened hair around her finger, all I had to do was sit still, batting away the tears when it pulled. My dress for the first day was a new dimity, blue with matching ribbons, and it had a long sash for Dolly to untie all day. Every time I moved to get up it was undone, dragging in the dirt. I'd fix it without a word and settle back into my seat, go on with my work. To this day I feel the nearly imperceptible tug, hear the stifled titters all around. When I tripped in front of the class the teacher's voice rose above the resulting uproar, suggesting my mother dress me in something more suitable to come to school. My face flushed hot as though it were blistered and it affected me so I was home in bed a week.

When I went back, Mother was with me and had me changed to the other class, skipping right into second grade. I was already reading and knew my sums, because Mother had taught me at home, and she would have gone on giving me my lessons if she'd had to. But after the first I got along all right. It didn't take me long to learn to ignore a bunch of dumb-bunny girls who had nothing better to do than torment an innocent person, spreading their lies. Once, somebody put a bloody rag, which was probably you know what, in my lunch box. By then I was old enough and didn't tell Mother, just threw the whole box in the garbage and made up something so she bought me another. Even then I told myself their meanness was ignorance and jealousy. That was one thing I could teach Francis's girls to help them while they're growing up.

When they get treated like that I'll tell them what happened to me.

Margy was already taller than I and clearly in charge. She wasn't even fourteen, but she could almost have been mistaken for a matron, her dark dress overlong, dragging unevenly at her ankles, like she had a big stomach sticking out in front, which she didn't. Worried frowns passed over her face, telling Ruthann to pull up her socks, cleaning Tommy's face with her slip. They'd had good upbringing as to manners, reaching out to shake hands, saying, "How do you do, Mrs. Stevenson," almost dipping a curtsy. Francis says the poor things have been alone so much they act more like miniature adults than children, almost as if they might have been coming to meet me dressed in little Pilgrim outfits, saying thee and thou.

Tommy seemed strange too, hardly able to remember who I was with the girls hanging their heads and being so formal. I reminded him of the ice cream we'd had at the dairy store, the movie we saw, but he hid behind Margy's skirts, peeking out like it had all been something I dreamed up.

"He's just shy," Margy explained, as though I didn't know him or anything at all about children, as though next she would kindly but firmly give me permission to use the girls' room. Francis says she's too big for her britches but how can she help it, considering how they lived, pillar to post. No wonder they find something enviable about a small town where everybody knows everybody else's business. Francis says their whole life has been a procession of shabby apartments in the run-down sections of different Southern cities. He knows I would never want to live like that, but apparently Phoebe didn't mind, her head in the clouds. She never cared if she had matching towels, if all her cups were cracked and they ate their meals on a wooden crate. Drape a dish towel and sing a song. They say she was artistic, sometimes performing at supper clubs, then getting a bee in her

72

bonnet to knuckle down and take up classical again with a serious teacher.

I guess she never knew just what she wanted; following after Francis one minute, moving out on him the next. Dragging that piano everywhere. Doing whatever came into her head. I know she hurt him too, thinking she had to have a job all the time, trying to support herself and the children. Making him feel like half a man, a poor provider. Francis likes to complain and say he's not important, but I know that's mostly modesty and what he needs is somebody to support him in a good opinion of himself. Even though he didn't stay with his music. Seems to me Phoebe let him down. She was a mighty discontented person, if you ask me.

Not that she wasn't devoted to the children. Anybody could see they adored her. I guess she just didn't think how it was for young kids to move every little while because their mother got restless, couldn't meet the rent, or found a better job. Or had some troubles with her husband. Francis would come home to find them existing on peanut butter and jelly, coats piled up on the beds because the coal had run out. But Phoebe wouldn't call on him, though he'd begged her to settle down in a real home they would make together. Especially after Tommy was born. But she refused. Married more than ten years, she still couldn't make up her mind.

Mother came out of the house then, bustling past those stuck out ''How do you do's'' and ''Thank you, ma'am's,'' hugging all three children in one scoop, right away telling the girls how pretty they were. It never bothers her if people think she's trying to butter them up, handing out compliments wholesale. And most people warm right up too, wanting to believe the things she says. Wouldn't anyone want to be handsome or beautiful? Even when I was a little girl I couldn't be like her, couldn't think of the things to say to make people like me, especially after I'd learned how critical they can be while they're smiling into your face. Smirking behind your back because you didn't wear play shoes on the hay ride or calling you teacher's pet because you won every spelling

73

bee. Before I'd scarcely opened my mouth to the children, Mother was ushering them along to the raspberry patch, encouraging them to chatter away, leading them on with compliments and questions while I tagged behind. I never know what I ought to ask anybody: in case it's rude or I'm butting in. If people want you to know their business, I figure they'll bring it up.

It was evident what Francis meant about Margy being excitable. Her shoes flew off any which way—you were lucky you weren't in the line of fire, and she was telling Mother some tale at the top of her lungs. Ruthann, smaller and quieter, was still awfully jittery, her elbows stabbing out so sharp and snappy it looked dangerous to stand beside her. I smiled to myself and I guess she thought it was meant for her and smiled back. With her gypsy eyes she was the image of Phoebe, from what I'd been told, and I caught my breath. Her face fell back into the sour expression Francis says is typical.

I asked Tommy to come in the house with me for a drink, while the girls were in the bushes getting berries he couldn't reach. "We have some Coke," I urged, but he turned his back, sucking on his fingers. I hadn't seen before that he had any of those bad habits and I wondered if it made him nervous to be around the girls. All that embellishment and display.

"Say, no thank you, ma'am," Margy told him, and of course he chimed in, grinning as if he knew it was silly to have someone telling you everything. I felt so sorry for him too, the middle of July, dressed up in a woolen sailor suit. He did look adorable with those golden ringlets, but I knew he must be about to burn up. No wonder he was cranky. Probably the girls hadn't thought, wanting to make a good impression. Just young girls, and who knows, maybe that was all he had that was nice. Francis has made no secret of the hard time he has making ends meet. He's warned me I better pull in my belt. In fact, he held off a day or two before he first popped the question, afraid he had no right to ask me to take on so much, three children and not much money besides.

But I know that won't be any trouble for me. I've always lived on what I've earned, or what was mine, except perhaps for a few extras now and then that Mother might give me. Money has never seemed that important, not if there's love in a home. I've tried to explain that to Francis, although he looks skeptical. He's afraid I may miss living with Mother, losing Michael's trust, small as it was. The holding pattern at the National Airport adds a new dimension to everyday life, he says, plugging his ears, and there are kids in the neighborhood who seem to survive mostly on knuckle sandwiches. But just because I've never lived on my own, it doesn't mean I can't do as my husband does and together we can make a better life. Someday we can move if we want to. Francis may find to his surprise that some women, when they vow to love, honor, and obey, mean that from the depths of their being.

I never would have thought I'd have ended up living back in this town either, but I have. Life isn't entirely a picnic. I always thought I'd be the first to get away, passing through school like a whiz, skipping grades and going over to the normal school after graduation with the recommendations of all my teachers. Not that I was a grind. It was just easy for me, so that even while I was in school I started doing some modeling at a big department store in Richmond, earning extra money. Soon as I got my figure a lot of the fellows were interested in me and they took me all over the state, to dance and have dinner. By then I wasn't going to let a little person like Dolly get under my skin. Not when most of the girls were starting to act nice. Probably they wanted me to get them some dates. They could see I was good at that.

I intended to make something of myself, more than being thick with the people I'd grown up next to. It was nothing to drive to Charlottesville after work, or stay with my cousin and take summer courses at the university, acting roles in the local theater, even some Shakespeare. It seemed that life was going the way I thought it would, but then I didn't know what was going to happen to me, that I would lose my husband in the war and end up working for Ray Edwards at Southland Chem. But it didn't take a genius to see that knowing something about the world would give anyone a better life. Some people might come to wishing they'd treated you better.

In spite of my training, I didn't want to teach school. Those memories of early days in the grades were too vivid, I guess, and what I really wanted was to go on modeling. The money was good and I liked the other girls, though we were never close, coming from such different backgrounds, just good pals while we zipped each other's dresses and fixed our hair. Sometimes the dressing room would feel like a room in a big house, full of sisters.

But I knew my daddy would never approve. In fact, I'd never told him a word about it. The look on his face when a woman came into church wearing a lot of makeup frightened me, and one time he'd gone into my closet at home and taken a new red dress I'd bought, cutting it to shreds with scissors. Then he made me stand beside him at the trash barrel while he burned up the pieces, that whole time without speaking one word to me, or even glancing at me, although I cried as though my heart would break. But it wasn't the dress. My daddy was always the most gentle man in the world to me, except when something like that happened.

I couldn't have said why the modeling was so important to me, why I enjoyed so much passing up and down the aisles, over a small stage, smiling, turning this way and that. The women in the audience were usually having their lunch, everything gleaming under the crystal chandeliers, china and silver laid out on starched linen, napkins perched like miniature desert tents in pastel colors. It was like a separate and timeless world, the women's faces peaceful, softly lit and pretty; lit further by the hope they might look as good as we did in those clothes they would buy later. Maybe it was my imagination but it felt as though they were smiling back at me too, not with envy, but in profound gratefulness, as though I was actually giving something to them. But my days were numbered. On the rare occasions when a man was sitting at one of the tables, for an instant I'd think it was Daddy and my blood would run cold. Finally the deceit was too much and I took a job teaching fourth grade for the fall term.

I'll be able to help the girls with their clothes and appearance. After all, modeling taught me a few things. I'll take them shopping, teach them to choose things that will be flattering and make good values. In a sensitive way I'll suggest to Margy that she pick skirts to be slimming so she won't look as if she has great big hips. Ruthann will glow in some bright colors. She must get pretty disgusted, hearing the raves about her sister's fair coloring. After we're done shopping I'll take them for a soda, before we go home, so they can model for their daddy, show off the clothes I helped them buy. And I'll explain to him how I helped them save money.

I wandered over to where the girls were picking berries and stood there, smiling when they happened to glance up. When I pointed out a loaded stem to Margy, she gave me a handful. I didn't need any but I took them to be nice. Francis has told me about her problems with her weight and he hopes I'll be able to help her so she doesn't get fat. Certainly I won't be baking fattening cornbreads every night the way their housekeeper did. I'll cook what Francis wants and try to make things that please him and keep the grocery bill down—I know they're used to canned stew and fried Spam, which I imagine I can serve in an attractive way. But I've told Francis he worries too much about Margy's weight. Once the fellows take an interest, she'll see there are a lot of things more fun than eating.

" 'Tain't no flies on you, cutie pie" was his teasing answer to that. But I knew that in his heart one of the things that would mean most to him was having a woman in the house who would set an example for his girls. Someone helping them develop into confident, independent women.

Tommy, copying his sister no doubt, came over to me with a berry stuck out on the palm of his hand like a speck of blood. "Margy," I said, "would it be all right if I took him over town to buy a cotton shirt? He's just

77

running with perspiration." I wanted her to see for herself how hot he was so she wouldn't think I was just trying to interfere.

"Do you want to go with Mrs. Stevenson?" Margy asked him. I wondered if she might insist on calling me that when I was living with them. I imagined Dolly hearing it—what she would think. No wonder Tommy shook his head no and when she coaxed him, flung himself flat on the ground, stiff as a board, holding his breath and kicking at me when I got down to talk to him. I backed away, not knowing what to do. Margy said, "Just let him alone and he'll stop. He does that all the time."

More's the pity, I thought. Later I'd have to explain to him that if he wants me to be his mother, he'll have to treat me kindly and understand that I want to help him. Otherwise I couldn't stay there. I decided to let the shirt go. If he pulled a stunt like that when I had him out in public, people were likely to think I did awful things to him when no one was looking.

Francis said he knew Tommy was getting spoiled, what with the housekeeper giving him his own way the instant he peeped and the girls doting on him. It nearly made Francis despair, having his son grow up in such a mixed-up way. His own life had been odd enough and he was barely hanging on by his fingernails. When Tommy finally sat up, Margy removed that hot jacket and he did seem to feel better immediately. Perhaps the heat was what made him throw a fit when we were supposed to be having a party. Although it could be a boy didn't see the thrill in drinking tea out on a porch. I always did feel I had more in common with boys. I would a lot rather have been out on a football field making goals than jumping up and down yelling "Sis boom bah," which made me feel dumb even when I was fifteen.

Living out in the world, modeling and observing other women, I'd learned to dress with some style and I didn't let go of that. These women from around here go into the dry goods, buy some dress off the rack, have a local girl pincurl their hair, popping them in and out from under the dryer like baked goods. Then they see me at the country club with a good-looking man or receiving at church and their eyes shoot daggers. As though I'd done them a personal wrong. As though I should have been wearing widow's weeds till the day I died. "What a lovely dress, Gloria," they purr, insinuating I flew to Paris to buy it and a dozen more, selling my body for the fare. "Belike you mean to make a puppet of me," I repeat inwardly, my smile never wavering. "Sis boom bah, knock 'em in the tar." They wouldn't be able to imagine what goes through my mind.

It doesn't take a lot of imagination to drive over the river thirty miles to shop in a town of some size with a few dress shops. Magazines for a quarter carry the latest hairstyles. But some would rather use their time to drag me through the mire. Paddle in a backwash and blame anyone with some gumption. I keep smiling right into their eyes. "Why, thank you, Emmy Sue. Your hair always looks so nice." The difference is, I mean it. "And how are your children? I saw where Fred Junior took first prize at the science fair." That child had the cutest red cowlick up over his forehead—just the way I remembered his daddy at nine. If people would stop to think about it they might realize my life hadn't turned out exactly the way I wanted. But then, whose does?

Francis and Phoebe had been separated a good part of the year preceding the terrible accident that took her life. Apparently, she died immediately, which was a blessing if it had to happen. Nobody could imagine why she would take it into her head to walk out like that in a thunderstorm, going for a bottle of milk that could have waited. That poor man who hit her; they said he wept like a child. But I guess Phoebe was that way. When she had her mind set on something she just went ahead and did it.

He buried her in Richmond, where they'd been living at the time. There wasn't any extra money and the break with her family had been irreparable. After they'd turned her out when she was pregnant with Margy, she'd never forgiven them, never even notified them when Francis and she decided to try marriage. Someone that willful could be frightening to sleep beside, Francis says. How could you let your guard down? Of course he's always saying something like that to get a laugh. I know he must have loved her very much.

He admits he wasn't the best husband himself. Even in the short time we've known each other we've shared so much of that kind of thing, knowing we could trust each other, probably because we've both known what it is to suffer. But Phoebe didn't give her marriage the chance she might have, I'd say. She couldn't give up her girlish dreams even after she had a family. Didn't want to help her husband with his profession and learn to budget so they could make do on one income. And she never forgave her own parents, who must have taken it hard when she came home that way. I know I would rather have died than bear that disgrace to my daddy. It will be so very different for Francis and me. We're older and there's nothing I want more than a close family. To be truly a "helpmeet," as God intended.

I never did see Phoebe, not that I remember, although she visited in town with those friends of hers and Francis's, people connected with the academy across the river, nobody I ever went around with. Friends of mine had seen her; they said she was pretty, although in a severe way, most of the time with her hair pulled back in a bun, wearing long, dark skirts.

It could have happened that I saw her, without knowing it. I might have gone over on High to pick up something at the store, looked up, and seen her. Maybe even the children, that dear Tommy still a baby in her arms. No doubt I would have noticed her good looks, although her hair was gray in her twenties and Francis said people always took her for being older than he was. We could have remarked each other in that way women have, neither of us knowing our lives were headed on a collision course with that car speeding right toward Phoebe, the driver never dreaming. Even thinking that makes me want to get down on my knees.

It was a little like that, the way I first saw Francis, not

knowing he was going to be anything to me. He was riding by on the river, lounging on the deck of a big speedboat, dressed in whites, debonair, red hair catching my attention like skywriting. Later I found out Francis had taken that ride to catch a glimpse of me, before he made up his mind about coming to the church social to meet me. But that first impression has stayed with me and I've thought since it was as though I were seeing my own twin brother passing by, the little baby that died right when I was born, looking the way he would have grown up to look if he'd lived. Mother saved a lock of his hair and it was already a true auburn shade.

At the time I thought of a movie star. I know many a redheaded man appears effeminate and Francis had his troubles growing up, boys wanting to whip him to show they could. It didn't help that his mother had to raise him alone and made him study at the piano like a child prodigy. Francis says he was supposed to make up for everything. But any woman seeing him on the river would have known he was all man, slouched against the cabin with the steady appraising gaze of a snake charmer. I recall a funny feeling, one that the roar of the motor and the waves slapping the bank were part of, a secluded private thrilling that goes with an omen.

The very last thing I expected was to see him at the social. I was only there as a favor to Mother, who wasn't able to come, taking her place overseeing the setup, the tables and chairs arranged on the lawn where the churchyard opened up to the river, crepe-paper decorations strung up and pretty enough, twirling in every breeze. Although for my taste it could have been more simple with just the plain cloths on the table and perhaps paper cameo roses for color. Standing there, looking everything over, I recognized Francis making conversation with the minister who had taken Daddy's place, knowing that red head from the back before he turned around. Immediately I had that woman's instinct that tells her a man knows she's around, like a warm hand on the base of my spine. I wanted to laugh out loud. I mean he was the last person you'd expect to be making conversation with old Fish-Flapper. It wasn't a bit nice, but we'd always referred to Reverend Gossage that way because he gave you his hand like it was something dead in the water, even if he did take his training at Duke.

I daresay Francis was amused too, but not as surprised, since he'd had a little preview from the river. His old friend, a woman I knew in town, was pleased as punch with herself for bringing us together, hiding in the cabin when they went by in the boat. Not that men had to be conscripted and hauled in by barge to date me. I had plenty of chances, but after a few dates, generally, I'd call things off, knowing I wasn't going to fall in love with just anybody. And if they were young, I knew they'd want to have a family. But Betty Jo had a hunch about Francis and me and the next day Francis told her that when he saw me close up in that white dress with the aqua polka dots, made in a sheath that showed off my figure, he'd nearly shouted hosanna, only he was afraid they'd throw him in the river and he'd already been baptized. Francis makes me laugh with his jokes, although the flattery doesn't go that far with me. For a long time I've known men to appreciate my shape and I've learned how to dress to enhance it without making myself cheap, something any woman could do. Even when I was modeling I'd think it was a lot of fuss over wearing a dress, although I kept it to myself since I was being paid for my trouble.

Shortly after Francis and I were introduced, we found out how much we had in common. We were familiar with many of the same towns. I'd attended house parties in both Richmond and Baltimore, and he'd heard of some of those families. And right away he let me know about his being a widower with three children. Of course, first thing I'd been wondering if he was married. He didn't wear a ring, but not every man does; often a good-looking man doesn't want to advertise that he's taken, though that doesn't mean he's a runaround. My eyes filled with tears when he told me about his loss. I couldn't help it, seeing in his expression the sorrow and responsibility he carried. I mentioned about my husband too, and it was as though immediately we could understand for each other in a special way. He said he'd been stationed stateside for his duration, but he could tell I thought serving your country was honorable, no matter what you were doing. It felt deep between us from that moment on.

We were still standing together when the reverend was called over for the cake judging. "Violet Kramer," I whispered to Francis while we watched him stand in front of each cake with his mouth open like a baby bird's for the taste.

"Pardon me," he said. I think anybody watching would have seen how much we enjoyed each other, the quick way we appreciated a joke. I took the cigarette he offered, wordless, noticing his eyes darken briefly, as though something he'd suspected and hoped about me was true. I was a minister's daughter who would smoke a cigarette and take a drink. The way a man is, the next thing he wonders is what else you'll do and when.

"Violet will win," I said. "I mean, she's the youngest and prettiest this year. I know, because not so very many years ago I took first prize—two years running." It was my turn to be serious. I wanted him to know I wasn't fooling anybody about my age. After all, I'd lost my husband in the war. That's the kind of experience that leaves its mark, a few lines around the eyes. I knew I was still plenty attractive, but I wasn't eighteen. Perhaps I knew I was already falling in love, the way I spoke to him so directly. In my heart I felt about eighteen, standing there by the river with the colored streamers broken loose in places and the ribbons entangling like on a maypole. When four ladies from the choir stood to sing "Blessed Assurance," and beside me Francis joined in, in a soft mellow baritone, singing every word to the end, only for me to hear, I knew that he had been raised a Christian too. It was all happening so quickly I was afraid to meet his eyes. He struck a match and the sharp sulphur made me sneeze. "God bless you," he said, almost a benediction.

Violet received the blue ribbon and Francis and I had to step away from each other, not to disgrace ourselves laughing, although no doubt it had occurred to others before me, since Reverend Gossage had been doing the cake tasting since he was assistant minister under Daddy. I went to help out at the punch bowl and was holding the glass dipper when Francis came over to say goodbye. The gravity with which he removed it from my hand, he could have been asking me to step into it, and I trembled as though everything depended upon the fit, needing his touch so much it was as though he were taking something out of me by stepping close. They say loving somebody is a gift, but at first it feels like a loss. It does to me.

He asked if he might call me. A man who will come straight out and let a woman know he likes her has always appealed to me. If he lacks that much gumption it's more than likely he'll fail you every step of the way. I even prefer a man who has a streak of arrogance. It's part of being high-spirited and generous, makes it easy to arouse him with a word of praise. My first husband was as particular as could be about how he was treated, anywhere he went. At a hotel you would have thought he was royalty, room service for a tube of toothpaste, shoeshines and shaves. Michael would complain to the management if he found a hair in the tub. I don't think anyone resented it, not the way he tipped. He was always the gallant with me, intent on surprising me with signs of his thoughtfulness, though of course with only three months to live together, it was still somewhat as if we were dating. It was hard for me to believe his mother hated me that much. Calling me on the phone. Whispering. Trying to wound me, as though I was to blame for the loss of her son. It affected me deeply and I never went to visit her or sent her any kind of a card until the day she died, even though some would have reminded me she was my mother.

After Francis had gone I was sailing on a clear stream, moving tables and chairs like they were feathers, breezing back and forth into the church hall, dividing up leftovers. I gave an extra big hunk of cake to Dolly. No doubt it was ashes in her mouth, mean as she'd always

84

been, but I felt I could forgive everybody. I bet Dolly never thought she'd end up an old maid. It had always hurt me especially that she was at the funeral parlor, grieving, when Michael lay there and I couldn't be with him, lying in the hospital bed losing our baby and nearly my mind. Somebody came and told me about Dolly, how she carried on, falling on Mother Stevenson's neck. I didn't breathe a hint of my feelings, not until I was alone, when I took the pot of chrysanthemums Dolly had sent and removed every single petal, one by one, letting them scatter by the hundreds to the floor. When I was done, I shoved the skeleton under the bed. Such a look the night nurse gave me, but I only stared her back. I noticed she didn't lift a finger to clean up but left it for the colored orderly who came in the morning. Maybe in my condition I shouldn't have gotten out of bed, but it made me feel ashamed to see somebody old and bent having to clean up after me and my temper, and I did what I could to make it easier.

All the space around me felt enlarged, because of my meeting with Francis, as though it was opening as I opened, the evening light thick and buttery like something winged you might catch in your hand. Times like that, you know your life really is planned out for you, the way Daddy taught me, and when I glimpsed the sanctuary through the church parlor I whispered, "Thank you, Jesus," the way I did sometimes. And I blew a kiss out the window to Daddy's grave, where the carved wooden angel maintained her doleful muse. My heart was tumbling around loose inside, needing someone to take hold. I really hadn't realized up until then how lonely I had been.

The last to leave the church, when I got out into the parking lot, carrying a bunch of stuff in my arms, I could see from way off that something was pinned to the front seat of my car. I couldn't make out what it was until I was on top of it and then I nearly dropped everything in my haste to get it loose and tucked away in my purse. Whatever had people thought of that, the blue ribbon spread out plain as day.

For quite a while I sat in the car, pulling myself together before I drove home. I even had a cigarette alone, which I rarely did, gazing out at the river running with the sunset colors like a rainbow rained to earth. Anybody driving past would have wondered what I was doing there for myself, Earl Masters's daughter. I had such a giddy feeling too, as though I didn't care, even after I was driving along the highway with stolen property in my purse. Imagining the state police coming after me, blasting their sirens, setting up roadblocks. I turned up the radio to blot them out, moving faster and faster, as though they'd never catch me and I would cross the state line and go on and on, until I was in some new place where nobody had ever known me, my life a mystery no one would ever even try to figure out. When I did get home I didn't mention a word of what happened to Mother. This was mine, to keep to myself a little while, private and special. Soon enough I'd be the talk of the town.

I knew I must be smitten, because I'm known for my honesty. Just like Abe Lincoln, I'd walk ten miles to return extra change. But I never for an instant thought of returning Violet's ribbon. They'd have to come and get me.

After a while Tommy got over some of his bashfulness and came to talk with me. I told him I'd take him to the cartoon show at the movie house, and seeing the girls look on, I invited them too. Before Ruthann could reply, Margy said, ''Thank you, ma'am, but I don't like cartoons.'' So of course Ruthann said the same. I just smiled—whoever heard of children not liking cartoons. Well, if they'd rather sit home and frown, so be it. Tommy let me take his hand, and it was so sweet and trusting, his warm little palm lost in mine, as though he'd go anywhere with me. Again I had that sensation that he'd been placed in my arms the day he was born. In time I would be able to help Ruthann develop a mind of her own. She might find things she liked which had escaped her sister entirely.

Mother has a way with kids. They came trooping out

of the berry patch, all smiles, fingers purple and pricked. Margy had torn her dress, but when I offered to get a needle and thread she only laughed and showed me where the briars had torn her leg and puckered her socks. Those were the rough ways Francis worried about, and no wonder. Anyone could see she made the most of them.

We all walked together to the tea table. Leave it to Mother, everything dainty, little party sandwiches, rabbits and chickens stamped out with a cookie cutter. Lemonade fresh-squeezed, with the pulp and rind floating. The girls ate and ate and I didn't know how they could hold that much. One sliver of strawberry pie filled me to the brim, especially with my stomach in knots. How fortunate to be young girls with nothing very much to worry about. Your life before you.

I knew it would be difficult. Francis didn't deny they were a handful: too much for him. I excused myself and went into the cool dark kitchen to take aspirin. Usually I just grin and bear it, but I wanted to feel good on that occasion. Probably after we were all settled down together, those troubles I'd had would fade away and I'd be glad I hadn't mentioned them to Francis. Anybody would be upset when one day a telegram arrived and told you your life was over. At least the life you thought you had.

When I got back outside, Margy was telling Mother a story about her mother and daddy having a water fight in some apartment they'd lived in, the floor sopping wet when the girls came in from school. I suppose she thought that was entertaining, since it was all she'd known. It made me feel so sad and left out to hear that stuff; ashamed, too, in front of Mother. I hoped the girls wouldn't talk on and on about their mother. Francis says Tommy has already forgotten and no doubt it would be better for him not to get confused about who his mother is. If the girls keep harping on Phoebe, I might bring up Michael, talk about marriage. They would see how it feels to be constantly reminded of dead people when nothing in the world will bring them back.

Later I told Francis about Margy talking like that in

front of Mother, bragging about the different schools she'd attended, about how peculiar her life had been, and he admitted she has a big mouth. "Her mother encouraged her and perhaps I have myself. But don't you worry about them. Leave the girls to me." He said he'd see to it they treated me with respect or know the reason why. I'd be tops on his hit parade if I'd agree to marry him. In a thousand years he wouldn't be able to repay me for my sacrifice. He looked as though he meant exactly that.

Before the children left, I was able to lure Tommy away, playing hide-and-seek across the yard until I had him in the house. It was shaded and quiet and I knew it felt peaceful to him. I took him up to the study and showed him the World War I medals, introducing him to the hero, my father, looking down on us from the fireplace. It looked so cute to see Tommy grinning up, the little sailor saluting the soldier. I knew my father wept in heaven to see me with that child after I'd waited such a long time. He and I were always more alike, more emotional than Mother. Sometimes I thought she didn't understand either one of us, greeting and serving everybody herself the day of Daddy's funeral, while I swooned behind my veil as though I inhaled a vapor.

I gave Tommy a German mark from the box and he ran straight with it to Margy. I realized I should have had something for the girls too, although I wouldn't have known what. Girls seemed harder to please. Mother saved the day by asking if they'd like to see the house, and when they spied the piano they seemed to forget everything else, sitting right down to play. Mother was praising them on their hand positions and technique, even for simple melodies—going on until I figured she was trying to dig me because I'd never wanted to learn and quit as soon as she let me.

Margy, ever vigilant, stood up in the middle of a song and announced it was time for them to be going. Mother and I stood on the porch, watching them walk away, waving again when they reached the corner. "I'll marry him myself if you don't," she said, as if Francis would just be waiting for her to give the word. "Their mother must have been a wonderful person. You can just tell."

"Don't talk nonsense," I snapped, and went off to my room to rest. Sometimes, the fuss people make. It's enough to make you want to step in front of a car.

I did feel somewhat disheartened after that day, not certain I'd fit in with the family, no matter how much Francis and I might care for each other. My promise wasn't given yet and I was brooding about what to do when Mother came home from town and told me what she'd heard, what people all over were saying. I turned to ice in the middle of an August heat wave, though for once my head was clear as a bell. My fury drove even Mother from the room. Anyone who has seen me that way is surprised, for most of the time I appear mild-mannered, even sweet-natured. Which I try to be. But I feel things on the inside and sometimes they almost tear me apart. I've just learned to control myself, at least most of the time. Daddy said people like him and me bore an extra cross.

About noon that day, when Francis called, Mother did what I'd told her to do and said I wasn't home—not sounding very convincing, since she hated to tell a lie. But the truth was, I wasn't home to him. Never would be, not after what he'd done. I heard what she said from the top of the stairs, tiptoeing back to my room before Mother saw me. When she knocked, I didn't answer, listening to her footsteps going away and not even feeling guilty. I was still like a statue at two in the morning, lying there with eyes pasted open, when I heard pebbles beginning to strike against the windowpane. It was Francis out in the drive. He'd hung up the phone and gone straight to the car, driving clear through to get to me. As quickly as he could. Not such a total surprise to me— I've known more than one man to value what he thought he might lose.

I went down and got in the car with him and we drove off, going for miles along the river. Just the sight of him, sheepish and whipped-looking, made me want to leap at his throat. I yelled at him until my throat was raw, banging my fists on the dashboard so the ring Michael gave me dented the wood. Calming myself briefly, I would only find myself starting up again. My good name was all I had. I never had been able to bear it when people dragged me through the mud, telling a bunch of stuff they didn't know about. If Francis wanted a tootsie, let him stick with his Richmond woman. Since she didn't mind what he did. See how eager she'd be to nursemaid his haughty daughters, scrape by on a small-time administrator's salary; scrimp and save, doing without and calling him a big man. See how she liked a small-time two-timer. I felt if I'd had a gun, I would have aimed it. "This is my home," I kept repeating. Finally, all I could do was sit beside him, shaken, flinching when he tried to put his hand on me. All my life I'd heard of men who didn't give a damn for a woman, who she was, where she came from. Use her up and move on. Spit her out. I quieted, facing away from him toward the river.

"Gloria." At last he spoke my name, his voice husky and emotional. "I kept wanting to tell you myself. Everything. So you wouldn't think I was leading you on. I just didn't know how to bring up certain things so you wouldn't want to quit on me. I know the kind of woman you are, believe me, and I respect you more than you know. I wouldn't ever really want any other kind. But I'm a weak mother's son and I don't know what I'd do if I didn't have you." By that time I was drained of tears. Empty. I felt so tiny it was like when I was a child, looking down at my noonday shadow. "I guess I've been keeping her like money in the bank. Just not able to think you'd really want me. Miserable cur that I am."

Up on the bluff Francis parked the car and we got out. The moon was very bright and it tinged the world with a greenish cast, as though I were seeing it through those X-ray machines that show how your shoes fit, with your bones glistening like wet marble. I believe Francis had been crying a few minutes before I was aware of it. It touched me, and automatically I reached out my arms to comfort him, the way you'd do for a child, humble that he was so moved. Then he really did break down, sobbing so desperately it was actually frightening. I'd never seen a man get like that before and I knew right then and forever what an intense and passionate person he was, how emotional, in spite of his surface bravado. It was as though the moonlight were indeed X-ray and I could see into him, and nothing he would ever say or do would be unexpected.

One minute he was begging me to marry him. The next he swore he was no damn good and would never deserve my love. Underneath I'm certain he did dread that one day I would leave him too, the way Phoebe was always doing. But he still had a lot to learn about me. Time would show him what I'm like.

He didn't try to deny what was said. He had been seeing another woman, although it wasn't what I thought. Not really, more a friendship, something from their past. And he had wronged Phoebe. He wouldn't deceive me about that or evade his own guilt. Young and weak, he'd been tempted more easily than some, being a lusty son-of-a-gun. He was ashamed and always would be, not that that was an excuse. The fact that Phoebe had done the same thing herself was only after she'd put up with him for a long time. Longer than she should have, he said, taking the blame, still speaking in a strained, harsh voice. All that while I held him close against me.

"There were times I could have sworn she was throwing me at other women. She'd go off to bed, driving away in a huff from wherever we were, not even telling me she was leaving. Whenever we went out, there was always a bunch of women around. She had lots of friends. I'd just get drunker after she'd leave, thinking, Oh, you kid. Christ, she wasn't even with me the night I hurt my hand when supposedly we were celebrating the big audition. The one that was going to make my future." For a while he lay against me, opening and closing his fists, on his face a look of painful bewilderment, and I felt as though I was seeing him when he'd been hurt, young and full of hope for the future.

"The fool story is too boring and predictable for me to repeat—a scholarship to a Northern conservatory, big

91

opportunity for small-town boys. Although by then I was old enough to know better; I didn't have a snowball's chance in hell. But Mother was going to be sitting there in that purple hat with the curved feather. In my mind's eye I watched it wilt like some other tokens of outworn pride.'' By then he'd sat up, his elbows on his knees, smoking a cigarette in gulps. The bodice of my dress was soaking wet, stuck right to me where his head had lain. He wasn't seeing me, though, his eyes fastened on the distance as if the moonlit river vanished into the notch at the bend, bearing the past away.

"I don't even remember the fight, just waking up at the hospital with my hand bandaged, Phoebe beside me. We'd already been through a lot together. I told her she ought to get out. The handwriting was on the wall. But I guess she felt sorry for me. Women are good at that—they want to help. I stayed on and received my master's degree, then couldn't find a teaching job to save my soul. In Baltimore I enrolled in some accounting courses and Phoebe took work as a secretary. Nine months later we had another child.''

Francis reached over, taking my hand. "Do you feel sorry?" he asked, his head lifted toward where a whippoorwill was telling his sad story. As though I were a woman so easily trifled with. I drew myself up, making my little shoulders as square as possible, throwing back my head.

"I most certainly do not. You have a lovely family and an important job. I'd have given everything if I could have held my own baby in my arms." Like that, he swept me into his embrace. I was thinking how happy we could be together. I didn't mind a bit that he wasn't a great famous musician either. A respectable and dependable position was plenty good enough for me, and every day he would see my pride in him as I found ways to prove it.

I would try to forget the sordid tale he'd told. Not that it was anything new. Those kinds of things happen everywhere, maybe even more often in a small town where there's nothing much to do. Although I'd never known personally a woman who behaved like Phoebe, not to talk to, I mean. One or two of the girls I'd known at school ended up consorting with different men at waterfront hotels, country girls who didn't come from any kind of family to begin with. I suppose they were nothing but whores, though I hate even to think a thing like that. I didn't overlook or take lightly what Francis had done either. It was a great wrong. But there was no denying the responsibility a woman has to her husband, to treat him with the utmost love and respect, seeing that he is never disappointed or tempted into evil. I know my father would rather I was hung on a tree than not do right by myself and those who love me.

"And I've got you, baby, don't I?" Francis whispered into my ear, his tongue giving me a tingle. "Say I do and I'll never be sorry again. Otherwise—" Francis sprang forward, climbing to the top of a huge boulder that hung at the cliff's edge, bent over to take the plunge. Laughing, I had to wrestle with him to pull him to safety and he was still straining when I said I'd marry him, if he really meant that his wife and family would come first in his life—after God. I promised too that I would help him every way I could. I knew how important a man's career is to him, the status it conveys—laying my finger on his lips and refusing to hear when he began to demur. Francis was apt to call himself a has-been, the school he worked for a loony bin, his colleagues dingbats. I thought he might change his tune when he got some nice promotions and raises, when somebody stood beside him who believed in him all the way. After we'd given our word, Francis watched me steadily and I saw a little shiver pass over him as the hour tolled from the Fort. It was a solemn moment and I know both of us were thinking of Phoebe. She wasn't the only one with a mind of her own. Francis could see that and it made me proud, as though I'd earned his respect. Something I knew he had for Phoebe in spite of everything.

It was my turn to confess then and I told him how some of the women in town had treated me, the gossip I'd endured. They said I took Michael away from Dolly just to show that I could, that I'd never really loved him. Then he was dead, three months after our wedding day, and I was carrying his child. To lie in the hospital, losing our little boy, Dolly taking my place at the funeral. I was sick a long time. It was a miracle I got well, the doctors said. And maybe it was, for Dad prayed for me as hard as he could. He even promised God that if I got well he'd never drive a car again, and that was a man who would drive three hours to Roanoke for no reason at all, speeding most of the way because he knew the traps, where he had to watch out. But the sacrifice meant nothing to him compared to my life, and the moment they knew I was going to live, although I would never have a child of my own, he went down to the courthouse to hand in his license. That was the kind of love I was used to, what I depended on.

I told Francis something I'd never before told anyone, not even the doctor at the hospital, about how I used to be afraid at school. There was a woodstove in the room the boys would stoke red-hot. I couldn't get it off my mind that one of them might take my hand and force it against the stove until it would melt, doing a terrible thing like that for no reason. Sometimes I'd have to stay home from school, I'd be that terrified. Although I couldn't tell Mother, for she might get it in her head that something was really wrong with me. But I wanted Francis to know my deepest secrets, to know what I'd suffered and how, after wanting to die, a person could go on and live a happy life.

He said the worst blow had been finding a letter among Phoebe's things from a man urging her to get a divorce so they could marry. Something in his tone made Francis think she would do it, but then the accident had made it a moot question. Although it had left him with a bitterness he couldn't get rid of. Until he saw me.

I had a surprise for Francis then. Something I'd been saving to tell him until we were engaged. I had a little money, some from Daddy, and I wanted to give it to him to help buy a new car. If he wanted one. I've never known a man since Daddy who likes to drive the way Francis does and I thought he'd really appreciate that gift. It's always nice to be seen in something new and prosperous-looking—like begets like. We'd keep it nice too, and I didn't think his pride would suffer that much—not enough to turn it down.

When it was over and we were quiet, I bowed my head. It seemed natural, feeling my daddy's presence, his Christian example. And I knew, too, how much Francis regretted and wanted to change. And I could help him. Looking up at him when I was finished, smiling, I murmured, ''Until death us do part.'' The mist sweeping in off the river with dawn's approach distorted his features. One instant he appeared to leer, the next to cringe. I just took his hand. ''Let's go home and tell Mother.'' The whippoorwill still called down the valley as we walked to the car.

When we actually did go off to get married, we made up our minds quite suddenly, everything about our meeting and coming to love each other providential, as though it was out of our hands. Mother was gone, visiting her sister in Nashville, and Francis was staying at the house while Ruthann recovered from her ordeal. Margy and I were having fun cooking meals and taking care of the house and Tommy, as if we were already a family and belonged together. Tommy let me read him his bedtime story, and when I stroked his forehead he fell asleep before I'd finished and didn't even ask for Margy. The letters from their trip came, and Francis read them out loud. Everybody laughed and agreed that Ruthann's was just like her—that was before we were entirely certain if she was simply feverish from exhaustion or had come down with a bug besides.

The night we left, I was coming out of Tommy's room on tiptoe when I met Francis in the shadowed hallway. The look in his eyes told me we shouldn't wait another minute. It was plain foolish that I was taking care of his children, seeing him all day, then at the end of the evening the two of us parting and going off to separate ends of the house. I knew Francis wouldn't have wanted me to give myself to him unless we were married. He'd been through that kind of thing once before and this time he wanted to do it right.

In a glance we knew it was time. It wasn't as though we were children and didn't know what we wanted. It wasn't as though we didn't know the difficulties, how at best it was a leap in the dark. I could never have known about Michael if I had dated him for a millennium. It took Mother Stevenson to call me at the hospital and ruin my life, saying Michael had never loved me, it was Dolly all along, until she'd turned him down and he thought he'd get back at her by marrying me. Then he'd run away to war, to get away from me. "Why else would a young man enlist? Throw his life away?" The phone fell out of my hand when she said that, her whispers boiling on at my thigh. He had told me he'd been drafted and I believed him. The trouble was, he was always a stranger to me, so that really I'd never known if what she said was true or just something mean to hurt me. Although when I thought about it later, I realized most young men considered it an honor to fight for their country.

Francis and I stood in the hall, those things behind us, settled for all time, our vows made. He went in to tell Margy to take care of things, leaving her the doctor's number, although Ruthann was clearly on the mend. Hurriedly I packed an overnight bag, slipping in a rope of pearls I'd been saving for this night. It was exciting, almost like sneaking off down a ladder. Wouldn't we cause a stir, everybody wondering. But I never could have stood up in front of a bunch of people to be married, letting them stare, knowing what they think about. I didn't even want Mother there. Any gown, white as snow, virginal, netted and tacked with pearls, might just as well be spun of glass. As I left the room my eyes automatically looked to where the little snapshot of Michael used to be stuck in the mirror. I'd noticed it was missing after I came upon Ruthann in the hall outside, that time she first came to the house. Now I was saying goodbye to him as my husband for good.

From the start I'd felt the passion in Francis, the heat

of his desire. It hungered in his eyes, seeming to creep around like vines, smothering me in a cloud of red jasmine. I would bring out my pearls, and weak all through from wanting him, I imagined the hold that would come when I gave myself to him, the time that would be ours when I bared my body, took my white breasts in my hands and held them to him. I wanted to see his face when he knew he had only to open his mouth to receive, to have them filling him, had only to reach out to tumble himself upon me. A woman's body, freely given to her beloved, can hold a man forever.

Even though Francis hadn't told Margy where we were going, what we were going to do, she looked shy when we said goodbye and seemed to sense something. We just ran out the door, waving, got in his old car, and slammed the doors. If Mother wondered why we were in such a hurry we couldn't wait for her to come home, I'd remind her that Francis was a pretty good catch. She'd said so herself. Then, gunning the motor, both of us laughing, we spun out the drive, taking the turn so it spilled us together, heading us down the highway to Kentucky.

PART II

The Tennessee Waltz

I STEER THE MOUNTAINS. DAD SAYS I'M DOING SEVENTY-five, they'll never catch me. Old Seventy-five the oats eater wasn't worth crow bait, good for glue. When Dad went on parade he was lucky Seventy-five didn't roll. Seventy-five wasn't going nowhere in the hot sun. Giddy-up, horsy, step on it, we're leaving laggards in the dust. Banana splits on the rail, it's Beetlebaum.

I check the rear to see Margy taking it. Dad says she costs him a pretty penny with her appetite. Margy grins and takes it. Dad says she's getting to be a stranger. She's got secrets. Must be the boys. He tips his hat and steps on the gas like we're going to catch one. Margy wouldn't be caught dead and stares out the window. Once upon a time Dad ran away from home. He was the soldier boy. He had the stiff upper lip and the horse that didn't have no name, only Seventy-five. Dad was a cowboy too, sometimes an Indian. After he was on his own a while he didn't care what he was; every place he took a different name. Dad says he's Running Still.

Your mother laughs. "I don't know how you could stand being around all those horses, Francis. There must have been a terrible smell." Two clothespin fingers snap off her nose and I have to smile. I don't look at Margy, who's going off someday to live on a horse.

"This is your mother," Dad said. "She's my bride and your mother. Be good to her and you can't lose. Anyone around here who doesn't like it is free to go." Dad looked around at the girls to show them the door. Your mother

101

gave Dad a new car. Dad gave her a family. Dad said how lucky can you be.

I didn't have a mother and once I kicked the new one in the leg. "You aren't the boss of me. You're not my mother." She got the suitcase out of the closet and was sorry to have to go. But if I didn't want her to stay. Her eyes were breaking and I said she could stay. Dad didn't have to know, she said. Before I didn't have a mother, only Margy. Your mother always wanted a little boy.

Dad says she got something extra. "Two girls into the bargain. Whether you want them or not." When you get a girl you leave her out in a tree to get a cold, but a boy gets the whole kit and caboodle. Ruthann said I was lucky I got to keep all my wiener. It's even got the skin. Dad said, "It's a boy. Hooray, we'll keep him. He'll need everything he's got."

"Bring out the mustard, I'm having a hot dog," Ruthann said. I cried and she laughed and I tried to sock her in the stomach. Dad said she was a nasty little girl but he couldn't blame her. A girl was bound to be bitter. "It's the way of the world, son. Keep the upper hand." I'm breathing with Dad while we're riding down that long, dusty trail. Margy says it's attached and I don't have to worry. She sang me a long song about the cowboy on the streets of Laredo and I went sound to sleep.

Dad keeps a sharp eye on Margy in the mirror to catch her daydreaming about the boys. Everybody wants a boy. Ruthann can't get my wiener because she's off visiting the mother-in-law. "She comes with your mother," Dad said. "Can't have too many grandmothers. Everything's coming up roses."

"By golly, I miss that Ruthann," Dad says. "There hasn't been one good fight since she left town. The rest of you are all sweetness and light. I long to see the fur fly." Your mother laughs and Dad says she's a good sport, half the reason he married her. The other half—can't say. He gives her a wink, his hands holding the steering wheel at the bottom in case I make a false move.

"We'll be home soon," your mother says. "After we

eat. You must be hungry, Margy.'' She smiles at Margy in the back seat.

"Don't say 'home,' honey. Your home is with me now, or have you forgotten. Anyway, to answer your question, of course she's hungry, although if I had my way there would be no eating on this trip. Not when I'm about to hit pay dirt at the mother-in-law's.''

Your mother laughs. ''I don't believe you'd do that, Francis. You're just kidding. Walk in on someone and eat up a lot of food just because it's free. I've always thought people who did that were a mighty cheap bunch. I'm not all that hungry myself, but kids get hungry. They're still growing.''

"More's the pity for some.'' Dad tries to nab Margy in the mirror, but she's looking out the window. Dad tells your mother he's a new man since she's given him something to live up to, although he's not going down without a fight. The hell with Emily Post, he will still use a toothpick in public and once in a while he intends to burp. If only for old times' sake. Your mother's lips make a line, her eyes heading down the pike. I'm driving to the mother-in-law's to get a quarter in my pocket, when I don't know. Sometimes candy. I don't check my pocket when somebody might be looking. Your mother says other people might wonder what your hand is doing in there.

We're driving right up to the man in the road with the red flag. "Whoa,'' Dad says, and stops the car on a dime. He leans his arm on the window. ''How much more of this stuff, buddy? My pilot wants to know.'' The men ride on their tractors like it's a wagon train going West.

The buddy grins at me. He sees Margy too, nodding into the back, where she sits up straight. Water slides in his hairy chest and two slit eyes peep out from in there, giving me the wink. ''We had a washout in here, sir. Mean job on the road, as you can see. We're sending folks back to Centerville, or you can go onto the dirt and cross the mountain on this side. Pick up the highway at the junction. Right pretty country in through here."

"Not a bad idea. Fifteen miles or so?" The man nods his head. "Any place to feed and water my posse? They're threatening mutiny." The man grins at Margy in the back, where she's twisting a piece of her yellow hair.

"Roadhouse near the junction's popular around these parts. Mrs. Blues. She's pretty famous for her cooking. Band Saturday nights." He leans down on the window where Margy is and then there's a rose in her lap, pink on her blue dress. "I know now, miss. Who it is you look like. I knew it was somebody. Ingrid Bergman, the movie star." The red flag is poked in his hip pocket and his teeth shine like a movie in the dark.

Dad slaps the car like it's Seventy-five. We jump in our seats and the man pulls back on the double. "So long," Dad says. "Thanks for the tips." We leave him eating our dust.

"That was rude, Dad," Margy says, her cheeks pink as the rose.

Dad stops the car and puts his arm over the seat, ready to back up. "Why, I had to protect my elder daughter. I thought he was going to climb right in and help himself. Raises my hackles. But if you want to go back"—he laughs at Margy trying to hide on the floor and then he's done with that and we're heading up the dirt road, popping stones.

"He was a cute fellow," your mother says. "Well spoken too. Probably he's been away to school somewhere. You can always tell. I wonder who his family is. It's too bad we have to be on this dusty road after we just washed the car."

"It beats backtracking a half hour. But if you want to—say the word. I never do anything that doesn't please the little woman." Dad's looking for Margy in the mirror but she's having a sulk and isn't talking to Dad. "I'm curious about this Mrs. Blues too. If my wife and daughter don't appreciate me, maybe I'll make a hit with her."

"Francis." Your mother shakes her head. "I'm not finding fault with you. Whatever you want is fine."

"When will we be there? When when when?" I'm singing a song and Dad raps me on the noggin and says, "Never. Now shut that up." We're steering ruts and dust is blowing in the windows so we have to close them up tight, stones knocking around like they want in too. Dad says nothing's perfect.

Dad can't find Margy in the mirror. He sighs and it tickles my neck. "I keep forgetting your sister's at the marrying age. Hormones that won't quit. Every time I see a motorcycle my heart skips a beat. We may lose her at the junction." I look back. "Keep your eye on the road, son."

"I want in back," I say. Dad's bones are hard like I've landed on a paving stone. I slip over the seat to be with Margy. She kisses me. Your mother smiles and smiles. My legs are itching. "Sit still," Margy says.

"I want a dog."

"Over my dead body," Dad says.

"I know you do, dear. I think every little boy should have a dog. It teaches responsibility." Your mother smiles in my eyes and we have a secret. Someday, she says. When when when? When I'm old and gray.

"I'm afraid of dogs," Dad says. "I'm not the he-man I appear to be."

The cousin took me into the field. He had a big wiener, he said. It was the biggest. Didn't it scare me? He could make it bigger than anything. I could watch if I didn't tell nobody. Didn't it scare me? I couldn't be a man if I was going to be the big crybaby. Both hands couldn't hold on to it when it jumped and some of it was in his hand. Then it was little, going away. He said that would happen to me if I was a tattletale.

"Speak up, boy." Dad slips a look over his shoulder to catch me thinking. "How do you expect the world to sit up and take notice if you mutter? You're among friends here." We're starting to go over a bridge and Dad stops. It's only a two-ton, Margy better get out and walk. We laugh and ride on.

"I'm hot," she says. "Can I open my window a lit-tle?" Stones pop and dirt is in my mouth, with my head stuck outside. Your mother ties a scarf around her head.

"We've hit a mine field," Dad says. In back his cow-lick sticks up like he's got a red hackle himself.

"Maybe if we went a little slower," your mother says, "we wouldn't raise so much dirt." Dad stops the car on the road and we're hanging upside down on the roller-coaster.

"You can take the wheel anytime, if you think you can do better. Probably you think you own us lock, stock, and barrel since we got this car. For two cents I'd be drop-kicking the old heap again." We start backing down the hill, but I don't look at Dad. When we go up the hill nobody's talking. "All right," Dad says. "I'm sorry. Sometimes I forget where my bread is buttered." He reaches over to rub your mother's cheek while she doesn't bat an eye.

I pull up close to her seat. "Hi, Mom." I show her my muscle. "Come sit with me and we'll read *The World Book*, dear." She makes room and I'm in her lap. Her fingers tickle tickle my legs like grass blowing. Dad says, "Sit on the seat, son. You're too big for a lap child. Besides, your old man's a jealous wretch. Can't help it." Your mother squeezes to let me in and we read. *The World Book* is for me when I'm in school. The girls didn't have one. Dad took them to the library where everything was free for the asking. They'd never take a thing for granted.

"Show me some soldiers."

Your mother does what I say, only we don't have the letter *S*. Just the letter *A*. "We'll look up Army instead," she said.

"Your sister wants you to look up Adonis," Dad says, and your mother has to laugh at that, and we're friends with Dad again, except for Margy, who reads and reads her own book while your mother hugs me with her arm. She's reading but I don't hear a word. Dad lifts her arm up. "I bet he likes those earmuffs." His eyes move on the road like he's reading a book.

When Dad stops with a bump, we look up and wonder if it's another two-ton bridge; only he says, "Howdy," and a boy is standing there on top of us, staring in with his mouth open. Margy slides down the seat and I'm on my knees to watch him eating our dust. "Well, what d'ya say about that one, daughter? A bit of a hayseed if you ask me, but I don't know your taste."

Margy's up and laughing. "Dad, honestly." She rolls the window up.

"Honestly what? I'm only trying to help." Dad shrugs. "I want to get you hitched before I have to ride shotgun. He looked kind of dim, but appearances can be misleading."

I go back to be with Margy. She has the rose pinned in her hair and I give it a good sniff for a sneeze. "She'll be gone soon," Dad says. "Enjoy her while you can."

"Francis. The way you talk. Margy doesn't want to get married at fifteen, for heaven sakes. Do you, Margy?" Your mother laughs into Margy's face and gets a smile back with a roll of the eyes.

"You know Dad, Gloria." I call her Mom, or she'd be too sad to go on. She always wanted a little boy and God gave her me.

"To know me is to love me," Dad says, his eyes sneaking in the mirror. He gets to rub your mother's cheek while she licks her little smile.

"I'm hot," Margy says. "May I open the window a little bit again?"

"Ask your mother. She's the boss. Especially when we're riding in her car."

"Why, Francis. I am not. I only thought we should have them closed when it was so dusty. Of course you may get some air, Margy. But you know, Francis, I'd be a little careful in through these hills. It's wild country and some of these fellows aren't all that nice. I've heard of terrible things they do to people. Take them out of their cars. It's even in the papers. They've got stills back in here too. Probably it's not very good for the car either, when you brake fast like that. It's bound to be extra wear on the tires."

Dad stops the car. It must be time for my spanking. Then with a sigh he drives on again, making a weary climb. "You can't beat married life."

The dead dog was in the woods, lying on the ground. The cousin said he was the one that killed it. "See, it don't got no wiener." Mine's still there. Your mother says it's not polite to check. The cousin said I wouldn't believe what happened to girls. "They ain't got nothing."

Dad's driving the car like we're never going to get there. "You can tell the honeymoon's over. Already I can't do a thing to please you. I feel as though I'm in my grave."

"Francis, that's not true. You know I think you're a wonderful husband. I just think people should take good care of their nice things. So they stay nice."

Dad pats her on the head. "The trouble is, I'm not used to nice things. They make me uncomfortable."

"I want all the money in the world, Mom." I put in my two cents. She wants to give me everything.

"He's insufferable," Dad tells Margy over his shoulder. "All boy and there's not a thing to be done. Lucky you can have one and not be one."

"I wish I lived out here in a cabin all by myself. With a horse and a dog," Margy says. "I'd have a garden too. These ridges are so beautiful."

Your mother says, "I don't believe you'd really want to. Not if you knew how backward everybody is in these places. And you say you don't like dogs."

"Besides, why be in such a hurry to leave your home, daughter? Free room and board. Where can you get a better deal?"

"I don't have a home," Margy says. Dad's jaw pounds like he's got a fist inside. He's heading down that long, lonesome road. Maybe it's time for my spanking. Margy doesn't have a home. She comes from the old time when the old mother was here that I'm not supposed to know.

"I'm sorry, Dad," Margy says. "I just mean we've moved around so much. All the different places I've lived.

Someday I want to settle in one place and stay there. Never move again.''

"You might find that pretty monotonous too.'' Your mother's smile jumps and plays like a puppy that won't lie down until it's told. I get over by the window and make V for victory, the President riding by.

"I admit, you do hurt my feelings, daughter. I know you think I don't have any, but you're wrong. I just try to keep up a good front. However, if that's the way you feel, I can't help it. What's done is done. Out here it won't be any trick at all to find you a hubby. Just say the word. These boys go for your type in a big way. They won't even notice you're a bit on the hefty side. They like a woman who can get out the wash. And that blond hair. They take to what's gaudy and fancy-looking.'' Margy used to stand out in the snow hanging up the clothes, everything flying in the wind. My dog will be sleeping in the old washing machine that's pushed back in the corner when Dad tries to give it a spanking, we'll run him through the wringer.

Dad stops the car and I get on my knees to laugh and see who's there, but it's only a cow switching its tail. "All right, Margy,'' Dad says. "Let's see what you're made of today. Maybe you'll make twenty-five. Pretend you're getting away from one of those desperadoes your mother's expecting. Or trying to catch a man.'' Old Seventy-five the oats eater was a mule in the road. He wouldn't budge. When Dad went on parade he brought up the rear. No wonder he never made corporal.

Margy's the winner. At school she even beats the boys. I'll be a winner too, your mother says, if I drink all my milk. She opens up the egg and drops it in. It looks up at me while I'm having a drink. The dead dog didn't have no eyes. "You tell,'' the cousin said. "See what happens.''

Margy gets down in the road for Dad's racing start. He teaches her in the yard so she can always get away. Dad ran and ran to get away from his home. He ran along beside the freight cars and grabbed hold. In a fight he lost a sliver of his ear. The bad men took his money and left him in a creek to drown. When the corn was high Dad thought he could go on forever. He had a lot to learn.

Dad draws the starting line. There's nobody for miles and miles, and the hills blow up and down like they're moaning a sad song. Dad says this is where he wants to be buried when his time comes, in the long grass where the wind never dies. It's something to look forward to. I get back in the car. Your mother looks at her watch. "I hope your father won't take too long. I don't want Mother to have to worry." Across her forehead a blue vein squiggles. "Shazzam."

"On your mark." Dad starts the count and hops in the car, slapping it like we're whipping up old Seventy-five. "Go!" We're off and running. I tell him he forgot "Get set." He asks if I want to drive.

I steer the miles. Your mother smiles and smiles like we're alone, just one, two, three of us. On her pocketbook her fingers go writing. It's a letter to God, thanking Him for her wonderful family. Once at the motel she was crying in bed while Dad walked up and down in his birthday suit. Dad said, "I don't think I'm the marrying kind." Then he went in the bathroom and shut the door. All night I didn't move a muscle.

Margy's face comes beside us in the window, looking at nothing. Dad says she's florid as a Flemish housewife—better watch her blood pressure. She pulls ahead and Dad calls, "What a gal!" leaving her behind. I flash Ike's V for victory. Dad waves while we go faster and faster until we've seen the last of her. "I guess that girl knows when she's licked," Dad says. I don't see Margy. "Keep your eye on the road, son."

"Keep your eye on the ball. Don't be like the butterfingers, godblessem." In the yard the butterfingers waited to catch Dad's high fliers. They stood with their eyes peeled and their hands up in the middle of the yard. Then the ball was coming at them and they screamed and ran away. Fell on the ground and had a laughing fit. I wanted to roll all over them. Dad said he was dumbfounded. He's been throwing to them time out of mind and they had yet

110

to catch a single ball. He was losing hope. They'd never get ahead.

"We're afraid," the butterfingers yelled, and twirled. Dad shook his head. "Let them be a lesson to you, son. They can't work their way out of a paper bag."

"Where's Margy?"

"I hope you took a long last look, son."

"Margy."

"Francis, you're scaring him."

"I can't buy a break."

"Don't cry, Tommy. See, there she is now." Margy's rising over the hill, slow, the yellow moon at the bend. She's taking her time. I wave and wave but she doesn't see. The rose in her hair, she comes along and walks right by us as though we're thin air. Dad drives to catch up. "All right, get in. The party's over." He stops the car. "Your mother's in a hurry."

"Why, Francis, I am not. I didn't say a word."

I get on the seat beside Margy and stick my nose in for a whiff of the rose. "My Margy, my Margy." An ant is crawling in the petals and I try to pick it out. Margy says, "Let that alone," and holds me away. I lie in wait with my head on her lap, but I forget and the dead dog rises up off the ground, good as new, following me all around, the wind in his fur, frost in his eyes. When he growls the earth shivers.

Dad's brother works at a filling station somewhere, only it's different every time and I never get to see him. We go by while I'm taking my nap and when I wake up I've missed it all. "Too bad, son. Maybe next time," Dad says. I can't help being a crybaby. Margy says, "It's all right. I don't believe in Dad's brother anyway."

"Don't listen to her," Dad says. "She just thinks she knows it all. Ask to see her report card if you don't think so." Your mother believes in Santa Claus even if the girls don't and she says I can too. Dad says we wouldn't believe his brother: the number of times he's been in jail, first cousin to Billy the Kid, the one Dad looks up to. Dad has to keep a close eye on our gal Sal—his brother

111

has it all over him, close to six foot seven. Her earrings shake like tiny bells at Christmas.

"I want a brother," I say, and cry some more. Margy tries to hug me, but I put my dirty shoe on her skirt to serve her right.

"Thank God, we've made it," Dad hoorays and stops the car. "Quit your crying, boy—the famous Mrs. Blues. You can have a brother the same as me, only you're better off this way, the only one." There are blue pinwheels spinning in the blue flowers leading the way to Mrs. Blues. "She seems like a cheery gal," Dad says, "in spite of her name. Although you can never go on appearances—I'd be the first to know." He gets out of the car and walks away. I cry in a deep voice.

"Your father's getting angry, honey. I'll buy you some ice cream if you'll stop crying." The cousin said, "I bet you pee the bed all night long." I get up to act like a man and Margy wipes my face on her skirt. I put my hand in hers and your mother takes my other one while we walk up to Mrs. Blues. We see Dad waiting at the bottom of the porch where there's a white dog standing, its fur raised up like a collar. Dad looks around and then he walks slowly backward around the side to another door. Your mother calls, "It's all right, Francis," but Dad's gone. The dog shakes itself and then slinks off, diving under the porch through a broken board. We walk over it into the restaurant, taking our time, brave as can be.

Inside the restaurant it's so dark I can't see a thing and Dad is lost himself until our eyes get used to it and there he is, up at the bar on a stool, drinking a beer. Minding his own business, he doesn't look when we come up. Finally he shakes his head. "Haven't I seen you folks somewhere before?" He tries to figure out, tapping his head with a finger.

I hang on his arm and beg. "Dad. You're foolin'." He whispers and everybody hears: "I'm pretending I'm single. Maybe it will improve my disposition." Your mother says he's a funny man and gets up on the stool beside

112

him. "The things you think of, Francis. I can't believe you."

"You better start," Dad says. He's hunched at the bar like a folded newspaper nobody else can read. He asks your mother if she's a pickup. "May I buy you a drink, miss?" She laughs and tells the waitress she'll have coffee.

Margy isn't talking and walks away into the next room. Dad says she thinks she's too good for the rest of us—he can't imagine where she got such a high opinion of herself. Certainly not from him. I go to see. She's in the room with the jukebox and we read the songs. "It's country," she says. "Hank Williams, Molly Bee." We don't have a penny.

"Play 'Lord Randall,'" I say and she laughs. They don't have it. 'Lord Randall' is Margy's song to sing at night when I'm off to sleep. Ruthann plugs her ears and hums so she won't have to hear. Ruthann wants a fast tune to snap her fingers by.

"Anything you want. Name that tune." Somebody talks over our shoulders and we jump. It's the man from the highway, jingling coins in his pocket. The flag is tied around his forehead like an Indian, holding his wet hair. He's wearing a blue shirt now, all clean and tucked in.

"You made it all right, I see. Nice place, don't you think?"

We nod our heads, reading the songs. Margy's hair spins blue-and-green cocoons in the light. The cousin said Margy was a bitch. He bet she was hot. He bet she did it all the time what I was too dumb to know. When we were walking the plank over the pigpen I made a fast move when he took a giant step and he fell in. He cried in the mud. "You goddamn, go home. You. Fucker."

"Choose something," he says, showing us his money. "Time and a half Saturdays." Margy's lip quivers like she's going to cry or do something. When Margy and I drank all the milk and there wasn't a drop left for anybody's breakfast, Dad swung back his arm and knocked her on the floor. Before he could get to me, Margy was up, yelling, slapping Dad, clawing at his face. He tried

113

to laugh, holding her away while she was fighting. "I don't care if you kill me. Don't you ever touch me again." She ran away to her room while we were wondering what to do next. Your mother helped Dad wash the specks of blood off his lip before he got any on his clean shirt. Her lip was shaking and she had to sit down she was so dizzy. She never in her life saw a girl act that way.

Margy steps back out of the colored light. "I don't know," she says, her hand going up to her hair, and there's the rose. Her eyes open like she's pricked herself on a thorn and doesn't know what it will mean.

"It looks real pretty. What's your name?"

"I'm with my family. I better go eat."

"Margy," I say.

"Margy. How 'bout you, boy. Anything you want to hear?" I can't think of a thing. "Tommy," I say, and he grins and ruffles my hair.

He's watching Margy, leaning back on the jukebox with his hands opening clear up toward Margy. "Say, you want to go honky-tonking, or what?" Laughing when she drops her head, smiling. She backs away toward the door and I'm along. Before we turn the corner she says, " 'The Tennessee Waltz,' " twirling off to where Dad is.

"Time to eat, kids. You weren't here so I ordered for you, the cheapest thing on the menu. Potluck."

"Boy crazy, boy crazy," I'm singing to myself with the lady who lost her darling to the Tennessee Waltz. My big hamburger faces me like beat the clock. I have to make a sneak attack and pour on mustard and ketchup.

"You're spoiling my appetite," Dad says. "Stop messing with that and get busy." "The Tennessee Waltz" plays again like it's somebody's favorite song.

Margy stands up. "I'm not hungry, Dad. I'm sorry, but I didn't order it. May I be excused? I'll wrap it for later." She pulls some napkins out of the holder.

"I can't believe you don't want to eat, Margy. You're always hungry, it seems to me." Your mother holds her hamburger in her folded napkins so her hands won't get it dirty.

114

"I'm just not."

"Ordinarily I don't speak to strangers," Dad says, his mouth slipping sideways along the counter. "They might be after my money. But is something wrong with you? Do you feel sick?"

"Look over there." Your mother nods her chin, her two hands keeping the hamburger safe. "There's that cute fellow we saw on the road. The one without his shirt. Remember, Margy. The one who said you look like a movie star." Margy keeps her head down, with her hair falling like a curtain.

"He looks as if he eats his Wheaties. You've got some catching up to do, son." Dad says I'll be able to take him in no time. He's felt puny ever since they discovered he was fifteen in the Arizona Volunteers—farewell to the oats eater. "I wish somebody would give that jukebox a kick. That song's driving me nuts."

"I'll wait outside, Dad," Margy says, looking toward the music as though it's following her. "I'll eat it later. Okay? I'll pay for it if you want."

Dad gives himself a slug of beer. "Don't make me out more of a cheapskate than I already am. But stick around. We'll hit the road before long. Maybe your mother will let me drink another beer." Margy heads toward the door where I saw the man walk out. When I start after her, Dad has me by the collar. "Oh no, you don't," bringing me back to my meal.

While Dad eats, he stays bent over, talking to the bottles lined in front of the mirror. He says he's frightened for his daughters. He knows too goddamn much about men. He gives me a buzz with his eyes. "I'd rather you ended up in a straitjacket than see you waste the time I did chasing tail. Spell that t-a-l-e." Your mother catches a wink. Dad says he's going to show me how to write my name in the snow now that I'll be learning my letters in kindergarten. Then I'll know there are other uses for my pecker than the one I don't know about yet. Ruthann says it's might handy to have on a picnic.

"Why, Francis," your mother says, smiling at me. "I've known fine men all my life. You know that. Look

115

at my daddy. My husband Michael. All my fellows were.''

"All my fellows were." Dad's face jerks around like somebody's serving marbles with his eyeballs. Your mother drops her smile into the hamburger's cozy nest. I want to get out of town and drink my milk in one gulp.

"Now why don't you bawl over that. I'm sick to death of your fool yak-yakking. Why don't you just shut it." Dad gets up fast, with his stool wobbling behind him. I duck, but he's gone by.

I make a bite go down after my milk. "See, Mom," I show her, chewing in her face. She looks up and tells me I'm the best boy. It makes her happy and she's not crying. She can't imagine how tall I'll be, big and strong.

"I can't imagine how fatuous he'll be if somebody doesn't cut him down to size." Dad's back. Margy's the fatso if you ask me. He's chewing on a toothpick and claps your mother on the back. "Sorry I lost my temper. I've told you I'm not reliable. Don't pay any attention to me. And besides, I'm sick of paying for food nobody will eat." I have a French fry.

Your mother won't talk. Dad tells me to watch out for the women folk. "They've got staying power when it comes to hurt feelings. Emotional distance runners. Crawl on your knees and beg—God rest my good mother's departed soul. Before you know it, you're pussy-whipped." Dad's leaning on the bar, standing over your mother. Nobody else is around.

"While you're chewing on that, son, go get me another toothpick. I think we may have just seen the last of Seventy-five." Your mother's hamburger lies under a bunch of napkins, buried alive.

When Grandma was dead Ruthann cried and cried. She wanted to go to the funeral, but Dad said Florida was too far. He didn't have the money except for himself and he had to go. She was his mother. He went over the budget so Ruthann would see how tight things were. Never mind cigarettes and beer—without them life wouldn't be worth living. Ruthann said she was going to

116

hitchhike and Dad showed her the door. "If you're that self-destructive—so be it."

When he came back from Florida he had Grandma's music box for Ruthann. It was shaped like a piano with tiny keys going up and down. Ruthann said her heart was broken. Dad shook his head. Girls were so full of feeling he was at a loss. Who would have thought one old woman would make such a difference? After that he sent Ruthann on the bus to visit the other grandmother, who would have to do in a pinch. I'm glad we're getting Ruthann back. When Dad was mad and told her to straighten up and fly right, she told him to straighten up and fly left. Then everybody laughed.

Dad takes the toothpick and tells me to stop eating. "I can't stand the sight. Besides, I need the privacy. I'm still working overtime on your mother. We aren't leaving here until she's forgiven me—if it takes all week. I've offered to buy her anything on the menu, long as it's under five dollars. And go see what the blonde's up to. Maybe she's eloped." Your mother gives me a tiny peck of a smile. When I'm leaving I hear her: "I still can't believe you'd speak to me that way in front of your son."

Outside, I'm staggering in the light. It's like a dark morning, blue and gold, with Little Boy Blue asleep in the hay. A bunch of big kids are in their cars with the doors open, playing radios, laughing and blowing smoke. I see Margy then, walking over the grass with her hair tied up in the flag. She's with the man, swaying, like they're dancing the Tennessee Waltz, going down the hill into the sky, and it's like I don't know her anymore. I can't even say her name while she's going away.

"Son." I jump, but it's not Dad. "Want to see the pups?" He's an old man in his droopy overalls and he leads me to the porch where the white dog scared Dad. I stay quiet because I'm not supposed to talk to strangers; they might want to take me away. "They're in there." He lifts the board and I skid under, into the sandy dirt where it's shaded and cool and I think I must be dreaming. The white dog is lying there, panting, watching me, and I'm not afraid. When she sighs her fur ruffles like a ghost passing over the grass. When she knows who I am she's not afraid either, leaning her head on her paws, light hanging in her eyes like two moons at night, taking it easy while the puppies eat their dinner. She has more babies than Carter's has liver pills and I wouldn't be in the way. Dog milk would taste like canned milk, I think. Something a man could get used to.

I hear Dad coming talking to your mother as they walk on top of me and the dog. "You've got nothing to worry about. If that was Mrs. Blues at the register, there's not a dish in the world that could tempt me." The white dog perks up her ears, standing while the pups spill all over the place. Wobbling around, they don't know what hit them. The mother wiggles out, snapping her teeth, leaving me in charge. I heard her claws click on the boards and then a long, deep growl and people stepping fast. Then some lights come on outside.

"Y'hear, Belle, Stop that. Y'hear." It's the old man yelling. "I've got her, sir. There's no call to kick at her. Just riles her the more. She's got pups, keeps her on edge. Sorry she give you a turn. I'll hitch her while you go on yonder. Easy, there. Easy." Dad's shoes are going down the stairs right under my nose. "She won't hurt you, Francis," your mother says. "See, she's wagging her tail. Oh, she licked me. I'm going back to the ladies' room to wash my hands. All right, Francis?" Dad doesn't say anything, his shoes walking away, while her heels click back up the steps.

One of the pups sniffs all over me, and then he wants to climb under my shirt to hide and lick some more. He likes it in the dark, nothing but slivers of light getting through. I hear Dad calling so I tuck my shirt in tight, holding the pup, scooting out into the dark blue night with a papoose. "Hi," I say to Dad, holding a breath, going fast to the car.

"Where you been, boy? Seen your sister? Time to roll." Your mother's coming again. I shrug my shoulders toward the field, going along, shrugging, and not breathing. Dad comes too, watching me while he sticks the key in the door. His face wrinkles up. "What the devil have you got in there, Thomas Henry? What in hell is that?" The pup is having a fit, scratching, trying to bust out while I'm trying to keep my shirt on. Then Dad's coming at me like gangbusters and my pup has to run away. He hits the ground, bouncing, then jumping everywhere.

"Get in there." Dad grabs me, pushing me in the door, hitting me one on the back of the head. The pup is trying to crawl up your mother's leg while she's stepping fast. "Get down, down. My stockings." Dad snags it by the skin of its neck, dangling it to take over to the man, dropping it without a word. I flop down onto the seat, hiding my face in the dark and not answering your mother. I won't cry. My pup is white and brave. Someday he'll be big, with his yellow eyes, and when he sees it's me coming along his growl will welcome me, his brother. Better than Dad's brother.

Dad yells, "Margy," getting in the car, slamming the door with a kick so we all jiggle. "I don't know what gets into that damn girl." He blows the horn. "It doesn't seem she has the sense she was born with."

"It looks as though she's walking, Francis. Along toward the river. With that boy, the one from the road crew. He's running now. Coming this way, I think."

"Christ, woman. I'm not blind. He ought to be headed the other way, if he knows what's good for him. One of your cute fellows, you fool." Dad starts the engine with another kick and we bust loose. I get down on the floor and I don't have to know.

"Francis. Don't do that. She'll come any second. Don't, please. Don't leave her." Your mother cries like nobody loves her while we're making the getaway. I don't have the sense I was born with and reach up, pulling the door handle down, the wind in my face. I'll find my way back to Margy if it kills me. Your mother screams and screams but I'm not going anywhere, Dad hanging on to me by the collar, the car bucking and rolling like we're in the rodeo, going down the hill. Dad doesn't let go, even when a crash brings us up short, rocking and heaving. When I look, we're driving up a tree into the branches. ''Hanging's too good for him,'' the cowboy said. ''He ain't nothin' but a low-down horse thief.'' Then Dad's resting his head on the steering wheel and it's quiet, only the leaves brushing over the roof, the wind blowing in the trees like we've come all the way to Dad's grave.

Sam the Man

W HEN I GET OUT OF THERE INTO THE PARKING LOT, Sam's leaning on a car, his eyes blue, reflecting the evening sky, moistened, deepening, a final molten glow. Lean hips, a loose-jointed stance that seizes me by the throat. From before, when he stood by the road, I re-member the hollowed shadow above his belt where I wanted to lay my head, feel him warm, his pulse drum, close enough to know what he would be like. Pretending I'm not noticing him, I gaze off to the river, depending on my nature-loving style to pull me through. I hope Dad doesn't see, glancing behind at the restaurant door, which shudders on the air hinge, the exhaust fan blasting a gulf of greasy stale heat, walking a little farther away toward the field. Still, sideways, I sense Sam's attention, his musing, as his open gaze shifts to follow me. I feel his slant against the car. It's embarrassing to know how your hips sway and I slow down, holding my stomach in a vise, one step from a sideshow and not fooling anyone, my flush at high noon. Ordinarily so backward I'm con-sidered stuck-up, here I am in an open lot with a guy I just met, unable to conceal how he makes me lose my head. Certainly Dad would guess and I want to get where he won't see. Dad thinks he wrote the book on me. Once he said, "In spite of your stature, something tells me you won't live a long life." It's haunted me. I wondered if he was thinking of Mother.

I hope Sam won't ask if I have a boyfriend. It must be evident that I don't—or none I admit to. When the other

121

kids know you have a crush, they can't let you alone. Whisper and plot, until it seems it's theirs, not yours. Before you're out on a date the thrill is gone. And at home it's no different: prying and smirking, we might as well be having dinner in the school cafeteria. I pretend to be made of stone. No doubt I'll live to regret this, following after Sam, no idea of what might happen next and out of my range. It was like that when I went on the hayride with Brooke, nothing as I expected. Then it turned out I'd misunderstood everything. Gloria keeps bringing up his name, as though she'll get me to confide. But I don't say a word. I wouldn't want to be reminded, dawn to dark, how silly girls can be. I wouldn't want Dad to know.

A breeze smelling of water and sweet like cane stirs up with the cool of evening, crackles a blaze of light and shadow over the grass. The poplars at the wood line would ignite if they could. Sam won't speak but I feel his eyes. Sideways I catch the red of the flag, dragged through his fingers, his hair fallen loose. He begins whistling "The Tennessee Waltz," and I can't help grinning. He's leading me on.

Probably nothing about an overwrought girl is lost on him. He's laughing up his sleeve, betting all along he'd see me tripping over the sill. Still, something in his eyes is curious and he looks as though he's enjoying himself. One of the waitresses used his name as though they were entirely alone, and the bartender said, "Sam the man," with a wink for me. He must affect every girl this way, drive her to the limit with a longing for him, a desire that he would turn to her and ask for something he wants. And she can dare to dream how she could make him happy. I turn as though I can walk away and never give him another thought.

"You aren't hungry," he says. I like his Southern drawl, the time he takes to speak, his eyes slow too. Luckily Dad isn't here to set him straight on my appetite. All I can do is nod, a big hot girl like me. Inside the restaurant I was too flustered to name a song, actually unable to think of one until the end. No further along than I am in school, at the board with a piece of chalk, writing on a downhill slant, stumped by the simplest math problem, all thought blocked on the exposed dimensions of my behind, its hapless spread, its blameless endurance. I clench my stomach with such a counterforce, no wonder I can't come up with a square root. Once, I wrote f-l-o-r-e for "floor," saved by a girl in my class, Deborah, who I hope will someday be a close friend. She made an excuse to pass me at the board and whispered the correction before I fell on the f-l-o-o-r. Now I can't lick my parched lips because it might appear provocative, ludicrous in someone with my confusion. Although I've watched girls who can do it with their eyes wide open, as though any shame would be in the eye of the beholder.

Gloria says she wants to help me come up with some confidence and I let her show an interest, going along. She can't imagine my torments. But it amuses her when I throw them up for laughs, throwing her off the scent with my bravado, parading my peculiarities. She knew I was wild for Terry Baker, until he told Sally Sadler he liked me and spoiled the whole thing. Everybody knew. Then after waiting an hour for Jon Able to come out of the movie I walked off before he saw me, nose in the air, as though I had an appointment with destiny. Gloria laughs a lot in the wake of my misadventures, while I race full speed, doing housework, cooking meals, setting the table, my heart pounding full tilt, in case I've said too much or the wrong thing. Sooner or later everything comes up at the dinner table.

And I know I'm afraid of what she might tell me. I can see when she's been crying or has a headache. The night Dad didn't come home she sat and waited on the couch all night, eyes wide and baffled. Days can pass and Gloria doesn't speak unless spoken to, while Dad stays locked in their room. Once I heard him, thick-voiced, "I wish I knew what I could do to get you to go," furious from the dark, where all the shades stay pulled. Gloria's kind to me and I want to help her, although it isn't enough, and to make up for it I work all the harder to be her friend, dream up things to tell her, compliment her

123

dresses and hairstyles. I know we've let her down. When I've done as much as I can, I excuse myself to get to my homework, up in my room lying on the bed and doing absolutely nothing, drawing deep, calming breaths.

Sam's broad tanned fingers sift through his hair, which, fine, drifts across his forehead in fawny threads. He comes over beside me then, the lowering sun flamed in his eyes, half smiling, around him his strength humming like an aura, a force field. Next I'll be groveling at his feet. Where else can this lead?

"The food seems good," I say, to say something, clumsy, because he knows I didn't eat. I remember Dad and walk farther on, trying to appear nonchalant, someone with her own life. As though I might at a moment's notice leap on the back of a passing motorcycle with the aplomb of a paramour. I may not be the most fun a girl can be, but inside it's a thrill a minute. When I'm alone I'll conjure him in full, dwell on the fine points, the rim of white teeth beneath his lifted lip. Far below, the river coils through the valley like a stalled shipment of gold. A breeze defines the dampness at my hairline and between my breasts. They ache.

I want to say, "Give me a moment not to be scared." Mother played the piano when I was falling asleep. Once, I woke later, hearing voices, and wondering if Dad was home again, I went to the stairs. A strange man sat with her on the bench and together they looked up, solemn, eyes unfocused, and I felt myself whirl off to be alone. The next day I picked a fight with Mother, vowing I hated her and hoped she'd die. Then I cried and cried until she made me tell her what was wrong, rocking me as if I were a little girl, with my legs trailing off her lap and past hers on the floor. "Margy's mother worries about her. She seems too serious for a child her age," the teacher recorded in my folder, which has followed me all the places I've lived. I read that last year when I worked in the principal's office, sneaking into it on the sly. It read like a proclamation from the dead.

Brooke admired my seriousness, my attentiveness to

the Bible lessons. When I walked into the church basement and saw him for the first time, sitting alone in the
circle of folding chairs, his Bible on his knee, I felt
something in me come to order. He rose to shake hands
as one by one we introduced ourselves and sat around
him, his greeting grave with responsibility, as though he'd
felt in each hand a soul. A student at a seminary near
Lynchburg, he'd come to take over the Sunday-evening
Bible study and fellowship as part of his training. What
before, under our regular minister's leadership, had been
mostly refreshments and Ping-Pong, an easy excuse to
get out of the house, became the center of the week, the
time I lived for. After Gloria saw Brooke she referred to
him as "that handsome young fellow you girls like so
much," angling—no urgency in the bare bones of a
name. But since we'd gone all year there wasn't much
she could make of it.

Dad said, mainly for me, the family big mouth, "I
hope you aren't disgracing us with half-baked notions of
free thinking," hardly paying attention, with so much
else on his mind. I doubted he knew what I thought about
anything. He was busier at the conservatory than he used
to be, teaching night courses for extra money, coaching
a barbershop quartet. At dinner, when he announced that,
he swaggered ironically, to conceal his mortification, he
said—a far cry from his old wolf song. God help him,
he'd be hung for a Booster. He and Gloria did do some
faculty entertaining, picking out a new rug and couch
before one party, and another time Gloria enrolled in a
flower-arranging course. I came in from school one day,
and absorbed over a bowl of iris and pussy willows, humming under her breath, she didn't hear me tiptoe away.

Brooke was tall and slim, dressing neatly in trousers,
a white shirt and tie, although his eyes were too small
and close together for him to be exactly handsome. Still,
they glittered darkly, and when I talked in class I suffered
under the strain of his attention, searching for words and
ideas that would impress him, at home poring over the
Bible lessons, imagining his response. What I said always came out jumbled and confused, but he didn't con-

125

tradict me mid-sentence, listening carefully; sometimes bemused as though he'd anticipated what I would come up with. It was a relief when he turned to someone else, and when he talked, in his deep Kentucky accent, I felt I had fallen facedown in a summer garden, drowsy with sun and flowers, the earth holding my heart. Unhurried and sonorous, he read from the Bible, on his face the excess I heard in his voice, the wild fidelity that ranged in me far and wide.

During discussions, Brooke would refer back to something I'd said, making it sound important, and that kind of attention gave me courage to say more; made me hope the A I'd received in ancient history wasn't entirely an aberration. Although I could still lose my wits when it counted most, and my achievement scores prompted the guidance counselor to suggest I take typing and shorthand as a backup to the college preparatory curriculum. I said, "Thank you, ma'am."

I could see that Ruthann watched me, and I thought maybe she was impressed, noticing a difference in me, but I was afraid to ask outright if she thought I was smart. When I'd asked her once if I was pretty, she'd considered the question, matter-of-factly looking me over, then announcing, "Not pretty, but not ugly either," her verdict unalterable, eyes sealed with the sad truth. At least I didn't beg her to reconsider and ask for a dispensation. I'd learned a thing or two about her moods.

But those nights, walking home from church under the milky sky of winter, the paddle wheel of the constellations seeming to propel us beyond ourselves, in rhythm passing the lighted houses, we two who had come so far together, I wanted to tell her about Brooke, my feelings for him and hopes that he could like me. To say his name out loud. Tears would stand in my eyes. I didn't dare, though. Ruthann might tell Dad or Gloria. Or she might retort, "Ugh, he's old." Twenty-one didn't seem old to me. In fact, as a serious person I thought I might not have any other choice.

During the social period after Bible study one night, Brooke played checkers with me and, when it was time to leave, offered Ruthann and me a lift home. She hopped out when we got there, but it seemed impolite since Brooke was talking, so I stayed. He was explaining the doctrine of infant damnation and I followed the best I could, trying to avoid thinking of his mouth, its vivid cut, his eyes set so far under his brows, in the gloom of shadows he could have been wearing a mask. I must have frowned in concentration, because when he'd finished talking, glancing at me he said, "So serious," tracing his finger between my eyes. I shivered, biting my lip. Behind him the lights in the new house, which had been built where once a patch of woods had stood, blinked out all at once, as though his pronouncement was for all time. The light from the streetlamp shone on my face like a spotlight.

"You and Ruthann are different from the others. I know, because my mother died when I was born. It leaves its mark. 'And the doors shall be shut in the streets, when the sound of the grinding is low, and he shall rise up at the voice of the bird, and all the daughters of music shall be brought low.' " In the silence, after he had spoken, I kept my face held to the light, unhidden, his deep voice vibrant in me, in the tranced dark.

His sharp laugh opened my eyes. "Wake up, Margy." He reached over to pull the door handle, a little push to get me going. "Rise and shine. Beware false prophets—context is everything. Look it up, Ecclesiastes 12. Beware the sin of pride. 'A worm, a mere nothing, and less than nothing.' See you next week." He laughed again, and in the headlights, knowing he was watching me from the idling car, I stumbled on the walk, shy and exposed for a simpleton. Determined to read the Bible cover to cover, blushing hotly for my pride and ignorance.

That next Sunday I found a bookmark in my Bible, a purple-and-gold velvet cross. I thought it was just for me until Ruthann showed me hers, puzzling about where it came from. I shrugged, crushed to have to share that with her, although I felt certain mine was special. It had to be. Brooke just couldn't leave Ruthann out, since she'd lost her mother too. The only thing I'd ever heard her say about Brooke was that he drove a swank car, something I hadn't noticed.

A girl calls, "Hey, Sam," and they smile and wave. I know he had his choice. I don't want to forget and be hanging out all over the place when there are a million cute girls who could take him away with the flick of a finger. Gloria's friend said, "I believe Margy likes to be different." That, with the emphasis on the "likes," was related to me complete with Georgia drawl and knowing smile. I suffered visibly—the transparent sham who does everything for effect. Besides, I was guilty too. Sometimes I lorded it over Gloria and could hardly blame her for getting back. In fact, I do like to be different, although I don't feel it's entirely by choice. Nothing seems to come natural.

Across the river some horses are grazing on a grassy knoll and I decide I'll make conversation, do or die. "This is horse country, isn't it?" My heart whacks me as though it has taken my threat literally.

"You like horses, Margy?"

"I love them. At least I think I do. To look at, anyway—the way they shiver. They smell good too. I mean, I'm sure I'd like to ride, but I never have. My dad says horses are dumb. But I don't know. They don't look dumb." I trail off—what do I know?

"That so? I wouldn't say that. I've got an eye for horses, been around them all my life. To me they seem more high-strung than anything." He stretches up his arms, folding them under his elbows, the muscles bulging, the light hair on his forearms silky. "You got to show them your respect. So how 'bout you, Margy. You ever get the shivers?" He grins while I wonder if I seem like a ninny to him. "How old are you anyway, seventeen, eighteen?"

"Sixteen," I say, adding, "Almost," in case he finds out. I always feel like a criminal. He can take off now. "Nice seeing you." Take off and roam the wide world over and I'll not show it's anything to me. Our eyes hold while he fumbles across the front of his shirt for the

128

pocket, going after his cigarettes. Milky, his could be agate, their colors blended in clouds. I shake my head no about the cigarette, while above a high light sails, Sam's polished cotton shirt gleaming in patches, like mirror cloth, where unexpectedly I might eye myself.

In spite of the warmth my arms prickle gooseflesh. Someone just walked over my grave—wherever that may be. Mother's buried someplace in Richmond where we never go to visit. When I'm older I'll take the bus and get it cleaned up, plant primroses and peonies to bloom every year, even when I'm not there to see. I wonder what it might feel like when we get that close again. Once, after Mother's accident, someone called. "I just wanted to say I'm sorry," he said. "And if there's ever anything I could do." I didn't know what to say and he was quiet a moment too. "Your mother was a dear friend of mine. Goodbye, Margy." He must have felt that it made us both too sad, because he never called again.

Sam shakes out a cigarette and lights it. "You could be older." The smell of burning grips me, something that has been inside Sam entering me. I feel his arms as though they hold me, the heavy twisting veins along the sides like bonds. Nearby I smell milkweed in flower, sweet heavy clusters, clunky and waxen, like cheap jewelry on an old lady's bosom. Along the riverbank below, daisies nod, blown up on the grass in a surf, and I imagine Sam and me swimming, coming up cold in each other's arms.

When I was riding in the truck with Brooke, the other kids behind us in the hay wagon, he reached over and took my hand, holding it all the way to the state park where we were going for our cookout, long after it was numb and I had to see with my own eyes to believe it was happening.

I'd even been worried that Brooke was angry with me because I'd argued with him the week before about marriage. We were studying Titus, Chapter 2, and he asked what I thought. "I don't like the part about 'obey,' " I ventured, blushing to be outspoken on an intimate subject with my newfound derring-do. "I mean that a woman

129

should be submissive to her husband." My neck was splotching with heat, a small itchy place rising up. Ruthann rolled her eyes at me.

Teasing, Brooke said, "Who should she submit to, then?" asking the others their opinions. The girls didn't know or wouldn't say, and the boys liked the idea. Somebody had to be boss in a family or nobody would know what to do. We all laughed when Randy said, "So I guess it might as well be me," thumbing his armpits and crowing, all five feet of him.

Brooke turned back to me. "Margy, I can see that as a human being you wouldn't like the idea of obedience. It's against our nature. But God doesn't ask us what we think. It's not a matter of efficiency or preference. It's what He wills. Perhaps you'll understand better if you read what God requires of husbands in marriage. Let's look at Ephesians, Chapter 5:25. Margy." He waited for me to find the place.

" 'Husbands, love your wives, even as Christ also loved the church, and gave himself for it.' " My voice thickened and trembled audibly, the way it always did when I talked about something I cared about, and when I finished I lifted my eyes to meet Brooke's.

"How much is that?" he asked, holding my eyes. "What level of devotion does our God require?" Something insatiable glinted, calling me, passing quickly into his smile. "Maybe that would be enough even for you, Margy?" Everyone laughed while I stammered and decided to let it go for then, although afterward I thought of different arguments, reading other parts of the Bible and taking notes. But when he took my hand in the truck it seemed maybe Brooke was right and I didn't understand. Maybe that feeling was part of what made it work, a part of God's plan.

During the fire making, games, and singing, Brooke and I didn't talk to each other, though it wasn't the silence of indifference. I knew he was busy running things and I didn't want to intrude, but mostly I was trying to protect what had happened between us in the truck, holding myself suspended until we would be alone together

130

on the way home, imagining what might happen then. Although I couldn't get beyond the precise moment when he would reach for my hand, as though that would be an ending rather than a beginning. A culmination. I set it up in various ways, letting him take my hand when it lay on the seat between us. Or I would be reaching out to put something on the dashboard. It preoccupied me in its myriad variations, including the arrangement of the stars out the window, so that I ignored the relay races and treasure hunt, helping around the fire like one of the chaperoning parents, serving food, picking up trash, getting through.

In the park's bare, barnlike restroom I met Betty Clark, a girl I'd never talked to; in fact, it seemed odd to me that she came to our fellowship regularly, the way she dressed and wore makeup suggesting she was a little fast for us, with livelier things to do. But she was friendly, just the two of us standing in front of the mirror under the dim gas lantern hanging overhead, letting me borrow her lipstick and comb. She asked if I minded if she smoked, which I didn't. I looked ghastly pale and she suggested I rub a little color on my cheeks. Standing back appraisingly, she said the bright orange shade of her lipstick was flattering to me.

"I've got it bad," she confided, almost a moan. "Paul Miles. Oh, God. All these weeks I've been coming to these stupid meetings. Tonight I swear he's going to kiss me if I have to sit on him. Who do you like?" she asked, turning on me the spray from her tiny vial of Tabu, which her mother claimed was irresistible to men.

I felt a great longing to break down and tell Betty about Brooke, pour my heart out even if she did think the meetings were stupid or would think that I was, to like someone so old. From her averted look when she said Paul's name I thought she might not condemn me, no matter the shame, but my silence was part of me, like a vow or even a nail I wore in my shoe. "Nobody." I shrugged. The alertness in her face died, her eyes even hostile, as though she knew I was lying.

* * *

Sam can stay in one place, quietly taking his time, noticing what's around, while I traverse the globe, the past and future, finding it hard to concentrate. He feels steady, a plant that can't hurry, like it or not, ninety days to harvest. The sun sinks in a mist of rose gold, in beauty so innocent and unaffected for a moment I recover my ideal mood of graceful abandon to life's inequities. I know I must look hot and blowsy. I will never make a neat appearance, can't wear a red dress or a pageboy. If I could stay in a meadow of simple flowers and grass I might begin to cool, take on an aura pale as seed. As it is, I'm like a rusted hulk of iron ore, battered by the elements and attracting extra attention. Soon Sam will scratch his head, wondering how he got into this. I hope he can see in the way I gaze to the distance that I'm used to it. I don't expect anything. Won't create a scene when finally he is able to break away. Which reminds me, and I scan the parking lot—the way I pass a mirror, a glimpse in case there's been some improvement. Before I rush on.

"You just got here, Margy. What's your hurry?"

"My dad will be out soon and he'll want to get going. We're on our way to pick up my sister in Fort Crossing."

"We'll stay where he can see you." Sam flicks his brows, a shift in his expression as though he's accepted something about me. Probably he can tell I'm jittery but doesn't mind that much, at least not until some normal girl comes along who isn't at her wit's end. In gym class when we were changing clothes, I overheard a senior girl say her boyfriend thought the sexiest thing about her was this big mole on her back. She couldn't believe he meant it. I sneaked a look and I couldn't believe it either, although when she got pregnant and dropped out of school, it was the first thing I thought of.

I know I must make a person nervous. I leaned forward to retie my tennis shoe, shaking my hair to hide my profile. At dinner Dad commands, "Chins up!" That's for me, because I turned out moonfaced. I'll never look wistful no matter my misfortunes. No one will ever feel sorry for me—I don't have the bones. Right before it was time to get back in the hay wagon to go home, Ruthann fell and twisted her ankle. I could see it hurt, her face cramping with pain, tears wobbling at the rims of her eyes.

Brooke knelt at her knees, his voice chiding gently, "Now, why'd you go on and do that, little girl." I stepped back, feeling as though I was listening in. Brooke went on to explain to Mr. Ames, one of the fathers, that he felt responsible for what had happened to Ruthann. He'd noticed some of the kids jumping off the picnic tables but hadn't really paid attention. And now someone was hurt. Tenderly, his voice a soft murmur so I couldn't hear what he said, he held Ruthann's foot in the palm of his hand, where long and thin it lay like a blade. Magnified by the tears, her eyes loomed, all darkness. He wrapped her foot in his own handkerchief, fitting a sock over it inch by inch.

"Get me my jacket, will you?" Brooke asked over his shoulder, and whirling to obey I knocked into Mr. Ames, who gave me a strange look as we disentangled. Then he looked at Brooke, who nodded and said, "Margy's always working overtime. Powder and paint for a hayride. I guess it is Margy?" He craned his neck as if to see me better, but his eyes passed along without curiosity, remote as though we'd never been introduced. When he looked back at Ruthann she dropped her eyes. I'd forgotten about Betty Clark's lipstick. Probably I did look hideous, especially in the car lights that had been beamed toward Ruthann, but I didn't do anything to wipe it off. Conscious of my lips as though they had erupted, I exhibited burnt orange, in a dress rehearsal for Halloween. If Betty Clark could do it, I could too. Brooke never looked at me again the rest of the evening anyway.

Before we left he had us form a prayer circle. I didn't say an audible prayer as we stood holding hands in the dark, but then I never could, the simple humility it took was something I'd lost, if ever I had it. When it became quiet, Brooke, holding Ruthann's hand to include her, gave special thanks for her protection. Then, clearing his throat, as though emotion was clotted there, he exhorted

133

us to search our hearts. He knew all of us harbored impure thoughts and ungodly impulses. Some among us were set for a snare. We knew who we were. "Pray that you may be forgiven, according to His will. We are standing, burdened and alone, standing in need, polluted and lost." I stood with unbowed head, watching Brooke. His eyes were closed but I sensed that same shadow I'd seen once passing through his eyes, now lurking in the cadence of his voice, unappeased and almost a sob or a song. When he said, "Amen," I walked with the others to the wagon, everyone quiet and subdued as though I wasn't the only sinner grateful for the darkness to hide in. Mr. Ames helped get Ruthann settled into the cab, to ride home with Brooke. She never lifted her head off his shoulder.

I pulled myself into the hay, lying down close to the railing to stare through at the night, letting the rushing dark cool my painted face, the sweet merciful grasses hold me. I didn't think God hated me. Gradually, around me, the couples found each other, moving steadily closer as we got under way, farther from the prayer. I had to make a conscious effort not to look toward Howard Grover, the only other unattached person, until after a while it seemed he'd gone to sleep. Betty and Paul, on the far side of the wagon bed, cuddled together, probably her dream come true. Apparently Tabu was not to be counted on, a charm working for some and not for others. I knew I could be too hasty, presumptuous. Even my adored kindergarten teacher had called me "Copycat," as I breathlessly had tried to please and imitate her. Still, Brooke didn't have to wriggle his nose, his cold smile on me unwavering, as though my scent wafted from Babylon.

At my house I was perched to jump off the end of the wagon, expecting to slip unnoticed into the house, when someone said, "Bye, Margy. See you at school." Betty sat up in Paul's arm, waving. I took heart, briefly, that someone with her confidence would want anything to do with the likes of me, and returned her good night before I ran to tell Dad he'd better go out and help bring Ruth-

134

ann in. I was already in bed, pretending to be asleep, when he brought her up, ignoring it even when Ruthann sang under her breath, ''Don't ever laugh when the hearse goes by / For you may be the next to die.'' Right then I felt like I wanted to.

I don't know what Ruthann thought when abruptly I stopped going to Bible study. Probably she didn't ask why because she was afraid I'd burst out with something hysterical, like I didn't believe in God. But after a few more times she stopped too. From the first she'd said it was boring, and once, she'd called Brooke ''Milord'' when he asked her to read. Betty and Paul weren't going either, she said. When I'd see Betty in the halls at school, or smoking out in the parking lot at noon, she always waved and spoke in a friendly way; though after that there never seemed a way for us to say more.

Any second Sam will be embarrassed to be seen with me. I'll forget myself laughing, blare my whole gumline where the exposed tissue segments into second-story teeth. Mother hated her thighs. They slapped like rubber sails, she said. I'd see her in her slip, pondering them with a rueful face. When she wore a party dress, who would know, her head thrown back, silvery hair to the waist like a cape, playing every request. Ruthann and I went to see her, sitting in the dark at a little table, drinking soda from wine goblets. It was as though Mother had forgotten we broke her favorite hair clasp snapping the daylights out of a magazine, and blew the car horn the whole time she was in the market. Afterward Dad yelled, ''I won't have my wife singing for a bunch of drunks. Doing I don't know what on the side.''

''Oh yeah,'' Mother answered, low and hoarse, but I heard. ''You're just jealous. You won't do what you could do. It's not Carnegie Hall—what would precious Mother think?'' I meant to listen, in case Mother needed me, but I fell asleep, and in the morning everything was all right. Dad was gone, dollar bills and coins scattered in the hall. Mother would be getting a day job again and we'd have someone to watch us after school. I always begged her to hire a colored woman rather than the high-school girls Ruthann preferred because they would play games and talk about their boyfriends. In the presence of a colored person, I felt something different happen to life, as though their accumulated suffering had honored me with a visitation.

When Sam has gone I will console myself, recapturing his smile when I toss my head, imagine that beneath my clothes I feel his bones bearing on mine, his hands move, formal in their slow knowledge. Now I must wait. I pick a stem of buckwheat and nurse its green-cud acidity. The flowers of the field stream in bright clarity before the dusk. The poplars reverse to silver, ripple and gleam like fountains. A stone, warm against my foot, seems to be the earth's first heavy fruit. Sam's lips are the velvety texture of red raspberries.

"Want to walk on down with me, Miss Dreamy Eyes? On over there?" Sam points toward a clump of evergreens, his tanned arm an inch from my breasts. I'd never thought a compliment would go quite that far with me. "There's something I want to show you." I sense his weight of bone and blood increasing, as though with night he gains mass. It's a solemn occasion; I feel moved that he would want me, not laughing or trying to get away. His hair webs with light in the afterglow of sunset and I imagine it melting with a whisper, my face coming down. I can feel myself against him, the way it would be, sliding into his shadow. Against my skin his is red like a bank of clay. I glance up at the car.

"The Olds, right? Snazzy. I'll keep an eye out. We aren't going far." He grins as though he could mean that in some other way. I know I'm too grateful. When Jon Able called to ask me out, just to the movie, I said, "Oh, thank you," about a dozen times according to Gloria, who couldn't stop laughing. She says I need to learn that the fellows are just glad if you say yes. They don't need to be thanked. Sam moves suddenly and I flinch as though I expect to be violated, but it's only his finger meeting the tip of my nose. My breath catches, but I go ahead and do it, waggle the buckwheat against his cheeks, sprinkling his faint shadow of whiskers with a pollen wash.

"You're coming down to earth, aren't you? You know, you kind of give me the shivers, Margy. When you smile. When you don't." How long can this go on, Sam not mentioning that I'm a little plump, especially in the hips? Maybe he really wouldn't mind if I had a big mole somewhere. Maybe he would take it in his mouth. Standing in front of me, he snaps the red caution flag straight out and wraps it around my forehead so I'm Pocahontas, coming right at him. He smoothes my hair in his hands, and I could linger forever, formed and re-formed.

"No one will miss you now." He grabs my hand as though he's willing to do that, get me going by know-how and persuasion as though it's worth it, and we go walking off. It seems I understand just a little how two people who are strangers might meet, walk across the land, or sit down at the piano to sing, making something between themselves, something neither of them had imagined.

The last light pierces the horizon like a passage to a realm where there is no night. My eyes find Sam's. His, like the wild birds that interpret the earth and know where to fly, know me on some obscure level. I drop my gaze to hide myself, the feeling that deep down inside I'm flushing.

Mother had her bearings in the out-of-doors, springing up to explore ponds, gathering cattails and wildflowers. She said her rightful name was Laughing Water. Once, we slept out in a borrowed tent, cowering and screeching by turns. When we were quiet we heard the hoot of the barred owl. Mother said it took her back to her childhood in Michigan, where her family came from. I knew her parents were dead, and sometime later, when it was just the two of us, she told me more.

"Your father and I weren't married yet, when we knew you were coming. My parents were quite religious and when I told them they were upset; in fact, we had a huge fight. It ended with them telling me to get out and not to come back. So I left in a great huff. Then, before we

137

could patch things up, they were dead of influenza. I think because they were older when I was born, and had given me a lot of freedom, encouraging my music, they blamed themselves for what happened between your father and me. I've come to understand more with time." Then Mother showed me the bankbook that had money in it for Ruthann and me, for when we were older. Her parents had left it to her, more than four thousand dollars, enough for college someday, music lessons. That had been her parents' wish and even Dad didn't know about it. After Mother died and we were moving, I climbed up and took it out of the vase on the high mantelpiece, hiding it among my things. I was excited and a little scared. Although it was mine to take, Ruthann's and my names printed inside the cover, I felt guilty, carrying Mother's secret all alone. Sometime, when Ruthann was older, I'd tell her about the money and how we'd come to have it.

Trying to appear only naturally curious, once I asked Dad about Mother's family, beginning to blush and feeling like a liar when he answered, "Cut her off without a cent. All because of yours truly." He stared me down, taking the blame. He wouldn't want me to think he'd ever been sorry or cried over spilt milk. Probably he thought the truth would have hurt me or shamed me, but instead it made me feel special, to think I was a love child.

"What're you worrying about now? I won't let you down." Sam puts his arm around me, directing me toward the river, away from the parking lot, away from the past if I could just let go. We descend diagonally on the hillside, our footsteps mired in moss and flowers, and it feels as though we could let go and stroll the purple evening and then pass on into the purple sky to heaven— there to face the music.

That was Brooke's opinion, and Gloria too believes literally in heaven and hell, six days for God to create the heavens and earth, everything exactly the way it is forevermore. During one of our discussions she admitted that when she was younger she'd had moments of doubt. She'd had so many fears. At school she'd been certain she'd see devils if she looked into the fire and had dreams that the boys forced her hand against the woodstove when it was white with heat. But that was being young, and now she never had any doubts. I couldn't tell from her smile whether I was the lucky one or not, being young.

Since she came to live with us we've had to go to church every Sunday, like it or not. It was part of the bargain, Dad said, something he agreed to in the early days of their marriage, when Dad said he was giving things away left and right. Things he had no right to give, I informed him, although I do my part and don't make trouble, going to Sunday worship; in my begrudging fashion refusing to bow my head for the prayers or sing the hymns, sitting alone in the back pew, unless Ruthann comes to join me, although she thinks it's odd and mostly sits with Dad, eyeing me over her shoulder, wondering what I'm up to.

Mostly it's an act I put on, for I like to be there. It's peaceful and makes me remember Mother and Grandma, and inwardly I pray mightily for the gift of faith. Before Brooke came to teach us, I was already reading the Bible every day, at night praying for the living and the dead. At school I made friends with a religious girl and she arranged to take a carload of us downtown to her church in Washington, where in the cement basement they set up a projector to show films about the life of Jesus. It was Holy Week and for three days straight we went down into the dark to share Christ's passion, the greatest story every told blaring through the tinny sound system, swelling music and Technicolor moving our hard hearts like stones before the garden tomb. Afterward, we rose choking with grief and blinking up into daylight, as though we'd come into the glare of our transformed lives.

Our friend Deborah, who is Jewish, went with us. I didn't think about it until she broke down in the girl's room one day and confided in me that Ann Leominister had called her the night before, distraught over Deborah, who she said could die at any moment. If she didn't make her decision to accept Christ that very instant, she would go straight to hell. "No one knows the hour," Ann had

139

warned. Deborah's drawn and sallow complexion, her eyes sunken under the flight of curly black brows, told of her night watch. "Is it true? Am I damned forever?" she asked. "Do you believe that?"

My outrage at Deborah's anguish drew from me an unregenerate confidence and I answered forcefully, "It's utter nonsense. God loves you as much as anybody. I know it." Straining, I added, "Besides, I don't even believe in hell." Brave words, but Deborah brightened so visibly, at first I didn't feel any fear. For once in my life, for all my wild striving, I had actually managed to make someone feel better. Someone I admired too, who spoke in a soft voice, took ballet lessons, and sang in the girls' chorus. Now I hoped we might become closer; although later, more calm, I prayed our friendship would not be bought at the expense of my own soul.

Since then I've felt even more of a backslider, though I still show up for worship, taking my solitary seat in the back by the clear-paned window, looking up and out. In my heart of hearts I still pray for the gift of faith—the approach of a Stranger at the well, divine madness on the way to Damascus.

"Do you live around here?" I ask Sam, making a renewed effort to pay attention, although it seems a dumb question. Where do I think he lives, Tipperary? Before he answers he leans over to rub out his cigarette, a pause and sigh that makes me feel he's annoyed, but when he stands he points over the river. "I used to live right over there. Almost directly across, behind that baldish mountain. A little spot in the road called Peachtree. That was when I was living with my wife."

He turns to look at me, but I don't see or hear, in my head such a roaring it's like a last updraft of the embers of consciousness. I just walk away, off across the dark field, off to break a leg, anything, if only I can vanish along with the spectacle I make, hopes soaring at a nod, everything blown out of proportion.

Sam is yelling, but I don't listen. I just want to go away and I think I'll circle back up to the lot and sit in the car to wait. Where I belong. But then it comes through to me that Sam's running toward the road, that he isn't even calling me. "Hey. Over here. She's here. Hey, you!" His arms cycle as he lopes strongly up toward where I see Dad's head, jolting at the wheel, vanish with the car going on down the hill. I give up, fall facedown on the grass, and I'm not scared, consider myself dead and buried.

Sam comes along beside me, panting. "Jesus. He heard me. I know he did. I'm sorry, Margy." I wait for the earth to split and swallow me. I ought to warn him. Off somewhere I begin to hear splashes and then connect them with Sam, his arm drawing back, the forward thrust. He's what I think about; want him to go, want him to stay. When I sit up, he lays a stone in my palm and another, and I keep throwing into the dark until my arm hurts, although I never hear a splash.

"I'm better," I say. He straightens me out, brushes off my face, repeatedly pressing his hands along my temples, stroking. I close my eyes and let it happen, my face swollen and tender as though I'd been crying. It seems like years and years since someone touched me, since I looked at myself in someone's eyes.

"Quite a guy," Sam says, and I open my eyes. "He'll come back." It could be a question and I nod. When I looked up and saw Tommy in the parking lot looking for me, I should have gone back or called to him. He seemed so small and alone, the sky behind him, like once when I'd watched Dad leaving our place, after a fight with Mother, humping his duffel bag and walking down the railroad track, not even turning to wave, though his eyes as I imagined them were transparent, apple green, stark with betrayal.

"What's with him, anyway? He heard me. He even saw me." Behind us, from the parking lot, I notice the din of the radios, laughter, cars arriving, the lights sweeping over us.

"He already did it once today."

"He did."

"Drove off and left me. Earlier, when I was racing the car."

Sam pushes his hair flat with his palms, puzzling but grinning down slantwise at me, so near the lashes fringed on his cheek seem preternatural, a drift of petals. "What is this, some sort of a game you folks play?"

"Some sort. Like paying to use the iron except once a week or proving you can support yourself and not asking Dad for any money." I put a finger on Sam's arm for him to listen, and I think I'll tell him my life story, but I don't feel like it when he looks at me, his eyes in the night like the enigmatic orbs painted on Egyptian figures, almond and full-view in profile. "It's partly my fault, I guess."

He covers my hand with his warm one. "That's going some, don't you think. But it's worth it, if you ask me. Meeting you. Let's go up, though. We wouldn't want to miss the next move." He pulls me to stand and I lean on him, quietly waiting for him to say what's next, singing when he does, " 'I remember the night / And the Tennessee Waltz.' " My feet are soaked now in the cooling grass. "What were you going to show me anyhow?"

"Nothing much. I keep a horse down there is all."

"A horse." I was that close to a horse and I didn't know it. I couldn't have been more amazed if he'd said a schooner or his army. "I'd love to see it." I hear my voice hitting the higher ranges.

"Maybe next time, little passion flower." He whistles three shrill blasts and the answering whinny is immediate, sounding up the dark, merging then with a round of hoofbeats I seem to feel inside me. "He's running in circles, like some of the rest of us, huh?" Sam grins like the fond parent.

"I'm jealous of a horse," I blurt out. Then Sam turns and pulls me against him, kissing my mouth. The whinny, a time or two more, plaintive and imperious at once. Before I'm over the shock he's yanking me along.

When we gain the restaurant lot, Sam keeps my hand, going through the groups of kids who stand about with sideways looks, seeing who I am, trying to figure out what's what. For once I feel glad to be among them, feel we have things in common. But we only nod and go on, out along the drive to lean against the pitted granite boulder that marks the entrance. A car speeds by, skidding the graveled shoulder, flashing the summer leaves thickly overhead. In the quiet after it passes Sam and I move closer together so we can touch along the length of each other. From the recesses of Mrs. Blues someone says, "Testing," and a few screeches from the microphone resolve into a guitar's twang. The lot empties with the crowd moving inside for dancing. I feel as though I've been waltzing for hours. The pinwheels twirling along the lighted walk could be in rhythm, too.

"How old do you think I am, Margy?"

"I don't know. You're married. A hundred, maybe."

"Feels like it some days. I'm nineteen, smarty-pants. Next port, Seoul." he shrugs. "Tokyo, Berlin maybe. Someplace, I don't know. It was either that or the mines, and this way when I get out I can grab an education."

My stomach drops as though I've taken a fast elevator into the bowels of the earth. "Korea. You're going there?" Somewhere. Tokyo, Hiroshima, Budapest. The night wind moans, laced with roses from the fields, fainter than in the afternoon when I was running along the high road in the heat, no one else in sight. Ever more blooms, until the wind would rise that left only the sepals behind, gleaming like the bare bones. I look back at the restaurant in its rounded clearing, cut out of what is otherwise meadowland and forested mountaintops, set there serene and protected. Above, the vast starry abyss where the thin lonesome music, the sprinkle of lights drain swiftly into the dark and no wind at all. The people we hear moving and talking inside, where will they be, at every moment separated from now, from their youth—the loveliest times of our lives pass unremarked.

Korea. At school a girl wears a green satin jacket every day, a present from her brother, who was stationed there during the fighting. Its embroidered serpents with flaming tongues stand out from far down the hall, against the rows of metal lockers and white shirts and jeans. Sometimes the boys brag about Russian roulette, and there are

143

rumors about parties with guns and scary games, although the only certain account was in the paper, the victim a boy from a Washington academy. I think about writing Sam, imagining him leaning against a ruined temple, someplace where people flood past in drab padded outfits, their faces as I'd seen them in magazines, harrowed with exhaustion and terror. I would send him a picture, hardly a pinup, but wearing my best and giving him the only smile I have. A passion flower of sorts.

"It's all right," Sam says. "I've given it my best shot around here. Probably I shouldn't have come after you the way I did. It's hard not to, though, when you've got a case of the shivers. The way you looked, sitting there in the car." Sam's long, hard legs, going down with mine, exert a force that's their own, like a tide. I feel myself yielding and I want to say, "Don't ever leave me," when the red light spins up out of the trees and a police car slows on the road, turning in the drive, drawing both of us to our feet.

The officer nods. "Sam." To me he says, "You Margery Clemmons?" Before I get upset he tells me it's all okay. "Your daddy's had a little accident is all. Nothing that much. Sidled up to a tree on down the way. Everybody's all right, 'cept your momma's taken a right smart clip 'side the head. Hop on in and I'll run you along."

Sam squeezes my hand, opening the car door for me with a little bow of farewell. "Take care of yourself. Now I know your last name," he says softly, as we pull away, and I don't have time to tell him I'm glad, too; that we met. I'll look for him everywhere. All I can do is wave the flag out the window, long after he's passed from sight. I'll keep it a secret if I have to eat it.

I didn't get to tell him that I don't have a momma. Or about Tommy, who might someday be in the army, too. That Dad was once a soldier. And I can't talk to my sister, because every time her eyes glaze over, and I can see she doesn't listen. But already there are things Sam knows about me that nobody else ever has. He's had a taste of me. Probably he'll figure out that I'm going to worry that everything is my fault—including the Korean

144

War. He knows I like him and I'm going to think about him even if he is married. He knows I've never had a moment to myself except on borrowed time. Before the car comes into view, I see it's Dad coming after me, because of the crazy way one headlight flares, leading on toward me with a kind of wild wall-eyed gallop overhead through the trees.

D for Divine

"ATTENTION!" DAD SAID. "WE CAN'T HAVE YOU up there on a stage disgracing the family." I yanked my shoulders back without a scowl, for once as eager as Dad to conceal my blemishes and right my wrongs in time for the high-school beauty contest. The mists went rolling by the window, adrift from oceans and frequent partings, as the November sun sank for good. Dad forgot all his troubles and said, "Turn off the lights. Wouldn't I love to be a cowpoke again." Margy flipped the switch. "Oh, it's lovely. Someday I'm going to live in the mountains by myself and have a horse and a dog." We used to be in love with snow. Now it's mist. Gloria isn't having any of it, including a fire in the fireplace, which according to her pulls the heat straight up the chimney, along with the money in Dad's pocket. No small matter to Dad, so now we have a gilded fan propped in there instead of logs. The flue has shut with a bang.

"I never in my life knew such peculiar people." Gloria laughed, egging us on. But I was on my best behavior and beamed her my beauty-smile, without a brain in my head. "I don't think you can imagine at sixteen, Margy, how lonely that might be. Off to yourself, how strange anybody would get." Gloria shook her head, while Dad and Margy exchanged looks that said it was not given to everyone to perceive companionship in a wildflower, the rendezvous implied by a falling star. Doting on themselves. I felt like bragging that I was peculiar too, but I had other concerns, with the beauty contest coming up, so I jiggled my eyebrows at Gloria and looked to heaven.

Tommy piped up: "When I'm big I want to live with Margy and be a fireman." Which is how much a first-grader knows.

"We need one of those right now, son. Two crazed teenagers, aflame with desire. Smarting with resentments. 'Nobody understands me.' " Dad boohooed and wiped his crocodile tears.

Margy scoffed. Love wasn't going to get its mitts on her. She was going to live by herself and not give a fig for anybody. Besides, there wasn't a single boy who liked her and it was embarrassing at school, the teachers asking all the time why she wasn't going to the dances when she hadn't been invited. I could have mentioned several who liked her, but that wasn't the point. She didn't like them. Little by little I was working my way back in Margy's good graces. I wouldn't have told who she had a crush on if they'd tied me over an anthill, a torture less likely than a long session with Gloria telling me I'm lucky I can buy all my clothes on a two-dollar allowance, learning to budget cradle to the grave. When so many others . . . .

"You girls are both so attractive," Gloria said, kindly including Margy, who hadn't been chosen for the beauty contest. "You can't imagine all the fellows you'll date, the places you'll go." The fabulous story of our cheerleader's younger days, the dances till dawn, the football games she left on a stretcher, dates booked a year in advance. She says a girl doesn't have to sit around in a car smooching to be the belle of the ball. *She* never did. Dad nods his head and agrees. We all know about Molly Schroeder, the girl he respected the most because she loved him to distraction but wouldn't come across. When Dad's out in the cold he has respect.

Gloria asked if we could have the lights back on. She had no interest in hiding in the dark and it was time to clear the table. Then we were blinking, coming to our senses, while Dad was sighing over the persistence of the mundane. Mist, that gossamer illusion, in modern times a noxious gas. November, portal to winter—hard to care with no wood to split, no salted meat in the larder. Gloria said what she missed most was pickled pigs' feet, and I laughed along with her, to stay on her good side.

Out in the kitchen, she was counting over her dates like rosary beads, the dresses she'd loved best, some of which she still had. Any one of them, compared to mine, was divine, but I had my eye on a pale green number for the contest—with, granted, a little help from the Kleenex box. Altogether Gloria had the confidence I wanted for myself. So far, the secret of her success: Never disagree with a man and never give a female an inch.

From the beginning Dad said Gloria would bring a ray of sunlight into our darkness. He warned us to find the same star—win her heart or hitch up to the next wagon West. Sometimes it's dazzling, Gloria up in the morning, dressed to the nines for ham and eggs. Ready for a date if one should come knocking, lipstick prints on the coffee cups. Gloria has done us the great favor of leaving her wonderful home and responsible job for a thankless task. She did it of her own free will, including giving up smoking, although I think nothing is quite what she expected. Still, she can say, "I always wanted a family of my own," real tears and her smile breaking together. I can't think what it will come to and I wring my hands, avoiding her eyes. Sometimes she says I'm laughing at her, but I don't think so, although I don't always know what comes over my face when I'm not looking.

Gloria has a short memory. Just when she's sitting pretty, counting her blessings, one of us jumps up to set her straight. Even Tommy rolls on the floor and screams that she's not his mother, as if he knew. I wish I could remember Mother better, like Margy does. From the start she told Gloria, "Like it or lump it, you're going to be my best friend." A privileged position, in my opinion, but Gloria doesn't know when she's ahead, pestering Margy to call her Mother, when I'd give anything if Margy would bend over backward to be as nice to me.

Dad shakes his head about Margy and calls her the mystery woman. But he's willing to let well enough alone, never one to look a gift horse in the mouth. If ever she gets married, Margy's perfectly happy to elope. If she goes on to school, she'll pay for it herself. With her far-away eyes and shining face, her look as though every-thing happened a long time ago, I know she's waiting for the day she will leave us behind and live on air if she has to. Nothing around here touches her any more than the mist blowing by at the window.

After Margy had gone to her babysitting job, Gloria brought the conversation back around to the contest. "Yes, Ruthann, you may borrow my gown, so you can stop hinting." She and I were in cahoots. Beauty had brought us together and my former resistance to her in-struction had flipped to the opposite pole.

"Though I'm not at all certain green is your best color. The bosom will be large of course and you must be very careful about your perspiration. Probably you should give up those potato chips you eat all the time. In fact, if I were you I wouldn't have a single thing that's chocolate or any sweets until it's over." We smiled intently into each other's eyes. Gloria wanted only the best for me—she was the first to say so. Ordinarily her helpfulness clashes with my self-respect, but already, on my own before dinner, I'd scrubbed myself so vigorously Dad himself noticed and allowed, on second thought, there was merit even in a dog show, since it brought the mutts in for a bath.

When Dad came in from work before dinner and heard about me and the contest he said, "Congratulations. I always said you were a beaut. I'm happy for you, but you and your mother are on your own. The prospect of a bevy of pubescent girls parading their wares is too much for an old man. I'm sitting this one out." He wanted daugh-ters who could man the oars. Margy had his coveted in-vitation to join him in the garage, dirty her hands, plant her feet in cement, and lick her wounds. She wasn't picked for the contest. She'd waltzed in from school with her nose in the air, superior to beauty, *The Girl of the Limberlost*.

Gloria was abashed, gracious from her perch on a

homecoming float still going 'round. "It doesn't make any sense. Nobody's any prettier than Margy."

"Some are thinner," Dad said, patting Margy on the head. Margy thanked Gloria for the compliment and then went back to her mountaintop. What did she care for hurrahs from the multitude, for crowns and transitory pleasures. Leave that to those who wander in the dark. People like Gloria and me. Not everyone can like the smell of sweat.

That evening I stayed friends with Gloria throughout dinner and until every dish was dry. For all we knew, this was my long-awaited capitulation. A redhead body and soul, flushed from her afternoon under the hair dryer, Gloria fluttered her knowing glances upon our newfound companionship. Whether some would admit it or not, bound as they were to mock the vain and frivolous, Gloria knew what was what. She told me she doubted Margy would have refused to appear in the contest if she'd had the chance. I could imagine Gloria's whole thought: Well, I suppose, if one must put a beauty contest and reverence for the Lord on balance scales, there would be no comparison, days holding what they do and all other things being equal.

While the garbage disposal chugged she said that no matter what Dad might have to say, he always noticed a woman's appearance first. Not every man read through *Vogue* magazine. "Your mother was a beautiful woman." It seemed shocking for her to speak of the dead. But there was no denying, her gray-green eyes sparkling with that wisp of tears always brimming and her red waves, Dad's second choice fulfilled the same condition. "Your father doesn't even like me to wear my glasses."

Dad appeared in the kitchen door with his paper and a weary look. "Must you make sport of my weakness and cupidity. Mock my every effort at transcendence." Dad was never very far away; in fact, the house felt like a pincushion, tiny, with walls of straw, sharp points everywhere.

"If you don't care about a woman's looks, Francis, then I guess I'll gain a bunch of weight and get a bifocal lens. Since you wouldn't notice." In the doorway, Dad fingered his earlobe as though it was a tissue sensitive to the approach of prey. He said he feared Gloria was doomed to the confusion of the stubbornly literal-minded.

"It is my belief—" he began. Between them, my back to Gloria, something passed and Dad's lip curled up to frolic off with his belief, the whim of a moment. After all, he had lasted only twelve years at the piano, six months at the seminary. He retreated to his reading chair with a parting remark: "I just think a girl of fourteen should be left in peace with her pimples and growing pains. I'd rather she went out for debate. But I'm outnumbered." Indifference fell like a shadow along with the news of the day.

I didn't go in for our evening chat, me on the footstool at Dad's feet, boring him with my reliable excellence, taking up his time with my papers. Giving Gloria another headache. Instead, I let Gloria help me with my French, a subject she'd studied, along with the great Shakespeare, bettering herself in night school. We were laughing and conniving, not ten feet from Dad, the best of pals. I told her the one about the man who wanted to show the lady his power tool and Gloria laughed more than she had to, just to be accommodating.

It worried Gloria that Margy pulled a disappearing act at the very mention of sex, frowned on every dirty joke. Dad called her an old woman—wondering if a female eunuch was a contradiction in terms. If he could redesign the world, women would live at one end, men at the other. In his typical fashion Dad has said all he means to on the subject: any daughter of his acts like a guttersnipe, he'll knock her up against the wall.

Gloria would say more, a lot more. In fact, it's mostly what she and I talk about when Margy's not around. How girls ruin their lives, the unbearable scorn of the righteous. It's almost too exhilarating to bear. "I know my father would rather I came home dead than pregnant," she said significantly, as though she had commented with distinction on the past and future.

A beautiful woman, born under an open star, Gloria is

no match for our intricacies. One day Margy confessed, eyes glazed, cheeks puffed with blood. She had read all the books. She had taken sex education in school, heard it more than once. Gloria didn't need to worry. She just didn't want to talk about it. Wouldn't!

Gloria was relieved, she said, that Margy was not entirely naïve. But, Gloria urged, there was more to the subject than the bare bones. Margy looked a hole through her. Anyone could have seen she meant what she said. But Gloria and Dad keep bringing it up. Everything reminds them of it.

They don't mess with me. The mere hint of a penis and I'm laughing my head off. To hear me telling my jokes, flying in the face of human decency, you'd think I had a one-track mind. Gloria joins in the fun, explaining to Margy as she's leaving the room that there's a great difference between jokes, some are smutty and some are merely cute. That is not Margy's opinion, and she's gone, leaving with Dad's approved posture, which could see her over Niagara Falls with a book on her head.

Gloria's smooth forehead furrows and she knits perfectly penciled brows in bewilderment. Maybe she's worried that her preacher father wouldn't approve—he was such a lofty soul. I haven't read a single book on sex and the stuff they teach us at school might as well be Greek. Enough to know it's better to come home dead than pregnant. I don't have to hear the sorry details.

Even Tommy couldn't get Gloria away from me during our French translation. He thrashed on the floor while I mouthed "Ha ha" behind teacher's back. Finally Dad called him away. I wasn't under any illusions that I was anybody's favorite, but for once the wind was in my direction. Tommy really does seem like Gloria's little boy now and eventually he will have to buy everything wholesale. I'll pick and choose. Before the beauty contest I would venture all in a mist of My Sin, the atomizer hidden deep in Gloria's dresser, where it ought to be. She'll accuse me of snooping—and while we're at it, did I take that little picture of Michael out of her room that time?

I don't know what she's talking about, unless I'm caught with the goods. Then I'm as sorry as can be.

Dad stuck to his guns, and the lone light in the upstairs bedroom declared his whereabouts when we drove in after the contest. Margy said she was going next door to watch television and Gloria drove off into the garage, giving me my opening, and I ran upstairs to Dad, burst in, locking the door behind me. Already the tears were streaming and I knew I was going to feel better. I had a right to talk to my own father. Across the room the tasseled lamp shade hung over his head. It looked as though he was under a hair dryer, like some silly woman wishing for the moon. "Oh, Dad."

My mouth was hardly open before Gloria was at the door. I should have locked her in the garage. "Francis. Francis. Open the door." Knock knock. " 'Open the door, Richard' " went singing through my head as I removed the key and hid my hand under the evening gown. Satisfaction smacked in my mouth like Dad with his crackers in bed, down the hatch whole with nary a crumb.

"What in the world possesses you, girl?" Evidently he was kind of pleased and amused after his quiet evening at home, his eyes moving deliberately between the rattling at the door and my appeal from the bedpost. It was like entering a peaceful den, the closed blinds and fog of cigarette smoke, the one dim light. I'd never known there were worse things than cigarette smoke, like perfume, squealing girls and overwrought mothers, the simpering strains of "A Pretty Girl." Dad was right, it was no different from a sideshow. Let Gloria serve beauty and fashion. Dad knew better. It seemed the longest time since I'd gotten to him in his own room, and I longed to curl at the foot of the bed in the maroon satin comforter and never have to leave. I went down on my knees by the side of the bed.

"Oh, Dad." I searched for his eyes as I had searched and searched to find Gloria and Margy beyond the extending plain of the stage, the dazzling floods blotting out the world beyond. His lean face was losing its bemused calm, his jaw muscle ticked. In a second he would have made up his mind. I lurched closer, scuffling the gown along the wooden floor, my hands folded imploringly—Bess, the landlord's daughter.

"Francis." The door handle shook and rattled. "Let me in there." I leaned to find Dad. "Don't, please. Give me a minute," I wailed, throwing myself on his legs, holding on for dear life as he began to stir. Behind me Gloria's fumbling grew noisier, more urgent. "Francis, why are you letting her treat me like this?"

I sobbed, trying to find the words so he'd have to listen and, unabashed, speak out the plain truth once more. Hadn't he known? Hadn't he said from the beginning it was all a bunch of foolishness and cheap vanity? Wouldn't I do better to stick to my studies and advance the race with an idealism befitting a creature of intelligence, the recipient of the Word? I longed to hear him speak.

Dad began to lift me. "Get off." Fitting his two hands under my arms he held me off his legs, swiveling himself out from under the covers while I slobbered into the sheets. "Don't. Please, give me time."

"Son-of-a-gun. What on earth are you doing, girl? What's the trouble here? Did they give out a booby prize?" He gripped both my arms so hard it hurt. I closed my eyes and went limp, a dead weight latched to him by a foot.

"Francis, I shouldn't be kept from my own room." Rattle rattle.

"No one is questioning that. I am coming, my dear. Right now I have my hands full." Dad was considering what to do with me next. I peeped at him through my armpit, veiled in green net.

"She's bound to feel bad. I don't blame her, but I only tried to help her the best I could." The handle sounded loose now, as though the whole thing would fall off. "Easy on that, Gloria." For the first time I heard the wind in Dad's teeth; he can't take it when things break.

"If you'd only listen to me, Dad. She said . . . she wants me to be ugly, that's what." Now I was in for it.

154

That only came out because she couldn't give me a single moment with my own father.

"That is a lie, Francis. I said no such thing. You know I wouldn't." Gloria never told lies and Dad knew it. Everybody knew it. I was sunk. "I did everything I could to help her. It certainly wasn't my fault what happened." Why couldn't Gloria just give up and go away? Had I misjudged her of the dainty wrists, the sneezes that were like irrepressible gasps of laughter?

Perhaps "Until death us do part" was exactly what she meant. My legs slipped off the bed and feebly I grappled with Dad for the key, watching my tears stream through his hairy shins. We walked along, me carried on the whirlwind, to the end of the bed. "You don't love me," I growled, my teeth ready to sink in.

Dad jerked me sharply backward by the hair. "Lucky you didn't." I lost track of the key and it spun across the floor. I let myself follow and lay sprawled, the dress knotted into a rope around my middle, some Kleenex giving away the secret to beauty. Who cared? They already thought I was a freak. When Dad opened the door, Gloria's counterweight nearly landed her at my feet. "Welcome," I wanted to say and make bright eyes, but one glance at her face silenced me and I turned away as the cold fresh air rushed in.

Dad sounded calm and collected enough. As though he'd seen that look before. "Okay, okay. Steady now. No harm done. I wish you girls would each wait your turn."

The slap, sharp as a signal, following immediately, whipped my head around to see what was what. Dad stepped back from Gloria, his hand pasted up to cover his whitened cheek, but it didn't hide all the scratch that zigzagged to his chin. Gloria's head was up.

"You see. You see what she's like." Blood tasted on my lips, but I scrambled up, stumbling on the gown, arms flailing. Dad was sure to take pity on his bleeding daughter. He wasn't afraid. But then he had me by the elbow, two fingers clamped in a vise, escorting the Whore of Babylon into the outer darkness. "Cover yourself,"

155

he said, lifting a withered lip. My dress was down to my waist.

Over my shoulder I watched Gloria sway on her perfect legs and plunge, catching herself just barely on the edge of the bed. I didn't know whose blood got to her, Dad's or mine, but I automatically reached out to help, butting into the flat of Dad's outstretched arm, which pitched me toward the stair railing, where a heel caught and I flipped to the side, cushioned in the net overskirt, toppling head-first as though into a snowbank, grounded, second step from the top.

Dad was already helping Gloria to lie on the bed while I looked on, wishing. In spite of everything I could have gone right to sleep. "Another episode like this, young lady," Dad leveled at me, "they'll ask me to identify you in a lineup and I won't remember your name."

"Blood," Gloria murmured. "Dizzy. I'll be all right. You know I've always told Ruthann she is a beautiful girl." Her two white arms stretched up, Snow White kissed alive by the Prince.

"Jezebel," I yelped. It was quiet and then their door slammed. I heard Dad: "This is a living hell." I let myself coast to the bottom of the stairs. When Tommy's door opened he was whimpering "Margy," like he does when he's had a bad dream, as though she could change night into day.

"Queer bait," I whispered. Dad's door opened and he called in his little fair-haired boy. "All hope abandon, ye who enter here!"

"Of course Ruthann feels bad"—I heard Gloria beginning her side of everything. I crawled away, out into the night to catch my death in November. Dad would feel sorry. He didn't mean for me to hurt myself. It would worry him to think of me out in the cold, maybe getting pneumonia or croup, like when I was a baby. He'd never thought twice about buying milk for me or extra cod-liver oil. In the olden days he fears I would have been taken off as an infant, prey to epidemics and dysentery, finally left somewhere at the side of the trail, my end marked by a wooden cross. He's grateful to modern medicine,

156

although the faith symbolized by that cross would at least have lent comfort to the grieving. Now there is nothing.

Next door Margy's hair was spiking up in the darkened living room, flaring with the voltage of the television as though she was featured in black and white. We didn't have a television but we would soon, Gloria saying that we were becoming a nuisance to the neighbors. Dad said he was holding out as long as possible—this way he killed two birds with one stone, got rid of the girls and saved money to boot. Anyway, he was suspicious of newfangled inventions. For all he knew, watching television made you soft in the head. A car slowly passed, a man at the wheel, maybe out looking for a runaway. I could have gone off with him. Dad says he'll keep the upper hand with us or know the reason why. If we don't like it, we're free to go.

I don't know what Margy thinks. All she'll say about Gloria is: She does the best she can. A bone I'd like to pick, but Margy says she promised Gloria she wouldn't talk behind her back and, heaven knows, her word is her bond. She tries to get me to join her in the good life, and her talks are so inspiring sometimes I decide to reform. All goes well for a while and I get to thinking Margy and I are the same wonderful person. I'm nice to everybody and volunteer for extra chores. To myself I vow that the next time Nevada comes looking for me, I'll cut him dead. He can keep his money. At school I'll stop prostituting myself to get in with the popular crowd and seek out friends of inner beauty and sterling character. Until, with no warning, my good intentions are gone with the wind.

Apparently Margy has become reconciled, not only to sex, but to all that fate may bring down upon her head. No matter how it's happened that she's landed on the lone prairie where children never supposed they were anything more than extra mouths to feed, hands in the field, and agreeable companions. When she first got her period, it was a deadly secret. Now it's become a privilege. And after all this time she's used to me sleeping in the next bed, watching her every move; although I have no doubt it's thanks to me she hasn't turned into some kind of a lonely pervert.

I heard Margy coming then, humming her way over the grass. I couldn't imagine someone so cheery being a nuisance to the neighbors, even if once she was asked to leave or stop snickering at Liberace.

"Edgy as a bred mare," Dad says, and Margy jumped about three feet in the air just because I was sitting there quietly in the dark. "Darn, you scared me. What are you doing out here acting moony?"

"What did you watch?"

Margy stood before me with her shoes in her hand, out for her death too. "This is where you belong in that gown, Ruthann. The sequins twinkle like you're dressed in stars. We saw this play about a man who loved a woman. Don't smirk, it was good. It was during the war and he had to go off and leave her. They were separated for years and she didn't even know if he was alive. Or married. Then years later they met again in that same place, in the exact room. You would have liked it. You should've come over." I saw right then that much as I wanted to be like Margy it would never happen, her face anguished and proud, as though she had just emerged from that room of hope and surrender. And even if she never earned anybody's respect or paid anybody back, she was going to hold out for love and her right to a wholesome meal. It made me feel so lonely I would have laid my beauty on the block to keep on believing it was possible.

"Come on in, my feet are frozen." Margy was prancing up the steps and we went inside, Margy flipping the door lock. Then we sneaked upstairs, avoiding the third and sixth steps, which creaked. Dad's door was locked and barred, a room so silent and dark they might have fallen off the side of the house. Beside my bed I let my finery slip away and kicked it all under the bed. See how Gloria liked that. Then I got in bed naked, the dirtiest thing I could think of.

I shivered; Gloria's glowing and furious eyes seeming to float over the bed, disembodied, the way they'd looked

158

when she hit Dad. While he stood, sad and bewildered, instead of smacking her back. Then I heard their door open, Gloria's robe swishing the length of the stairs, and the chain bolt slid home. Such inflamed watchfulness worked like a sleeping draught and while she ran the water in the bathroom I grew weary of it all. Let them take us in the night, lead us into the forest. Then Margy said, "Don't feel so bad, Ruthann. It was a dumb contest. Look who won. You're a hundred times better looking." Rosemary Phelps and Margy had once tried to be best friends. Even way back then, when Dad nicknamed her "Dishwater," she'd been at work on her prizewinning hobby—collecting key chains.

In the morning I was first up, dressed and spying from the living room. I had one of Gloria's headaches and probably I could have stayed home for the day, but the thought of what Gloria would have to say would have driven me out the door with a gaping wound. Catching my eye in the fireplace mirror, I blew myself a kiss. I've got eyes.

Up in the hallway I heard Gloria talking to Margy. "I don't like to lie. Your father is in there with the shades pulled, just pretending. He won't get up and then he makes me call the office and say he's sick. I can't even go in to get my clothes. I don't like to lie. I wasn't brought up that way."

Some of us come to it naturally. Gloria likes to take the credit for being the first to catch up with me, as though before no one ever cared or was smart enough. "You don't appreciate it now," she says, "but the day will come when you'll be glad I treated you like my own child."

Dad's on the spot when my lying comes up for discussion. I tend to think Dad's always liked me the way I am, something he could take the credit for. Sometimes he tells Gloria he always thought my tendency was more in the opposite direction, hostage to the unvarnished truth. I let them work it out.

I wanted to yell up to Gloria, "Tell the shirker to do

his own dirty work," but then I heard Dad himself in the hall. "You're off the hook, Gloria, so you can quit tattling to my elder daughter, poisoning her against me. I'm up and at 'em, raring to go. Where's that miserable excuse for a beauty queen? Now she'll listen to her old dad." Any ideas I had of sneaking into the inner sanctum to spend the day with Dad flew out the window.

"I hope she doesn't think I didn't want her to win. I certainly did all I could, didn't I, Margy?" I imagined Margy nodding, agreeable to the final hour, taking the noose with a smile. Dad says if she gets any more resigned we can watch her levitate. He wishes he'd been a better father, admits Tommy has a better deal. He regrets Margy and I are lost to him, although that's the way of the world, nothing working out to suit anybody.

He sounded like himself, ready to forgive and forget. That's how Dad is. When he chases me out of the house at night, the next morning he's up bright and early. "You wouldn't be telling a lie, my sweet. I am sick. Sick of living. Sick of playing nursemaid to that bunch of befuddled *artistes*, pretending I give a damn. But to spare you an uneasy conscience, I'm dragging myself from the arms of Morpheus to face another day." Morpheus, as opposed to any woman, holds a man tight and feels grateful for anything he gets.

Then Tommy was up, jabbering to Margy, taking a stroll along her prone body, beginning the Dauphin's day of prepared meals, ironed briefs, and a pony cart to school. Every morning Margy and I darn our socks, which are worn to holes by evening. We have to pack our own lunches, Velveeta and mustard, at dawn. Dad says we ought to be able to understand that Tommy seems more like Gloria's own child. He was very young when she came and doesn't remember his mother. I want to protest, "I scarcely remember her myself."

When I set out I hadn't heard a peep from Margy, queen of drudges and babysitters, chief moneylender. Lucky for me there's nothing she wants. I live off her charity, and before I left the room I borrowed another dollar—"Put it on the tab," so to speak. Even Dad hands me an extra dime sometimes, for when my face lights up, he says he finds it possible to forgive himself for every mistake he ever made with me.

Out on the porch a little wind devil of dry leaves spun up, nudging my leg like a stray dog. Suppose around noon I showed up at Dad's office? Would Mrs. Johnson pound and holler and order me to get out? Would she turn mean? Gloria's afraid to go up there with Mrs. Johnson in charge. She won't even let her, Dad's own wife, go through to Dad unannounced. I guess in the daytime Mrs. Johnson figures Dad belongs to her and she doesn't want Gloria on the other knee, messing with his papers. Once, Mrs. Johnson had the nerve to tell Gloria that being Dad's secretary was heaven on earth. Probably Gloria wished she could say the same for her end of the day. At dinner she said, "I think everybody should be their very nicest at home with those they love." Her eyes filled and I looked down. My arms flapped at my side. What could be done, Gloria takes the world so to heart. A locked door, an unlocked door, Tommy's sniffles. Dad said, "Ho-hum," and yawned.

I'd get on Mrs. Johnson's good side, lick her stamps, answer the phone. She and I could be Dad's little daytime family. "Sorry we're in conference," I'd tell Gloria when she was calling. Eventually she'd give up and go away, back to where she was always so happy. She could take Tommy with her. He hardly seems like my real brother anymore.

After I've struggled over the bridge to Washington and climbed the hill to Dad, my brown eyes purpled in the shine of my blue-black hair, faint from the long, weary trudge, Dad will smile and yank on his ear, ask, "What can I do for you, little brown girl?" Dad says I'm always after something. "I just want to be with you," I'll say. He and I never get to be alone.

I stepped out of there, onto the mailed heart of the earth, the door left ajar, no word of farewell, looking for all the world to see like an orphan, a child of the workhouse, no coat, in my oldest gunnysack dress, overlong with a ripped sash, a secondhand Orlon sweater. Like the neighbors would naturally imagine: the father pre-occupied with his lady love, the older girl grown strange and dreamy, the little boy reeking of mustard plaster in case of a bad cold. Everyone would know.

At the corner by the Church of the Evangelical Pente-costal I took five steps in the direction of the four winds, my eyes closed. Each time I had to say "Amen" five times. The answer on the sermon signpost struck me: "If I were hungry, I would not tell thee." Psalms 50. Just as I thought. I turned my back on school and Manassas and headed on the old route toward Washington. My grades would hold up if I was gone a year. Far down the street the gaze of the Saviour followed me, arms out-stretched, the lost lamb cuddled at His feet among the glass-pale lillies.

There were grimy little settlements all along the way, strung out along the highway into the city. Dad went there on Saturdays to do his errands, taking his shirts to the Chink, buying pastry from the Krauts. The shoe-maker was Giuseppe. He said he felt almost as though he was in Baghdad, trading at the bazaars, where for the price of a Fig Newton he could purchase his own dancing girl.

In the old days, Dad had offered Margy the chance to become a tap dancer. It didn't even have to come out of her allowance, and he sacrificed his Saturday mornings to wait out in the car, reading the paper and smoking cigarettes. I waited with him until I needed my gas mask, then went inside the Quonset hut to watch Margy dis-grace herself, holding her big leg up in the midst of in-fants, blushing and intent, ballet included as a part of the lesson. She was always in the beginners' class, because we always moved before she could be promoted, until finally one time, when the newest member sucked her thumb, Margy came out and told Dad she was sorry but she was quitting. She couldn't do it anymore. Dad slammed down the paper and drove home with a white mouth. His parting remark, "Don't you ever let me hear you belly-yakking—'Why didn't you *make* me?' " He'd heard that from dozens of nurses and bored housewives.

That was in the time when Margy and I walked to the library every Saturday afternoon, after our work was done, taking our books into the movies, if we went, or into the dime store for our shopping. Both of us took three, which was the limit. Margy always read hers cover to cover, while mine went back unopened. Now that Margy was a junior and had her babysitting and friends of her own, we went our separate ways. My ways had taken their toll, although I couldn't believe it when Margy said that if I weren't her sister we probably wouldn't be friends. I wasn't her type. I must have turned pale, because Gloria looked concerned and later confided that someone might have to be Jewish or at least unconventional to get Margy's attention. I guess Gloria felt left out too.

I would have to sail in fast, take Mrs. Johnson by surprise, get to Dad before she sent out the alarm. In spite of my headache I would throw my shoulders back and smile for all I was worth. A man likes to see something coming at him that won't add to his misery.

The dime store was my favorite place and I could have bought a jug of Blue Waltz or a pet mouse with my eyes closed. But it was too early for it to open up, so I strolled along the sprawling highway to Washington, to mix in with the colored, where nobody cared if you went to school or not. It didn't surprise Dad that colored kids had washed their hands of separate but equal education. He didn't take them for fools.

My first class of the day would be getting under way, Miss Hildebrand, who was about a hundred, set to hum all the parts of *Tristan and Isolde*, her hands folded over her dreary heart. One night I repeated the whole long tale to Margy and kept her spellbound—any tale of love, doomed or otherwise, is what she lives for. Dad, sniffing the wind, has offered her a bonus to elope, formal weddings in his opinion on a par with beauty contests, women celebrating their downfall. For which not one penny will come out of his pocket! Miss Hildebrand will miss me. I sit in the front row and pay strict attention, a nice contrast to the boys in the back of the room who use the time to gab and copy my homework. Miss Hildebrand sings just to me. I don't mind, I have a world of patience with romantics.

One time Margy, missing the point, asked Dad's permission to skip school. "My God, girl. What do you take me for? Not only am I a father but I have at least a semblance of professionalism."

I bet Margy was wondering what a lifetime of doing the dishes got for a person. Dad went on to cast aspersions on her judgment, bringing up a subject like that in front of youngsters who looked to her as a guiding light. What kind of an ignoramus was she? A lifetime of that had undermined Margy's position; doubtless it hadn't occurred to her that she was anybody's example. Nor to me. "Yeah, you should talk. You play hooky all the time"—I put in my two cents.

"Yes," Gloria chimed in. "And he makes me call his office and say he's sick. I don't like to lie." Some things bear repeating. Once, when I told Dad I was going to run away, he asked if he could come with me.

"I might do it anyway," Margy said. "You're lucky to have a daughter like me. I don't even smoke." Margy reached for Dad's pack. "And I want to." He drew back and raised his smacking hand.

"You call that luck. I wouldn't put up with the other kind for five minutes." He eyed me to be certain I knew the score. Not that I want to smoke. When I disappear with his cigarettes it's to throw them in the garbage. As far as I know Margy never did skip school. She didn't want to take the consequences. I've been asking for them all my life and they come, one fast on the heels of another.

I could have breezed in and out of Washington with a blindfold on. It's one favor Dad doesn't mind. He follows the highway, going along the old route and across the bridge, dropping us off at art galleries, libraries, museums, anyplace that's free and uplifting. He'd as soon read the paper at the Reflecting Pool. "Take your time," he says, and he means it—he's seen it all. Margy climbed the Washington Monument twice in one day. When we return to the car we detect crumbs on Dad's coat, candy wrappers left about. Dad grins as though they're feathers, but we can never catch him eating.

Washington would be full of sailors and colored people, so I'd know when I was in the heart of D.C. When Margy's along, they stare. You'd think they'd never seen a blonde. Without her, I might get a little attention, though I'd probably fit right in; when we're driving around in Washington, cruising 9th Street, Dad says it's tempting and slows the car. He's going to let me out. Gloria laughs and says I'm not that dark. On the way back we see the signs to St. Elizabeth's, where Dad says we would all be at home.

The streets were getting filthy, a sure sign I was on my way into the nation's capital. Next I'd step in something disgusting. That's something Gloria couldn't take. Anybody's foot gets restless, seeking a table or a footstool, her mind gets to circling. She can't help imagining where that foot has been. She comes by it honestly. Her father wouldn't eat a banana before it was washed and her mother disinfects the phone where people have been breathing. Clorox goes in the dishpan and the laundry tub. Soon everything will be white. Gloria says when you think about it, germs are everywhere. When I think about it, I'm always cold.

A man passing by in a car called out. Another admirer off to work for the government. I didn't look up fast enough, probably unnerved by the beauty contest. Gloria would count that a blessing. In a taxi once I got chummy with the driver, edging up, jiving to the colored music they bring in from D.C. "Feel so good. Now that you're here / come let me hold ya / Come let me squeeze ya." Behind me the air around Gloria glowed, and after we got out she had to find a place to sit and get water for her aspirin.

Dad was brought in for the crisis. Didn't I know the difference between courtesy and courting danger? My smile kept introducing itself, living a life of its own, and out of patience, Dad whacked me. Gloria winced.

165

"Francis, don't do that." You would have thought she'd never seen such a thing in her life.

It shocked Dad to be tormented in the Roman manner. "What in God's name do you want from me, Gloria?" The wild horses had severed his spleen from his backbone. "Just tell me. Show me a better way." I hated to see his white face with pinchy red eyes and I started to cry. I was sorry. I'd be good. Now it seemed that somewhere along the way Gloria had taken to our ways, the red mark down Dad's cheek something I never thought I'd live to see.

So many dark folks on the street was like the mural we were doing for extra credit in Brewster's class brought to life. It was going to hang in the front hall by the principal's office, for parents and visitors to see. Bright and happy-looking, we were showing the world a better way, man in a free society, with desegregated schools. There flew the American flag to show you where you were. In Dad's opinion it is the shame of progressive education that the superior student gets a diploma knowing how to color and count change. Also they teach us to cooperate.

Some refuse to learn. Once I found a Confederate flag stuck in my notebook and before I turned it in to the teacher I outfitted it with a swastika, four capital *L*'s to the four winds. When the teacher discovered those hopeless bigots had been busy on the mural, tits on the ladies, the colored people changed to monkeys, she appointed me and Pearl Rosen to be in charge, erase that stuff, and restore human dignity to the mural. Something impossible for me, since I've never progressed beyond stick figures, so I perfected my coloring and told other people what to do.

It's no secret I'm a nigger lover. I said right out in Current Events that I'd marry a Negro if I loved one, if he'd have me. News like that travels like wildfire in the Old South and soon perfect strangers called me "Chocolate Drop." Even Nevada Baker came up to me in the hall and said, "You're full of bull," and according to him we've been engaged since kindergarten.

Gloria doesn't know my best side, imagining my loy-

166

alties would be for sale. "You must remember, Ruthann, you are in the South. If you want to have friends you must be sensitive to the feelings of others, even if they differ from your own." Et cetera, et cetera.

I know how she figures. When Margy broke up with her best friend, Rosemary, Margy maintained she was sick to death of fighting about segregation every day to and from school. Gloria found it hard to believe that racial equality was such a burning issue and insinuated that their differences had more to do with Margy's being in the academic program at school and looking for new pals. Besides, Margy was taller than Rosemary by a foot and needed to find taller friends who would make her look better to the boys. Another indigestible truth, harder to swallow than a goldfish.

I told Gloria, "Before anybody's friends with me they'd better know I treat everybody the same regardless of race, creed, or color."

Her eyes snapped for the red, white, and blue. She didn't need Miss High and Mighty to tell her right from wrong. She'd been raised a Christian. And she had news for me: the colored wanted to be left to themselves. They weren't interested in a bunch of do-gooders messing with their business. Gloria had had the confidence of one or two maids. That sort of thing doesn't wash with me unless I hear it from the horse's mouth. Gloria ended up, "One drop of color and you're a Negro. All the sarcasm in the world doesn't help."

She's practice for me. By the by, not just on Lincoln's Birthday, the subject comes up in Current Events. Since it arrives out of the blue, the class is always slightly heightened, an undercurrent of expectation holding the boys in the back, busy copying homework and inscribing answers to quizzes up and down their forearms, alert, one ear out.

At bay, those world authorities on the colored races display the social and moral standards of respectable housewives. You wouldn't think, to look at them in their skin-tight jeans and greasy ducktails, that they were devoted to Clorox and the straight-edged lawn. No one can convince them there's hope for the downtrodden. Their usual smirking indolence evaporates as though it had been a pose. They bully and threaten. Student monitors throw tantrums for order. While the discussion rages, the louts ascend in volume and rancor, mount their desks in defense of white supremacy, blare and bleat. The South will rise again. All the murals in the world are lost on them. They know they don't have a snowball's chance in hell, and damned if anyone else will. Once I went home with Terry Brown and he made me take off my underpants and leave them behind. Clearly he will be a desperate man.

Now I would see it all for myself, down with the colored in Washington, skipping over drunks, getting the nod from drug dealers. A girl about my age in high heels and tiger-skin shorts sashayed by. I tried to meet her eyes to let her know I understood, but nothing doing. She knew it was too late in the day. Every shadowed doorway stunk of cats and garbage. I didn't suppose it was any different when you went inside. The boys at our school regularly pissed on the hot-water radiators. They hadn't asked to be there either.

"Yo. Yo, girl. You lost?" I had as much right as anybody to be heading into Washington, but that didn't stop me from turning around, skedaddling back to where I came from, although not so fast people would think I was scared, throwing a casual glance over my shoulder. A colored boy was coming after me, not scared, that was for certain, sauntering along and grinning. One of those fresh know-it-all, seen-it-all types in sunglasses and a checkered cap, his jacket opened up and swinging along with him like he never was anything but warm. He looked as though he'd gotten to be sixteen by fearlessness and grace, like maybe he was the first and had the keys to the city.

"You find trouble if you be lookin'," he called after me. That's how much he knew about me. Dad says I wouldn't know trouble if it came up and hit me in the face.

He seemed a lot friendlier than Grandma's maid.

Margy and I had tried to be friends, showing up in every room with a dust rag and a smile, but she must have told Grandma we were in the way because we were sent to the store with a long list. She never even turned to wave when her taxi came. That boy was the one who should be looking out for trouble, coming into my home territory, the louts out beating the bounds. I never would have thought I'd start to shake and tremble, jerking on the inside too like I was up on a stage in my evening gown, just because a colored boy spoke to me. That was a long way from a wedding. Unhurried, he drifted along after me, slouched under his slouched cap. I patted my hair all around to see it was fixed. There was no telling what was happening to my face.

Gloria said maybe the judges had thought I was a little simpleminded, smiling and blinking while the contest was going on. She'd been looking funny, under the ceiling light of the car, her eyes so full of sympathy I lost all mercy and demanded to know the truth. I could tell, all the girls avoiding me, even Nevada Baker not coming up afterward as though our engagement had been broken off. The woman sitting next to Margy had even told her she should have won. Gloria said she knew it was just nerves, the different expressions I'd been making, all the fidgeting. Then the pasted smile, once I'd latched on to it. No one up on the stage was any prettier, she said. But it was unfortunate, especially when Rita Cantwell recited "To be or not to be," while I smiled all the way through. Gloria thought maybe after all it was a good thing Dad hadn't come.

My arms oared at my sides, the most telltale thing about me, aside from my expression. I dashed headlong from a clothesline flapping sheets in the breeze, pounding like an invading army. The colored boy vanished, then reappeared like the faint sun, breezing in and out of the clouds, everything running together. Maybe he would have a knife. I wasn't as dumb as I looked, my dumb look something Dad says I put on to buy time. I don't know. Sometimes dumb's exactly how I feel. At last, back at my own dime store, I leaned safe on home base, hook-ing a heel on the display window, and turned straight to face the boy when he came bopping up beside me, making himself at home, in broad daylight in a lily-white suburb.

He tilted the glasses onto his forehead and light fell into his eyes like an avalanche of snow spilling into a rock fissure that had been dark forever. I wondered if I would ever stop shaking, as though deep parts of me had shifted too and I was breaking up. He'd never before seen the likes of me, the impetuous sword-swallower, rope-dancer, beloved of the unvarnished truth. His nostrils dilated as though he scented me, and he slid out of his coat, handing it to me. "You cold," he said.

I snuggled deep inside.

"You a Mexican jumping bean."

I guess it didn't take a judge to see I was a nervous wreck. I ignored him, keeping some style, and brought out my lipstick, angling to see my face in the mirrored case, keeping a watch on it. The curve of my lips lifted my spirits and I went to coloring them to bring out the gutsy bow. Maybe he would think it was a little pouty bee sting or a droplet of honey. I slithered my eye sideways to see if he was watching, grateful for my looks. Without them I would have to rely on my personality, not my most reliable commodity. A car passed with the radio loud in the morning street, Little Richard bearing the lamentation of the people. "Got a gal name Daisy."

"She almost drive me crazy." I mouthed the words, licking my lips, wrapped in the sheltering coat, my eyes on the prowl, checking through my purse for this and that.

"Now. How you know that? They play that cross the border? You the limit, gal." I kept snapping my fingers, wiggling in time, painting my mouth. "Tutti Frutti Ah Rutti." Making myself the living end.

It rattled Gloria. When she married Dad she expected the radio, heaven knows. After all she knew kids, forty years in a Sunday school. But she'd expected the top forty, not the colored, wailing and screeching like banshees, out of the nation's capital. She knit her brows, perplexed.

170

Dad said, "Tell them to turn the damn thing off. Who cares if they hate you?" He knows what matters. Gloria said, "I'll just take some aspirin." Behind her back, Dad gives me the wink. Sometimes it's in Gloria's smile—she suspects Margy and I are putting on, just to be different. Could be. We play it constantly, getting at something.

"I know," the boy said, pointing his finger for a clever guess. "You from a island where it's warm all the time. Blue waters. Coconuts on the trees. Be dancin'." He dangled his hands before him, dark graceful maidens, half dressed, the cuffs of his green shirt the skipping waves. He made it look so nice. "Cat got your tongue, señorita?"

I laughed and twirled off in a jitterbug on the sidewalk, keeping my secret origins. Our bedroom was like an island in troubled waters, small with high-backed twin beds from the Depression era crowded in where Margy and I sat side by side to do our homework on our laps, the radio thumping between us. Margy's looking for a way out of there. She wants to get a job and save money. Then if she decides to go on to school, she'll pay for it herself and not have to take favors from anybody. If it turns out she's not smart enough and has to drop out, she'll be the one to lose. I can't ever imagine feeling that rich.

In the same breath she mentions Mother's bankbook and I go blank. Long ago I figured out that there was nothing to it, just another one of Margy's dreams of what might be. Like getting somebody to take her to the Howard Theater to hear Billy Eckstine, somebody like her married friend who's five thousand miles away. Or Brooke, the old stuffed shirt from church, another dreamboat. I can't get her to open up on those subjects, even if I compliment her speaking voice, which along with her posture is her pride and joy. If she thinks I'm the same person who blurted out at the dinner table that Margy got caught hiding in the shower during gym class so she wouldn't have to dance with the boys, then she hasn't been paying attention. I'm known as a liar because I've learned to keep the bitter truth even from myself.

That fresh boy, probably noticing that my attention

171

wandered, leaned over and offered me a stick of gum. "Why you so sad?" he asked. What was he after? I was wiggling and flirty. "Got a gal name Sue. She know just what she do."

The cold fell across me with the shadow when it came. I waited for it to pass; then, when it didn't, followed along the blade of it to the curb where Nevada Baker was seated on his motorcycle, scowling blue-bloody murder. I couldn't hear myself think. I raised my lipstick case to hide my mouth and went on with my artwork, showing my white teeth like pearls on a string, under the flickering intrigue of my glance. Not letting on that I'd ever seen either of those boys before. Beside me the colored boy waited deep and still. Nevada seemed to have captured both of us in the beacon of his remote and galling eye.

He stood before us, his motorcycle hanging off him like something studded and silvered he was wearing, his ironed and starched blue jeans taking on some of that cold metal sheen, spurs winking off his cowboy boots. Nevada hadn't been west of the Mississippi since he was born but he thought he'd invented the style. In fact, concentrating on me, hunched forward and doggedly stubborn, he was like a dray horse beaten to death in the street.

"Ruthann. You get on over here. I'm taking you where you belong." Nevada knew I would never ride on that thing between his legs. I couldn't abide the smell and its infernal racket. At the first turn I'd be carsick. But he just had to keep asking. I took out my comb, fluffing my hair, stroking the bangs with a wet finger. I primped the brow over my almond eye and winked. In no time I'd be riding the rails again—when was up to me.

Nevada and I met in kindergarten when once long ago we'd lived in Washington with Mother. He said he remembered her, bringing that up when we met again at the high school, and I must say my heart skipped a beat. His father had run out on him before he was born, he'd reminded me, a harsh acknowledgment of rank in the scheme of life's misfortunes. All I'd remembered about him was that every day he'd been dropped off in a long white car with a uniformed driver, and left the same way.

I went ahead and applied my eyelash curler, so he wouldn't think he could get to me, staring and glaring. According to Nevada, back in kindergarten I'd promised to marry him. He'd kept after me with the same cussedness that kept him right then astride the motorcycle, immobile, stolid, as though if he moved a muscle to approach he'd lose leverage that was his by right.

When he was sitting on his motorcycle, his crooked leg from childhood polio didn't show. He'd gladly give up walking for the advantage to his appearance. At school he kept to himself, periodically erupting from sullen reveries in a spit of resentment, unsettling and not quite coherent. The others, suspecting he marched to a different drummer, didn't give him the time of day and he was always alone, even at the lunch table. I leaned my head from side to side, tilting my hair, arching my back, one eye caged in the curler like a monocle.

"I mean it, come on here. Durn you, Ruthann." Nevada cut the motor and started to dismount. Then his spur or something caught and threw him, the motorcycle wavering, then crashing, just barely missing Nevada, who scrabbled sideways on his back along the walk.

So long! The first time I do something I take myself by surprise and I don't have a thought in my head. The colored boy was there with his hand stuck out when mine flung in his direction, as though we'd caught each other for balance. And we began to run, had already been running on the inside to escape the sorry, sorry boy, leaving Nevada amid the glittering heap of the downed motorcycle. I'll make it up to you, I thought, taking one last peek to see that he was able to stand up. I'll let you buy me that turquoise ring—tell Dad I got it in Cracker Jacks. You can pay my Girl Scout dues for the decade, since you wanted to. We turned and fled along the narrow dark of the alleyway beside the dime store, as though our lives depended on it, following the line of blue sky flat overhead like a trail to the open sea.

I'd never known there was so much beyond the high-

173

way—back streets, twisting alleys, hills, fire escapes, and garden plots. We lurched beside high fences, broke into yards where children turned wide eyes to wonder. Dogs joined up for a frolic, cats yowled and scattered. When we stopped in a doorway to rest, the boy moved his cap and glasses to my head. "What you island girls named? Pleased to meet you. I'm Bobby D." He took a deep breath, slithering his shoulders. "D. for Divine." He dipped a slight bow.

In the stillness of not running, my teeth chattered. I hoped I wasn't going to be bothersome, feeble from the cold. "He telleth the number of the stars; he calleth them all by their names." Above I saw the daytime moon, a pale wafer and distant, meager as the November sun. Two heavenly bodies and still I was freezing to death.

"All right, señorita. Tell you what. We'll go dancing. Warm up in no time. Why you so scared? He your boy?"

Bobby D. took out cigarettes and offered me one. Oh, baby. I threw over a lifelong aversion for a moment's diversion and had one. When I couldn't get it to light, he exchanged it for the one from his mouth. My lips were shaking in a plague. The smoke snaked up my nose in a blue coil while I had to hold it live and burning in my hand. I could have swallowed it whole. Bobby D. watched me through the match flame while he lit his own. "You having a good time," he said, letting smoke out long and slow. His lips were mobile and sensitive as fingers. The little fire did warm my hand but it would never add to my beauty. Dad's fingers were yellow and carbuncled as an old squash.

"Wait here," Bobby D. said, taking me by the shoulders, placing me against a warm brick wall and stepping on my cigarette. "You wait now. Hear?" He ran off toward a little corner store, glancing back, worried. He wouldn't be the first one to have me disappear—he'd search and wonder and never forget, feel sad the rest of his days. When he came speeding out of the store and saw me waiting, the sun broke out in his smile, as though he'd had more than one thing vanish on him before, and he presented a box of candy cigarettes, wrapped up in

174

cellophane. I wouldn't cry for him and bared my teeth like a snapping dog. But he looked so pleased I figured he took it for happiness, and when I got one out of the box, I sucked and blew from it, shaking my hair, drifting my eyelashes. The melting sugar splashed through my mouth, twinkling in the dark.

"'She got everything Uncle John need. Oh baby.' Let us flee to our island hideaway." When he looked at me that way, like Icarus in his flight, I really did smile back. Bobby D. took my hand again and we went sliding through the streets, me behind my disguise, following like a blind person. Finally we ducked into an alley, and at the end was a door, set in the brick like a secret. Bobby D. found the key wedged between the doorframe and a loose brick and opened it. Would I grow tall or small? The door fell into the dark. He bowed for me to proceed, and as the door staggered shut the light eclipsed. From somewhere I heard a murmur of voices and balls clicking.

"We're here," he said, his hand light on my arm. The smell made me feel dizzy and I held my breath. When Dad opens a beer I leave the room. "That's my daughter," he calls, "thin as a garter and just as snappy."

"This is my uncle's place. He's got the establishment next door," motioning with a shoulder toward the muffled clicks behind the wall. "Pool hall. Sometimes I come here, long as I leave it nice." He flipped a switch and in the back a jukebox lighted up like an idol in a cave, dripping colors like limewater. Little Christmas lights bubbled around the mirror over the bar. There were stools there but the tables were pushed off to the side and piled with chairs. At the end was a raised platform. Bobby D. ran over, jumped onto the stage, and sat at the drums, brushing out a rasping rhythm like a catch in the throat. "Welcome the señorita, ladies and gents. Prettiest gal on the street of dreams." His voice brushed out soft too as he drummed me toward him through the half dark. It helped the part of me that was still a part of the world to make the trip and step onto the stage, throwing out my

175

hip, swishing my hair, trembling. I thumbed my nose to the jukebox, which sat overseeing, impassive as a judge.

The dancing got me going, warmed me up. Twisting and twirling, the coat fell away to the floor and I forgot it, forgot about the sour beery smell, casting myself into the air like a throw of the dice. A jitterbugging fool. Dad says I've got rhythm. When we're dancing Gloria bosoms her way in to make Dad her partner. "My times are in Thy hands." I rolled my eyes and didn't let go.

Bobby D. knew how to make the jukebox play without any money. We punched all the tunes, dancing the fast and the slow. He taught me to dance "the stroll." The first time he pulled me close I held my breath. He gave me a tiny poke in the ribs, grinning. "I take good care of you." I didn't know how not to smile, not to be cold, not to be sad. When nobody was looking maybe Bobby D. felt sad too.

"We got the moon. Nothing to worry about." Over the bar a lighted clock showed a scene, the moon shining down on a colored man playing a banjo. The clock had only one hand, set at midnight. I stayed close to be warm. I could have touched his cheek with my lips. In the mirror I watched my lips almost doing it. "You a sweet girl," he said, his breath as sweet as milk, lifting my hair. The dark of the room clung like water all around, held us, molding like current. He brought my wrist up to his mouth, touching the vein. Somewhere I was opening up, somewhere I didn't know. "You better sit down. Are you feeling okay?"

We sat at the bar on stools, our eyes meeting in the mirror while he lit a cigarette, and I couldn't think. I could see what was in the mirror, his eyes when the red coal sparked, the smoke writhing, the eyes of the girl and the boy in the mirror, dim, floating, watching back from the mirror, like phosphorescent creatures in a dark sea.

"Sometimes I think," the boy said, the girl not thinking, just listening. "I think sometimes I got to go away. Get to someplace. Someplace like Africa before it goes away, see the giraffes stepping along the plains, taking

176

in the long view. That place would be maybe a million miles from my worries.''

I had forgotten about Africa. A long way from Virginia. I couldn't know about Africa, rising up in my mind like the whole of the endless black mirror where four little eyes were almost nothing, never knew, never were. He crushed out his cigarette, which had burned down in his hand, turned and brought my face around to look straight and closely into his face, a finger caught in my lip. ''You know. I ain't goin' t'smoke these with you. You don't like them. I believe you fixin' to be sick.''

He led me over to the corner by the jukebox, laid the coat down for me to sit on. That made it like a separate little hotel room where a neon sign flashed outside the window, a hotel where exhausted people came to sleep for a night after they'd been riding buses away from all the places they used to know, the people they used to care about. In such a place you could tell anybody anything, because nobody would know the difference and you'd lost track of who you were supposed to be.

Bobby D. said he was going to go out for us, get something to eat. Maybe a Coke would make me feel better? I couldn't think. I'd forgotten what I liked or didn't like. I tried to smile. I wanted to ask him to stay but didn't know how. He said he'd be gone only a minute.

''Ruthann,'' he said, standing over me, ready to leave but holding back. My own name went through me like a shock. ''Let's stop this. When I come back you start talking to me, tell me who you are, where you live. If we goin' be friends.'' He reached down and stroked along my bangs before he walked across the room, turning at the door in a shaft of light. ''At first you look so dark, I thought you was mad. But when you smile, you the prettiest gal I ever saw.'' The door closed slowly, marking the fall of his footsteps along the bricks of the alley, the absence in our parting.

I left the cap and the glasses on top of the folded coat and got out of there fast as I could, not feeling cold, not remembering. I went a long way along the streets and I was shivering again, but it was an outside cold, not that dry racking shiver that rose like fever and came from a deep-down part not holding up. It was as if I'd died somewhere and didn't know it.

Compliments didn't work with me. He was never going to know my business. All the time pretending he really thought I was from an island, until I almost was believing it myself, playing along. Taking me in and tricking me so that I'd forgotten Nevada said my name. As though anybody would believe him. I guess he'd learn—just because he was smart it didn't mean he knew all there was to know about just any white girl, how to cozy up and get on her good side. I kept going along through the shivery afternoon, glad to have something real, like weather, to complain about. The sun shot fast out of the clouds like a comet traveling on. I'd been tricked and tricked. Bobby wasn't the first to try and get in with me. I asked my way to the highway from black and white along the way, one and the same to me.

Hearing the motor, I knew it was Nevada coming to the rescue, but I didn't give a flicker, just happening to stop and lean against a storefront, bringing out my lipstick. My pale ragged mouth shocked me. Anybody who said that was pretty was sure enough out for something.

"Where have you been? I've been looking all over for you." Wouldn't you like to know? I showed one tooth like a skull and crossbones but he didn't even wince. Then, as suddenly, I snapped the lipstick shut and was on the bike behind him, before he'd even thought to start begging. I like to surprise a man. "If I take the wings of the morning, and dwell in the uttermost parts of the sea."

Nevada gasped, "Ruthann," and nearly overturned again. For a year he'd been pestering; he knows I'd rather smoke a Havana. Before we'd left the curb the vibration sucked me in like I was riding a drill and I laid my head on his back, closing my eyes. One thing I'll say for Nevada, he doesn't smoke. If he did he'd be blowing the stuff in my face until I said I loved it. And he never tells me I'm pretty.

We broke loose from the curb as though from a hitching post, rearing onto a back wheel. I was clinging to

178

him, my head down, when he turned and wahooed. "Durn nigger" came from him in a shout, joyous and humble together as though he'd won something fair and square for the first time in his life. Wrenching back, I saw Bobby D. standing, one foot lifted toward me, arms outstretched, his lip jerking up, lifting for words he couldn't speak, in grief and dismay, as though one time in sight of blue Africa he was on a ship that pulled him fast away. Blue smoke fogged up between us and the bitter taste of metal ran in my mouth. "I'll come back," I whispered against Nevada's shoulder, knowing it couldn't be true, for I'm not like Margy and I know that when once you've seen something sedate and timeless step out upon the plains, in wrappings flaxen and dappled, it's for once and you won't ever have it again.

My backbone was collapsed, maybe severed, but I delivered no protest even when Nevada roared twice past the principal's office, home from ranging the Galaxy on a mean stallion. School was out anyway. When we got to the field behind the shopping center, where there once had been an estate, remnants of its ruined gardens and stone walls still scattered about, I slid from the idling motorcycle, a paving stone for my pillow, turning my face away. Nevada switched off the engine and the silence fell like a lid. Off in the distance life went on at the shopping center. A plane flew by overhead, on its way to the airport. I didn't know if I was cold, didn't know if snow-bearing winds had covered me in drifts. The motorcycle died like a foundered horse. Somewhere behind what I could feel, Nevada moved, the weight of something blanketing me, smelling of skin, its warmth sacred as that of an albino buffalo robe from a fatted calf. He tucked me in like a child into its grave.

"I'm sorry, Ruthann. I'm sorry. I know I'm no good. I wouldn't blame you if you never spoke to me again." One by one I counted the methodical snap of his knuckles to ten. When I was asleep I wouldn't have to care. Next he'd be talking about his "injury," which was how he'd come to refer to his polio, the way he bragged to everybody at school about cattle drives, when his mother had left Reno before he was born.

I couldn't be with Nevada long before I'd begin feeling his leg, from the one time when I'd seen and touched it, hating to but begging, until he rolled back his jeans and showed it, his face stiff, held away. I remember the terrible thinness of it and how it stayed cold. It seemed, too, I could feel some of what he'd gone through when he was little and there hadn't been any medicine for it and the pain was like bones growing backward, twisting and crunching. And how he and his mother had waited for his father to come, tracked to a boardinghouse in Salt Lake and notified. But he didn't.

Nevada was crooning, "You awake, Ruthann. I've always tried to take care of you, you know. Ever since that first time I saw you come into the kindergarten holding your mother's hand." I couldn't remember. Maybe he made it up. Probably she held on to me because she thought I'd run away. Or she already knew she had to be leaving, and I was supposed to hold on to her.

I cried into the ice smell that was the no smell of the cold earth. Nevada said he felt as bad as I did. It hurt even more to have no memories at all. He started rubbing my bones, their stone hearts luminous in the dark, binding me like stays. Grandma used to lie on the bed on top of her pink corset, tying herself into a tidy package with the silk bows. She was the one I remembered, the one I missed last and maybe the most of all.

He lay down beside me, pulled me into his arms and against his damp cheek. I knew he couldn't help himself. "I love you, Ruthann." He pressed up against my leg with his hard legs like braces, starting to move his hand down, his zipper opening, then the warm skin on my leg where it went sliding and sliding, his words running in my ear like water so I wasn't hearing, my head flat on the ground, from below the rushing sound filling me, the tides in the rock swelling beneath, and I was carried on the waves through dark and fire, winds of granite blasting through the earth with a roar that was like the vast herds of Africa sinking to their rest.

180

Sometime it was over. I didn't know. He fell away from me, his eyes shut on their yellow anxiety, his cries subsiding. I didn't want to be around for the "I'm sorry" part, Nevada telling me how we were almost married because we were so close, as good as married. I left him lying under the jacket and didn't look back, going off toward the woods beyond, under the pale moon which rode the darkening sky, making the most of a purple heaven over grass, lime-green, as though it had absorbed the flavor of the moon. For an instant I dreamed a bird flew out of the dark trees, an orange-and-gold parrot moving in a free dance upon the face of the deep, coming to take me for a partner. I stopped and yanked my socks out of my shoes.

The day had not lasted any set length of time but had gone on until it was finished. I started for home. It was too late to visit Dad. He'd have to wait his turn like anybody else. In the hollow of a dead tree, the last safe place in the world, I hid the candy cigarettes. Then I walked on straight through the woods. The year before, a man had killed two schoolgirls who were walking along with their books, their lunches under their noses. He came down on them swiftly with his knife and they, although they were two, had not screamed or struggled. At least, not one sound was heard by the mothers who lived in nearby houses and feared for all children the rest of their days. I was in no hurry, but made myself stand still and say the Lord's Prayer twice through, the little house lights coming on like altar candles, blinking through the trees. Before I let myself walk on. It was dark when I emerged into the lighted pavilion of the shopping center to continue my way home. Amen and amen.

Gloria would be waiting. I had myself put back together and was ready to deny everything I ever knew and be sorry for the rest. A million times I could look blank when she asked about the missing picture of her husband. Finally she will be amazed: I'm the best child she ever knew for not holding a grudge, letting bygones be bygones. Call me a liar; as you will. She will tell me I am beautiful and it will be as though she never raised her .

181

hand to Dad and left him white and shaken. Gleefully, I will call her Mother, tell a joke, dance cheek to cheek to her old Duke Ellington record, and celebrate a hollow victory.

At dinner Dad will be glad to see me looking good. We'll say grace, thank God for our blessings, that we're white and Christian, which can't be said for everyone. Dad will thump me between the shoulder blades for old times' sake—beauty being infinitely desirable until you think you have it. I'll help with the dishes and afterward pour the evening grease into a can we fill for the neighbor's maid, who lives on our charity and is always back for more. Anybody can wave a hand in front of my face, point-blank, and I won't flick a hair.

Here to stay, Gloria will smile around at her wonderful home and family. She cannot imagine how she got here. Somehow I always end up here too, like every time I'm with Nevada and it happens again, I end up crying, telling myself there's nothing I want that money can buy. That I'd rather be dead than stuck with him, while he's thanking his lucky stars we're as good as married, considering how close we are. Wouldn't it be just like me to end up with a cowpoke.

PART III

Everybody Works
but Father

"THIS HERE'S MY FOREMAN. YOU GIRLS WILL CALL him boss. Either that or captain. Men rise to the top—like it or not." Dad liked it, holding me by the ear, eyeballing Ruthann. Her eye close to the mattress was rolling and pitching, where Dad couldn't see. She was snoring. "Your ceaseless complaints will go to him. I want a peaceful day."

"This little shaver." Ruthann's finger bone came poking out of the covers like Hansel's through the bars and flicked my other ear. "I'm calling him 'Tadpole,' that's what." She jabbed my ribs.

"Shut up, you dummy. I'm eight. Dirty neck, dirty neck." I was aiming a kick, but Dad let go of my ear and I hit the dust with my ear hanging low. Margy didn't come up for air and I rolled away under Ruthann's bed.

"Enough poor-white talk. Show some respect for your elders, boy." Dad's pointy brown shoe came poking, giving me the feelies. If I grabbed on, he'd be a goner. I cleared my throat.

"Come out of there. You rowdies are to be up and dressed, on the line with your mops and pails by the time I get back. I'm going to work you till you drop and plead for the iron mills. Hit the deck or I'll hire scabs."

"Yeah, where's the dough?" Ruthann was kicking on the bed over me. Something white was stuck up in her mattress. I wasn't supposed to know. I crawled out of there and up over the side of the bed, the human fly, getting under the covers with Ruthann, knocking in her knees, pinching for side meat.

Then the wild bronco was rearing and we buried down deep when he came speeding from the bathroom with the water glass full and dripping on the sheet, bringing the Chinese water torture. "Grown men break and squeal for mercy," he yelled. I was quaking in my boots laughing. Ruthann snorted and bucked. "Doesn't hurt."

"This is dumb." The ghost sat up in her bed in front of the window, covered in the sheet, except her face.

"Great big sourpuss," Dad said, and all the water splashed in Margy's face. We came out to see the old woman sputter, the big lummox get what she was asking for. One nightgown strap was broken, drooping over the covers like a pink flower, like the flower somebody tossed in Margy's lap when Dad was driving us like crazy. I wished we were riding in the car again and would never be there.

"Insubordination." Dad shrugged and grinned—he couldn't help himself. "You know what you get." His hands smacked his hips, like Margy smacking on her girdle. "About face! Just what are you going to do about it, Blondie?" Dad was marching with his gun. "Talk, talk, talk. I've heard more women talk. 'Oh, that man is so mean.'" He was a sorry sorry man, laughing. My men were climbing over the ramparts, hiding in the ivy outside the window.

Margy was hot under the collar, with a red splotch on her neck. "I don't care, Dad. You turn on the radio sky-high at dawn. You don't care. You think it's funny I'm trying to sleep after I was out working half the night." She wiped her face on the sheet, shaking water like a dog coming out from a swim. I tailed a drop down her neck, where it slipped like a pearl inside her nightie. I went over to be with her. At night Margy's head was at the bottom of the bed, right under the window, everything upside down like taking a rest in China. Dad said Margy had to get her thrills the best way she knew how.

"I warned you not to take that job, sister, but you

wouldn't listen." Dad told Margy everything. Ruthann stood on her knees behind Dad, shaking her finger, three feet tall.

"I told you it would be too much. With all your other responsibilities. I told you to make do with your allowance and babysitting—you never could finish your homework even before you went out to sling hash. You ought to take a lesson from the half-breed." Dad whirled around and aimed a swat at Ruthann and she fell dead on the pillow. "Work your old man for what you want. Get yourself a meal ticket. You won't see her flipping burgers." An airplane was going by and Dad gave a wave out the window to his brother. He would sure be missing us when we crossed over the line to Arlington. With our fancy new address, we'd be the ones not speaking to him. He wouldn't see us again until he saw us in our graves.

Ruthann started singing, " 'The stars at night are big and bright / Deep in the heart of Texas,' " slapping the clapping parts on the bed with her feet. We could hardly hear her over the screaming jet. "Dirty neck, dirty neck," I sang, twisting a fat pinky ring with Margy's strap. Once, Dad and I went to Margy's diner to eat and she was our waitress. I hardly knew her in her white dress with the brown hairnet. Dad called her Miss, and asked if he had to leave her a tip, considering how much she already owed him. On the way out he slipped a quarter under his plate and gave me a nickel for mine, like when we were in church. We stopped in the kitchen to say hi to Jake, who was the cook and Margy's friend. Dad shook his black hand and I saw something flash. Dad said it was his pinky ring. Jake told Margy to wrap up a piece of pie for me to have a midnight snack. I thought maybe sometime I could go back and he'd let me wash the dishes all night long.

Margy was reading again, giving us the cold shoulder. Dad said he couldn't bear to think of the trash she was filling her head with. How cruel it was—the disappointments to come. "I'll be with you in apple-blossom time"; he had me again, scooting me over the floor by my ear, the ring unwinding like a cord. "Cut that racket

187

out, Ruthann,'' he called from the hall. ''Your mother's trying to catch up on her beauty rest. No telling how long it will take.''

In my room he whispered, ''We have to be nice to your mother. The girls don't like her.'' He let go of my ear. ''Now get dressed and stop lollygagging with the milk-maids. Next, they'll have you in a pinafore. And stay out of their beds before you're brought up on a morals charge.'' Dad struck up a smoke. ''Whatever you do, keep your blood pressure down. Don't go near cigarettes. If the women get to you, get out and mow the grass, and if the snow's too deep, carry coals to Newcastle. And stop clearing your throat. Sometimes I think I'm back in the corral, about to saddle up old Seventy-five.'' Dad had his back to me, smoking, his eye out the window. I gave Pete's Sake a sprinkle of goldfish delight. That miserable freeloader was going to eat me out of house and home.

I checked outside: yep, it was still spring, no snow to shovel now. Luther's blind was shut so probably he was still in bed with his dog. Wait till he heard about judo. I checked out the corner too—no car waiting, the guy maybe with some candy. Sometimes I shut my eyes to see if I could make him come and go like The Shadow. When he talked, he slid his mouth sideways, gritting his cigarette. Once he slanted my way, under his baseball cap. ''Hi, bub.'' I couldn't move a muscle.

''You're my best man,'' Dad whispered. ''My under-cover agent. See what the girls are up to, will you? They're in cahoots. A nickel for every piece of hard in-formation you come up with. When it's time for college you'll be glad you saved up.'' He clapped my shoulder to make a man out of me. Next door, Sydney, the grownup girl who was the government worker, came out and got in the car. She slid in, scooping up her legs, and they shone like nets pulled wet from the ocean. We listened to her radio going away. Dad said he wished he had a date for breakfast. Or lunch, or dinner. I'd know someday. ''Now see if you can rout your mother out of bed—tell her it's moving day. The girls have her buffa-loed.'' He gave Mom a rap on the door as he went by. It was time for Pete's Sake to have his meal, and he swam over to say thanks. He was lucky I didn't take him out and shoot him.

Those girls sing and dance. They've got time and time alone. They've got the radio. It's playing and they're whispering. Pete's Sake and I can't hear ourselves think. "Someday the radio will be yours," Dad said. "When the girls are gone. I can stand only one at a time." But how did you get them to go when they had such a deal, free room and board, a weekly allowance? How did you bump them off the gravy train? Dad said they might be on our hands the rest of our days.

I yanked on my T-shirt, zipped my jeans. Then I went into the bathroom to starch my crewcut. Dad said mostly it needed dusting but every day I looked like more of a military man to him. "Perfect the square meal, son, you'll be halfway to West Point. Halfway to the pinnacle of the welfare state." Dad said he was working to get a congressman in his pocket. He had to do something. "If that miserable excuse for a music school goes broke it will be all up to you. No amount of time your mother logs at the bridge table will save me. God knows those weak sisters don't pull their weight." I heaped on the wax Mom found to get rid of my curls. If I could manage to get the girls in a knockdown, drag-out fight, Dad said he'd give me a bonus. In the hall I didn't hear anything but "I'm all shook up." Dad said you knew you were in trouble when your daughters were aching to take up with a sick man.

Mom's door was shut. *Dragnet*: This is the police. Come out with your hands in the air. Under the door the dark caught in my throat. "Who is it?" came the sigh of the wind along the lonesome plains. Margy told me to write another poem like the one for her birthday. She loved it. Dad said, "Over my dead body."

"Mom." The little poet was me.

"Yes. Come in, dear, it's not locked. What are the girls doing? I hear that music they listen to all the time."

Dad's smoke clamped a hand on my shoulder. Anywhere could be a pitfall. Once, Margy came home late from working and Dad was there, standing in the dark hall without a sound—keeping her on her toes. Judging by her nerves, Dad thought maybe he'd overdone it. When he reached out of the dark and put his hands around her neck, she couldn't stop shaking. Dad said she ought to know by now.

"If you ever do that again—" Margy said in the morning, smacking her hands on her hips.

"Yeah? You'll do what!" Dad had his hips in his hands too. Margy just turned away. Dad already knew what Margy could do. Once, she was hitting him and crying and he was laughing. Holding her back. Later he told Mom she probably had her period.

I peeked under Mom's bed. "Hi, Mom, it's me." She couldn't see a thing, wearing the mask. Dad said if I'd loan her my six-shooter he'd be Tonto. Margy didn't believe in guns. "Why should she," Dad said. "She's never had to face up to anything." He couldn't believe Margy—living in that dreamworld. "Anyway, she'll be gone soon to take up her chosen profession."

"Dad." Margy couldn't help laughing when she heard that. "I'm not going to be a waitress forever, you know." Dad didn't know and shook his head. "You look fetching in a hairnet. Tips stay good if you keep smiling. Just hope bunions and varicose veins don't force you into early retirement. College is not for everyone." Margy was in the pitfall, her lip jerking, but she wasn't talking to Dad. He nodded at me. "Let her be a lesson to you, son. Pride cometh before a fall."

Margy was mumbling.

"What's that, girl? Speak up. Revile your old man openly."

"I said I might go to college someday. Pay for it with my own money."

Dad shrugged. "Save up if you like. I'm not laying out that kind of dough on a maybe."

"Have the girls used the bathroom yet? I don't want to be in the way. I've been lying here awake all this time. Listening to your father squealing and prancing. I can't

190

see the point in getting up to stand in line to use the bathroom.'' I don't see Mom when she's in the bathroom. The water runs and runs. Dad says he can't imagine what she's washing—the water bill has gone through the roof. Toilet paper has become a major expense—three women peeing. ''Be glad you're a boy.'' Ruthann bent over and ran next door. She couldn't hold it another minute. Mom said, ''If we had two bathrooms I wouldn't hold anybody up.''

I was on a mission, balancing the end of the bed, gathering information, taking peeks out the window. Maybe the car would be there, the boy leaning forward to the mirror, slicking his hair with a comb. I never knew when. I told Mom, ''Dad says we have to be dressed in time. When he gets back we have to work all day and into next week. Turn this pig's ear into a silk purse.''

Mom said Dad was a funny, funny man. The funniest—making so much over waxing a few floors. As though that was all people looked at when they bought a house. She'd be up soon. She took off the mask and I let go of the window shade. It flew up and snapped the light into my eyes like confetti. Once I saw a ghost; maybe the old mother coming to get me. Margy said it was only the curtain blowing.

Mom's elbow made another mask. ''Hand me my dark glasses, dear. The light scalds my eyes. In a minute I'll fix your breakfast. I'm certainly not one of those women who can't get out of bed with a headache.'' After the car hit the tree, Mom saw two of everything. It wasn't anybody's fault, just the will of God. Dad said maybe that was why she was turning gray so fast, everything coming in by twos.

The Desert Rat was making his move, his whiskers twitching like radar, finding out where this was and that. If anything was moved. In the back of the drawer, the overturned jar buried in pearls. A sock in the closet set on a marble. Some things I wasn't supposed to know. I found Mom's ring when it got lost. She said I was amazing.

Once, Ruthann caught me on the prowl in her room

and pinched the skin on my arm. "Get out of here, you little sneak. And stay out. Can't a person have any privacy?"

"No, you can't," Dad said. "I know I read anything I get my hands on. I wouldn't trust a soul." I showed him the nail slits where she'd pinched me, tiny buttonholes. "That one's mean," he said. "We have to watch her all the time."

Ruthann said that wasn't true. She was as good as anybody else. Nobody gave her a chance. Everybody said she was lazy when she worked as hard as anyone, scrubbed the kitchen floor every week. Dad said she ought to give the same attention to her person. Then she got huffy with Mom. "I'll clean my own room, thank you. Nobody asked you to go in there."

"Your father might read notes, but I certainly wouldn't. I just like to mop the closets and under the beds, Ruthann. You girls leave stuff around. Things can get pushed to the back and get to smelling."

I was grinning like the wise guy who knew what was smelly, but Dad said he was drawing the line right there. If I said anything vulgar, he'd knock me up against the wall. His final word: "Burn everything you don't intend to share." Mom said she and Ruthann would have a private chat someday, just the two of them. Ruthann would understand everything.

I told Mom all the things I was going to eat for breakfast. "Rex King's a dead man." He was my archenemy. Mom called his mom to tell about my colds. Rex shouldn't take my hat and sit on me every time I got a cold. Mom knew a boy who got wet and² didn't live through the night. When she put on the mustard plaster my eyes couldn't help the tears, but that wasn't me. Dad said next it would be lard and turpentine. He was afraid to look out the window. Mostly I was belly-up with some mother's son on top. He'd take Rex himself but the neighbors might talk. "Ask Margy to do it—she's got the brawn."

I'd get Luther to do it and he didn't even need judo. When I left the lawn mower in the middle of the yard and went over to Luther's house, I forgot to come home. Then it was dark and Dad was calling. I went into the dark yard and Dad smacked me up against the fence, ringing it like a bell while nobody talked, Dad shoving me over the grass, giving me kicks in the behind, getting me to the mower. From out of nowhere, Luther was there, standing beside me. With his white face and dark hair, he looked like a man looking up at Dad. We stopped in the yard, and after a long time Dad said, "You want a turn?" His voice was squeaky. Maybe he was trying to laugh.

"No, sir," Luther said, sounding like his father, the Marine. Dad walked away, up the steps and into the house, not looking back, and Luther and I pushed the mower together and finished the yard, side by side, pushing on without saying a word but moving forward and making square turns like we were off to pass inspection. I looked out over the yards as far as I could see and never wanted to be done.

Mom says I have a good build, even if I'm not a tall man yet. Lucky to have broad shoulders and a deep chest. She looks me over good. Probably I'll have a deep voice too. "It better boom like a gong if he's going to save his hide," Dad said. He gave me a dollar to save. "That's one kind of power. Some say the best. Don't tell the girls. They'll be an endless drain if they know the well is flowing. Let them find husbands."

"I'm not going to get married," Margy said.

"Not if you don't wise up, you won't. Learn the ABC's of flattery. 'Poor little me.' Ask your sister—she knows the score. Brünnhilde makes a man feel puny."

The front door opened and then Mom and I heard Ruthann racing down the stairs yelling, "Dad. Wait for me." Making her getaway. We popped up and went speeding to see out Margy's window, Mom putting on her robe because the girls had such a cold room. Margy said, "Hi," flipping the page and turning off the music. I sat on her legs for a free ride.

"You don't have to turn off the radio on my account,

193

Margy. I'm getting used to that music you like." Mom was stretching out her neck to see Ruthann get in the car on the driver's side. Mom knocked on the window, calling Dad, but he didn't answer. Rap, rap. He was getting little rides back and forth to the garage. "It's too bad you can't learn to drive, Margy. I know I could teach you if my eyes didn't see double so much of the time."

"That must be awful, Gloria." Margy looked up from her book with a red face, then off to the sky like she was saying a prayer to the will of God.

"You wouldn't know how awful, Margy." Mom sighed because nobody knew. Then her lips flipped the other way. "But a person has to go on, doesn't she?" In her dark glasses Mom was the Green Hornet, who knew everything first.

Margy shifted on the bed and the springs went tilting like we were in a boat. I was paddling through a mine field dragging Luther to safety. "Probably I'll never learn to drive," Margy said. Dad said he wasn't giving her any more lessons. He was too scared. That telephone pole would live in his dreams—fifty miles an hour in reverse. He almost had his wings. Somebody more daring would have to take over. When I was big I'd drive Margy everywhere, the way Dad used to do. He'd be the one left at the side of the road wondering where his next meal was coming from. Dad told Margy, "You better keep that sweet disposition if you're going to survive on handouts."

Mom rushed out of the room and down the stairs, calling to Dad as the car zoomed away in the nick of time. Margy picked up her book. "You better go down."

I wasn't taking orders. She fitted her book at the end of her stomach, sighting down the barrel. "You're always reading," I said, plopping down on top.

I didn't have to know. Mom's eyes hurt. At the doctor's they put in drops and her stomach flopped inside out. She hoped she wouldn't go blind. I closed my eyes to see how dark that would be. When Mom was coming up the stairs I got up in the dark, edging along the wall into my room, where it was so quiet I heard Pete's Sake swimming. I gave him a snack for good behavior.

Mom was telling Margy on Dad. I didn't have to know. He was waving and Ruthann was driving, both of them laughing. I heard Margy reading. "I guess Ruthann has a secret to tell her daddy. She has a great many these days, don't you think?" I heard Margy nodding. Once Dad was drinking some beer, talking to Mom. "Ruthann better stay away from the booze. She's the type to lose her head and jerk off the football team." Mom frowned at me but I wasn't clearing my throat. Dad had more beer and said he was a damn mean drunk. "Nobody should pay any attention to an old duffer shooting off his mouth." He gave me a tap on the head. When I was a football player I'd wear my pads and helmet and Dad couldn't get through.

"I think she went with him so she could drive," Margy said. She was the one who figured out what everybody was doing, like the house detective. I went in to be with her and rolled somersaults along her body, up and down, slow, so I didn't kick her in the chops. She had her book up to her chin.

"Well, I think it's very nice you and Ruthann can be such good friends these days. I guess you don't feel the way you used to. Remember you said if you knew her at school you wouldn't even speak to her. But it helps when you have a sister to talk to. I never did, you know."

"You're the only one," Mom said when she came to be my mother. Her own real little baby didn't get to be born and her husband was dead in no time. Margy's stomach was gulping and I went posting over the jump.

I went off to my closet to clear my throat before Dad came home. When Dad was a little boy he was locked in the closet until he could be good. Dad told Mom I could put my fingers anywhere I wanted to and leave them there a year and a day. The alternative was the whip and a hair shirt.

Mom was coming out of Margy's room. "I'm hungry," I yelped, and burst out of the closet into a new day.

"Just let me use the bathroom first."

"Do you want me to fix his breakfast, Gloria?" came Margy's voice.

"For heaven sakes, Margy. I guess I can get a meal on the table. I'm not that down-and-out." Mom's bare eye gave me the wink. "You girls." She shook her head, going in the bathroom. The water was running. Once, Margy came out of the shower without her towel. I couldn't forget. If I was a blindman I would have walked right by.

One bite of old man egg and I was up against the wall. Mom paid me dimes until I got it down. If I drank all my milk I could stay up and watch *Playhouse 90*. We got the television so the girls would stay home, but they still go to the neighbors'. "They don't like us." Dad shook his head at Mom and me, sad to say. Mom said it couldn't be true, we were all they had. "Maybe they'll like it better at the new house with the recreation room."

"I voted for the piano," Ruthann said, and folded her arms.

"They never forget." Dad said he and I ought to va-moose. We'd find utopia. Form a eunuch band. Anything so the women couldn't come. Mom said, "You wouldn't have any fun." Dad winked his eyebrows over a pair of snake eyes. "This is fun," he said.

After I ate I gave Mom the slip. Margy was reading on her stomach, like she was getting a suntan. I sat on her butterballs. Margy wanted butter all the time. Dad bought oleo—he wasn't springing for frills. Besides, any difference was in her head. He would prove it with the blindfold test. I took it too. We giggled when the taste was coming on the spoon. It might have been something to poison us. Three times Margy couldn't tell butter. She said she got flustered, like when she was driving the car or taking a test at school. She knew she still liked butter best.

Dad tossed his head back in her face and said she was

a dumb cluck. I climbed up, holding on to her waist with my knees for a spin upside down around the world. Butter would have to come out of Margy's tips, Dad said. Or maybe she could pilfer from the diner, slip those pats in her pocket. Either way she was never going to earn his respect, always fooling herself.

The car wasn't at the corner yet. When that guy raced the motor, I felt it pull as if I was holding on, riding water skis. Luther was playing in the yard with his dog. Sometime, he said, I could come water-skiing with his family. When I yelled hi, he stood still and held up one hand like he was saying the Cub Scout oath. I took Pete's Sake on a stroll around my room, splashing water on my shirt, covering it up with a sweater so Mom wouldn't know.

Once, Rex King pushed me down in the snow to give me a cold pack. After he let me up, I walked home in a sock and was the disgrace that couldn't stop crying. "I'll bring you a little dog to play with," Ruthann whispered. Her eyeballs were hard, as though I could have pressed them with a finger and she wouldn't blink.

The puppy was in a box in the dining room when Mom came home. She couldn't believe the surprise. "Why, Ruthann, I thought you didn't like dogs. You girls say you hate all animals. Like your father."

"I like this one." Ruthann folded her arms. She let me hold it all the time and he crawled up under my shirt. "I love this dog," I told Mom. "It's like the other one."

Mom frowned. "Ruthann, where did you get this dog?"

"Found it." Ruthann told us the story of walking down the street, the puppy coming out of nowhere to follow her. She knocked on some doors, asking, but it was a stranger. She couldn't just leave it crying. Her arms were folded. Mom was afraid it might belong to somebody who was crying now. "I'm naming my dog Belle," I said, and Ruthann approved. Boy or girl, this was Belle. She stood by my side like an Indian who only said, "How."

The next day Belle was gone. Somebody called. "Ruthann took too much on herself. Of course that puppy belonged to somebody. This is worse than no dog at all." I was bawling again.

"I'm not deaf, you know. If you have something to say to me, say it. Just because I gave it to him, you took it away. And that's the durn truth."

"That will do, Ruthann." Dad was there for the rescue. He'd escaped by a hair—he didn't believe in dogs. "All's well that ends well," he said when Pete's Sake arrived the same day, right at feeding time. He was my responsibility and I was supposed to give him one square meal a day but I gave him extra. His thin pale lips were never still.

He was mine, so I could boss somebody too. Those great big girls around. Dad said he'd just as soon swallow Pete's Sake—one of the more valuable things he'd learned in college. Then I could boss him and be a paperboy for fun—earn money to boot. Mom said Boy Scouts were just as good as paperboys, only they didn't have to get up so early in the morning, especially when they got colds and needed their rest. While I was getting my rest, Luther went out every morning in the dark to deliver his papers. Pow! I heard the papers sock up and down the street. Take that and that.

The Desert Rat never slept. When Mom called Margy into her room for a talk, I scooted my paw into Ruthann's mattress and came out with an envelope. Maybe this was the deadly secret. I was behind the couch listening to Ruthann and Brooke when they came home from miniature golf. I wanted to hear them kiss. "Sugar," Brooke said in his deep, low-down voice, "it's hard for me to believe you really love me when you have secrets from me." He got up and was standing over by the door, breathing hard.

"It's only one little thing. Something I promised Margy a long time ago. Something she asked me. Really, Brooke. It's nothing you'd care about. Come back over here, please."

"It's the idea of the thing. But if you want us to be

198

like that, holding things back from each other, I guess that's how it will be. If you'd rather be close to your sister. I wanted to take you by that store this evening, where I saw the rings, but it worries me. Maybe you don't have the same kind of married life in mind that I do. It's almost as though you lied to me, Ruthann. I swear it is. Sometimes I wonder if you really do love me.'' The handle on the screen door squeaked and Ruthann got up, stumbling a little, making a cry.

''No, I don't lie to you. I've told you. You know how that hurts me. You're just like everybody else. I've told you and told you.'' I couldn't believe Ruthann was crying and my throat got all itchy. ''It was a promise, for a long time. About Mother. That's all. I gave her my word.''

Ruthann was making soft noises while Brooke was begging her to trust him, a lullaby rocking us to sleep. ''I can't help it that I love you so much. I know she's against me.'' Then they were kissing. Ugh. Boys hate kisses. Lucky they got out of there and I cleared my throat as the car blasted off, a new red convertible Dad said made you wonder what else Brooke was hiding. Ruthann said he got the one she wanted.

When I heard Margy coming back to her room I tried to fit the envelope into my pocket. She was calling, ''I'll talk to her, Gloria. I know she gives you a hard time,'' rounding the corner and nearly running right over me. ''Watch yourself,'' I said, shoving the envelope under my shirt, pretending to be scratching.

''What are you doing in here?''

''Nothing.'' I was scratching.

''That's a likely story. Well, stay out unless you're invited. You've been told before.'' She gave my cheek a love pinch. Something I hated. She'd been told before, and looking around, I spied her book, grabbing it and racing off to Mom's room, dancing behind her, skidding around the bed, over it. Reading *The Last Days of Pompeii*. Mom was laughing at me trying to read that.

''Pomple, purple, pimple.'' I slid under the bed and through the door. Finally I was clear out in the yard yelling "Pimp" for the neighbors to hear, waving the book. Margy was grounded at the door in her nightie, her hands stabbed on her hips. A plane flew over and I waved to Dad's brother, but Margy didn't laugh, moving away.

Then I knew the car was at the corner, light sparking off the hood, parked at the turnaround. Once, he held something shiny in his hand. I sneaked away while I could get away, goose-stepping into the house like the Desert Rat into his tank. No telling where the secret envelope got to—vanished without a trace. Up in her room Margy was reading again. "Hi, Pimp," I said. She had my *World Book*.

"Give that back. It's mine," I yelled. She held on for a tug of war, until I put her book on the bed and she gave me mine. "Don't you read about anything but war?"

"That's for me to know and you to find out." I gave her the raspberry and went to find Mom. She was dressing, wearing her bra with her gown drifting down from the middle. I was peeking out the side of one eye, the other one casing the joint for the lost letter. "Stop poking in my drawers, Tommy. Although I know you're not the only one who gets in my things. I can tell when they've been moved. Today I'll call Luther's mother about judo." Mom was going to pay for judo with her own money. Then Luther and I could stay pals, maybe ride our bikes to visit, when I was in the new neighborhood. "Don't tell the girls," Dad said. They never had bikes or judo or anything Dad could think of except a hard time. Mom said they wouldn't mind. "And won't they be surprised when you can toss a grown man in the air. Snap a board in half with your bare fist." Mom pulled up her gown to fit on the garter belt, the long straps swinging. Dad said that was the stuff of a young boy's dreams. "But look too long, you turn to stone."

Once Dad told Margy she was stonewalling. He was on a quick visit to her room, standing by the door, smoke curling out the keyhole to me in the hall. He cleared his throat, since he's allowed to. "Frankly, your mother thinks you're too young to go off by yourself to work. She may not be your real mother, which, God knows, you never let her forget, but she does take an interest. And besides, with the move coming up, she needs your help. What's that look supposed to mean?''

"You said I could, Dad. You promised. And Deborah's counting on me. It was my idea in the first place and I wrote the letters and everything. What do you want me to do?''

"I wouldn't mind if you stuck around a while. It means a lot to your mother. Someone for her to talk to. You know she gets lonely, no close friends around here. She's a pretty insecure person, if the truth were known. I'm just asking you to think it over. It doesn't hurt to have one peacemaker in the family.'' When Dad left, I sneaked in to sit on Margy's stomach. The book she was reading was shaking up and down, her eyes staying in one place.

Ruthann came roaring, wheeling Dad home in his buggy. Dad said it was lucky we lived on the Indianapolis Speedway, a hell-driver in the making, although she ought to watch it. The whole family seemed accident-prone. More bad luck: he saluted a plane flying by. He couldn't make a deal to save his soul. In spite of a wax job we might have to give the house away. First he'd advertise at Gallaudet.

We carried the supplies in and Dad sure was glad to have my muscles toting in the waxer he rented at the store. They had doughnuts too, but I was full. Mom said she'd save mine in the buffet where the girls wouldn't know. They were the hungriest girls. Dad asked Mom, "Why the blackout? Hiding behind those goggles nobody knows what you're thinking. You could be packing your six-shooter.'' He tried to raise her dark glasses up for a kiss, but she turned her back. "What'd I do now?'' he begged everybody, brushing his hands together.

When the phone rang, Ruthann and I raced and it fell on the floor. She stepped on my hand. "Don't mess with her,'' Dad said. "I keep telling you.'' He was asking Mom to tell him her troubles, saying he was sorry. "I waved, didn't I, honey? Don't tell me you can't take a little joke?'' He grabbed my ear, warning Ruthann,

"Don't talk all day." She was bending in, whispering. I hissed "Kissy, kiss" as I went by.

We followed close behind Mom on the stairs, aiming at the back of her skirt like a bull's-eye. Dad pretended he had a rubber band. He said he preferred the world before there was a telephone, when a man could keep better track. "And you can hear the worst news too, innocently picking the thing up. Hear you're out of a job. Your wife has flown the coop." Dad's eyes dropped and I gave a blood-brother call, like I was clearing my throat. Without a never-you-mind Mom shut the door to her room.

Dad stepped back, stung by the Green Hornet. Then he sighed and knocked politely. "Honey, you take it easy today. Do whatever it takes, as long as it doesn't cost money." He winked at me. "I have a houseful of kids to do the dirty work. What else are they good for—unless it's to offer a ray of hope." It sounded like Dad was dropping stones in a deep well. He whispered to me, "That's how it's done, son. Sooner or later they come around."

We went in to get Margy started. No kidding about that! She was his number-one helper. Always had been. She'd scrubbed more floors, washed more windows— hanging by her heels. "And for that matter," Dad looked at me, "changed more diapers."

"Change your own diapers," I told Pete's Sake, and gave him food while Dad was talking. If Margy saw fit to stick around he'd see to it that she got into a typing course, evenings at the high school. Shorthand too, although he couldn't read a word she wrote as it was. Too bad she hadn't been more of a student all along so he'd been shamed into sending her to college before he bought a new house. "But you can always hire out as a drudge, I'll say that. You don't quit."

"I don't mind. I like to work."

"I believe you do. And if you didn't have such a lofty tone, I'd pay you the compliment. As it is, I'm simply going to ride herd." I sneaked in for a ride on Margy's back, hanging down into her face to be near the most valuable player.

Dad made me get off and we went to making the fur fly, down on our hands and knees. Dad wanted to see a shine that would bring in buyers off the street, money down—before they went to the basement. He told us to notice the grain of the wood, take pride in our work. Then he went down to see about that shiftless Ruthann. She better keep her grades up and get a scholarship. She didn't amount to a tinker's damn on the line. He gave Mom's door a how-do-you-do as he went by.

They were back in a minute, Ruthann looking like Dad had her by the ear. "I swear if I ever hear you use a word like 'hickey' again, I'll lock you in your room and throw away the key. I thought, supposedly, you were a Christian."

"Dad. For heaven sakes. It was only Priscilla." Ruthann's cheeks were pink, her eyes glittering like sugar over her hand holding her mouth.

"Glad I amuse you, daughter. I may have to keep you home tonight to show you I mean business. Big date or not." I checked at the corner. The boy was taking a snooze, his head back with his cap yanked down. I blinked and he was still there. When Brooke came to wait for Ruthann in the living room, sometimes for hours while she was getting ready, I didn't go in there alone, not even for a Whitman's Sampler. I was afraid to see his long teeth, his lips red as lipstick.

Ruthann's hands made a prayer and her eyes were sorry. "Please, Dad. I won't say it again. I'm sorry." She got down beside Margy with her dust rag spinning. "Okay, Dad?"

"You betcha. Humility, or the semblance thereof, will take you far. What I want to know is what that yo-yo can give you that I can't. Besides the fact that he has more money than I do. You'd think he'd have a clue—I can sniff out a fortune hunter at fifty paces. No matter what you might say about your mother, you can hardly accuse her of that. But Brooke seems a little square, if you don't mind my saying so. How old is he anyway? Twenty-nine, thirty. Robbing the cradle.''

The girls were laughing and scrubbing. Dad sent me up and down to be the gopher while he took his turn with the whip, settling back against the wall. Ruthann said Brooke wasn't an old man yet.

"Careful," Dad warned. "You're on sensitive ground. Maybe he's just naturally a bit on the prissy side."

"He's religious, Dad. That's all." Ruthann put on her glasses and carrying the Bible went limping out the door with a weary load. The overseer snapped her with the whip, a nylon stocking. Sometimes he wore it over his face to be a burglar. He said Brooke looked to him like he'd already been double-yoked, his eyes lost in so much bone and hair. The girls were laughing. "Any malingering, I'll sell you down the river. Then you sisters will weep and moan. So, what are the young man's intentions, now he's ordained? Pretty soon he ought to be speaking to your pappy. Unless a rich man just helps himself.''

"Dad." Ruthann looked down at the floor and bit her lip. "I told you, he's looking around for a parish. New Orleans, Mobile. And he's not really rich. Just some money from his grandfather, for school mostly. Can we have some new rags?" Ruthann's was full of hairs and dirt, with a bobby pin stuck in there.

Dad whistled, handing out rags. "Those dens of iniquity. Must be the moth to the flame. He'll find worse than a few books in the library to tickle his gonads.'' Brooke told Ruthann not to read any books unless she cleared them with him first, to be sure they were Christian. One day, out in the trash barrel, we burned her love comics so Brooke wouldn't find out. Margy wasn't supposed to know.

"Everybody works but Father," Dad sang. "I'm a song-and-dance man. What a pity, I've offended my daughters. 'Gonad' is a perfectly good word. Look it up." Margy and Ruthann kept working and frowning.

"Now"—Dad winked at me—"what I'd like to know is why Brooke doesn't lasso somebody for your sister.

Why should she languish on a Saturday night? Maybe a nice Jewish boy would haul her out of the deep freeze. I imagine that search-for-the-meaning-of-life crap would fly right out the window. Or''—Dad was tying the whip into a bow on top of his head—''maybe a big black buck.''

Margy slammed down her rag and stomped out of the room. As she went by, Dad ducked, in case she knocked him one. ''Ho-hum,'' he said. ''I guess I've gone and done it. Alienated my chief cook and bottle washer. What's the scoop on those two anyway? Your sister seems mighty eager to get to work every night.''

The Christian was making wide, sad eyes, looking up and down. ''Nothing, Dad. They're friends. Jake's nice to her. He says she's smart and that she ought to be going to college.''

''Flattery will get you anywhere. He'll have her in the broom closet and she'll think they're riding on the underground railroad.'' Dad settled back, clasping his hands behind his head. ''Why don't you clue her in? You're in the know, aren't you?'' Ruthann twisted her rag, staring down. ''Answer me. You don't think I fall for that 'I've been saved' routine.'' He slammed the bow in her face and I rolled under the bed.

''Dad. You make everything dirty.'' The runt of the litter put a piece of dust in his mouth. Dad stood up, tucking in his shirt. ''Why, damn it, girl. It is. That's what I keep trying to tell you. I try to be a father to my daughters. What do I get for my efforts—stonewalling. I'm going down. Strike up a fag, lick my wounds.''

When he left Ruthann rested on the bed. On top of me the springs were rocking and creaking, like a hammock. Pretty soon Margy was back and shut the door. She had the radiator brush and sat down with her back to us, zinging the pipes. ''Why do I ever say a word to him? Ever. Why, why, why,'' playing the organ. Ruthann sat up, the springs bearing down on me like the coffin of nails. I poked a finger in the mattress hole and something was up there, maybe the letter back again. Elementary, my dear Watson.

"I think I hear him blabbing to her right now. Blab, blab, blab. Every little word. He could never keep a single thing to himself if his life depended on it."

"What did Dad mean about Brooke speaking to him?" Margy was scratching a red place on her neck, using her shoulder bone. "I don't know why you can't just tell me right out. One day you like him, the next you don't. I don't know what's going on."

"I never said I didn't like him." Ruthann was sitting up, about to squish me. "Brooke says you don't like him."

"That's not exactly true. I don't like some of the things he does. Making you wash makeup off, and stuff. Not letting you get a Toni. I don't like that." Margy was using her wrist for a head scratcher, her hands coated with dust.

Ruthann flopped down, kicking on the bed. "I can't please everybody, you know. This place is enough to make me want to run out the door and never come back. I wish everybody would just let me alone." My throat was closing down.

"Leprosy. My God, I've got leprosy. There goes my eyeball, right into my highball." I burst out with "Jealousy" at the top of my lungs.

"You little rat." Ruthann was coming after me headfirst and I squiggled out, making for the door. "Jerk off the football team," I yelped as I was leaving.

The door slammed, then opened. "You have a filthy mouth, boy." It slammed. "Missed me, missed me." I went in my room and fell in the closet. On second thought, stupid old Pete's Sake came too. The day might come when we'd both be blind from too much time in the dark.

"Psst, psst." The girls were calling. I put my fingers in my ears to see if it was a dream. Along came Ruthann with her finger moving like a magic wand. The Desert Rat stood by the door, in case.

"We want to be friends," Ruthann said. The girls were sitting on their beds, facing each other, knee to knee, like they were wading in a little stream. Ruthann pulled me to sit beside her and I went sinking into the soft mattress. The radio was murmuring low like the wind in the willows.

"Tommy, we want you to do us a favor. Find something Dad has that belongs to us. He took it and we want you to get it. Then we'll really be your friends and you can come in anytime you want to. Sit in here, listen to the radio, and be cozy. Have a drink of tea. It's partly yours too." It was the way it was when we had the dog and Ruthann let me hold it. Like I was hearing a story from before when the other mother was here and put me to bed in a basket by the river, and Margy took care of me.

"Promise you won't tell. On the Bible." Ruthann held out hers that was a gift when she became a Christian, white with a gold cross. Mom said Ruthann always was a Christian, only she liked to get extra attention, making a fuss. I put my hand on it and got a tingle when I said I wouldn't tell. My other fingers were crossed behind my back.

"It's a thin, tiny book. Dark blue with numbers in it. And our names. Do you know where it is?" The little stream was bubbling. I was nodding my head, drifting and dreaming.

"You do? That's terrific. Can you get it?" The Desert Rat came sniffing out of his hole, scratching his belly. The radio was brown with a plaid window. "I want it sometimes. For in my room."

"Why sure. That's what friends are for." Ruthann's curvy lips puckered my cheek and I wiped it off, a little. "Okay. Mum's the word." The bed was jiggling, Ruthann's foot tap-tapping. I was nodding to sleep in the sun, floating along.

Margy got back to cleaning the radiator. "I don't want you to get in any trouble, Tommy. So maybe if you'd just tell us when the coast is clear, one of us could go get it. We'll still be friends."

"Margy, you're going back on what we said. He won't get in any trouble. Dad had no right to take it." Ruthann's arms were folded. "Mother gave it to us."

The other mother gave the girls everything. Sometimes Margy showed me her little picture, which she kept in her Bible. When it made me cry, Dad yelled at her and called her a tearjerker. The past was past. Mom had to read to me a long time, holding me in her arm, Mole and Ratty having adventures. Mom said I could take judo with Luther, be a Boy Scout. Go on fishing trips to the Smoky Mountains with Luther's fine military family. His father was a decorated hero, like her father, and they were Christian too. Even though she would miss me very much, Mom wanted me to have the best times in the world so I wouldn't ever feel left out. I was such a sap, I didn't know what I'd burn first: the little picture or *The Wind in the Willows*.

"Is everybody happy?" Dad came back to let bygones be bygones. We had to work and work—no rest for the weary. He separated the girls so they wouldn't have secrets and gang up on us poor men. In my room Ruthann whispered, "What did Dad say about the football team?" When I told her, she lay down on my bed with the pillow over her head until Dad came and she hopped to it. She was working so hard, Dad said he was tempted to re-evaluate her character. Maybe she would do more than snag a rich husband. "Albert Schweitzer better watch out or he'll have a beauty queen to add to his miseries." Ruthann didn't talk back. Dad said she was rising in his estimation, moment by moment. "Now if we can wipe that smirk off your puss."

The old wax came off with the petroleum cleaner and Dad had to hold his poor head out the window to smoke so we wouldn't vaporize in the fumes. Next it would be time to lay on the wax, and last came the shine. Dad said he was proud and hoped we'd find a way to please him forever so he could always put a roof over our heads. The girls were going to have to swear to forgive him for all slights, real and imaginary, before he'd let them get away.

"Lunch is ready," Mom called. Dad checked his watch: one-thirty. "I'll give you an hour." He barred the stairs with his body. "I mean it, girls."

"We forgive you, Dad," they said. Dad made Ruthann say it twice because of the supercilious expression on her face. "The queen herself would have trouble passing muster with these two." He passed out Vaseline for our itchy, stingy hands. "Don't thank me. It's in the budget."

"The girls are laughing," I told Mom. She said girls were like that, always whispering. They didn't care whose feelings were hurt. Well, other people could have secrets too—which reminded me of mine. "The Case of the Purloined Letter."

The sandwiches were set on the table and Mom was in the basement doing some wash. Dad called her and she said to go ahead without her. She wasn't hungry. After two bites Dad said he couldn't do it. He was altogether too sensitive a man, appearances notwithstanding, to ignore hurt feelings. Gloom hung like fog. He'd have to go down and see what he could do with Mom. Maybe they'd picnic on the dryer—heaven knows it had cost enough to do double duty. He went toward the basement stairs on tiptoe, his two hands out before him like the strangler, giving us the wink as he rounded the corner. The girls looked at each other, pressing their mouths. We started passing jam and eating out of the jar. Ruthann said Mom would never know the difference—even the kitchen dick couldn't smell germs.

Margy got up and turned on the radio in the living room. The announcer called everybody Daddy-o, and was in a good mood, playing fast songs while we chewed faster, tipped back in our chairs, blowing bubbles in our milk. "I love this one." Ruthann jumped up to dance, whirling around the table in a blur, passing into the living room, then coming back, begging Margy to be her partner. Margy laughed and said she couldn't dance. "I'm too fat."

"You are not." Ruthann dragged Margy up and I landed in the middle. "I'm the man." Ruthann said she hadn't danced in ages and was never going to stop. Brooke didn't believe in dancing, except the two-step. We were jiving and twirling, slip-sliding on the bare floor. Margy started to pound boogie-woogie on the table, so I did too, tapping on the pedals. Ruthann was breathing heavy on a saxophone she grabbed out of the air, waving it up and down, bending low. Dancing and singing along. "Good golly, Miss Molly. Sure like to ball. When yo' rockin' an' a-rollin', Can't hear yo' momma call."

Dad came by, shuffling, shaking his poor old head. "I don't know if I'd call it music, but it sure gives you a charge. That bozo's larynx seems in the final stages of hopscotch. Whatever happened to Nelson Eddy?" Ruthann chased him down, taking his hands. "Hi-ho, Doctor Daddy-o." She got him spinning, shuffling his feet, pumping his arms. I jumped off the couch. "When yo' rockin' an' rollin' / Can't hear yo' momma call."

Mom came looking. She fitted herself in the middle between Ruthann and Dad and they stopped dancing. Margy sat down at the table and I rolled under. Somebody's gum was hung in the rafters.

Mom stamped her foot and was about to walk on Dad's toes. I saw Margy sneaking out the door. "You won't ever dance with me, Francis. You say you don't know how." Mom was stamping again.

"Miss Molly" ended. "For heaven sakes"—Ruthann's voice was screechy in the quiet—"can't you let us do anything," going to follow Margy upstairs, but Dad got her by the elbow. "Keep a civil tongue in your head. Apologize to your mother." Another man was singing soft and low.

"You should talk," Ruthann muttered. "Mother, I'm sorry. Now may I go?" Her big toe was sticking out of the top of her tennis shoe. Dad said it wasn't his fault she wasted her money on idle pleasures, wouldn't babysit and save up for necessities. Ruthann said she got too scared, staying alone in different houses late at night. Dad said she'd have to find a way.

When she was gone Dad said, "We can't dance to that racket, Gloria. We're not spry enough."

"Why, I've danced all my life. I used to go everywhere. I was the last to leave. Though I doubt Brooke would want Ruthann acting that way.'' Dad was trudging, going upstairs to get the troops under way. Mom stopped talking, smiling to herself. Upstairs the waxer started humming, tuning the whole house for a song and a sleep. When I came to, Ruthann was coming by the table. ''Mother, can I talk to you about something? In private. And really, I am sorry.''

''Of course you may. And I have something to talk with you about too, Ruthann,'' Mom said. ''Let's go in here where we can be alone.'' They went in the kitchen and the door swung back and forth until it was quiet. When I got my arm stuck in there, Margy was pushing the wrong way to get me out and Dad had to knock her down.

''Tommy told me about what Dad said. I hate him.'' Ruthann was crying again. The little squealer went out to sit on the porch. The car was at the corner, the boy sitting sideways, unwrapping a piece of something. It was like the two of us were pals, sitting around together. When he lifted up his arm, mine went up too. When he dropped the wrapper in the street, I let a piece of grass fall. I jiggled when he did. Once, after he'd gone, I went over to see. I didn't have to go with him even for butterscotch. When Dad caught up with me I'd be dead meat.

Ruthann came out the door behind me, her eyes open but not seeing anything, not even me. I was going to say, ''Watch yourself girl,'' but she looked like a ghost that didn't hear, floating down the steps and over the grass, walking faster when she got to the curb. By the time she was at the corner she was nearly running, and when the car started she jumped straight up like she hadn't seen it before. Turning back toward the house, her mouth opened until it was breaking, not making a sound. Then she ran on and hopped in the car. It took off like that guy knew what he was waiting for. I listened to the tires skidding around three more corners and then it was gone. It was either him or me.

''What in the world was that?'' I jumped when Dad came out of the shadow behind the screen. He sat beside me while I was hugging my arms. ''You've got the birthright free and clear, son. Use it wisely and you'll make a bundle, I know you're nervous." He put his hand on my knee like it was a shoulder. "And frankly, as the middleman, I don't blame you. But if you don't stop fluttering your uvula, I'll have one of those sisters buss you. Then God knows how you'll turn out." I got away for a trip around the house. Someone might think they heard growling.

Mom came out wearing a sun hat to shade her eyes. She sighed. "I don't hear the girls. I wonder what they're doing."

Dad winked at me, giving her a pat. "You wouldn't want to know. It would be too shocking. How's your head, honey?" He drew her close in a hug while I was poking a stick into a flower's heart where Dad couldn't see.

"I'm not as easily shocked as you think, Francis. I took some aspirin and I'll be fine. Why make a fuss when it hurts pretty much all the time anyway? I want to take my turn with the waxer and help out the way I always do." Mom was tickling the back of my neck with her fingers where the hair was shaved to the bone.

"Thank God, I'm not as alone as I thought. Boy, go upstairs and see what powerful Katrinka is up to. Besides nursing a grudge. I hardly blame her. Her sister's got the glasses, the driver's license, the figure. Beaux lined up at the curb." He winked at me. "Ask her what she's got." Dad told Mom he pretty much regretted everything he'd ever done. Except marry her. She batted her eyes at him. "I think you like to hear yourself talk."

Margy was lying on her bed, staring out the window. I rolled under Ruthann's, stuck my paw in the mattress hole, and came out with a plum. The little blue book. Now where did that come from?

I held it up for Margy to see, between the beds, bopping it back and forth. She took it and then her head came down until she was standing on it with her eyes getting bloody, looking at me like I did something. "She told me Dad took it. Liar." She bounced back up to lie down. "She had it all the time."

212

"Yeah," I breathed. "Liar." We were quiet.

"Let's get this show on the road," Dad called up the stairs.

Margy sat up, brushing her hair with her fingers. "I'm going to hurry up and finish before it's time to get ready for work. Here. Stick it back up there for now. I'll talk to her later. Where'd she go anyhow?"

"It's mine too?" I said.

"We'll talk about it later, okay? Right now I'm too mad." When Margy came out of the bathroom with her shiny face and rainy hair, I was giving Pete's Sake his snack.

"You feed him too much, Tommy. He's going to get sick." I kept on pouring the box until it was empty. Then I slammed the door in her face.

In a second Margy knocked and handed me a cup with a spoon. I could see sugar in the bottom from her tea. It smelled like perfume. She had the waxer by the throat and gave me a wave as she went down the stairs, the way she waved from the corner on her way to work, looking for me in the window, so it was like I was going along with her. When the waxer started in, I scooped out the extra food while Pete's Sake went swimming for dear life.

I tiptoed into the girls' room and slipped the book from its hole. Even though my name wasn't in it, finders keepers. Sometimes, when Dad didn't know anybody was there, he looked so sad I thought we were riding the hills again, looking for his grave. It seemed nothing would cheer him up but a dollar in his pocket. While I was at it, I dug around and came up with a little green ring and a snapshot. When I saw the man was a soldier, I clicked my feet together and returned his salute: "Aye, aye, sir." I took the radio too and headed for my closet, where I fixed a place for everything. I shut the door and turned up the music, but then I had to go back out for a dumb fish. When the girls came waltzing back, banging and pounding, saying what was what and yelling for their rights, the little squealer wouldn't have to hear a word about it. They could take it up with Dad. I thought maybe

213

that was the end, but I had to keep making quick checks at the corner in case somebody was waiting or waving. Then I heard a fast horse galloping, but it must have been the ghost horse, Seventy-five. When I was grown up I was going to be a pilot like Dad's brother. Then everybody would be watching for me.

Weak Sisters

"YOU WOULDN'T KNOW, MARGY. YOU JUST
wouldn't." Weary as I was with it all, I had to
smile, that smooth round face furrowed, as though a million wrinkles could make her as smart as she thinks she
is. Wait until her husband said he didn't love her anymore, or raced off to the store to be alone with his daughter. She'd do more than drop her eyes. But I knew she
meant to sympathize and I told her I appreciated it. But
how could she have the least idea; I mean, a young girl
with her life before her. When her time came she'd have
more than a case of hives.

Francis wouldn't care what I told her. "Go ahead. Say
what you will. It doesn't matter what she thinks of me—
if it makes you happy." Big talk. What if I told her he'd
robbed a bank or was a queer? Much as I needed someone to confide in, it hardly seemed Margy was the right
person. Once, she asked, "Do you think it would help if
you went away for a while, Gloria? Sort of a trial sepa-
ration to see if you feel any better." As though I was an
unwed mother. As though life was that simple. When she
was afraid to make eyes at a fellow and couldn't learn to
drive a car to save her soul. There was a welt raised up
on her throat right then, but she'd rather scratch herself
raw than speak her mind. As though I might do something terrible to her. I'm not exactly a wild animal; in
fact, I never harmed anyone in my life that I know of.

And what did I get out of her. A simple question: "Is
Ruthann getting her diamond?" Suddenly her nose is in

a book. As though her sister wasn't leading her around by the nose—like everybody else. Probably I'd be the last to know, or they'd like it that way, and it annoyed me enough to remind Margy, "Seems to me once upon a time you kind of liked Brooke—a little bit." She read all the harder and I knew I'd hit home. But I didn't want her to stay mad, for really I did think she was a very sweet girl and couldn't help being shy and insecure, so I confided in her, telling her that after I had lunch with the president's wife he'd called Francis into his office, saying he was recommending him for a good raise, mentioning how highly his wife thought of me. Those things matter. I know the girls resent my clothes and probably the new house too. But they wouldn't if they thought about their daddy's future. Any man wants to be important in his community, invited to join Rotary and that sort of thing. I slipped in a compliment for Margy too. "You've got the most lovely hair. So glossy." She could tell I wanted to be her friend, especially since she'd never let me be a mother to her. Compliments never hurt. When I wanted to know what Ruthann told her father, I'd ask. Francis doesn't believe in secrets.

A little later I walked into my room and found the envelope lying on the floor by the bed. I picked it up, although I feared it was God's judgment, the note or some proof that would expose my husband, and my hand faltered so the paper ripped as I opened it. Although it had been years, if I saw Dolly's handwriting I'd know it as positively as a sample of Palmer cursive.

When I held the snapshot, slick and cool, it appeared to jump in my hand like a live thing, until I realized I was the one who was shaking. There was almost a sensation that it was wet. It took all my control, clutching the bedpost, to lower myself to the mattress, certain I was having one of my spells. Trembling all that time I realized, when at last I was able to lean back against the wall, when the murmuring I'd thought was blood pouring through my head turned out to be the bedsprings gradually subsiding, sinking to rest under me, lending me support. Although I couldn't help remembering that Phoebe had once slept in that bed. Sometimes I'd wondered if she spent her nights staring at a wall. Later I would call Dr. Wilkie back home and tell him I needed some more sleeping medication. He always helped me, for he understood the troubles I'd had.

From the beginning I'd warned Francis about our bed. I knew the kids would hear us and think awful things, the jiggling like a drum tattoo across a jungle. Especially on a Sunday afternoon—crestfallen when we left them behind, they were soon on tiptoe and breathing in the hall outside the door. As though they could imagine; the girls no doubt smirking as if they could and Tommy just following along, trying to fit in. I found a key for the door, only to have Ruthann inform me her parents had never locked their bedroom. True enough, since usually they were all together in one room; when they weren't divided by different cities. Probably both girls thought I ought to live the same nomad life their mother did, with a piano instead of a couch. Margy would have it all turned upside down, making it romantic to live over a railroad yard. It didn't seem a bit odd to me that I would want my privacy, no matter what they thought they had coming.

What the kids thought didn't inhibit Francis. He was on his honeymoon, wanted his wife, and that was that; grabbing me with the turn of the key. "Now, you said you were taking a nap." I'd pretend to be cold and pull away, watching him tense. Before my hand found him. It made me smile. If the day ever came when he didn't want me, I knew it wouldn't be that I'd given him cause. I didn't have another man and I would never have to feign a headache, one that was real enough pounding with no urging. But it calmed with a nod from Francis, that gleam in his eye. All those long times we were together in the room, the rest of the world locked out, my heart, mad with excitement, was in the palm of his hand; as though under siege we had only that little time to hold each other before the enemy broke through.

It gave Francis a charge too, he said. Almost like the good old days in the rumble seat, the moonlight atomized on his pale and striving behind, at any second the police or some outraged father giving voice like a pack of hounds. He thought I wouldn't know about such things, but just because I'm not a poet doesn't mean I've spent my whole life in the Sunday school. Just because Dad was a preacher didn't mean he didn't drive a fast car and like to hunt. Didn't know what it was to protect a daughter. There wasn't any sound more anxious and needy than a pack running the woods at dawn, that hoarse cry. It would come back to me, boil in Francis's whispers, merge with the working springs to blot out all the petty hindrances, until it seemed I was one in desire with those shameless girls, moving to his hand their secret and dripping thighs, moving under him like current, tumbling like ruins. Until we sprang, smothering our cries in the bedsheets.

I wouldn't know all that went through my head in the time I rested on the bed with that picture in my hand. My blood seemed alternately to freeze and vaporize. I recalled Dr. Miles teaching us in school. Just a backward country school, but I don't suppose anyone ever had more fire. "Howl, howl, howl, howl! O! You are men of stones!/Had I your tongues and eyes, I'd use them so/That heaven's vaults/should crack." It hadn't been anything for Rosalie and me to leave class white as paper, tears streaming, best friends in each other's arms. I made the mistake of repeating that to the girls; their smiles flickered behind the dark of their eyes like a movie reel while they went on to posture that Shakespeare was boring and old-fashioned. They knew I'd taken parts in some local theater back home too—how dreary. I let them dig in their heels. The day would come—they'd express themselves in the wrong circles.

The picture of Ruthann soaked up my headache like a sponge. I forgot all about aching sinuses and a sleepless night, grateful to be alone in my room so I could think clearly and decide what to do. Where had it come from? What was its meaning? I just knew it was providential that it had fallen into my hands; although I wasn't exactly a diplomat you could have stuck what the rest of them knew about life in a thimble. All rush and show. Regardless how much they might have to say.

The car, back home from the hardware store, got me on my feet. Suddenly the house was alive, Francis braying, "Is everybody happy?" It was a wonder Colonel Lewis at the corner didn't salute and run up the flag. I reached quickly into my bra and hid the picture. Not long ago it wouldn't have been safe there for five minutes, Francis at me the second the kids turned around. Given any time at all he'd have my underclothes unfastened, my breasts hanging free for his hands and mouth. We'd ended up by the washing machine more than once and I hadn't known if the musky smell was the two of us or the dirty sheets piled at our feet. If I heard the dryer tumbling or the kids pounding the stairs. He denied it, but I knew some little tramp had taken his eye, was giving him a tumble. When I got to her I'd tear her hair out, expose her for the whore she was. Every pocket might hold some clue. I called the office at all hours, putting up with his fanciful secretary: "The king is in the counting house"; her attempt at levity, presumably, but I wasn't in any mood.

When I confronted Francis with my suspicions, he snorted. Yawned in my face and said he couldn't help it. He was slowing down. Getting to be an old man. Old at forty-one. Hardly—a man like Francis, married only four years. He had been spry enough to walk off from the country-club dance with Dolly last time we were back home. Disappearing for more than an hour while I endured the painful whispers of everyone who'd ever known how she'd treated me. Since then I'd turned down any suggestions from Francis that we drive down to see Mother. As if I'd throw them together. He denied there was anything to it; they'd just walked along the river and talked, according to him. What would the two of them have to talk about? They didn't even know each other.

Ruthann and her father racing off in the car was now a distant memory, more pathetic than stinging. Neither one of them with the peaks combed out of their hair from the night before—what a pair of birds, doing business at

219

the hardware store. Francis would have laughed out the other side of his mouth if he had a clue. Mr. Know-it-all. Imagining the worst would be one of his precious daughters dodging some work or out on a date past midnight. When that picture had been taken in broad daylight. Ruthann lured him away to confide some worthless secret. Lulled him to sleep. Probably he wouldn't smell a rat until he heard its mew in the upstairs bedroom.

Seemed to me I'd always known what was going on, which girls were and which weren't. The fellows were dying to tell, after they'd get excited, kissing and hugging me. They'd confide whatever I asked, hoping I guess. Some of them would have jumped off a roof. To make a gesture—not because I'd ever give them what they were after. They knew who my daddy was. After some of their tales, we'd get to giggling and couldn't get stopped. Just the thought of somebody like that stuck-up Selma Grimes locked out of the car without a stitch on made me want to scream.

It was my family that kept me from going wild, and I'd told Francis the home had to set an example. You couldn't expect a girl to hold back out of thin air, and it was no secret what Francis thought of the trash he'd used. My own dad wouldn't allow a deck of cards in our house and on Sundays I'd had to sneak off to go anywhere but church. My whole life, all he'd had to do was look at me sternly, as though I'd disappointed him, and I'd want to die, I'd feel so wicked. If Francis was going to cheat and play around, what could he expect of his daughters? What was I to do? I'd threatened to tell them what I thought he was up to.

"Go ahead and tell," he blustered. "Since you're aching to. If I don't like what you say or I think it's unworthy of me, I'll call you a liar. See who they believe."

There were times I thought I couldn't stand it anymore; on top of everything, Francis taking sides with Ruthann. Struggling to manage on the little bit of money Francis made, doing without so many nice things other women had. Then putting up with the noise of jets from the airport, trying not to mind. Not that those things

220

would have mattered, if our marriage was all it should be. That snobbish bunch at the women's club wouldn't have gotten to me with their Arlington addresses, their private women's colleges and colored maids, not if I'd had something appreciative to go home to. And I only joined in the first place because some of the faculty wives at the conservatory belonged and I knew those contacts would help Francis get his raises and extra recognition. Once, I told him I was leaving.

"I wondered what it would take" was his reply to that. My suitcase was packed, but then I didn't want to give him the satisfaction, not if my head split in two. "Maybe you don't want me," I said. "Or the girls, for that matter. But I have a son." My chin was up. Later he begged me to forgive him—he didn't know what got into him sometimes. To treat me so coldly, to forget all I'd done for him and his children. I wouldn't ever turn down someone who needed me so much. I've always had a very soft heart.

From the time we started our life together, Francis told me not to interfere with the girls. He'd handle them and I could devote myself to Tommy. Back home, when I'd taught in the Sunday school, I'd gotten on with boys, but I'd never understood what girls were up to.

"What's to understand? All you need is the temerity to face them down." That was Francis, jingling change to conceal an empty wallet. I wanted to answer back, "Maybe they could use something more substantial than smart talk," but I'd let him discover that for himself. His eyes would open up. But the thought of Francis face to face with that picture made me weak all over. I didn't know what he might do to her. I'd always told him I couldn't stand it if he hit the children. I'd walk out. And for Ruthann to be seen like that by her father; it would be unnatural, something unfilial.

The picture shielding my heart, I walked into the kitchen and stood among them while they leapt and scavenged at the bag of doughnuts, spoiling any appetite I might have had. "Save me a jelly," Margy yelled from

221

the stairs while Ruthann snatched and bit one, her eye-tooth snaggled raspberry. I'd told them how that snapping and swallowing whole went down with the fellows, and as an example, I ate my meals slowly, one hand in my lap, pressing the napkin to my lips: inciting them further as far as I could see. Someday I'd like to be a fly on the wall; one of them would guzzle from a fingerbowl or knock over a glass of iced tea—send her admirer running. More than one fellow had told me he dropped a girl because of a disgusting habit and I'd seen my daddy leave the table without paying if the waitress served him a hair. Even though Francis had always told the girls he would never pay for their weddings, it was clear Ruthann would be angling for a white dress and all the trimmings. So she could parade around and feel important. It seemed ludicrous, considering. She had a great deal to learn about the behavior proper to a wife, the inner purity that needed no veil.

"Cat got your tongue, honey?" Francis asked—although how would he notice in that cacophony, arguing with Ruthann about what time she had to be home that night. Probably he felt guilty too, about running off, but I had my own thoughts and told Tommy I'd call about his judo that very day. He was such a patient little boy and so loving, his eyes sparkling when everybody else was laughing, joining in whether or not he knew the joke. Just to be part of things. I'd told Francis not to worry about him. He'd stop that nervous habit of throat-clearing when he grew up some. Any child would feel nervous after all he'd been through. Who wouldn't be anxious, so many large noisy people demanding their own way?

"I'm a mother," I'd said to Francis more than once, and his eyes widened, dark with feeling when he hugged me. He remembered what I'd done for him, I guess, the sacrifices he'd asked me to make. When he was alone and had no one else to turn to. He had vowed he would thank me all his days. I didn't have to ask Francis, "Why did you marry me?" We both knew, but then that wasn't so different from most people. Wasn't it a normal thing

222

for people to fall in love and want to raise a family together? It had to be more than a thrill.

Ruthann was casting her sultry glances to the four winds, seeing whom she could rile. For once, someone she dismissed as beneath notice could have given her a taste of her own medicine, and when her gaze intersected mine, I smiled and fluttered my eyelashes. She resented it. "Pardon me for breathing." But I was tired of her lording it over everybody. If she knew somebody was onto her, maybe she'd stop pinching Tommy. She defended herself, said he'd kicked her. That little shoe. I'd told Francis she was mean to Tommy and he couldn't deny it. "She's always been that way," he declared, nodding his head in the affirmative, as though they'd formed a club.

Next a private little chuckle pealed out of me and they all looked startled. They thought they had a monopoly on a joke. Francis scratched his head. "What'd I do now?" The center of the universe. After that I frowned— see what Holmes made of that. "When Fortune means to men most good, / She looks upon them with a threatening eye." Naturally I kept that to myself. If I quoted Shakespeare they'd only think they could do better.

Throughout the day I retreated to my room, locking the door, and took out the picture, the only way I could be certain I hadn't dreamed it up. Once, Francis came and pounded on the door. "Do you have someone in there?" I had to laugh, about as excited as if I did. Since the car accident when I hit my head, my neck half frozen, eyes crossed, stomach on fire—I'd thought I couldn't be any more confused. But that picture had done something to me and it seemed that any time, like my cousin Helen, I'd find myself out in a tree with a bird's nest on my head, begging everybody in sight to arrest my husband. Although over at the county home it turned out she didn't even have her name on the deed to her house and I'd never be that stupid. But I did hope that the move to a new house, one I'd chosen and helped pay for with some money from Mother, would make me feel more like my old self again. Certainly Francis was grateful to me for my help. He could never have afforded it on his own.

223

Gradually the room Ruthann was sitting in became clearer to me, familiar in detail, as though I'd been there: the slope to the ceiling, a shell pattern on the faded wallpaper, one glass pane repaired with cardboard and tape, and on the wall a black-and-white photograph of a naked woman. Sideways, so you were supposed to think it was artistic. Ruthann's picture must have been taken on a cold day, her chair drawn up to the radiator and the window behind her steamed up. A stained mattress was on the floor beside her and next to it a bottle of Coke had been tipped over and left to lie. She'd kept a blanket over her lap and maybe under there she still wore something. When I examined it that closely I had to stop and make myself take a deep breath, as though I could have caught one of those sinful diseases at that range. It was that tawdry and forlorn, like the end of the world, like Ruthann had been in that much trouble with no one to help her.

But someone was there, to hold the camera and aim it, snap the shutter. Some fellow, no doubt, calling it something it wasn't. Some lowlife. I knew Ruthann would never have made that kind of mistake with someone she wanted to impress, any fellow she might want for something. I was sophisticated enough to know there were men who liked to look at such pictures, who bought girlie magazines to get their kicks. I would never have reacted that way, looking at a picture. But I couldn't help imagining how that boy felt, following Ruthann with his eyes, seeing her movements as she removed her blouse and then her brassiere. Had she lingered, the coquette, teasing him the more? Chills came over me at the thought of her danger, as though I witnessed her whole ruined life trailing into nothingness. Under my hair my neck prickled, the same as if I'd gone to get into my car while unbeknownst to me a man was there, concealed behind the seat. Any garage can be scary. Margy could vouch for that, riding in with Uncle Orville, after they'd pitched horseshoes all evening. Then he was pawing her in the dark so she had to force her way out of the car, still pretending it was a game. One of those country relatives Francis thinks are the salt of the earth.

Brooke would never have to know about his precious Ruthann. The best solution would be a hasty marriage. They could go off while there was still time. I'd known plenty of young girls who had been saved, turned over to decent men who wanted them, after their families had given up. Girls who could not or would not take care of themselves. It was arranged; quickly and secretly, before there was any open disgrace, the marriage consecrated and the young couple set up in housekeeping, months going by before people stopped counting or realized they might have missed out on something. Of course Francis has his reservations—Brooke's tight-ass smile gives him the willies. He thinks a big grin would prove him long of tooth. Francis is the first to admit he can't take the competition. And of course Margy's opinion amounts to sour grapes.

No matter what she had done herself, Phoebe would want me to look after her daughter. It was my sacred trust. Francis said that when he got to the hospital that night, after she was already gone; only the position of her head would have told you that she had other than fallen asleep, her only wound hidden by her heavy hair. I had never seen my own poor young husband. They said his wounds were too terrible and the coffin was kept closed. Still, he'd gotten confused in my mind with Phoebe and I imagined him like her, just asleep, his head drooped like a broken flower, his face with its cleft chin. I'd even forget and see him with her gray hair, when his was black as the raven's wing.

Of course Ruthann wouldn't know what was best for her if she met it decked out in brass and leading a band. A carat diamond would excite her for about a minute. It wouldn't stop the girls from laughing, making fun of Brooke because he took his Bible with him in the car, for bringing flowers to the house, taking time to talk with me. They couldn't imagine that, a young man taking an interest in an older woman—made me wonder where they'd been. And just because Brooke didn't fall over every Negro who came in sight, Ruthann was ashamed and made me promise not to tell Margy. She was going to change him. It never occurred to her there might be some changes she could make.

Ruthann confided in me how she teased Brooke, laying her hand on his thigh when they talked, grazing his arm with her breasts. Of course it was a riot that he wanted to make her his wife before he jumped on top of her. That he had principles to guide his life. He knew I understood, because of my father, and in our private conversations he'd assured me that his intentions toward Ruthann were entirely honorable. I had his solemn word that he would never endanger her immortal soul.

I'd let Ruthann find out for herself—Brooke would give her more than she bargained for. I knew a passionate man when I saw one. The way his eyes penetrated when he talked of Our Lord gave an indication of how he'd be with a woman, and his voice had none of that oiliness that made so many preachers seem like eunuchs. Tired as Ruthann is, I think many a night she'll be trying to manufacture a headache; although Brooke doesn't seem like the type to take no for an answer. And God help her on those days when he's home sick from work.

I could stand naked before my lawful husband and let him see me because I knew it would please him and make him want me more. But that was nothing like having my picture on film, something for them to snicker over at the drugstore. Though that wouldn't ever happen in our family, because Francis wouldn't own a camera. Even when Tommy was so adorable, standing up on a box and giving a campaign speech for Ike. I wanted a picture of that so much, but Francis says it's just another way to spend money. Hard enough to feed a family without having to pay for pictures showing them eating the food. More than likely wearing new clothes to look good in the pictures.

Or not wearing them. It was the sight of Ruthann's bare chest that startled me as much as the fact of it. I'd never seen either of the girls naked, the door slamming in my face, or ''Just a minute,'' if I knocked. Sometimes I'd imagined their faces if I barged right in. It was odd

226

though, seeing Ruthann that way, as if I might not have recognized her if I hadn't come across the picture on my own bedroom floor. Her expression was unfamiliar, not like a magazine at all, but contemplative and melancholy, eyes downcast, fallen to one side, more the way I would have expected her to look afterward when she realized what she had done.

It was flattering, I had to admit, Ruthann's normally sallow skin radiant and smooth, not a blemish visible, her black hair shiny clean, tucked under in the wave of a pageboy. I'd advised her to keep her oily hair up off her forehead and back, on account of her skin, but she'd always insisted on being with the styles; peeking through the bushes, Francis is apt to say when he's after her attention. But it did look nice in that light, the slight forward hunch to her shoulders, probably some latent modesty, drawing out the bones of her throat, taut and polished like ivory stays, taking away the scrawny look she had sometimes. I couldn't help but think she looked like her mother just then, with that wistful expression, almost as though she were visited by a spirit, her hands folded, almost reverent.

Partly it was her thinness, the small size of her breasts swelling from the child's flat and bony chest, that gave her a quality of innocence in spite of the wanton pose. The tawny tips, squeezed tight like diamond points, sparkling amidst the surrounding flesh, supple, diaphanous, any disturbance likely to set it aquiver. And once in motion it would dance and writhe. Such crazy ideas came to me when I looked at her, the dazed look in her eyes—hard to believe sometimes that she was an A student. Now Brooke could educate her with his money and Francis wouldn't have to worry. I'd certainly never expected my daddy to pay for my education—money down the drain as soon as a girl marries. Later on, anybody can take a course here and there, improve herself in different ways. I know I did.

The import of Ruthann's clandestine affair stayed with me the entire day, although I didn't feel afraid or overwhelmed by the responsibility, working along by myself while the others were upstairs, imagining how it would be when Ruthann and I had our talk. After her initial

227

shock, when she knew that I knew, she would give up her hostile defiance and begin to open to me. It had happened other times. When she had begun to menstruate but had been afraid to admit it, I approached her gently and patiently, and she had suddenly caved in, crying honest tears of relief while I explained it to her, and we had been close for once. That could happen again. She would confide in me, and after the shame and tears, we would even laugh together. She would tell me everything: what the boy who had photographed her had said. Who he was. What he'd asked her to do. And I would understand. Margy could rush around all day long trying to outdo everybody, then go off to kowtow to an uppity short-order cook. Fancy herself the great white hope. We wouldn't even notice she was gone.

Even when Ruthann flared up over the dancing I wasn't blaming her. It wasn't her fault, though Francis made her apologize. Give her something more to hold against me. It wouldn't occur to him that he looked foolish, prancing through the living room, his hair sticking up red as a cockscomb, in a frolic with young girls. As though he could dance. "Sometimes I wonder why I spend the lonely night." Francis had all he could do with slow time, though I'd never complained. But when I caught him shuffling, wagging his behind while some colored man insinuated "Oooh-oooh-oooh," he had the grace to blush—and blame his daughter. Maybe he'd resort to that when his next floozy had him asking for a divorce.

Once, when I was suggesting that maybe my headaches would be better if we didn't live anywhere near the holding pattern from the airport, because of the noise—something Francis mentions all the time—he said why didn't we call it quits. If I was so discontented. Since his mother's death he'd realized life was short. We'd rushed into something and we had to be adult about it, admit we'd made a mistake and go on. I wanted to ask him who "we" was, but I held my tongue. "Whatever you want, Francis," I said. To hear him tell it, there wasn't any other woman—he'd just had an awakening, had seen the dark at the end of the tunnel. He couldn't fool me, though. What man ever left a woman unless he had something else lined up? I was certain I hadn't made any mistake.

"You can't think of your own son," I reproached him.

"I have thought of him. You can have him if you want. In fact, take all three. I'm sure as hell no prize as a father either." It was like him to weasel out. He shrugged. "Since I've spared the rod they scarcely seem like my own anymore." All those complaints about Phoebe saving the spankings for him to administer when he got home. Making him the bad guy. Maybe he hadn't minded as much as he said.

After that it seemed I was ill most of the time, in and out of the hospital for tests, not that they could find anything. Although one doctor said he'd never seen anyone as nervous on the inside as I was. It was no wonder my throat burned. I had to begin to watch what I ate, mixing my food to a mush in the blender. It seemed they expected to find a cancer growing in me at any time and they hardly knew where to look first. In comparison my headaches were my salad days.

Not the most romantic scenario, but I could still get a rise out of Francis. I called him late from the hospital one night. "Hello, baby. This is the Big Bopper speaking," disguising my voice. I didn't have to ask him to come over right then and he got past security, coming up the stairwell from the service entrance. Sometimes Francis complained because I insisted on paying for a private room, never knowing who they might stick in beside me, but this night he had nothing to say. Mother had sent me a black lace gown that made it worth the expense, Francis creeping along the hall to get one of those DO NOT DISTURB signs for the door. The way it could still be between us, it was hard for me to really believe he'd ever want anybody else.

This time I'd find out who was after him. Then I'd go to her, make her see what she was doing to me and the children. I could tell her a thing or two about Francis too, open her eyes. At night I heard Francis breathing and sighing, pretending to sleep. Thinking about her. Once, I told him I had a notion to do like some other woman I could name and go out and find somebody else.

His face got all red and his eyes dared me. "If you had half a brain, you would. Actually, it's the most exciting thing I've had to think about in a month of Sundays." After that he rolled over and slept like a log.

I was surprised when Ruthann came looking for me, coming into the kitchen not long after the dancing and asking if she could talk to me, saying right off that she was sorry. Ruthann was like that, letting things roll off her back. At first I thought she wanted something, perhaps had discovered her picture was missing, but she burst out weeping. "Mother, Tommy told me what Dad said. I hate him."

I closed the door so we'd be alone. "Watch out for spite and malice when she turns on the waterworks." Francis couldn't imagine that somebody might really need a friend, someone to talk to, and I let Ruthann cry, feeling so sympathetic, the two of us together, sitting below the framed stitched sampler of young girls playing jump rope, an appliqué of yarn and fabric which Phoebe had made long ago. Once, I'd tried to take it down, after we'd painted the walls a fresh yellow. I was going to find another place for it, but Ruthann went to Francis and got him to put it back in the kitchen. Without a word to me. Nobody thought I might prefer something of my own that was more cheerful and modern. But now it seemed significant, almost haunting, as though Phoebe and I were the two older girls swinging the rope for Ruthann, who was the little one jumping, dark and skinny as a water strider, long arms and legs skidding out.

When Ruthann could get out what it was that Tommy had told her Francis said, about the football team, I could scarcely remember. Crasser than usual perhaps, it was typical: her father mouthing off, probably a little tipsy. Although I knew it could hurt and I told Ruthann I understood exactly how she felt. I was so sorry for Tommy too, hearing stuff like that in his own home, even though he was too innocent to understand what it meant. I reminded myself to call Luther's mother. They'd invited Tommy to go away with them for the month of August, up to their place in the Smoky Mountains. Right then I knew my answer would be yes. It would be a wonderful opportunity for a young boy, even though Francis vowed he was glad they hadn't invited him. The colonel led the family in morning and evening prayer, and every day he raised the flag over their dock, the Pledge of Allegiance before calisthenics—hardly Francis's idea of a vacation. But sometimes when I talked with Luther's mother, just out in the yard a few minutes while she hung up the wash, I thought I saw genuine sympathy in her eyes, as though she appreciated how hard I was trying to bring Tommy up to be a fine man. It wasn't just a vacation for Tommy but an example too. Although she was highly educated and refined in her speech, she was never anything but respectful to me, nothing like so many of the musicians I'd met through Francis, who expected everyone to know Beethoven's Fifth from his Fourth, when Francis said they had no more business sense than rabbits. It seemed that even if I had to turn my own son over to her, she wouldn't condemn me but would consider that I'd done her honor. I never had to confide these matters to her to feel that she understood. In fact, I never called her anything but Mrs. Lewis.

I told Ruthann I would speak to her father for her. Naturally she would have died of embarrassment. This was a graceful way to lead into the talk I'd wanted to have, a way for me to tell her the fears her father and I had, our worries about her future. We didn't want anything to spoil that; not that we wouldn't want her to have a good time. I could remember how it was to be young and I spoke to her as sincerely as I could, my eyes holding her wide tear-stained ones, that now seemed all softness, drained of their usual mockery. Hard to recognize this as the girl who yodeled in the background when I practiced my part in the Community Chorus; who once in a restaurant, when we were being entertained by an old friend of Francis's who had played with him in a combo, addressed me as "Lady Bountiful," calling attention to my dragging a greasy piece of chicken skin from my plate to Margy's so she could eat it. Afterward she denied she meant to humiliate me. It had just popped out. The next time her father sent her from the table for talking with her mouth full, I imagine she knew something of how I felt. Not that I thought that was any way to teach a child manners.

I told Ruthann I sympathized with her indignation at her father. Any decent girl would rather anything than to bring disgrace upon her family. A furrow slithered down her brow as though she didn't quite see the connection and was impatient, but I went on. For once I was determined to have my say, to speak straight from my heart. I knew how much a young girl needed someone to talk to, something I'd never had. All I had were the fellows pressing me, trembling against my heart, begging me and claiming they were about to die. I had wanted so much to give them what they wanted, I hardly knew how I could deny them. I'd wake at night with terrible dreams that I had done it and was lost forever—it seemed I was that close to throwing over everything that was dear to me, that I would trample the love of my family and make a grave of virtue.

Perhaps if my mother had talked to me as I did to Ruthann it would have been easier for me. I wouldn't have felt so alone. But I'd had to hear everything from the girls at school, all those sickening details, descriptions of loathsome disease. I became afraid to use a public bathroom and would scream myself awake, from nightmares I couldn't repeat as I lay weeping in my mother's arms. There were times I couldn't help thinking she was mighty dumb—what did she think had me so upset, having Mrs. James ignore my hand in class, my curl dunked in an inkwell?

When my period started I sat at my desk, afraid to move, afraid I was dying. My teacher sent me home with a note my mother blushed to read, although she didn't speak, even as she pointed out the cloths folded on the closet shelf, the belt and pins which she'd had waiting for me. While I talked to Ruthann I was glad she could come to me, that I could listen to her and be a help. I knew my mother hadn't been able to speak of such matters or she would have. She would have wanted to be close to me. There wasn't any use in being angry, although it was too bad. I had been growing up into a woman and it was bound to happen. But I'd thought I was dying.

In spite of our troubles, Ruthann and I had shared so much. She confided in me about the kids at school, told me jokes she'd heard, asked me to help her with her homework, to intercede with her father. Margy didn't need a thing—asking all the time if she could help me. It made me want to scream sometimes, nothing to say but "Thank you." I actually would have preferred that she fly off the handle and blow up, yell and throw things. It would have been better, even if she hurt my feelings. Feelings could be mended.

Francis shook his head when I talked like that. "My God, woman. Can't you let well enough alone? Why look a gift horse in the mouth? I feel close enough to give orders." But what would he know about wanting to be close? After a year or two he admits everything bores him. "I can't help it, honey. I gave up the piano. Lost my wife. Fell in love. And it's come to this." He turned and faced the wall. Played possum while I cried. It made me envy the woman I'd heard of who got up in the night and began to whack the daylights out of her husband with a bedroom slipper. I wanted to use ten-gallon boots.

As we talked, Ruthann's tears dried, glazing her face mother-of-pearl. I watched her eyes from the side as I talked and she stared out at the sky, their luminous surfaces transparent bubbles spinning under the spheres. Poor Ophelia went through my mind, Dr. Miles delivering Hamlet's epitaph! "Lay her i' the earth; / And from her fair and unpolluted flesh / May violets spring!" Poor Rosalie next to me gone ga-ga, as though he'd called for roses. No wonder she and I drew apart once the fellows began to notice me. She couldn't get over being teacher's pet with her bedroom eyes.

I dared to reach out and touch Ruthann, smoothed her creased brow where I fancied the frown lines formed the letter *M* for mother. I hoped my touch wouldn't remind her of the troubles she'd had with her complexion, though for once she seemed beyond comparisons, her eyes blank as shells, pale with light. Sometimes, to protect the girls with their oversensitivity, I'd do little things like hide my feet under me so they wouldn't notice their own large ones sticking out.

Altogether I'd given the girls more than their share of compliments, for the little bit of good it did. Sometimes I thought they were posing, insistent on their faults when anybody could see they were very attractive girls. And I tried to tell Margy how intelligent she was, even though her grades weren't as high as Ruthann's. Francis said it was a losing battle—and truth to tell, they were altogether too large and boisterous for his taste. Hadn't he picked a dainty little five-foot-two? But that was Francis talking. Let me say a word against them! Once I barely implied that Margy would be having more dates if she'd learn how to apply some flattery and tone down her opinions.

"That girl is a breath of fresh air," Francis said, and slammed out the door. Of course any father would like the status quo, his daughters all to himself, trailing after him, working overtime to impress him. When Margy declared, "Don't tell me about life, I want to find out for myself," he fell mute with admiration, full of the same baloney himself. Made me want to tell her everything I ever heard and then some. Stuff her like the silly goose she was. A sense of mystery! She'd find out the mystery was why she took so long to have a boyfriend. Another father would have flattered her into slimming down and learning how to apply makeup. Whether or not she was his type. Plenty of fellows liked a girl who was statuesque.

I never thought that much of my own looks, in spite of the fellows. Perhaps any face would begin to wear on your nerves if you saw too much of it. I could get to thinking my nose turned up like a snout. "Oink, oink," I'd whisper in the mirror. My lip would curl up too. But I kept it to myself—fellows can't see for looking, their eyes below their belts. There was a woman I knew at summer school whose teeth ran out in front like a loading fork and yet she had the best taste in clothes, showed off her figure, her hair just so. She ended up with the big man on campus.

I spoke to Ruthann as I would have wanted my mother

to talk to me, my eyes following hers to the window where the maples fluttered their new leaves that still held the crimson of their buds. It could have been fall, the color and mist of sunlight muffling and blending the world and time. Above us I could nearly feel the rhythm of the turning rope, the child's heavy shoes slapping on the dirt. "Down in the meadow, sweet as a rose," in the distance, unseen, the urgent scramble of the boys playing ball.

"We are all young once, Ruthann." I let myself go, not caring if she listened, just reaching out to her, feeling for once something of the bonds of family, if not exactly mother-daughter, then sisters.

"You see, I know about your diamond. Your father told me." Her arm lay upon the table, long, curved, and smooth as a stretched throat with its blue pulse at the wrist. "You could have told me, for it makes me very happy." My own little diamond winked like a tear and Ruthann turned from the window and looked, as though she was reminded that hers would be larger, worth a whole lot more; that I would never have the luxuries she would have. Even our new little house, modest and unassuming.

"Brooke is a wonderful fellow. So good-looking, and he'll be able to give you everything you want. A great catch." I could have added, "And he's real." As opposed to Margy's crushes, which were totally out of the question. But Ruthann would never tolerate a hint of criticism about Margy, viperish though they might be between themselves.

"You probably wouldn't think an old married woman would be that excited. But a new marriage is always a thrill to a mother. She knows it will bring her daughter close to her as she comes into her life as a woman. My being married to your father, with such a wonderful family, you might not dream that anything could be less than ideal. That I might have some troubles of my own. But any marriage is difficult at times. You can feel disappointed, bored. Maybe even cheated."

Ruthann's gaze appeared to sink inward, back into the past. "I want you to know you can come to me as your mother. Anyone can have troubles, can be tempted. No

235

doubt you think it couldn't happen to you. But you're very young still. No one is blameless, Our Lord said. You surely know that, now you're a Christian. I know your mother was a good woman too and meant to do right. Like any mother-to-be, she wanted Margy to be born. To make a home and a family. And she and your father decided to marry and begin their life together. I'm certain she intended to be a faithful wife, true to her vows through the bad times and good. No doubt she thought she always would be.'' I had to pause in the middle, out of breath and uncertain, now that I was speaking of Phoebe. I couldn't tell what Ruthann was thinking, or even be sure she heard, her eyes sealed on the floor, her girl's hair cast in threaded shadow on her face like a netted veil. Overhead the sampler chanted, ''Red Rover, Red Rover, won't you come over?''

I brought the picture out and laid it on the table, the visual manifestation of all I'd been trying to say. It was familiar to me now and I might even have smiled slightly, but the way Ruthann jumped up, it could have been a snake or she might have drunk poison, lurching, her hand on her throat. ''I wouldn't show this to Brooke,'' I began, but my mouth was suddenly dry as cotton and Ruthann had stood up and walked slowly from the room. It took me a minute to realize she'd had the presence of mind to take the picture with her. Perhaps she'd been after that all along. And now what would Francis think? Would he even believe me?

I sat at the table for a while, the jump-ropers' singsong overhead. ''There's rosemary, that's for remembrance . . . O! you must wear your rue with a difference.'' I recalled the little snapshot of Michael which I'd always believed Ruthann removed from my dresser the first time I met her. I wanted to pray then, but when I closed my eyes all I saw was a cozy bungalow on a quiet, dead-end street, windows swimming with light. When I went up to look in, to see who lived there, in every window was a little piggy face. Rue, rue, rue. My headache came down like a sentence.

The Evening Wolves

I DIDN'T KNOW HOW I GOT TO THE PORCH, AS THOUGH a tidal wave had picked me up and would set me down, willy-nilly, sweeping me past Tommy and the mountain laurel by the porch and on to the street. There at the corner Mack was waiting, a hell-sent vision with those baby booties crocheted by his aunt swinging in front of his astonished face, the engine rocking the car like a current. Everything was dark and at the same time aglow as though I'd been looking into the sun. Balancing then, high-kneed and blinded, I walked up the gangplank and sat beside him, jamming the picture out of sight into my pocket. He launched that baby. I knew I had to be one of those nymphos.

Mack probably thought I was horny—he should have all his dreams come true. He drove, the wheel seized in his arms like his love, teeth bared at his shoulder, one eye out for the vice squad. I was trying to pray: "Cast me not away from thy presence. Restore to me the joy of thy salvation." It was hopeless, spring pools sunk to glimmers in patches of rank woods, a high breeze whisking away the apple blossoms, pollen drifts at the curb. Dear Dad—Sorry I had to go before the work was done. I know you were waiting for the day I'd wash the car without being asked. Even though you never thought I was a lot of help, I did the best I could.

We drove and drove, getting nowhere fast while the afternoon pitched to nightfall, crossing the Potomac to Washington, following the avenues, the sights blurred at the speed of light, turning back toward Virginia at the Maryland border. The only one I recognized was my hero, Thomas Jefferson, the voice of reason, bewigged in his marble hall. When I was little I thought he and Dad were the same person, redheaded, standing straight and tall, smarter than anybody. Later Tommy came along, his namesake, Dad's reason for going on. "We hold these truths to be self-evident." Amen. The last I saw of Tom, the floodlight had come on, his loneliness for all to see.

Two months before, I went to the Coliseum to give my life to Christ. If He wanted it, He could have it. Even though the steely-eyed preacher looked like a holy messenger from God Himself, his words were lost on me. My mind was already made up and I was just waiting for him to be done, the lights to dim and the choir to hum. For the time when he left the podium to stand at the front, his arms outstretched, saying, "Come." I didn't need to be told I was a sinner.

Beside me in the stands, my friend Priscilla wept and clung beseechingly to my arm, as though I could console a pom-pom girl. As though she and I were in the same fix. Earlier, she'd pointed out Cathy Adams, president of the senior class, and a few other popular girls who had been saved the week before and were already down in front, singing in the choir. She could go on taking the credit for bringing me—whatever it took to keep her satisfied. But when I stood among them, singing in the choir and sipping grape juice in the vestry, I would know the difference. I wanted to laugh, not cry. "Fornicators and adulterers. Blasphemers and deceivers." I rejoiced when he called the roll.

That wasn't the first time I'd gone home with the good news and it didn't surprise me, Dad with his jaundiced eye and a host of problems only money could solve. Gloria, who already knew everything about everything. And I, with only the truth to tell, smirking as though I was pulling a fast one. I never did know what my face was going to do.

Dad looked up from his paper. "Well, little daughter, did the great man get to you?" Everybody knew about the Witness, the multitudes hungering for salvation. Dad flickered his eyebrows, red sails in the lamplight. "I guess it can't hurt."

"Oh, Dad." I longed to tell him but he seemed so far away, his lofty eyebrows increasing the distance. He couldn't know, his life nothing like mine with his worn brake pads, always the tide of water rising in the basement. "I'm a Christian," I said, witnessing for the first time and blushing, not exactly ashamed but lame, as though I knew it couldn't be true.

"Why, you've always gone to church, Ruthann. At least since I've known you. Surely you were a Christian before, unless you were just putting on." Gloria looked up from the real-estate ads, eyes of jade.

" 'For God so loved the world, that he gave his only begotten Son, that whosoever believed in him should not perish, but have everlasting life.' John 3:16." I'd been studying that all night where it hung from the rafters, printed on a banner. Maybe it wasn't the last word, but it shut Gloria up, at least for the minute. Dad said he was impressed to hear me quoting Scripture. Maybe there was something new under the sun, and Gloria nodded her red head that she'd always known that and more besides. I felt ready to fight the beasts.

Mack didn't take me seriously either. Not at first. But I stuck to my word, refusing to see him, riding home with Priscilla and cutting him dead if he showed up at school in the Chevy. Priscilla would have seen at a glance that Mack was nobody special, even if he was in college: his long ducktail and scuffed white bucks. Let him lurk at the corner the rest of his days, sullen and wheedling—one thing on his mind. Those days were over, I told him. He could see he was nothing to me.

He'd done everything but put it in; though, while breath remained, he'd keep at me, even though I'd told him in no uncertain terms I'd kill myself. As it was, I was sick with worry anyway, and every month I lost my appetite and could scarcely drag myself around, certain it was morning sickness and the end of me. Son of a bitch. In the school bathroom I stood in the stall, pummeling my fists into my stomach, lurching back out with a savage grin for whoever was there, panting over the rush of water into the sink. Maybe it didn't actually have to penetrate. In all their billions, one death-defying seed, as desperate as Mack, might slip inside and navigate upstream to spawn. But then, let my period, beloved curse, arrive and I was myself again, scoffing at my panic, considering the facts. He hadn't even put it in! Who did I think I was, the Virgin Mary? Then off I'd go with Mack, and do it all over again. I went downtown to the Witness and put an end to that.

The evening light behind the moving trees had hammered black by the time Mack and I had seen the last of Washington and wheeled into the drive at the fraternity house, parking around back under the spindly locust, tunneling into the heart of unpruned honeysuckle that wound halfway up the fire escape. It had been winter when I used to go there every afternoon after school to see him, when everything was bare. Now I drew from a blossom the tiny stamen and touched its nectar to my tongue. "In the days of Ahasuerus, the Ahasuerus who reigned from India to Ethiopia over one hundred and twenty-seven provinces." A dead halt: now even the solace of Scripture denied, as though I'd drunk from the river Lethe, my former dreams of winning the national Bible bee a mockery, departed with the hope of salvation. Stiff against my thigh I felt the dimensions of the picture, as though there it made its final imprint.

I hadn't been to the frat house since the night Margy sneaked up the fire escape and took the picture out of Jim's drawer, after we'd hidden behind the garage and waited for him to leave. After I'd broken down and confessed to her about the mess I'd gotten into. What Jim said I had to do. That was the beginning of Margy liking me again, in spite of my being such a brat to Gloria and having the world's most shallow friends. In spite of the picture. Obviously I was no match for Deborah, Margy's best friend, but Margy wanted to help me, and right away we figured out a plan to get it from him. It worked too and I didn't hear from Jim again. But here I was, all the same, looking up the twisting black ribbon of the fire escape. Chomping down, I tore flesh from my cheek, the floodlight blurring in a distant nebula through the sudden tears. Doomed to begin again. I saw myself going up and down, fated by blood and fortune. If Nevada hadn't ended up a spot on the highway, he would have found some way to be here too.

Margy had handed over the picture when she came down, her silence allowing it to speak its thousand words to anyone who would listen. I stuffed it in my pocket, but later when I got my first good look at it, I couldn't believe the sad lot of that lovely girl. I couldn't believe she was me. Up it went into my mattress, along with other unfinished business. Part of the old worried me. At night I went home to sleep a dreamless sleep, floating on my cares and woes, oblivious, like someone who keeps a ladder standing at the window for an easy way out, never suspecting someone could as easily come sneaking in.

Mack was doing his best to exercise self-restraint while we sat in the parked car, occupying himself by bouncing on the seat, thumping his size twelves to tunes on the radio, drinking off Cokes he stashed under the seat, tossing the crushed empties into the bushes. Dialing in Canada and Nashville, WWVA, by turns as they faded out. Finally, probably when he could see I wasn't making the first move, he heaved himself out the car door and came around to me, leaning in at the window, his pale hair slanted over one eye like a patch. There was a time. When the world was young. He was just a skinny guy with an Adam's apple that rode up and down in his throat like a lodged stone, but his lashes were double-deckers and in certain moods sparked his simple intentions with an air of mystery. Now I endured his touch, his lips a snarl of whispering in my hair. "I couldn't forget you, baby. Never for a second. I knew you'd come back. You had to." Even if Jim had told him stuff about me, Mack didn't care. His breath sweet and sticky from the Coke, beside us the honeysuckle dripping, alive with bees, peril either way. "Ya got any beer?" I asked, the old me, tough and full of surprises. He only grinned. "Anything you want."

I let him take my hand and he pulled me out, starting me up the metal stairs, where I collapsed on step number three, abashed, the eyes in the back of my head staring on up the dark spiral that ended in the black hole of his window. I was tempted to dive into the honeysuckle and be stung to death. Dear God—to finish anything feels like dying.

Mack tugged on my arm, striving upward with his foot. "Come on, honey. You don't have to do anything. Not unless you want to. Just be with me. I wasn't ever going to leave, you know, not until I got you back. That little brother of yours sure is something. We're getting to be buddies. Just come on. You can tell me about the Appalachian watershed and the Cumberland Plateau." Pearls before swine—trying to use that old stuff with me. His eyes crinkled, his lashes sweeping his cheek, recalling a thing or two from the old days. Sometimes on winter evenings we'd sat out on the top of the fire escape to watch the sun go down. Moments of forgetfulness and peace before I'd have to leave for home, and I would tell him different things I'd memorized, Indian myths, the names of ancient cities, geological formations from sea to shining sea—sheer poetry to a student of business administration. To someone who couldn't keep his mind out of the gutter. He was always bragging that I was the smartest person he ever knew—and there we were at the top of the world. I was surprised he remembered, though I regarded him with the white stone eyes of a statue looking down on ancient Thebes. Aphrodite, foam-born. Probably if he could have read what was in my mind he would have taken me by force. "Don't you want to?" he breathed.

He wouldn't know the difference. I would lie down beside him and never get up, the damage done. Above us the fire escape flaked its sour rust. Anybody could have been watching us under the floodlight, although I'd never given it a thought. Not until Jim said he had spied, watching Mack and me go up and down. Sometimes he'd stood in the hall outside the door. Pervert. I went down to the Witness and asked Jesus to come into my life.

Jim sent me the negative along with a note. "See, I'm not such a bad guy. Once'll do it. Now don't be long." So coy it was sickening; one glimpse told me I'd have to get my picture away from him, no matter what. His room was only two doors down from Mack's, but I'd never seen Jim until the day he stopped in to give me a message, supposedly from Mack. I'd never thought about any of the other guys; when I heard the knock on the door, jumping up to sit on the edge of the bed, checking my hair as I said, "Come in," set to flee from the window if it was the police.

He leaned in the doorway. "Mack says to tell you he can't make it. Not today. Something came up." Stood up, I blushed into my purse, bringing out my nail file. It was a rainy day and chilly in Mack's room, but I didn't get up to leave, jiggling my foot, which had on a holey sock, I realized, hiding it under the spread. Make yourself at home—and what of it. I met Jim's eyes as though maybe I'd come there on purpose to catch my death, shivering, aiming a rubber band I found on the floor, sighting him as I settled back against the pillow.

"How's it going?" The rainy light on his hair washed out flaxen strands. I realized he was good-looking, golden-skinned, muscles along his arms like a lifeguard, his chest rolling with them under his T-shirt. I felt myself weakening. He shifted his weight and the wall appeared to arch and sway as though gravity too were under his influence. "Seen you around."

"Yeah." I let go of the rubber band, which fizzled to the floor. Probably he thought he could get to me. When he offered a paper cup of beer, I downed it in a gulp. I hated the stuff, but at least when it was flat it didn't burn my nose. There was always plenty of that left from their party kegs. Margy could be afraid of everything: afraid to take a drink for fear she might start a riot, afraid to drive a car because she might have a wreck. Afraid to be alone with a really cute guy because she might do any-

243

thing he asked. I looked out into the rain, the fire escape suspended like a bridge over a canyon in the blowing mist.

"You'll warm up in my room," Jim said. "I get all the heat on the floor." He started down the hall without looking back to see me coming. When I arrived at his door he expected me, though, a chair dragged to the radiator, and he tossed over a blanket with Indian designs. "I noticed you. Thought maybe sometime you'd like to sit for some shots. You've got a good face. Lots of bone. You're dark too." He paged through a book of black-and-white pictures, scanning, restless, wiggling his leg. I could show him some cotton-pickin' bones.

"Okay." I shrugged. I didn't have any pictures of myself, except a tiny one from first grade, when my front teeth were missing, and another when I was a naked baby, sucking on a clothespin. Jim slammed the book shut, bringing out his camera, winding film, testing the light with a meter, forgetting I was there. I walked around, fiddling with the cord to the window shade, winding it around my neck, picking up his lighter and sparking the flame. I was nervous, as though I could feel free love stalking through the room and without my even asking I was going to get some. In fact, if Jim didn't say something pretty soon, I didn't know what I was going to be asking for, begging him to do, rolling and screaming so they'd have to carry me away. At the mirror I stopped and spit on my finger, arranging my bangs, wondering if I'd leave there alive.

Margy said it was like that when she went to the Pentecostal church. She'd felt so anxious and out of place she didn't know what she might do, like any second she'd jump up and heal the sick or speak in tongues, whether it was the Spirit making her do it or not. The girls at school were buzzing too. A lot of them excited about going to the Witness to be saved when it came to Washington, scared that maybe they wouldn't be chosen by God and would just be left sitting there like duds, knowing they were doomed to hell. I wasn't the only one living a double life, it seemed. Although they giggled about

244

the minister, who looked like a movie star, they were hoping for something they didn't talk about in public, only to their best friends. Who told only their best friends, until finally we all heard. Hoping that something would happen so they could stop themselves, the boys urging them toward a fate worse than death. Toward something they felt in themselves, distantly pounding. Priscilla had already decided she would kill herself if worse came to worst. At least she would have lived once. She would do it in the garage with the car exhaust and she'd even taken an old blanket down to stuff up the crack under the door. We had to go to the Witness, she told me. It was our last hope. I didn't appreciate her including me but probably she meant to be flattering. As far as she knew I'd never been to first base.

After Jim's flash started going off, I was blind as a bat. Sitting there, nearly on top of the radiator, like I was all alone, for all he paid me any attention. What a life to be a model. Thinking about the Witness, as though it really was my last hope for sure. Cotton Mather—we'd studied him in school, in a unit along with Emerson and Thoreau. Why not gingham or pajama. Ha! "His Divine Providence hath irradiated an Indian wilderness." I knew if I decided to be a Christian there would be no fooling around. Across from me, Jim was luminous in a cloud of light. I drank another cup of beer whenever he handed it out, still not saying a word. His hand came out of the cloud to fix the blanket too. He moved me to sit and lean, until he got it the way he wanted. When he spoke it was to tell me my neck would look longer if I didn't break the line with my collar. The camera held over his eyes, he mentioned some girls who had let him take their pictures without a stitch on. For artistic shots. Great, fun-loving, jolly girls. One of them was behind me on the wall—artistic like Marilyn Monroe. He lit a cigarette, suspending it burning on the edge of the desk like an act of faith. An Indian wilderness rose up inside me. Then one quick flash and it was done. Dear Dad—you had my number. I think I used to worry all the time although it didn't feel like worry. Counting and praying. There are

245

twenty-nine steps to your office door. If you never get out of debt it won't be the end of the world. Even Priscilla wanted a father like you and her father drove us everywhere we wanted to go. When she sat on his lap and nuzzled his whiskers, it was as good as rubbing a magic lamp.

I got back from the Coliseum and went straight to Jim and said, "Give it to me. Right now," holding out my hand, my face remote with prayer. He was lying on his bed with his knees tented, smoking a fag, hooding his artist's eyes. "It's mine. Give it to me and I'll go away and never bother you again."

"You don't bother me." He unfolded his legs, giving the picture a snap before he sucked in his gut and tucked it down inside his jeans. "Come and get it if you want it." His eyes dropped to where his zipper bulged, and he moved his arms up to clasp his neck, the cigarette dropping slantwise over his chest, the white ash falling. "See, no hands"—the joker again. He blew it away, ashes to dust, grinning like he was tied up.

I went to the bed and lowered myself to my knees, as at night I sank to the floor to say my prayers, quickly, before Margy would come in the room, like something I was sneaking. "Know and see that it is evil and bitter for you to forsake the Lord your God." The zipper twisted like an intricate brass gate, and deep into the hair of his stomach a tiny birthmark curved in a key. Suspended there, I felt his hand laid on my head, and I remembered Zion. I got up and walked out of the house and away as the Angelus rang from a nearby church. "You'll pay, bitch," I heard him call.

When I started down the white satin pathway to salvation, the shining stuff unrolled to lead the way down the wooden floor between the rows of folding chairs, the ushers stood at their stations in dark and sober dress, white teeth gleaming above starched shirtfronts, candlelight flickering in their obsidian eyes, the chorus humming soft and low, heaven seemed a black-tie affair for the Friends of the Symphony and I began to laugh. Once it began I couldn't stop, shaking with it and bent over,

246

stuffing Kleenex that prudent Priscilla had brought into my mouth, trying to stifle myself. Trying to pray and feel sorry. "Just as I am without one plea." Around me the great throng swept along to the front, weeping and stumbling, housewives and fathers, children and stricken youths, girls and boys, on their way to the preacher, who held out welcoming arms, urging, "Come. Come unto me all ye who are heavy-laden." Others came to stand with him, giving the call.

They didn't know the meaning of bad. The laughter rumbled on while I choked, rocking, my stomach in a knot, holding my nose and plugging my ears. Though nothing worked I kept to the road, in shame and dishonor for all to see, the laughter raging in a fire that would not consume, while I couldn't stop, going on and on.

Arriving at last, I stood convulsed, in front with a preacher, and he took my hand in his, laying the other on top of my head. "Blessed be the name of the Lord," he prayed. Then he drew back his arm and slapped me full force in the face, whacking the breath right out of me, so that with a loud cry I was restored, weeping in his embrace, pressed close to his stiff whitened bosom while he murmured in my ear, "God loves you, child. He is your father." Like that I was saved, washed in the blood of the Lamb, born anew into travail, into my true family with the hope of heaven to come.

He gave me to another man, someone who called me by name but whom I couldn't quite remember. This man seemed glad to be with me, patted my shoulder, replacing the sodden tissues with dry ones, telling me how happy God was at the return of every sinner. He too had renewed his faith, after a time of doubt and ungodliness when he had cried out for death. God heard every plea. I wasn't the only one, the whole place crowded like a train station with new arrivals entering in flocks, with cries of grief and joy, finding each other at last, laying their burdens down, with hugs and kisses welcoming each other home.

Then I remembered the man was Brooke, our teacher from church a long time ago. I'd never noticed before that he was tall, that his voice mourned, in his stricken eyes a dawn, like the start in hell of each new day of torment. I reached out to comfort him, my hand on his cheek, my smile washed by tears that mixed with his when, with a sob, he pulled me into his arms. "I'm no good, no good," he kept repeating even after, dry-eyed, I stood beside him with my hand on his shoulder, greeting my new brothers and sisters in Christ. "I'm sorry," he said when he was quiet. He didn't realize this was child's play for me, that of all the lost sheep, I had the most to be grateful for. For I knew where I'd been, out in the farthest reaches, among the evening wolves.

When Brooke got up, he squeezed my hand. It was time for him to go along with the other ushers, and pass out packets of special prayer guides, pledge cards, and Bibles to the new believers. "I'll take you home," he said, as though it had already been decided by a higher authority, and he looked certain again and proud as he moved through the room. While I waited I read over the schedule of prayer and Bible study, quickly memorizing a simple grace to be said before all meals. Brooke spoke briefly to Priscilla, who was circulating, solicitous and honey-tongued, as though she were hostessing at one of her mother's bridge luncheons, as though she'd always been there.

On the way home I sat up in front beside Brooke, Priscilla taking my usual position in the rear, looking on. Her eyes still rolling after one glance at the car and Brooke's impeccable manners. When she and her father rode up front, side by side, sometimes at stoplights he'd reach over to rub her neck or murmur words I strained to hear. It seemed possible that now, in my new life, I was in for the brand of attention that transformed ordinary girls into majorettes and cheerleaders. But, with Brooke beside me, I supposed such trifling matters would be seen for what they were: a snare and a delusion.

I didn't forget that Margy had liked Brooke once, when we went on the hayride. Back then Margy wouldn't admit that she cared and I'd let her suffer, going to the boring meetings at church a couple times after she quit, even though without her it was no fun at all. This time I would ask her straight out if she minded about Brooke, and I'd take the consequences. If she asked me, I'd give him up, wealth and social position down the drain. Reckless in the first flush of sacrifice.

After we dropped Priscilla off, Brooke took me home, walking me to the door. He asked if I'd go to church with him that Sunday and I said yes so automatically I knew my mind was already made up for me and everything was going to work out. I could sit back and not have to worry. But it felt sad and empty too, as though I'd said goodbye to somebody I used to know, and it was like that with Margy too. Just when we had been starting to be friends again. Sometimes, in the early morning, I'd wake up and watch her sleeping, lying very still in her bed, the covers undisturbed except for the line of her body, as though she lay in her coffin. The old me that used to wake her up for fun had passed away. Now, in freezing dawns, windows and shades flung to the limit, I scarcely breathed, a privileged witness to Margy's nightly communion with nature.

Later, Brooke said it had been like that for him too, knowing even that night coming home from the Witness that we would be married, that God had given me to him and his search was over. Not that much of a gift, in my opinion, but the ways of the Lord are mysterious. When I told Margy about my new love, she looked at me funny, as if maybe she was going to confess something about Brooke at last, but she didn't. She said she wasn't a bit jealous, except maybe a little of God. I told her she could have Him too—end of discussion. Brooke had warned me about Margy. Since she wasn't saved and had no intention of it, as far as he could see, it was better for me not to talk to her about my faith. It might mix me up. He could tell that I'd already been under her influence in different ways, sometimes I talked exactly like a left-wing Democrat. Frankly, in his opinion, the less I had to do with Margy the better. When we were married, I would have proper guidance and in the meantime, Gloria seemed like a fair and understanding person to him, someone I could confide in, instead of Margy.

As far back as I could remember, even when Mother was alive, I was supposed to do what Margy said. Now when she talked I nodded my head and agreed with everything—hear no evil, see no evil. Crossing my fingers, I denied anything was serious with Brooke. What's serious? I had my own troubles, for since I'd become a Christian, daily devotion had about taken me over. Just when I'd been thinking my life was going to work out the way I'd hoped, I could scarcely get out of my room for things I had to do to keep it happening. Prayers to say, Scripture to memorize. The top sheet of my bed folded down to a precise recitation of Paul's farewell to the Ephesians. The picture of Jesus with the rabbis demanded a ritual of such intricacy it almost turned me inside out, so that, despairing, I sometimes fell on the bed and beat my fists. Once Margy surprised me, walking in on that, giving me a funny look. But I couldn't tell her. Brooke wouldn't like it—although the family's free thinker seemed mostly a free talker to me, the chances very slight she would ever come home pregnant, in which case Dad would kill her and I'd never speak to her again. Mostly it was Margy's sympathy, fulsome in her golden-brown eyes, that threatened to be too much for me and I'd be back where I started from, tripping off to Washington, dancing the hoochie-coochie, striking up fags and holding a colored boy in my arms.

Signs were everywhere. One day, coming home from school, I saw a car parked on the street, and just as I was saying a prayer, asking God to deliver me from temptation, I saw something dangling from the door. It was a dead rat, caught by the tail and frozen stiff. I was trembling as though it belonged to the devil himself with his D.C. license plates, all I needed to redouble my efforts at self-mastery.

After Tommy told me what Dad said about the football team, I went to Gloria. It felt as though Dad was trying to undo all I was striving for, and I was crying before I even got a word out, relief coming in a flood with the tears. I wanted to go on and on, get it all out, even to Gloria, and I'd always been so mean to her. I wanted to tell her everything. But before long she was hardly listening, interrupting and changing the subject, starting in to sing Brooke's praises. Marry him yourself, I was thinking. "You'd knock 'em dead at a John Birch tea." I'd seen her fluttering her lashes during their little chats. When she came to visit Brooke and me in our mansion, we'd kill her with kindness. Brooke could drive her to kingdom come in our hot Cadillac. He'd be better off with me flat as a board, dead as a doornail.

What Gloria said hardly penetrated, rattling on about her marital troubles, subjects I have no patience for, until I was shocked to realize she was speaking about my mother. Telling me stuff I couldn't believe I was hearing, wicked things she had no right to say. As though I didn't know my own mother, like she was somebody bad. Like she didn't even love Dad. Then the picture was there on the table between us, and I, like Lucifer, fell from heaven as though I'd been pushed out. After all the time she had been with us and the nice things she'd done for me without asking, I couldn't believe Gloria hated me that much.

I trailed up the fire escape after Mack, ignoring his helping hand at the top, stepping over the sill into his room, shoving off the ramp which vibrated behind me. I flopped down on the mattress, in the shallow place between the walls, where the ceiling sloped down, folding my hands on my chest, prepared for the great ordeal. This time no fuss, no laughs or shivers. I wouldn't feel a thing. Once Margy gave a little family concert, singing the old war-horse "Lord Randal," her voice small and shaken but going on to the end, strumming the three chords she'd taught herself on Deborah's guitar. Dad stood and watched out the window, probably afraid he'd laugh, that former musician. Still, he clapped when she was done and said she had a good enough voice—he'd heard a million. Gloria said why yes, she'd always known Margy had a lovely voice, in fact Mrs. Rowland had said she was gifted. I confess a tear came to my dry eye,

Margy with a certain kind of nerve, singing her heart out in that mare's nest. The world's most dreary song for the world's most unpromising audience.

"Ruthann." Mack startled me from my reverie. He still stood at the window, and here I'd been hoping it was over. I stared back across the dark. What did he want, an engraved invitation? I pulled my blouse out of my jeans while I looked at him, and slowly the light dawned. He began to breathe so I could hear him, dropping the curtain over the window, his shadow moving on the red backdrop of the corner stoplight's shine upon the wall, Satan amid the flames, taking off his shoes. I hugged myself in my arms, turning to face the wall, rocking. At my feet he'd hung an old pair of patent-leather pumps on the wall, some I'd abandoned one night when a heel broke. Colored red and then green in the changing stoplight, they drooped like the Red Shoes Deborah had hung on her bedroom wall. Those, in crimson plaster, bunioned and crippled up like some poor dancer's feet, spoke to Margy like poetry, and she'd described them perfectly to me because, of course, I would never be admitted to that bower where the fair Jewish princess lay down to sleep. I was never good enough for anybody I'd ever wanted. I closed my eyes, rocking. Next I'd be banging my head against the wall.

Mack lay down with me, still dressed, and began to rub my back. At first I jerked and couldn't stop, clenching my teeth. A shadow fell over my grave and I shook harder. Mack gathered me up, turning me around to face him. I couldn't breathe. His hand touched the base of my spine, and I fell apart. "There now, Ruthann," he kept on, rubbing my face, his hands in my hair. "You don't have to. You don't have to do anything. Just this is sweet. Being here with you. The first time in the dark." Leave it to Mack to feel romantic at a time like this. I was numb in all the places his hand didn't reach. Dear Dad: I tried to hold out, but something lay on me in the night. Inadvertently, I stepped on your grave.

Some noisy boys tromped through the hall and whacked the door, their laughter and insinuations going away with them. "Christ." Mack flew up and slid a chair under the door handle. For all I cared he could charge admission. Already I could see what was happening, as though I were out in the hall, my eye to the keyhole, watching some other poor girl.

Beside me Mack was quiet, on his elbow and looking down at me, the curtain blowing in, colored in the party light. In his face, the set of his mouth, the amazing obstinacy that had possessed him and kept him coming after me all those weeks, showing up, against all odds, at the corner, in wind and rain, never doubting that eventually he'd get what he wanted. With higher ambitions he could really have made something of himself.

Heaven was empty without my mother. Hadn't she come to wait with me when I was all alone, sitting in the dark holding my hand to the end when I was asleep, perfumed with rosewater, in lavender silk, with her mermaid's silvery hair waved close to her cheek like scales? Although I'd done my best to forget her, who else ever snatched me bald-headed to comb out the tangles? She was the one who taught me to ride a cockhorse. No matter what she had done, cast out and reviled, she was my mother.

I gritted my teeth and hissed in Mack's ear: "You know how, I guess. You aren't all talk."

Mack came down on me like the Assyrians on the fold. I held my breath, crushing my remaining will, sparing no effort, tensed for the blind weight of centuries, the full avoirdupois. But a feeling I didn't know was there came rising up, lifting me until I was floating under Mack but supporting him, the two of us borne in deep water in a surging tide. When I smelled blood I would know it was time. It would flush and pool, warm around us, dark as wine in the night, a stain on his hands, salt on his lips. Lapping our thighs. I bet he didn't know there was a flower called love-lies-bleeding. On the wall the red light caught in the thrown weave of the drape, like droplets.

He took my hand, pressed it to his mouth, then guided it with him to unfasten my jeans, slipping in to where my body was hidden and waiting, his fingers drawing mine

253

to explore in a new land where together we might come upon anything, forests moldering, deer drinking untamed. I, at the edge, in warm shallows, prepared to hook a wily trout, which, pallid and smoothly muscular, inherently tricky, did flips and, running with the line, made for the open sea. I held to him, braced for the part that would hurt, the iron oar, the long drowning.

"Ruthann. Are you all right? You're pulling my hair." Crossing me again, propped on his elbow with his pinched, fretful face. "You're breathing funny too. And you keep sniffing." When I wanted a medical report I'd ask for one. When I had my strength back I'd help him out, shout instructions, exhort: Boil water, strap her down and let 'er rip. Now we're cooking with gas. On the wall the rainbow switched to green and slowly a car went by. It became so still I thought perhaps it was done and had been nothing like what I expected. Dear Dad—How often I've wished we were back in the car, going someplace, with me begging for food, feet stuck out the window, the open map giving us more of the world than I have yet to see. When will we be there? Those were my best days.

Mack sighed and rolled over onto his side of the bed, face down, holding my hand in his. "I'm sorry, Ruthann. I can't. I don't know why, but I can't." He squeezed my hand and let it go, his dropping limp. "I love you," he whispered, and was quiet.

I had to rest a while before I went on. Let Margy fall for that routine. I'd heard it all. I felt so weary, maybe I took a nap, for when I sat up I cracked my head on the ceiling, forgetting where I was, and I had to hold it in my hands to recover. Beside me Mack's breathing was deep and even. Lucky for him. I inched my way, flat along the wall, crawling over the floor to the window, where I stood to fasten my jeans, letting my misbuttoned blouse hang as it would. I had my pumps too, my mangy tennis shoes strung up in their place. Then I took out the picture and stabbed it with a pencil about ten times through the heart. Mack could piece it together and have himself a pinup.

I crossed over the sill and made for the bottom of the

stairs, my palms singed on the railing as I went along, setting the whole house aquiver. After a pause to set myself aloft on my heels, I started off, walking with care to keep the broken shoe in one piece. It gave me a swayback syncopation. Shake it, don't break it; so much for the sporting life. I didn't care who saw me—some girls couldn't give it away.

The dark was swathed in mists, like draperies I could push aside into hidden galleries of the coldest air. Pestering all the time, acting like they were dying of the deprivation, drooling over pictures, hanging out of cars and gasping, resorting to blackmail. But let the real thing come knocking—turned out without a prayer. Along the way the surburban streets and yards were empty and I took my time, going toward the highway, stopping to wade in little baby pools, the stars glimmering among my toes, a few turns on a lopsided swing set; the tricycle I pedaled drove my knees to my chin. It was my own separate toyland where I lived by myself and nothing would ever happen. But around me the other world grew and grew, houses surfacing, dark on the inside, shining from streetlights outside, becoming enormous phosphorescent creatures bobbing and luxuriating upon the deep while I watched from a place deep as the oyster beds on the floor of the sea.

When I rubbed my nose to see if I was dreaming, the smell of Coke and honeysuckle blended with another more secret, as though I'd opened up a shell. I licked one finger, as tasteless as seaweed. Dear Dad—I always wondered what they saw in me. I guess they saw me coming. You should have stopped the car more often and knocked our heads together.

When I got to Margy's diner, out on the side of the highway, perched there like somebody's little mobile home or a railroad car waiting for a pickup, I stopped and yanked my socks out of the heels. She passed by the window with her pad and pencil, taking orders for coffee and hamburgers from the world's unfortunates and happy to be there. The clock over the pie case said it was only ten-twenty and she'd be busy for hours. It was hard to see how love for the Negro could put a smile on your face twenty-four hours a day. When Margy apologized to me for not being nice to me for years and years, I just stared. If she said so—I hadn't noticed. She said she couldn't believe she'd been so mean and stingy—wouldn't let me borrow her cashmere sweater. Nobody in the world had ever made her laugh so hard, and who else knew all the words to "Street of Dreams"? I guess that included Deborah, unfailingly gentle and kind though she might be. She gave Tommy the record *Tubby the Tuba* for his birthday, while I spent a quarter on six colored pencils and no wrapping paper. When my best friend, Prissy Priscilla, never once invited me to sit up in the front seat beside her father and her.

Once, when we passed Margy in the hall at school, Priscilla whispered, "Your sister could be kind of cute if she didn't always hang around with them. So serious." She rolled her eyes at Margy's crowd. I had to sit in the girls' room stall for a spell of cooling off. "My sister doesn't want to be cute, you moron. She leaves that for nincompoops like you and me. You probably never heard of Cajun music or the hammer dulcimer. And why don't you come right out and say they're Jewish?"

I passed the diner by, going on the way I would pass Mother's grave, a thing of the past. I gave up my dreams of being Margy's best friend, living at the diner, sleeping in the booths at night, daytimes posing as a customer, with pie for breakfast, lunch, and dinner. Joking with Margy and Dorry Ellen, the other waitress, who supports five kids and Dad says is a tough broad. Dancing with Jake until dawn—one eye on Margy, who is always full of excuses. Once, he asked her if she'd go into the city with him to hear some music. He knows she likes R&B and anybody can see he likes Margy. But she said no. Not that she didn't want to, a guy working on his degree at Howard University who looks like Harry Belafonte; that look on her face of wishing. But Margy maintains you shouldn't play around with other people's feelings. If you don't have the nerve to marry a Negro and raise his children, then you shouldn't even flirt. I don't know who's talking about marriage but I'd be the last to butt in. I let my best chances pass me by. Someday I'd come back in the spirit and raise a marquee over the diner: LIVE. DANCING GIRLS— bubbles coming out of a glass. Once I had a dream that Dad played the piano again.

If I told Margy what Gloria said about Mother, things fast becoming dim memories, she'd remind me. "You knew that. I told you, remember. When I showed you the bankbook." Because Margy never forgets, dragging up that will-o'-the-wisp, telling me what I'd never wanted to know in the first place and put out of my mind in the second. If she wanted blood money, she could have it. If she could find it.

Brooke was after me and after me. I had to give it to him, he said, for safekeeping. How did I know there wasn't something to it? Maybe Margy would take all of it for herself. Black with shame, I stood there open-mouthed, the one who had told. I could have laughed in his face. Both of us knew who he was afraid might take it and flee to the ends of the earth. There was nothing to fear on that score, but he'd never have it either, and I shoved it way up in the mattress and said Dad took it. The same thing I told Margy—living on borrowed time. I knew then I had to get away from Margy. "No man can serve two masters: for either he will hate the one, and love the other; or else he will hold to the one, and despise the other."

I left the diner, limping on down the old route to Richmond, the wobbly heel pinning me to earth. Out on the open road, the gas stations and jive joints petering out, the cold set in. But I wasn't feeling a thing. Trucks whizzed by, blowing bugles, vanishing in black smoke with smears of rubber behind. Sometimes I was caught in their lights like a rabbit or a deer, shrinking and fascinated, the hint of a smile. Something they might take for a spin.

Then brilliant light was aimed right at me, so penetrating and searching I thought maybe I was having a vision for real and God might want me back. I stood still, rubbing my eyes, trying not to smile or seem too eager, getting my hopes up only to get a laugh in the face; in case He was as tricky as the next guy. But maybe redemption really was renewed every instant, maybe you couldn't get away. Oh, Dad. Brief were my days as a daughter, briefer still as a nympho. When I saw that snapshot I couldn't believe my eyes. It looked just like my mother. No wonder I was in the way, although she should never have talked to me like that. I guess I am just like my mother. My dancing days are done.

When I saw it was Brooke getting out of his car, coming toward me with his arms held out, I knew my trials were over and I believed again. It would be as he required. Brooke held me in his arms, eyes heavily swollen, his face puffy, the sad state Dad was in when he came walking home from the dentist's office with his wisdom teeth in his pocket, along with the money he'd saved skipping the anesthetic.

Brooke was crying. "Oh, Ruthann. I thought you were dead and gone. I won't ever leave you." His tears watered my hair and in that moment the power of Scripture was restored; my mouth watered. Like a prophetess of old I stood in the light, speaking of many things, the widow's oil, the unclean woman. The last words of Jephthah's daughter. " 'Let this thing be done for me; let me alone two months, that I may go up and down upon the mountains, and bewail my virginity, I and my fellows.' "

Daughters
of Jerusalem

HE HAD COME TO LAND ON THE SAND, NOW RESTLESS over a small fire he'd set to burn, blowing under twigs and wadded beach grass. "I gotta agree with what's-her-name. You're a dumb broad. Dumb as they come." He wore his bathing suit again and the maroon high-school letter-jacket, number 29 WILMINGTON CENTRAL, in white raised letters. My clothes had been strewn along the way, up and down the beach, and I stood naked and shaking. "What's her name there, Margy? I forget."

"Gloria," I said, watching his lips squeeze and open, rhythmically, gently urging the flame. Without warning it could start up again.

"Yeah, Gloria. All I can say is, you better wise up fast or it's gonna be too late." Darl perched flamingo-style, breaking a branch over his knee, laying it on the fire with deliberate care. "Lucky you ran into me."

I sank onto my knees, sideways, nearer the fire. Watching and not asking. To keep my teeth from chattering I locked my jaw, ignoring the bruises and scratches up and down my arms and legs. Darl reached behind him and the blanket sailed over the fire. "Here. Cover yourself. You look like a goddamn refugee." He grinned. "Well fed"; helping himself to a swig from his flask, wiping his mouth on the back of his hand. A thick hairless growth, it hung like a bunch of grapes.

On the way out from town he and Buzz had passed the whiskey back and forth. I told them I didn't drink, looking off while they exchanged a glance, toasting the kiss

259

of death. Darl ended up laughing and giving me a hug; although he said later that was his first clue that maybe the night wasn't going to be quite what he expected—what he goddamn had coming. Buzz's eyes in the rearview mirror pivoted and returned, set on a hair trigger. I stared to the horizon, where the red moon rode, shoulder to shoulder like a blood brother grasping the fringed mane of the world, praying for the ride to end, when Darl and I would be alone again. The theme from *The Wild One* came on the radio, and Buzz punched the buttons until violins were playing "Cry."

"Yeah, Margy. You had your joke. The party's over. Fucking broad. Cocktease." Darl stretched and sank to the sand, muttering, the flames licking up in answering tongues. His beardless skin appeared to weather in the heat. "I come out here. I'm thinking, Tonight's your night, pal. You got it made in the shade. Busting my pants. I guess you dames get some kind of a kick making a guy feel bad."

I had to say something; my silence infuriated him sometimes. "I told you, Darl. I wasn't thinking. I didn't know."

"Yeah. You told me. You never want to get laid. Now that I know, I'll treat you like my mother." He flipped over and began doing push-ups, still talking as he pumped up and down, puffing. "Buzz ain't gonna believe this. Where we come from I do all right—no matter what you think. Maybe that was it, Margy. You took a peep at Buzz and clamped down. Going for the older man?" He eyed me, panting on a hold, beginning to blink his eyes like he had sand in them, something I'd noticed from when I first met him.

"I told you. I don't. I never have. You got the wrong impression."

"Impression, my eye. Impression, my ass. You chickened out is what. I don't have it figured yet." He shoved himself up to sit, grinning at me. "Anyway, keep your shirt on"—a nod to me in the blanket. "I told you, I'm taking it easy." Cross-legged, he shook out a cigarette, lighting it with a burning twig, whistling a few measures of "My Lean Baby."

"I like a fire, Margy. A night like this. Keeps things away. You ever read those stories in English class? Wolves creeping up, like in Alaska. Just their eyes showing in the dark. Howling. Guys starving to death, freezing their balls." He lobbed a missile over his head, behind him into the dunes. I strained to listen but didn't hear anything coming from there. His eyes blinked, peering out across the ocean waste.

The fire blazed up when he poked it, exposing hair and gooseflesh on his legs, which were skinny for the rest of him. As though he knew it and was suddenly shy, Darl snatched his jeans up and trotted a few yards away to yank them on, fastening his tooled leather belt as he ambled back, shifting his shoulders. "Don't get any smart ideas, Margy. We're waiting right here for Buzz. Like I said, we'll drop you in town. See you home, Kathleen." He squatted, fueling the fire. "I like it big," he said.

"I want to get dressed, Darl. Couldn't we go back and look around for my clothes while we wait." My voice was flat but the whine was gone.

"When Buzzy gets here. I got a flash in the car. That's my buggy you came in. Bought and paid for by yours truly. Not bad for a working stiff. Your stuff's scattered all the hell over the place, you know. I hear there're cats that come out here nights. Wait'll you hear them. They go wild, roaming around. Seafood lovers, I guess." His laugh spurted and he began balancing a stick on the palm of his hand, hopping, dodging to keep it upright, cheering himself on.

The last time, Darl forced my head so far back, his hands in my hair, it seemed he would scalp me, and I fell to my knees, suspended, while he jerked my face under his, his lip twitched up with fresh blood oozing where I'd bitten it. When he dropped me it was combined with a shove that brought me down at his feet. Riding my hips, he ground into me, gouging with thick blunt fingers, wedging my legs apart with his knee.

I went limp, pronouncing my words carefully in a static undertone: "You are raping me. You're going to have to kill me next, because I'm going to tell."

He shimmied along me, straddling my waist, my legs pinned with his, his hands bolting my wrists. I felt him hard against my breasts, my eyes locked on his. "I'm telling," he quavered back. "Who you gonna tell? Your big strong daddy?" I worked my mouth to spit but nothing came. He smacked me lightly on one side of my head, grinning, daring. Another slap. With my eyes narrowed, the moonlight behind him flared like a war bonnet.

His eyes dropped away from mine, and just then a dark shape winged past, a bird hunting in the night. Darl flinched, falling off to the side as I scrambled to my feet and took off, running again; but when he didn't follow I stopped to rest, elbows on my knees, panting and glaring at him.

"You'd like to kill me, wouldn't you," Darl said, his visible eye beaming off the sand like a polished shell. He closed it. "I can see that. You want to kill me. We'll see what Buzz thinks about that." Wearily, he humped to stand, leaning down to pick his bathing suit out of the bundle, shaking it and finding the front. All evening he'd been careful to gather his things together, using the blanket like a knapsack. I didn't drop my eyes or turn away. He hung small. Then he vanished into the tunneled darkness among the dunes, reappearing in a couple minutes with his arms stacked with wood. I kept watching him, resting while I could, waiting for when it would start again.

In the hours I'd been running from Darl and fighting him, I'd covered miles of beach, but the ocean town where I'd come to wait tables at an inn was still an untold distance to the south. Deborah and I had come down after graduation, riding with a guy from school who seemed like a closer friend than he was by the time he dropped us off. A last familiar face, we feared, entering the lobby at the inn to announce ourselves. Hoping that at least we were expected.

We lived at the top of the inn, over the boardwalk, with fifteen other girls in a narrow attic corridor, sleeping on army cots lined along both walls, facing center under the steep-pitched ceiling. Looming just beyond the long bank of wavy-paned battered windows that faced the beach, the sea and sky merged, in daylight a blue and silvery slope, at night the ebony gulf over which streamed the perpetual winds, wailing on the sills, bringing in the waves that crashed and surged below. Telling of tides, an echo to the moon; beneath, the great herds lodged, blowing in their feasts, singing in the dark.

From the inland regions myself, there by the sea for the first time—I could not have imagined the thrill, kicking off my shoes and running down, standing in it, licking my fingers for a taste, breathing. It was as though I were severed, abruptly and irrevocably, from the land and all its ways, hired aboard a vessel and set out upon the watery life. Even my worn litany of memories failing, as though I could sail away from them too and never go back.

Every week I wrote Dad and Gloria, as I'd said I would, even though I was annoyed they didn't answer and tempted to give them the silent treatment. But I ended up dashing off duty letters in a large scrawl to fill the paper, describing the fancy dining room, hunting murals papering the walls, white damask cloths fresh for each meal, special forks for oysters, and a relish tray presented by a single waitress designated the relish girl. I mentioned some of the other girls Deborah and I were becoming friendly with, but I kept quiet about Cal, the chef I was getting to know. It wouldn't occur to them that I might just like someone and want to get to know him, no ulterior motive, no crusade.

Tommy wrote that he and Gloria were staying with her mother in Fort Crossing while Dad was at home overseeing the move, helping to direct a Gilbert and Sullivan production at the conservatory. I wrote and asked which one but got no reply. I described the beach, the miles of sand and boardwalk with amusement rides and games, delicious foods we could sample when he came to visit. I asked if anyone had heard from Ruthann but he forgot to answer that too. He said maybe he'd be going to school down there, no explanation, and he signed his letters "Love, Tommy C.," as though I wasn't the only one who felt very far away.

The first day the hostess took us into the kitchen to be introduced to the help it was like viewing a second sea. It had never occurred to me they would all be Negroes, including the twelve-year-old who washed the pots and pans. The swinging double doors that led back into the dining room could have been the entrance to the jumping-off place, the other side.

We waitresses belonged to neither place. Forbidden to sit on the veranda or in the lobby, or to visit with the guests, when Deborah and I started hanging around on the back eating porch after work, talking with Cal and some of the others, we were called in to see the hostess. Told that the porch was off-limits to us, except during meals. She overrode our protests. "Don't be selfish. They don't have any other place to go."

Cal said that it used to be spelled out on a big sign on the beach, along with other regulations, such as no dogs or alcoholic beverages allowed. But the city fathers must have realized it went without saying or was somehow in bad taste and took it down. They were right. It wasn't necessary. Cal laughed when he said that, and I told him it made me ashamed, which irritated him, and he closed the subject. "It's a waste of time, being ashamed." But by dinnertime he was teasing me again, reminding me not to put my hands in my hair, and when I rushed up to the range for something I forgot, interrupting a girl giving her order, he made me go to the end of the line.

Cal was thirty-five and married, his wife home in Atlanta taking care of their kids. He missed them, he said, and I could see he did, the quiet way he sat alone most evenings after work, smoking and staring off from the kitchen stairs. The others left quickly and noisily, men and women together, changed into street clothes, hair slicked back and a few younger women with theirs tied up in scarves with earrings, pirate-style. Sometimes three or four would run behind a beat-up convertible to get it going for a jump start, springing onto the seats as it caught. Cal would laugh and wave them away, half mockingly. Anyone would have wanted to yell, "Wait for me," and go wherever they were going.

Dad's postcard, breaking the silence of six weeks, announcing a brief stop to see me on his way home from somewhere, intruded on my idyll, brought me to my senses, as if while singing and dancing I'd discovered the house was on fire and the baby had run away. His cramped, minute script, adopted when he was thirteen to frustrate a despised teacher, made me feel ready to do penance. Willfully I had insisted on coming to Sea Breeze for my summer job, even after Ruthann had left, telling Dad it was enough that I'd quit my job at the diner early so I could help get the house ready to sell. And I couldn't let Deborah down. The morning I left no one was up in time to say goodbye. Now, just in case, I dragged my suitcase out from under my cot, emptying my bureau drawers, and I went out to buy homecoming presents for the family, as though I'd received a summons. When Dad was sixteen, Grandma, after six months of not knowing if he was dead or alive, traveled West to get him when he sent a postcard home. Now he was coming for me. I would go back and take care of Tommy, clean the house and cook the meals. Dad wrote that he missed his right-hand man.

It wasn't until I approached Dad, seeing him strange and remote amidst the others in the hotel lobby, pale and smooth-skinned in our world of suntans and salt crusts, that I realized how much at home I felt in this new place. The shock and force of that recognition distracted me while we shook hands in our customary greeting, what he was saying lost in the surge of blood through my head. I stood blushing, wondering if he could read my mind, covering my confusion with enthusiasm for the shell mortar of the fireplace, its Indian design, repeating what I'd

265

heard a guest say. I realized the tie I'd bought him was ugly.

But when he said Ruthann's name, I came to. He hadn't heard from her directly, but Brooke had sent a couple of notes, keeping him informed. They were living in Memphis, where Brooke had been called to serve as assistant pastor in a small mission church. Although Ruthann hadn't completed her senior year in high school, there was a chance she would be accepted by a Baptist Bible college on probation. Brooke signed his letters "With love in Christ." Dad shrugged and looked down at his shoes. With Ruthann in Memphis, there was no mention of an annulment—what's done is done. He finicked his fingers, his nails gleaming under his cuffs, the skin on his ears buffed and taut, catching light like diamond studs. "Lucky for him they don't have to take a vow of poverty—she'd be out of there in a second." He looked up at me and said, "You're looking good. Not too much color. Seems to me you've lost weight."

"The food's terrible," I blurted out. "What they feed us, I mean," I added, glancing about to be sure no one had heard, while Dad's slantwise amusement told me I'd never change. I had been careful about the sun, doing what he'd taught me, buying Sea & Ski and wearing an old-lady hat. I was thinner too, surprised he'd noticed since I wore a long man's shirt over my plaid Bermudas.

It was easier when we went out to stroll along the boardwalk among the crowds of evening tourists. The sea air's fish and salt enhanced by broiled and steaming sea-food cooked in the open, and there was a sweetness about the breath and being of those who had just dined. They might even have been deviled in seasoned crumbs, wine, and capers. I began to talk faster, mispronouncing *gratinéed*, with a shrug and rushing on to another subject. This time I could show him the ropes.

The little shops, opening in lighted alcoves off the walk, seemed just then as familiar to me as rooms in our old house, and I led Dad in and out. Could he believe plastic seashells stamped *Sea Breeze*? Vials of ocean water for a dollar! Who did they think they were kidding?

266

Dad pulled his ear and nodded politely, following after me. By the time we got to the imported laces, they didn't even look pretty to me under the fluorescent lighting, stacked in cellophane bags. I hastened to assure him I hadn't bought anything for myself, wincing to remember the tie. "I'm saving my money," I added with a touch of pride.

"What for?" he asked, as though he couldn't imagine there would be anything I might want. And had forgotten he'd spent a lifetime encouraging me in the pursuit of frugality for its own sake. College was on the tip of my tongue, but I changed it into a cough. I didn't want to ask right out for more of his skepticism. Or he might imply that only a lack of imagination could have me coming up with something so mundane. If I'd said a car, he might have fainted.

We made stops at the different food stalls and I tried to entice him. "I'll treat. Please." I pointed out cotton candy in pink and green, grills loaded with sausages and peppers. Wryly he suggested that I might be the hungry one. Of course I was hungry, I was always hungry. And to prove it I bought a box of french fries, sprinkling them with vinegar in the new way I'd learned. I went on, sniffing, gesticulating, acting as though I could serve up as readily the salt breeze and the half-moon, which floated out over the sea. Dad roused from his bemusement to ask if I had been hired by the Chamber of Commerce, then was lost again in his thoughts. I refused to be subdued, my enthusiasms my only hope, thrown up like so many sandbags before the day of reckoning.

Then abruptly Dad turned to the side, moving to the edge of the walk to brace his arms against the back of one of the wooden benches placed at intervals behind the iron railing, to overlook the water. I faced the sea head-on, as though brought up short before a wall. Bent over, resting on his forearms along the back of the bench, Dad glanced behind us, motioning with his shoulder. "What's all the excitement?"

I looked back and saw groups of kids hurrying along, weaving in and out of the crowd, arms loaded with blankets, food and beer, radios and newspapers, calling to each other and piling into cars parked along the walk, speeding off in the direction of the dunes.

"Mostly just kids who work here. Different places. They're going out to the sand dunes to have parties. Make fires, eat and dance. You know." I'd heard more than I told Dad, whispered conversations in the dorm, sometimes at dawn when the girls came sneaking in, shoes in hand, tangle-haired and blurry-faced in the wan light, at most an hour's sleep to catch before breakfast. Some with eyes smudged black as though already they'd been sleeping. Someone cried once, her head under the covers. And another girl left suddenly with her parents. For a while after that we'd had to sign when we went out at night and again when we came in.

"I don't go," I hastened to tell Dad, stammering, but I was proud, too, that I wasn't running wild like a horse let out of the barn. "I really don't want to," I rushed on. "There's a lot of drinking." A prude to my own ears, I could see what Dad thought of me, shaking his head, half in wonder, half amused.

"You make it too easy," he said. Protestations ran in my head. He'd always warned us about drinking, implying it was part of the trouble between him and Mother. But I kept my mouth shut. Let him think he knew everything. Like why I let him talk me into quitting a week early at the diner. It certainly wasn't to paint the living room, although for a while I told myself that, keeping myself from thinking about what had happened with Jake.

I'd been dreading the day as it drew nearer, leaving for the summer and having to say goodbye to him, not knowing what would ever bring us together again. Finally he was all I thought about and several customers got their soup with dessert, or worse. I thought I could feel him moving in the kitchen and found reasons to go in there and see him, knowing he'd look up. When I reached for orders at the pass-through, he'd be standing there. I'd watch my wrist tremble as I took the dishes.

I knew he had girlfriends, different women I saw sometimes waiting out back in the parking lot after work.

And between us there was nothing, nothing like that. We were friends. He brought in books for me to read. Politics and religion were what we had in common.

But one night, Dorry Ellen had to leave early, because of a sick child, and Jake and I were alone, closing up. The shelf radio was turned up loud while Jake worked in the kitchen and I swept up the front, then scoured the steel coffeepot at the sink, piece by piece, and slowly, like a preparation, knowing when I finished and headed out toward the back with the grounds, he was finished too and I might meet him. And I did, in the small back entryway with its dim yellow bug light. I could smell the warm sweet coffee, like his skin, felt his body's angles and stance, its narrow elegance. He put his hand on my arm, lightly, turning me toward him, bringing us close, his hand holding me, his breath tremendous. Both of us shaking, barely touching along the length of ourselves, as though it were that attraction that held us upright. Inside, I was lowering, centering, my haste and longing composed; brought to him like a gift while I looked up in acceptance. In that amber light his dark eyes held deep purple. It was a few seconds before I was aware of the car that had pulled into the lot, its lights dappling us through the leaves of the vine at the back window. Jake pulled away. I didn't have to look to know it was one of the women he knew, coming to get him right on time.

"Margy." Jake's voice was unsteady, almost harsh, as I pushed by his hand, rushing out to use the phone in the front where I could scarcely dial the numbers and then had trouble speaking loud enough to be heard, ordering the taxi, finding myself yelling, when abruptly Jake switched off the radio. I didn't look at him or speak, going to sit in a side booth and holding my head toward the window. "I'm not sorry," he said before he left, and I listened to him go quickly down the back steps. After a couple of minutes he came back in and stood across from me in the doorway. "What do you want me to do?" he said. I shrank closer to the window. We were like that a minute. "I'll go on now," he said after I didn't move or look at him and the taxi was coming.

269

"You've probably got it figured out," Dad said, turning again to face the water. "Why I've come here to talk to you. I wouldn't ask if I didn't think it was important. I can see you like it here and you've made a place of sorts for yourself. But your mother is pretty downhearted these days and sometimes we all have to give a little, think of someone besides ourselves. It's been hard on everyone—your sister taking off like that, free as a bird. How much do you know about what happened? Anything about a picture of some kind?"

I repeated what I'd told him before, what Gloria had said about Ruthann being upset over something Dad had said about her and then she'd just walked out of the house. I shrugged about the picture, although I could see it as plainly as I'd seen it by flashlight the night I took it from Jim's room and handed it to Ruthann. It had been exciting, both of us frantic that she might get caught. Now that she had been, it seemed different, sad and lonesome, and I missed her. Dad sighed, nodding and staring off. Maybe he did too.

"Well, your mother can't help feeling guilty, but I tell her she's crying over spilt milk. Something of the sort was bound to happen, only a question of time. Anyway, we're both agreed it would seem more like a real home if you'd come back. Your mother will be done with her tests soon, ready to take up at the plow. They can't find anything, maybe a nervous condition. It'll be pretty lonely, rattling around in the new place, trying to pick out wallpaper and furniture with nobody much to care. I'm not much of a hand at that kind of thing myself. It won't be for long, understand. A year at most." Perhaps it was Dad's unaccustomed seriousness that made what he said sound unconvincing.

Only his hands on the rail, clenching and loosening, the knuckles blanching white as teeth, conveyed strong feeling. Above us, around the high lamps that lighted the walk, moths hovered, beating their wings against the globe, whirling in the lint of their disintegration. "And I do have some affection for you," he added, "though I don't often show it,'' looking down and fussily brushing at the lapel of his dark jacket.

"How's Tommy getting along, Dad? We write, but I can't really tell.''

"Not so well, I'm afraid. He's a bit of a worry, some sort of asthma or something, so the poor kid thinks he's choking. Between him and your mother the AMA ought to be paying me dividends. You know how she is—'*en garde*' with the thermometer. He's gargling salt water like the Great Blue. Maybe it will do him good to go off to the Smokies in August and practice up on 'The Star-Spangled Banner.' Your mother's certain of it.'' He clapped me on the back. "I think he needs his true love back.''

Bent against the wind, he cupped and lit a cigarette, speaking on the exhale, his tone softening. "Your mother's lonely. She needs someone she can talk to. She can get some pretty funny ideas from time to time. Had me mixed up in some torrid affair with one of the gals from her hometown, just because we took a walk. She sure called that one wrong, although I wished I'd taken that walk a long time ago.''

Then he turned around to half-sit along the back of the bench, facing the crowd, which shuffled along, underneath us the boards trembling and shifting, creaking, as though we sailed on a lighted ship through the night, even the souls of those tramping by seemed paltry, so many phantoms. Dad smoked in thirsting gulps, the cigarette pinched in his bunched fingers, the muscle in his jaw jerking like it took electric current in bolts. I couldn't think what I should do, staring up at the moths, caught in their onyx eyes. Deborah said I muttered Jake's name in my sleep, although I didn't remember dreaming of him. I hoped I wouldn't rise up one night and walk to Memphis in my nightgown, or open my eyes to find myself in a park scattering corn to pigeons who would peck and moan and fly away.

The tap on my arm startled me and I looked down to see Dad offering me a small, thin book, scuffed on the edges like cardboard. "Here,'' he said. "Take it, it's yours. It won't bite." He pushed Mother's bankbook into my hand, clearing his throat. "Don't say I never gave you anything."

"But—" I stifled my confusion. I'd been so positive Ruthann took it with her when she left.

"Your brother found that in your sister's things. You have him to thank. Probably you know something about it anyway, but it sure was a mystery to me. I called the bank, though, and it's on the up-and-up, a bona fide passbook. Your passport to the future. Over six thousand big ones. I know you've never cared that much about filthy lucre, your principles being what they are—but even a Commie doesn't look a gift horse in the mouth. Now, if you ever figure out what your dreams are—they're yours. And if you don't, somebody will always have a hand out. When you're back home you won't have to part with a dime—maybe a little for board as a gesture. Don't worry about that other one. She vamoosed. Wherever she is, she's having a merry time. Picking somebody's pocket." Dad smoothed the sides of his hair, primping with the palms of his hands. Then, slanting an eye at me: "You might consider sharing with your brother. He found it, after all, even though he wasn't among the chosen. Your mother and he keep trying to figure out ways to keep me broke. Military school—a straight shot to West Point." Dad bit his lip and rolled it out tooth-marked. "I don't know who your mother robbed to lay aside that kind of dough. But then she was always holding out. I suppose you were too young to remember?" A mother is a mother is a mother, in his book.

I nodded and he sighed, finished with his business, with his wondering. I felt his weight settle more fully along the back of the bench. His long legs ran out in front, thin, expensive feet in polished Oxfords, special-ordered. Glancing about, he began to comment on the passersby, the shops, as though he were waking up and seeing them for the first time. "What's all that about?" He motioned across the way to a shop that sold jade figurines, ivory, Chinese silks. I answered vaguely, my turn to be preoccupied. Dad didn't want to know how Mother got the money. Or Tommy—the little sneak. Side by side at the bench, we stood facing in opposite directions, like the Roman god Janus. I was remembering when Dad came down to the railroad tracks where Ruthann and I were playing, to tell us about Mother's accident. How flattered I was when he put his hand on my head and said, "I'm depending on you."

Eye level with the fire, Darl lay brooding, his head resting on his arms, blond crewcut tipped auburn in a burnished fur. He raised onto his elbows, rousing himself with eyes blinking. "To tell you the truth, I didn't know they made dames like you. Not since the Bible. No wonder Gloria wanted to keep you at home. Throw away the key."

Sometimes he'd begged: "Come on, give it to me, let me stick it in why don't you cunt you close up on me some guys would slam you bitch it's grounds I tell you you get a guy out here treat him like a dog don't come across Christ you turn him into a beast I'm in pain it ruins a guy I won't ever be the same." Howling, he humped the sand, pounded his fists, one eye on me and ready to leap if I made a move.

He grinned, getting up, brandishing a limb like a sword before he dropped it on the fire. "Scared you, huh?" He sat down, cross-legged, baleful, rubbing his eyes when a gust of smoke blew his way. "Why couldn't you justa been normal?"

I looked off to the water, the last light of the moon falling around us, our little basin left dark like a theater, tucked in the shadow of the dunes. It seemed it would be the same at night along any sea, any time or place or tide, a desert waste, salt water as parched as sand for human thirst. I could imagine the solemn nights at Jamestown, ships anchored out beyond the swamp and the longboats rowed upriver with the tide, foundering with their half-dead cargo. Brought up to face the moon on the water and the ceaseless waves, not knowing America from Africa, for all they could tell, the cold moon a sun on that forsaken planet.

273

When Darl and I had walked around the dunes onto the beach, after Buzz left us off on the highway, I clung to my hopes even though sand and water stretched like the tundra, empty in all directions, no campfires or music. What I had been told about and believed would stud the dark with the bustle of a gypsy caravan. Absorbed in my new life, the routine of meals at the inn seven days a week, I hadn't imagined there wouldn't be any parties on a Monday night, everybody recovering from the weekend. Buzz's parting taunt still ringing in my ears: "Don't do anything I wouldn't do, Darnel," punctuated with grinding gears when he sprang away, Darl pounding his fists and cursing under his breath. I pretended not to hear. Earlier, when I'd said I liked his name, he said it was short for "Darling," grinning, his momma's boy.

Darl shivered, in spite of being nearly in the fire, beginning to whistle the theme from *Gone With the Wind*, "Tara's Theme." How had it happened that an afternoon had passed, swimming, floating in the trough between rows of breakers, laughing and talking, and I hadn't seen, hadn't thought? His eyes, beaded with water, flung off a golden haze. I'd noticed him blinking and wondered if sometimes he wore glasses.

Darl shed his jacket and stretched prone for another round of push-ups. Then he lay back, his head on his arm, playing the muscle up and down. "You're strong for a girl, I gotta say. And you don't quit. You can run too. I hand it to you, you don't seem the type. Probably you don't know that either. I mean if you're that dumb. The way you walk. I mean Buzz was drooling." He landed on his feet and built up the fire, grinning when I half stood up, ready to take off.

"Keep you on your toes. We oughta have us some marshmallows and wienies. Our own little party. Why couldn't you have been regular?" He shook it off, giving himself a rap on the head with the flat of his hand. Then he whirled two lengths of wood toward the dunes. "Hear that racket. Christ A'mighty." I listened but I didn't hear anything different. "It's enough to give you the willies. Wish I had my flash. But when your buddy asks a favor how you gonna say no. Buzz don't take no. Well, I owe him. You ever seen a ghost?''

"I don't know. Maybe. My mother's dead."

"Yeah, so you said. Gloria's your step. Right? See, I pay attention. You ever think she'd come back?"

"Sometimes I think I can feel her. It's like she's here." He'd been nice during the afternoon, sympathetic about my mother. Now it seemed odd that I'd told him, hanging out like a charity case. And I knew I'd made too much of it when up at the boardwalk he'd knelt before me, slipping on one of my sandals, looking up. "It fits." Waiting with the other one.

He yanked up his collar, snapping his jacket. "Okay. None of your tricks. My old man's dead too, for all I know. So if you call yours I'm calling mine. Probably she was some kind of Amazon like you. I'm good to you, ain't I? You got the covers." He stood up, pacing a circle, whipping rocks into the dunes. Then in an exuberant flurry of fire building he stood amid a rain of brimstone.

"So, Margy." He dragged a log over and settled down. "What would your old man think of Darl? Money in his pocket. Driving a sharp car. Man, I gotta let Buzz take it when he asks. Women all over the place. He can't walk with all that on the ball." Buzz held his jaw as if left to rest he would drool, and his long ducktail, more like a peacock's, had been carefully arranged over a bald spot visible to me riding behind him in the car.

"Sure you ain't holdin' out, waitin' for him?" Darl batted his eyes.

"I'm sorry about your glasses," I said. "Anyway, you're a lot nicer-looking than he is."

"Yeah. I don't wear 'em that much." He got up and stuck out his hand over the fire. "Truce." I reached up for a quick shake, holding my blanket. Then he got busy straightening the woodpile. His hand felt cold and damp and close up, beads of sweat clumped on his forehead. I'd thought he was going to cry when he fell and found his glasses crushed in his pocket. Then I was afraid he'd kill me.

He fired a couple of rocks into the dunes. "Yeah, I'm

not your worst guy. I'm taking care a'you, right?'' He sat roasting twigs in the flames.

I sat across from him and started poking in the fire too. ''Once my dad made Ruthann and me make a fire.'' My voice sounded hollow, but he was letting me talk so I went on. ''We were out somewhere in the woods and he wouldn't let us use any matches. We had to do it by rubbing sticks together, and of course we were there all day, trying. The whole time Dad stayed with us, smoking, making us laugh, telling stories about his life. A couple of times Ruthann nearly got his matches or a cigarette butt. It was fun, although we didn't get a single spark going, Dad finally using a match. Still, he said he was proud of us, saying how we could never tell . . . the day might come when hanging on was all that we could do.''

Darl was staring. ''I thought it was in the bag. I could almost taste it. Made me kinda crazy—you'd stick up your nose. Like you think you're better. Bitch. Laughing up your sleeve. What's with you anyhow? I can't believe you never done it. What're you saving it for? You want it to go rotten or something?'' His lip curled, but then it was jerking.

''I don't know. I didn't think, I guess. I wanted you to like me. I thought you did. I wasn't laughing.''

''Well, I'm done handing out compliments. So I liked you. What's liking gotta do with it. Jesus.'' He brought out his comb, glancing at me when he flicked off something that maybe was glass, stroking through his hair, arcing up the front. ''So this Gloria. She got big tits or what?'' He was beating his boots with a stick, grinning up under bony brows. ''I mean, it figures, your old man eating out of her hand. A lot of them broads from down there are lookers.'' In the afternoon he'd told me his grandmother lived near where Gloria was from.

I didn't answer that, starting to get edgy again, but Darl flipped over for push-ups, talking in short bursts. ''I keep myself good. One-armed too.'' Halfway down he collapsed, leaning back, tossing a smashed beer can

276

he'd dug out. "You probably thought I was a ninety-pound weakling."

"Darl, let's walk back to town. It's not far. Or just let me go. I don't need a ride."

He jabbed his stick at me. "Shut up. I told you I stick by my pals." I leaned back with a sigh he mocked. "You stop staring at me all the fuckin' time. Frigid bitch. How'd you know there's not something a lot worse down there? I'd like to hear you bellow, you run into one of them wildcats. You're so dumb you don't know enough to be afraid. Figure you'll dash off. Sing a song. You're too cocky, ya know that?" He wiped his forehead on something he took from his pocket. Probably that other thing was in there still, wrapped in foil. When I threw it off in the dark he'd had a fit, until he found it, raving that it was the only one he had. Not that he'd waste it on me. I deserved whatever I got. "Buzz'll blow the horn and I'll give the whistle." He gave an ear-splitting demonstration and then we both listened.

"Keep the home fires burning. If he has to he'll drive out on the beach and find us. He had a little somethin' in Bel Air. Just you hold on to me when he gets here. Nobody says nothin' doin' to the Buzz." Darl looked a little worried, as though he might not appreciate his car humping over the dunes. His whistle took up, something minor like a hymn.

I'd gotten away once and was fast leaving Darl behind, when a man stumbled out of the dunes calling, "What ya doin', girlie. Hey, momma, wait for me." Taller than Darl, he gained on me, seeming to rally and sober with the chase. Zigzagging, I headed full-tilt back to Darl, pulling him then to run with me, away from the stranger before he saw him. That time, when I started to fight again, Darl punched me in the back and I'd ended up kneeing him. Crawling on the sand he'd threatened to strangle me. After that I'd been afraid to get too far away.

"I have a friend waiting for me, Darl. She's going to be worried when I don't come home." I didn't mention the curfew—in the afternoon I'd told him what that amounted to. Deborah, when I'd asked her to cover for

277

me, telling her my plans with Darl for the evening, had said, "Do you think you should?" her eyes widening with alarm.

I'd wanted to slap her, as though she were Ruthann and it was she and she alone who had stopped me from having the life I wanted. "At least I'm not afraid to ride the breakers"—I had to bite my tongue to keep from accusing her. Instead, I pointed down the row of cots to Sally's. "He's her cousin," I said, superior and complacent. "She introduced us and he's very nice." Deborah backed down and I went on telling her different nice things about Darl, how he'd surprised me with ice cream. I even repeated what Darl told Sally, that I had the best figure he'd ever seen. So there! I couldn't go to the movies, in plain sight, plump in my full summer skirts. Out alone in the night, I'd be his dream girl, rising out of the waves. All evening, serving dinner, inside I was humming the melancholy theme Darl whistled when he seemed to have forgotten I was there. I told Deborah I'd wake her up when I got in.

"Sally knows where I am too, Darl." His mouth whitened and I shrugged. "I mean, maybe they'll call somebody to come out and see about me." I guess Sally had thought their little ruse was harmless, cooking up the cousins story so Darl could meet me. When they'd never seen each other before in their lives. At the time I'd wondered at Sally's friendliness; she'd never liked me since the first, when she said I talked funny, as if I were English.

"Yeah." Darl stood, flexing his hands, lacing them like a helmet around his head. "Another dumb broad. Let 'em come. Trouble with you, you think too much. Think you're gonna hear music. You're just gonna get laid." He pulled on the flask, lit a smoke.

"My father," I said.

"Your father what! Your father's a queer." He stretched back and let his eyes close, his chin weighted on his chest, the stick in his hand.

* * *

Dad and I had been silent for a few minutes when he took my arm, steering me around the bench to face his way. "Let's go take a gander." He nodded toward the kimono shop. "Your mother might like one of those for mornings in the new breakfast room. A little gaudy, but cheery, just the thing to put a headache to flight." He didn't seem to mean it sarcastically, more like a kid with his allowance in his pocket, his expression shy and hopeful. The freckling on his cheeks was rosy, freshened by the gigantic breath of the sea.

Both of us seemed relieved to have something to do, now that our talk was over, and we took a long time selecting an embroidered kimono with a bird of paradise theme, one we decided would please Gloria. Because of past mistakes we were both cautious. Once, for Christmas, we'd picked out a pearl necklace which was a duplicate of one she already had. Dad said he'd sure be glad to have me back, presents not up his alley. I remembered the only gift he'd ever given me, a large rectangular-faced watch with a dark leather band, surely one meant for a boy. Of course golf clubs on a tie were pretty silly, for someone who had no interest in the game.

Dad didn't ask the price until we stood at the register, when he turned to me. "You're paying, aren't you?" Confidential with the clerk: "She's an heiress, you know." He brought out his checkbook.

Setting out for the inn, I was worrying about what I was going to say, hurrying along and not seeing the sights now, as though already I'd left the place behind, when Dad did an about-face, taking my arm in tow and leading me into Paddy's Place, a ramshackle Irish bar that definitely looked its best at night under misty green lights. "Quick one for the road. Absorb some of the damage." Dad patted his wallet. "At least I'm saving on a motel." His plan was to drive on home for the night.

Inside, Dad's hair shone coppery in the light, and I easily followed him in and out of the crowd to an empty table against the side wall. "Guess they're trying to make it seem like it's raining in here. Makes the Irish in us feel at home." I forced a smile, slightly sickened by the

279

yeasty smell of stale beer. I thought of asking if it had to be raining beer, but I didn't know if that would be funny or just dumb, so I kept quiet, trying to think of something more interesting, when the waitress came over.

"You're a lot of fun, daughter." Dad grinned at her when I ordered a glass of water. She was short and pretty, with brown hair in a poodle cut, a half moon of freckles bridging her nose. "Don't you even want a Coke?" he asked, but I shook my head, embarrassed I hadn't thought of that.

Dad ordered a draft and the waitress pushed back her curls to find a pencil, her tongue poking out as she wrote it on the bill. As she walked off, Dad watched, tipped back in his chair, loosening his tie and opening his shirt a couple of buttons, snaking his neck free. I decided I would exchange the tie for handkerchiefs, something Dad could keep in his pocket if he didn't like them. The waitress looked over and smiled from two tables down.

When Dad brought out his cigarettes he half offered them to me before lighting up. "You don't smoke, do you?" Puzzling briefly about me while he took a drag. Then he shook his head as though, like calculus, I was too perplexing and not worth the effort. "There must be more to you than meets the eye," he said, glancing off to greener pastures while I dropped my eyes, hulking inside my anger. If he didn't watch it I was going to become a beatnik, never take a bath and speak only in bebop.

He caught me napping, pouncing when I didn't expect it, still with the harsh indifference grating in his voice. "You haven't heard from your sister, then?" I shook my head while he considered whether or not I was lying. Whether or not he cared. Long ago Dad had described me as intellectually dishonest, a verdict inexplicable at ten, still a mystery. But whatever it was, it was still part of our brief tense exchanges, during which I trembled as though for my life. Ruthann had strung me along when all the time she knew she was going to marry Brooke. She hid the passbook, and Tommy gave it to Dad. While I was running in circles. Dad and I retreated to watch the bartender's furious activity, his bottle-opening, glass-washing, lemon-slicing, and hand-wiping like a written score, with the finished drinks surfacing as grace notes.

Dad sighed. "I guess I don't know when I'm well off," his eyes resuming their restless survey of the room. "Maybe you blame your mother for what happened. I know grudges are your long suit. But I hope you won't chew on it like an old cow. She's done her best, and believe you me, it hasn't been any picnic, coming in cold to a free-for-all. I know I owe her plenty, even if you don't." I jumped when he banged his mug on the table, and his smile was bitter, as though he knew I'd exaggerated it slightly and could have chosen to sit as still as a post. I didn't know why I would blame Gloria in particular, but I didn't have it sorted out. Dad dared me to blame him, from his catbird seat.

"Hey, Margy," a guy said, someone I knew from the inn squeezing past our table, his jeans brushing along as he gave Dad the once-over. Probably he thought I was quarreling with my date.

"What's wrong with him?" Dad asked. "He got B.O.?"

"Dad! Nothing. He's just a guy from work. Besides, he doesn't know I'm alive." I glanced over and met his eyes, giving the lie to that, and my heart raced.

"That's what you think," Dad said, toying with his glass. "Don't get me wrong. You do all right and I'm proud of you. I appreciate the fact that you're shy. I'm a bit on the shy side myself in spite of my daredevil ways, if the truth were known. But I think you might try going out some with the other kids. Maybe to those parties they have. It won't hurt you to have a little fun. All work and no play, you know." We avoided each other's eyes, both of us embarrassed I guess at the thought of me having fun. As though there was something unnatural about it. "I don't know what happened," he added. "You were a pretty adventurous kid, as I remember." For a time we sat in silence, watching a disturbance at the bar, where two guys having a drinking contest were getting rowdy and the proprietor had to call the bouncer, who convinced them to break it off just by standing there.

"Your mother didn't want you to come here in the first place, you know. And I think we can both see why. It's a little fast for your speed. Just as well you come on home where we can keep an eye on you."

"But, Dad, I love it here. I'm happier than I've ever been. I'm doing all right. You said so." It sounded pitiful and tears stood in my eyes. When I looked down, one dropped on the table, a luminous bubble magnifying that forgotten fabled time when I was free and easy. Earlier in the day I'd seen two girls drive by, each at the wheel of an MG, painted identical canary yellow, tops down, hair flying, zipping in and out of traffic to stay together.

"Now, now. Don't get yourself all worked up. You're doing fine. I never was much of a diplomat." I smeared away the tear while Dad tipped back again, holding his neck in a cradle of fingers. "Maybe you don't go in for that kind of thing. God knows Phoebe didn't. Nothing doing there—no matter how you've got it fancied up." I felt him studying me but I kept my eyes down. Maybe I was all to blame. I remembered the first time I refused to kiss him, holding out my hand, perhaps ten, ashamed but determined. Dad had started to tease and beg, but when he saw I was adamant, he blushed.

Another impasse, another off-limits discussion. Dad struck a match and the sulphur afterburn cleared the air like incense. "I guess they have to wear that getup," he observed. "Keep the customers happy." He was looking over at the waitresses, who bobbed before the bar, yelling orders, filling trays, all of them, all sizes and shapes, dressed in identical green satin shorts with T-shirts printed with shamrocks. I did my part to let bygones be bygones, smiling and taking an interest, while under the table I traced the initials carved in a heart, figuring it out like Braille. Ruthann and I used to send each other messages pricked with a pin into paper—preparing for the worst, we said. When we broke our music box open we pretended to be reading music with our fingers along the cylinder while we hummed. Gloria said Ruthann had asked her questions about Mother when they were talking, but I doubted it. I couldn't remember that Ruthann had ever asked me a question in her life unless she wanted to get my goat.

A group of men, dressed alike, down to identical toupees, stood by the upright piano and sang "My Wild Irish Rose," their arms along each other's shoulders, pals to the end. The picture out front said they were brothers from Ireland. I joined in, singing with some of the others in the audience, closing my eyes to hear myself better.

"You should be up there." Dad was leaning toward me. "Show how it's done. I always said you had a good voice. Too bad you don't have the confidence to go with it, but then, why should you?" Our eyes held while he drank, the green of his divided into streaks of blue and yellow like match flames. The damage done. Like a genie the waitress refilled his glass from out of nowhere. "Cheap date," he told her when I refused a drink for the second time.

"You come for the regatta?" she asked Dad. The dimple at the corner of her mouth sank deeply.

"Too rich for my blood. I'm just a poor broken-down piano player." Tugging on his earlobe, Dad slid his eyes sideways to her shirt. "Lucky sign, the shamrock. Paris green, if I'm not mistaken."

Her dimple flew up like a bird seeming to perch in her eyes. "You better watch your daddy. He's a slick customer," and she went on, her smile diminished by confusion, although she was flattered by the very mention of Paris.

"From my artist days." Dad winked at me, his wet finger tuning the rim of the glass. "You should take lessons. You can bet she doesn't sit home on a Saturday night wishing for the moon. But I guess you can't be all things to all men. And probably you don't do that either. Bet, I mean." His eyes flicked at me and I leaned my head against the wall, closing mine. The cement block felt indented, as though weariness could wear away stone. No, I don't. I was steaming, thinking of the poker games on the beach and how I always said no. Trying to be good—for somebody who didn't care. Or so he said, until I did something. Then he'd care. My eyes opened on the

283

white arms of the waitress bringing me a soda trimmed with a slice of lime and a cherry. She topped off Dad's beer from her pitcher, murmuring, "On the house," swirling off to replenish the singers' mugs which they lifted high in the gloaming, beginning "The Blue Bells of Scotland."

"The least you can do is drink that." Dad's lips tightened. Blanched, the light gave them a chalky texture.

"I'm dizzy," I said, drooping my head, twisting the straw.

"Oh, hell." He grabbed it and gulped a swallow, lowering on a bounce onto the four solid legs of his chair, his face easing with the jolt. "It's time we were leaving anyway. Get out while the getting's good." He had some beer, standing up with a glance at me. "You do look kind of peaked, girl. Why don't you get some fresh air while I settle up." He was laying down change for the tip.

I made my way to the door, between the moist-eyed, middle-aged Irish lads and the close-drawn-up tables. "Keep the home fires burning, / While your hearts are yearning; / Though your lads are far away / They dream of home." I ended the song with a draft of the sea air, banging out into the tumult of the wet wind, Gloria's present flashing before me in a vision, under the table where I'd left it. I went wheeling back the way I'd come, through the swinging door, broadside into the raging pandemonium on the other side of the wind.

I made Dad out through the gloom, against the back wall, where he stood in conversation with the waitress, on his face a look I'd never seen before, a look at once insolent and beseeching, so fundamentally private nothing else existed but the two of them. She clung to him with her eyes, on her face two vivid spots of color, coppery, reflections from Dad's hair, it seemed. I scurried to retrieve the package, eyes down, slipping out to wait.

On the way back to the inn Dad noticed my shivering and tried to drape his jacket around my shoulders, but I sidestepped him, mumbling that I wasn't cold. And I wasn't. It was more as though I was burning up. When we got to the steps down to the parking lot, I led the way, greeting Cal, who was smoking on the porch by the kitchen, but going on without stopping to introduce Dad. I just wanted to get it over with; I would tell Dad I was sick and write him later about my plans. Then in the letter I would tell him that I couldn't come home. I'd make some excuse.

At the car, when I held out my hand, waiting while more hesitantly he extended his, Dad continued to be solicitous. "I hate to leave you like this when you're not feeling well. What if you really got sick?" He reached out to touch my cheek with the back of his hand, like I was a child again and he had aspirin gum in his pocket. As though I were faint, I wavered, my hand grasping his, and then he began to smile with pleasure, actually taking my hand in both of his.

"Say, Margy. I know. I've got an idea. You know what. You could just come along right now, drive back with me. Why wait around when you know you're coming home anyway? I'll go in and tell them you're sick, pick up a few of your things, and we'll hit the road. How's that for a taste of adventure?" He dropped my hand, moving to open the passenger door for me to scoot in.

"Dad," I gasped. "I can't do that." I felt so weak I leaned on the car. "I couldn't, I mean right now. I haven't given notice or anything. What would they do?" I slid along the car in the direction of the inn, away from Dad.

I watched disappointment replace his smile before his mouth whitened. "I'm sorry," I said. I remembered saying that to Jake over the phone, as though that would help.

"I don't see how you owe anybody here a damn thing. They feed you slop. Why look, you're already sick. And they can pick up another flunky in five seconds, believe you me. This world's full of losers. You can lie down in the back there, stretch out, and sleep away the miles. Get some TLC. Keep your old man company."

I was so limp that if he'd reached for my hand and pulled me to sit down in the car I would have gone. But he didn't touch me and I repeated myself, "I can't. I'm not ready yet. I have to think about it," I added. In spite of what he'd said about my job I liked it, and in the morning there would be four tables of people waiting for their breakfast. "I like being on my own," I said, dropping my eyes with the shame of that admission.

He moved in on me, seizing my arm while I shrank back, but he pulled closer, his eyes fixed and staring over the top of my head. "I'd like to know what your likes have to do with anything, young lady. All of a sudden everybody around here thinks they can just skip out on me." The sudden twist to my arm, behind my back, made me gasp, and I stooped, backing farther away, the car stopping me when with a jerk he brought my back against it, the door handle jabbing in. "Don't," I gasped, pushing back. "You're hurting me."

Nearby someone coughed, a deep low reverberation from the shadows. It snatched us apart like a hook and Dad dropped my arm, stepping away as I slid along the car, bent down and stumbling, passing Cal on my way to the stairs while behind me I heard the engine grind, then Dad peeled out of the lot, the sound of the car submerged in the pounding of my feet on the treads of the stairs leading up to the dorm.

At that hour the room was deserted and I climbed in my bed and under the covers with my clothes on, covering my head too. Eventually I calmed down and slept, and I didn't find the cup of tea Cal sent up with Deborah until morning, sitting on my bureau along with the bankbook which she said he'd found in the parking lot. Distantly, I recalled trying to force it into Dad's hand when he was holding me.

I stared and stared, as though by a miracle it had washed up from the sea in a bottle. The tea, stone cold, seemed the elixir of forgetfulness and I drank it to the dregs, knowing it wouldn't work for me. I'd be stone sober to the end. Whatever Cal thought, he didn't say, and I let both him and Deborah make a fuss over me, tending me through an improvised recovery from a mysterious illness.

* * *

The moon had set and Darl got up to feed the fire, as though it had withdrawn a measure of heat. "Christ." His worried laugh was forced when he flung some sticks into the dark. "They must be having some sort of convention." All I heard was a bird squeak until he started whistling, "My own true love."

"I promise, Darl. I won't tell if you let me go."

"Don't make me laugh. What's to tell. You double-crossed is what. Anybody in his right mind's gonna sympathize with me." Drawing a heart on the sand, a piercing arrow, he rubbed it out before he added initials.

"You know, Margy, I feel all right. Talking to a broad. You say 'boo' to my kid sister, she's yelling for the police. Jesus, sisters. Talking to the guys, you heat up. Don't know what you might do. Get to wonderin' if you are one of them rapists. A murderer. But I didn't even hurt you that bad. Not half as bad as I coulda. Some guys." He shook his head, batting his eyes.

In the car, Darl had been waiting in the back, the motor running. I hurried through the parking lot, the first time I'd been there in the two days since Dad left. It surprised me to see Buzz driving, the door to the back swinging open for me. Before we were on the highway, Darl had his tongue in my mouth. Struggling away, I met Buzz's level gaze in the mirror. Ancient eyes that had looked at everything. If I'd thought at all, it was to excuse Darl for showing off in front of his friend, and I sat forward to tell Buzz where to drop us off, eager to see the last of him. Then Darl would be the same boy I'd met in the afternoon, the gold cross around his neck, his secret hope to enroll in the state teachers' college in the fall. When I'd complimented his melodic whistle, he'd looked shy and startled, murmuring that usually everybody told him to shut up.

"Darl, I have to go to the bathroom." I had to ask as though he were already the teacher.

"Go on. But keep humming or I'll come after you. Ready or not." I followed the path around the dune, listening for traffic, but not a single car passed. I sang, " 'Sweet Betsy from Pike, who crossed the big moun-

287

tains with her lover Ike.' '' I hadn't mentioned the guitar
Darl said he'd bring when I said I liked folk music. Poor
me—I'd thought I could show off my singing voice.

When I finished I went around the dunes, back into
the sound of the waves. In the attic room where we girls
slept, close to the water, we heard it all night long, even
when we were asleep, so if somehow the waves were
stilled we would have risen in alarm to see what had
happened. The breeze coming in the window sailed the
curtains high over the beds, riffling the sheets and pages
of books left on the sill, letters from home and lists of
things to do. Clothing, hung on chairs and knobs, bal-
looned and fluttered. If my plight was known, if it was
possible to reach them, the girls would gather in their
robes and, carrying lamps, surge onto the sand to find
the one who was missing. I could envision Deborah, always late, hurrying for once, her dark hair salt-grizzled,
spread like a sail. I whispered her name as though I could
reach her.

Darl propped himself on his elbow when I lay down,
his eyes yellow through the fire. ''So, Margy. This Gloria. Was she nice or like in fairy tales?''

I could have been watching him burn, staring through
flame. ''Actually, she's quite nice.''

''You can bet it's tough. Either way. My old lady's
come up with some real ball busters—Mr. Big Man. Besides, it would give you the creeps. Maybe the other
mother watching. I mean, nobody knows. I used to think
about my old man coming back. When I was gettin' hell.
Showing up like Prince Charming.'' He waggled his stick
at me, grinning.

''You better hope she's not watching you.''

''You deserve it. Think you're perfect. I bet you handed
it out all over. Whore.'' A couple of stones soared into
the dark. I imagined one striking Buzz down like Goli-
ath.

Darl had torn my blouse, yanking down my swimsuit.
I crossed my arms while he stared at my chest, straddling
my waist. ''Don't worry. I wouldn't touch your tit if it
was big as a mountain.'' He gouged at me, offering to

pay. "Two bits, more'n it's worth." With his hand, he forced mine down to touch him. "Come on. The least you can do is give me a hand job."

"I wouldn't touch it if it was big as a mountain." I bucked him back, driving up with my knee.

Chafing his hands over the fire, Darl shrugged, beginning to whistle. He lit a smoke, eyeing me. "Wish we had cards. Make the time go. Five-card. You play?"

"No. But I could learn." I sat up. "Darl, you know, I'd like to smoke a cigarette. Would that be all right?"

Earlier I'd said I didn't smoke, but he only shrugged. "That's more like it. You may learn something yet." He lit one and handed it to me. "Don't inhale right off or you'll be puking." He stretched back, crossing his legs, opening the flask.

"Can I have some of that too?"

"Hot damn. I don't know." He held it up to see how much was left. "I guess. What's next?"—grinning at the possibilities that came to his mind. "Now watch yourself. It burns at first, till you get the hang of it." I held a drop on my tongue and trickled it back, my mouth numbed in its track. Did it again. "It's nice. Warm." We smiled at my whispery voice.

"It's not so bad being here with you. You're okay when you loosen up. We might could go someplace, you know. Hear music or something. It's lonely out here. About the loneliest I ever was, except when I got lost in the woods. I was gonna run away, but then I ended up in this swamp all turned around. My dog found me. The only one who cared. Ha, ha—just jokin'. I told you now, don't inhale." He oversaw me have a coughing fit. "I shoulda had you with me, Margy. You coulda been running around, starting a fire, reading moss on trees, looking for bear." I was thinking of telling him about Dad running away to the West when his father died, but then I thought Darl would take it personally, because he didn't get out of his own back yard.

I leaned to have another sip from the flask, treating it carefully like a medicine I had to get used to. "Sometimes I drink, Darl. A little wine with Deborah's father on Friday nights. It's sweet, like blackberries. Nothing like this. He tells me about Russia, where he came from. When he was a boy he traveled all the way from the Black Sea to St. Petersburg to study to become a rabbi. They were poor and it took all their money for the train, so when he got there he had to sleep in the park under newspapers. In the morning he would be covered with snow. But it was a great honor to study, and he was proud. When we drink he pours me a little extra. Says it's good for a girl to enjoy the pleasures of life. Calls me a daughter of Jerusalem.''

Darl's eyes dropped. When he looked up he asked, "How 'bout your sister. She retarded like you?" That gave him a charge, and he sprang up to spar with the night, left and right to the stars. "I coulda slugged ya, Margy. It woulda been curtains. That time you stuck me with the live butt it was touch and go. If I coulda caught ya. You oughta go out for the Olympics. I'll be your trainer.''

"I used to run. The kids called me Man-O'-War. I beat the boys too. My dad trained me in the yard and sometimes I'd race the car.''

"Yeah. We'll take you all over. Soccer's my game. I'm not that tall, ya mighta noticed. Got to be tricky. You got the legs. I saw that first thing, only I wasn't thinkin' about a race. Flaunting them. Sticking them in my face. Probably you ran all over those chumps while they were gettin' a loada your gams. Ask Gloria. She'll tell you.'' He opened the flask, squinting into it glumly. "I may not be a hundred but I know a thing or two. Here's looking at *you*, babe. Now, that was class. He didn't beg. I bet you think I'm a bum.'' He glared under brows that appeared bald in the firelight. "So your sister. She good in bed?''

He got a laugh out of that, rakish, shifting his shoulders. Tough Guy. When he lay back, I did too. Every star was out now that the moon was gone, the heavens opened up with light, like an Advent calendar with the last window flung wide on the great day. When you looked in there, it was usually a sweet baby lying in a manger. I was dragging away on my second cigarette, filling my mouth and holding it in, smoking my tongue. "Sometimes I think it'll be a miracle if I ever get laid."

"Don't get smart." He sat up fast. "I ain't never getting hitched. I get enough without the ball and chain." We drank to that and he lay back, his head pillowed on the log. "Plenty of 'em don't think twice. You'd be surprised with your notions. Take 'em out, bang. Funny thing, you carrying on like that. Like you got a jewel in there or somethin'. A guy gets to thinkin' he's missing out. You'd do better to lay back and take it." Sprawled full-length, musing, he began whistling "Spellbound." It was flute-like, reedy and poignant. We could have been two shepherds come down to the sea with our flocks. He didn't even know. That time when I got up and put wood on the fire, Darl didn't stop me.

"You're showing promise." He nodded, glassy-eyed. "Next you'll be asking me to be the father of your kids. Too bad I ain't the settlin' type."

I hunkered down almost in the coals with the blanket held close, tired, a squaw whose work was never done. The night was thinning out and it was as though I'd exhausted myself climbing a mountain to the highest pinnacle to reach that finer air.

"Never saw the old man. The one that got away. Thought that was your game. Wanted to lasso yours truly, turn him into some old pussy, drinking wine." His head bobbed to his chest. I tossed sand to scatter a crab before Darl thought it was an ambush.

"I liked you, Darl. I thought we'd kiss."

"Christ. What's kissin' but getting the ball rollin'. I think you're chicken."

"I guess you hate me."

His chin hit the deck, bouncing. "You must think twenty-four hours a day to come up with that shit." He struggled to his elbow, stuck a cigarette in his mouth, grumbling but adding another when I nodded. "Lousy habit." His voice was nasal, his lips held stiff. "One thing that was smart about ya. Kills your wind."

"That's how Buzz talks. Out of the side of his mouth.

Like a criminal.'' I mocked it: ''Let's talk turkey, doll,'' hiding my smile in my hand. ''I'm sorry.''

Darl's baffled eyes swung between surprise and insult. ''Shit. You got your laugh, didn't ya. You girls kill me.'' Glaring at the fire, his mouth shook into a sheepish grin. ''He is kind of a stiff, ain't he?'' Darl yawned, settling back, smiling to himself. When he opened the flask I had my hand out.

''Monkey see, monkey do. Next thing you'll be swearing like a trooper.''

''Sometimes I want to.''

''Well, I don't like it. It's not ladylike. Broads take over. No sense of moderation. Just be a girl, okay? I'll be the boy. I like you the way you are anyway. First thing, I could tell you had class. You know the way you talk, stuff about your sister, your brother, and old Gloria. Had to watch my mouth; no saying 'nigger.' Right off I figured you for a nigger lover. Right?'' He used his grin like a spur while I gave him the silent treatment, not about to compliment him for second sight. ''I woulda treated you good too. I'm thinkin' you're not as dumb as you look. Like you could tell I wasn't that bad a guy. When you picked me.'' When he drank he forgot to share, blinking.

''I saw your cross and I thought you were religious. You said you went to Mass.''

''So what if I did.'' He reached in his pocket and brought it out. Hanging over the fire, it swung wildly like an instrument seeking the poles. ''Go on, take it. It's yours. You wear that, Buzz'll think we did all right. He's kinda like Dracula. Anything religious cramps his style.''

''Thanks, Darl.'' I slipped it around my neck and he lay back, eyes closing. I paced, running the cool silky sand through my toes, spraying it in jets before the fire. Spooky, like a ghost story or maybe a prayer, I started to talk. Darl wouldn't be the first to be mesmerized by the story of a beautiful maiden.

''I guess Ruthann was always trying to get away and sometimes she'd do crazy things. On the way to Washington we used to pass this sign, faded and rained-on, stuck off in the weeds in front of a dilapidated house. We'd laugh to think anyone ever went in there. Even the front steps were gone. MADAM WANDA AND HER CRYSTAL BALL. PALM READING. But one day Ruthann said, she went up to the door and knocked, and after that she went a lot, dropping in to pay the old lady a call. Probably she reminded her of Grandma, who was a bit of a fortune-teller herself. At first Ruthann paid a dollar and got her palm read—stuff like she'd meet a tall dark stranger. Nothing Ruthann was interested in, and soon they forgot about that. Mostly it was a home for stray cats, and once Ruthann counted to twenty-eight before she got mixed up. She knew she acted funny because she had to breathe through her mouth all the time so the smell wouldn't make her sick. Still, Madam Wanda must have liked Ruthann, handing her a box one day, saying it was time for her to pass on her crystal ball to the next person in line. Only, when Ruthann opened it, it was the kind of glass ball you shake up and it snows. Madam Wanda said anything would do if you had the gift.

"Ruthann brought it home and gave it to Tommy, who looked in there and saw everything. He told me I was going to be a singer, he saw himself carrying a gun, and Ruthann was talking to a man in a long robe who must have been Jesus. Ruthann looked in at the two children holding hands and walking away and she said she didn't get anything out of it but a broken heart. She wasn't going back to Madam Wanda, the old faker. But maybe it'll turn out that Tommy's the one with the gift, after all, because I'm going to buy a guitar and find somebody to teach me. Then I'll sing any dreary song I want to, passing through this vale of tears."

I watched Darl sleep, then stooped to rake out the coals, spreading the ashes as though sand and water presented a fire hazard. The fire erased, the paling sky all around, Darl's weary face was ashen, although the faintest smile held something hopeful. Like any dreaming boy—Tommy after a day trout fishing in the Smokies, Deborah's father under the open skies of the divine, lost

293

city of St. Petersburg. Although Dad, rumbling away to the West, looked out from the dark of the slatted flatcars to see the Indians and the buffalo gone, not one reason he could find for going on.

"Maybe Ruthann doesn't want any gifts," I said, Darl's chest rising and falling. No second thoughts for him, no stunning regrets. I draped the cross over the log beside him, where it didn't make a whisper or a glint, drab as the driftwood before the dawn. A twitch, then he slept on. "I think," I said softly, walking backward toward the surf, "you're going to need it even more than I do. Because I'm telling, Darl." Veering in the direction of town, I kept my eyes on him while he faded into distance, to gray, to nothing. The waves pounded as though they brought the light.

The night Ruthann called to say she was married she asked to speak to Dad, but he wouldn't come to the phone. "Tell her 'tough luck,' " he said through the door of the darkened bedroom. "Congratulations," I said. "Dad's in bed." In a high-pitched and unfamiliar voice Ruthann said how happy she was. I asked, "Why did you take the bankbook without telling me?"

Then she was shouting, "Money, money, money. That's all you ever think about. I'm so glad to be out of that hellhole." She was sobbing and then Brooke was on the line. "Now, listen here, Margy." I hung up the phone, sitting there a long time holding it in my lap; for the first time ever, Mother's money seemed like something real, even though it was lost.

When I'd seen the last of Darl, I turned toward town and ran faster, thinking perhaps I heard a horn. It seemed I could go forever, the tips of the ripply water, in the clarity of new light, spiry, tremulous to show that what was around us were infinite temples bobbing over the abyss. Then slowly and with grace the sun appeared from the grave of night, enfolded in clouds like a seraph in its wings, its blush advancing over the deep as though such splendor wasn't fitting but couldn't be helped, a stain that must reach everywhere, strike upon the bars of prisons,

294

blare out the faces of all yearning in all dark places. I raced along, the blanket streaming.

A solitary car was pulled up alongside the boardwalk when finally I could see it begin in the distance, a gray track above the sand, the low pastel buildings of the beach town starting there too. I was almost certain the car was waiting for me, that Deborah had been worried when I didn't come home. I slowed to a walk, calming myself, the morning bluer now, the color of dawn drifting away like the petals of wild roses. The moment I opened my mouth I knew I'd be crying and feel too weak to stand. I didn't have to be told how foolish I'd been. Still, I was grateful to Deborah. One of the true daughters of Jerusalem, she didn't have to play with fire, for she already knew fire could come down from the heavens in the twinkling of an eye and sweep the whole world away.

DURING THE REIGN OF THE QUEEN OF PERSIA
by Joan Chase

A beautiful story of twentieth-century womanhood. Gram, the Queen of Persia herself, rules a house where five daughters and four granddaughters spin out the tragedies and triumphs of rural life in the 1950s.

> "Brilliant and compelling . . . a lush and lyrical world of unsparing reality."
> —*The Cleveland Plain Dealer*

> "Daily life exhilarated with the richness and evocativeness of poetry."
> —*The Washington Post Book World*

> "Absorbing and wonderfully written."
> —*Los Angeles Times Book Review*

DURING THE REIGN OF THE QUEEN OF PERSIA
SBN 31525,   Price $3.95